8/8/15

Royal Wedding

MEG CABOT

Royal Wedding

MACMILLAN

First published in the US 2015 by HarperCollins Publishers

First published in the UK 2015 by Macmillan Children's Books
an imprint of Pan Macmillan
20 New Wharf Road, London N1 9RR
Associated companies throughout the world
www.panmacmillan.com

ISBN 978-1-4472-8249-5 (MME)
ISBN 978-1-4472-9871-7 (OME)

1 3 5 7 9 8 6 4 2

A CIP catalogue record for this book is available from
the British Library.

Printed and bound by CPI Group (UK) Ltd, Croydon CR0 4YY

She will be more a princess than she ever was – a hundred and fifty thousand times more.

A LITTLE PRINCESS
Frances Hodgson Burnett

Royal Scandal:

Prince Phillipe of Genovia Arrested

MANHATTAN – Prince Phillipe Renaldo, the 50-year-old crowned prince of Genovia, was arrested early Wednesday morning for driving his newly purchased 1978 Ferrari 312T3 Formula One race car down the West Side Highway, according to a spokesperson for the New York City Police Department. No injuries were reported.

Witnesses say the prince was driving at speeds in excess of 180 miles per hour before being pulled over by NYPD Highway Patrol officers. A spokesperson for the NYPD confirms that the prince complied with all instructions given by the officers, including taking a field sobriety test.

Police as well as Genovian embassy officials declined to share further details regarding the arrest. Prince Phillipe has had no previous arrests, either in the United States or abroad.

It is illegal to drive race cars intended for closed-track use only on public streets in the state of New York. It is not known whether the prince, whose primary residence is the European principality of Genovia, was aware of this. The prince is said to have purchased the vehicle earlier in the day at an auction upstate.

New to Formula One racing, this is the first year the prince has taken part in Genovia's Grand Prix, infamous for its tight corners through the small principality's narrow, cobblestoned streets and precipitous cliffs overlooking the Mediterranean.

According to the prince's mother, the Dowager Princess Clarisse Renaldo, age unknown, this year's race will also be his last.

'The only place he'll be racing after this is down the aisle, with my granddaughter,' Princess Clarisse was overheard to say outside the Manhattan Detention Complex, where she was waiting to visit her son in jail.

According to the Royal Palace, however, there are currently no plans for a royal wedding between Princess Mia Thermopolis Renaldo, 25, and longtime boyfriend, medical entrepreneur Michael Moscovitz, 29. Moscovitz is founder and CEO of Pavlov Surgical, a successful medical robotics firm.

Princess Mia is the prince's only child and heir to the throne of Genovia. She was raised by her mother, American artist Helen Thermopolis, in New York City's Greenwich Village. Mia has stated in numerous interviews that she is thankful she did not find out she was a princess until she was a teenager, though it meant missing out on the glamour of being raised as a young royal on the Riviera.

'I was able to grow up in a fairly normal way,'

Mia has been quoted as saying. 'If I'd had a cell phone and constant access to the Internet like most kids do today, I probably would have caught on sooner.'

This is not the first unhappy event to strike the princess's family in recent months: her stepfather, Frank Gianini, passed away last year from congestive heart failure.

In his name, the princess founded the Frank Gianini Community Center in New York City. The center is designed to help children and teens acquire the skills they need to succeed in school or their chosen future career path. In a statement at its opening, the princess said, 'My stepfather was always there to help me with my homework, and my hope is that this center will carry on that legacy in his memory.'

Genovia is a constitutional monarchy and member of the EU, with Prince Phillipe having ruled as monarch since the death of his father over twenty years ago. He's also served uncontested as the country's prime minister for nearly a decade, but a distant cousin of the prince's – Count Ivan Renaldo – has drawn significantly ahead in recent polls, running on a campaign of economic and immigration reform. Genovia has seen a sharp rise in illegal immigration but a decline in tourism in the past few years due to the worldwide recession, losing revenue to better-known tourist destinations such as Paris, London, and Venice.

For these reasons, many are speculating that the prince's arrest could not have come at a worse time.

I don't know what's happening to me. I lie when I should tell the truth, and tell the truth when I should lie.

Like half an hour ago, when Dr. Delgado, the newly appointed 'royal physician,' was here, and asked if I've been under any 'unusual' stress lately.

I laughed and said, 'Gosh, no, Doctor, none that I can think of.'

You would think Dr. Delgado might have noticed the hordes of paparazzi gathered outside the consulate doors when he came in, and figured out that I was being sarcastic.

But no.

Instead, he said I shouldn't be concerned about the fact that my left eyelid has been twitching pretty much nonstop for the past week, which is why I asked for an appointment in the first place.

According to Dr. Delgado, this sort of thing 'happens all the time, and is not at all indicative of a brain tumor or stroke.'

Then he suggested I stop putting my symptoms into iTriage and instead get 'plenty of sleep and exercise.' Oh, and I might try eating healthier.

Sleep? Exercise? Who has time to sleep or exercise? And how am I supposed to eat healthier when I'm literally trapped by the press inside the Genovian consulate and can only order food from places that deliver near the United Nations (which are basically steak houses, Chinese restaurants, or gyro joints)?

It wasn't until he was packing up his medical equipment that I realized Dr. Delgado was immune to sarcasm and really intended to leave without writing me a prescription.

So I said, 'The truth is, Doctor, I have been feeling a little stressed. You might have heard about my recent family difficulties, which have led to . . .'

I pointed meaningfully out the window. Dominique, the director of Royal Genovian Press Relations and Marketing, says if we don't encourage the media, they'll go away – like stray cats are supposed to, if you don't feed them – but this isn't true. I've never fed the media, and they still won't go away.

'Oh, yes, yes, yes,' Dr. Delgado said, seeming to realize things were a little out of the ordinary – as if the fact that he was visiting me in the consulate instead of seeing me in his office hadn't given it away. 'Of course! But your father is doing very well, isn't he? All the reports I've heard say that he'll most likely be given a slap on the wrist, and then he'll be able to return to Genovia. The press seem to find his little mishap with the law quite amusing.'

Little mishap with the law! Thanks to my father's decision to take a midnight jaunt down the West Side Highway in his newly purchased race car, Count Ivan Renaldo, Dad's opponent for prime minister, is ahead five points in the polls. If the count wins, Genovia will be transformed from a charming medieval-walled microstate on the French Riviera to something that looks more like Main Street USA in Disneyland, with everyone strolling around in T-shirts that say WHO FARTED? and eating giant turkey legs.

'Oh, Dad's doing great!' I made the huge mistake of lying (I realize now). This is what we're supposed to tell the extended family and the press. It's not the truth. Royals never tell the truth. It isn't 'done.'

It's for this reason that I think I'm losing my grip on my sanity and can no longer tell the difference between what's real and what's a façade for the sake of the media (iTriage says this is called disassociation and is generally used as a coping mechanism to manage stress).

'Wonderful!' Dr. Delgado cried. 'And things are going well between you and – what is the young man's name?'

I swear Dr. Delgado must be the only person in the entire western hemisphere who doesn't know Michael's name.

'Is Michael Moscovitz the World's Greatest Lover? "YES!" Says Sex-Mad Princess Mia,' declares the cover of this week's *In Touch*.

Michael's dad thought this was so hilarious he bought dozens of copies to give to his friends and even his *patients*. Michael's asked him to stop, but his dad won't listen.

'You really expect me not to buy this?' Dr. Moscovitz asked. 'My son is the world's greatest lover! It says so right here. Of *course* I'm going to buy it!'

This could be one of the reasons for my twitch.

'Michael,' I said to Dr. Delgado. 'Michael Moscovitz. And yes, everything's fine between us.'

Except that's a lie. Michael and I hardly ever see each other anymore thanks to our work schedules and the fact that I'm being held a prisoner in my current home by the paps. I had to move out of my old apartment last year on account of my stalker, RoyalRabbleRouser, who enjoys posting online about how he's going to 'destroy' me for writing a historical romance novel (years ago, under another name) featuring a heroine who has premarital sex (he claims this is proof of how 'feminism has destroyed the fabric of our society').

The consulate is the only building in Manhattan guarded 24/7 by military police specially trained in the protection of a royal.

And now lately on the limited occasions Michael and I *do* find time to get together, we mostly just order in, then watch *Star Trek* on Netflix, because leaving the consulate is such a pain, unless I want to hear all sorts of horrible questions hurled at me on my way to the car by the press:

'Mia, what's it like to have a felon for a father?'

'Mia, is that a baby bump or did you just have too much of that falafel we saw delivered an hour ago?'

'Mia, how does it feel to know that seventy-four percent of those surveyed think Kate Middleton wore it better?'

'Mia, why hasn't Michael put a ring on it?'

I tried to show Michael my twitch earlier on FaceTime, but he said my eye looked perfectly normal to him.

'If you're twitchy, though, Mia, it's probably in

nervous anticipation at the prospect of going out with me, the world's greatest lover.'

'I thought we agreed we weren't going to read our own press,' I reminded him.

'How can I help it?' he asked. 'Especially since my erotic powers seemingly extend all the way to the Upper East Side, where they've rendered you sex mad.'

'Ha ha ha. You probably planted that story yourself.'

'You've grown so jaded and cynical since I last saw you. But really, Mia,' he said, finally getting serious. 'I think you're just stressing too much about all of this. I'm not saying things aren't bad – they are. But maybe all you need is to get away for a day or two.'

'Away? How am I possibly going to get away? And where am I going to go that the press can't follow me and ask about my alleged baby bump or how my dad looks in his orange jumpsuit?'

'Good question. Let me work on it.'

I know he's just trying to help, but really, how can I go away with Dad in so much trouble and the country in such an uproar and the election so close and Mom being a new widow and Grandmère as crazy as ever?

Plus my boyfriend having rendered me sex mad, of course.

No. Just no.

But of course I couldn't tell Dr. Delgado any of this. It's like my lips have been frozen into a permanent smile by all my media training (and compartmentalizing of my feelings).

'Well, that's fine, then,' the doctor said, beaming.

Fine? It's so *not* fine. Was it really so wrong of me to think that maybe, possibly, the palace physician might give me a little something to keep my eyelid from jumping around like a Chihuahua at dinnertime, or at least help me not lie awake all night?

And then when I *do* manage to fall asleep I have nightmares, like the one I had last night that I was married to Bruce Willis, and whenever Bruce got out of the shower, he would dry off his naughty parts while singing the song 'Chitty Chitty Bang Bang.'

I can't even tell Michael this. How do you explain it to the kindly old physician they found who is still willing to do house calls?

You cannot.

'I'll make sure the lab gets the blood and urine samples you insisted I take, Your Highness,' Dr. Delgado said. 'I should have the results in about a week. But I have to say that medically, I doubt they'll find anything wrong. Your pulse is strong, your skin tone looks even, your weight is within the normal range for your height. Despite this twitch you say you have – which frankly I can't see – and your fingernails, which I see that you bite, you seem to be glowing with health.'

Damn! He *would* notice my fingernails. I must be the only female left on the entire planet who doesn't get manicures because there's nothing left of my fingernails to file, let alone paint.

'Maybe,' I said, trying to keep the eagerness out of my voice so I wouldn't sound like one of those crazed Oxy-addicts on *Intervention,* 'I should be written a prescription for a very mild mood stabilizer.'

'Oh, no,' Dr. Delgado said. 'Nail-biting is a bad habit, but very common, and hardly worth treating psychopharmacologically. The worst that could happen from compulsive nail-biting is that you might incur an infection, or pick up a pinworm.'

Oh my God. I am never biting my nails again. At least not before thoroughly washing them in antibacterial soap.

'What I suggest you try,' he added as he packed up his bag, 'is journaling.'

'Journaling?' Was he joking?

He was not.

'Why yes, I see you've heard of it. Journaling has been shown to reduce stress and help with problem solving. My wife keeps what she calls a gratitude journal. She writes down three things every day for which she feels grateful. She keeps a dream journal as well. She says it's helped tremendously, especially with her mood swings. You should try it. Well, I'll be in touch in about a week about that blood work. Good day, Princess!'

And then he left.

Which leaves me here. *Journaling.*

Why couldn't I have lied to make myself seem more pathetic so he'd have written me a prescription for an antianxiety medication, or at least a low-dose sleeping pill? Even the veterinarian does this for Fat Louie when I take him on the private jet back and forth to Genovia, and Fat Louie is a *cat*.

Granted, he's an extremely elderly cat who now needs a tiny staircase to climb up and down from my bed and tends to revenge-poop on everything when he doesn't get his own way. But still. Why does a *cat* get tranquilizers but the expensive concierge doctor we hired will not give them to *me*?

Oh, dear, I just read that over, and it sounds a bit odd. Of course I don't revenge-poop on things when I don't get my own way. I'm simply saying that it seems a bit unfair that we have the one concierge doctor in all of Manhattan who refuses to prescribe antianxiety medication. I'm sure every other celebrity (and royal) is loaded up on them.

- *Note to self:* Check on this. This would explain a lot about their behavior, actually.

But if 'gratitude' and 'dream' journaling really does help with stress, I'm willing to give it a go.

At this point, I'll try *anything*.

Let's see. I already wrote down what I dreamed about. Here are three things for which I feel grateful:

1. I don't have a brain tumor.

2. My father didn't die in that race-car incident. ~~Though given how reckless it was of him to have been in it in the first place, he probably deserved to.~~

3. Michael, the funniest, handsomest, smartest, and most forgiving boyfriend in the entire world (even if every once in a while lately I've noticed there's something going on with *his* eyes, too. Not a twitch. More like something brewing in there. If I still wrote historical romance novels – which I had to give up, not because of RoyalRabbleRouser's threats but because I don't have time, between all my public speaking, running the Community Center, and worrying about Dad – I would describe it as a 'haunted shadow.')

I know it's selfish, but I hope if there *is* something wrong with Michael, it's that he's passing another kidney stone – even though he said the one he passed last May was the most painful experience of his life, and the nephrologist compared it to giving birth – and not that Mr. G's death has caused him to re-evaluate his life and make him realize he's with the wrong person. I'm totally aware of the fact that it would be much, much easier for him to be with a girl who could meet him for drinks after work at T.G.I. Friday's without it first having to be swept for bombs, or go to the movies with him without having a plainclothes sharpshooter sit behind us, or simply stroll around Central Park without being followed by a phalanx of photo-hungry press.

But I'm never going to be that girl.

And my worst fear is that someday he's going to realize it and dump me the way my mom dumped my dad, leaving him the brokenhearted, race-car-speeding, empty shell of a man he is today.

Honestly, what good is owning a castle if the person you love doesn't want to share it with you?

Tried to go to work at the Community Center after my appointment, but Perin called while I was on my way and said hordes of paps had shown up there, too, and were bothering the teens (and their adult mentors) by asking how they felt about my father's brush with the law, and whether or not I was 'carrying Michael's twins,' so maybe it would be better if I 'worked from home.'

So sweet, right? Who else has such kind, concerned friends?

And not just the kind who've known you since high school and so have no problem telling you that your bra strap is showing and that there's salad in your teeth. The kind who are willing to run the Community Center you just founded even though they could probably be making millions running a start-up in Silicon Valley instead.

(See? I am already taking the doctor's advice and practicing more gratitude in my day-to-day life.)

I said, 'Thanks, Perin, I understand.'

People everywhere pray for a job where they can 'work from home,' so I guess, going with the gratitude theme, I should be grateful for this opportunity.

I wonder how, though, when people get one of these jobs, they keep themselves from spending the entire day going on YouTube and looking at videos about baby deer that have been adopted by golden retrievers. Because that's all I've accomplished today so far.

Well, aside from FaceTiming Michael and asking again if he could see my twitch. Of course he asked if I could turn the camera lower, and then lower, and then unbutton my shirt . . .

And suddenly I realize what *else* people who work from home do all day.

Except that Michael does not work at home, he works at the company he founded, Pavlov Surgical, so we couldn't have quite as much fun as we wanted since his work space has glass walls and anyone could have looked in and seen what we were up to.

He did tell me though (later) that he'd read on WebMD that eye twitches are very often caused by a magnesium deficiency and that human spermatozoa are a rich source of magnesium.

'Is that so?' I said. 'I suppose you're going to volunteer to come over later to help relieve me of this severe nutritional deficiency?'

'Well, I don't want to brag, but I have been touted in the press as manly enough to render perfectly respectable princesses sex mad from several miles away.'

'Nice try, Mr. Moscovitz,' I said. 'I'm reporting you to the board of health for making unsubstantiated nutritional claims. Good-bye.'

His eyes actually looked as normal as he claims mine do, so maybe he really is okay, and the whole shadow thing is a figment of my admittedly sometimes overactive imagination.

I am going to order magnesium right now from the

grocery store down the street (to be delivered, although sadly I can't order it with my smartphone because the closest grocery store from which the Royal Genovian Guard will accept deliveries doesn't have an app for that. Also, I'm not allowed to have apps, except of course for iTriage, which I can't imagine doing any harm).

I'm sure the news of what I'm ordering will get out somehow and the next headline about me is going to read:

'Pill-Popping Princess!

CAN ANYONE SAVE HER?

Pope Swears He'll Try.'

TARANTINO'S,

Your Neighborhood Grocery Store

At Tarantino's, we're here to help! We know you have better things to do with your time than shop – play with your children, finish that important project for work, or just relax at home.

That's why we've made shopping easy with our home-delivery order form! Just check off the items you need, and we'll bring them to your door (or doorman) in ninety minutes or less (not guaranteed during peak delivery times, Monday–Friday 6:00 p.m.–8:00 p.m.).

Let's get started!
Check off desired items.

MEAT
Please give quantity/type desired
Beef:
Pork:
Steaks:
Lamb:
Veal:
Deli meats:
Other:

GOURMET FOODS:
Please give quantity/brand desired
Caviar:
Pâté:
Salmon:
Sushi:
✓ Spreads: *Cream cheese, plain, full fat, 1 small*
Other:

DAIRY:
Please give quantity/brand desired
Eggs (organic):
Cheese (kind):
✓ Milk (size): *1 gallon, 2%*
Yogurt:
Butter:
Margarine:
Sour Cream:
Half and Half:
Other:

PRODUCE:
Please give quantity/type desired
Lettuce:
Tomatoes:
Oranges:
Grapefruit:
Bananas:
✓ Apples: *2 Red Delicious*
Grapes:
Melon:
Potatoes:
Onions:
Peppers:
Mushrooms:
Other:

BAKERY:
Please give quantity/brand desired
Sandwich bread:
French bread:
Babka:
Challah:
✓ Bagels: *5 plain*
Muffins:
Coffee cake:
Dessert cake:
✓ Other: *1 container chocolate cake frosting*

DRY GOODS:
Please give quantity/brand desired
Coffee:
Tea:
Cereal:
Sugar:
✓ Cat food: *20 cans, Fancy Feast, Tuna and Chicken, Seafood Mix, Beef and Liver, Trout flavor*
Dog food:
Jellies:
Condiments:
Other:

PHARMACY:
Please give quantity/brand desired
Shampoo:
Conditioner:
Bath Soap:
Hand Soap:
Women's Sanitary:
Aspirin:
Vitamin C:
✓ Other: *Nature's Way Magnesium, 2 bottles; Tylenol PM, 1 bottle*

ITEMS FOR THE HOME:
Please give quantity/brand desired
Dish detergent:
Laundry detergent:
✓ Toilet tissue: *Extra soft, 4 rolls*
Sponges:
Other:

SNACKS:
Please give quantity/brand desired
✓ Popcorn: *Cheese popcorn, prepopped, 2 large bags*
✓ Potato Chips: *Corn chips, 2 bags*
✓ Salsa: *1 jar, medium heat*
Peanuts:
✓ Cookies: *Chocolate chip, 2 bags*
Candy:
✓ Ice Cream: *Rocky Road, 1 carton*
✓ Other: *Wasabi peas*

BEVERAGES:
Please give quantity/brand desired
Soda:
✓ Bottled water: *1 12-pack sparkling water*
Juice:
Wine:
Beer:
Other:

Please Note: If you are ordering beverages containing alcohol, the person receiving your delivery must have identification proving they are at least 21 years old.
It is illegal to sell or give away alcoholic beverages to:
1. Any person under the age of 21 years.
2. Any visibly intoxicated person.

The Surgeon General of the United States of America advises women who are pregnant (or considering pregnancy) to avoid consuming alcoholic beverages, as this may be harmful to developing fetuses.

I, the undersigned, agree I am over the age of 21.

X: *Lars van der Hooten*

Address: *Consulate General of Genovia*
31 East Sixty-ninth Street
New York, NY 10021

8:32 p.m., Wednesday, April 29
Benefit for the Chernobyl Shelter Fund
Waldorf Astoria Bathroom
New York City

Have to write fast because the ladies' room attendant is wondering what I'm doing locked in this bathroom stall.

But I *had* to jot down what this scientist who has been working on the project to build a containment structure over Chernobyl just told me (cannot believe all that radiation is *still* floating around out there, even though that nuclear reactor exploded almost thirty years ago).

So this scientist said that the very intelligent are sometimes bad at games like Trivial Pursuit because they dismiss knowledge they consider 'inconsequential' to make room for information they think we'll need someday (which finally explains why I'm so terrible at *Jeopardy!* Also sports).

(Of course I'm not saying I'm *very* intelligent.)

But why else do I know absolutely nothing about Chernobyl (or really what anyone is talking about here tonight, though I'm happy my presence is drawing attention to such an important cause) and so much about etiquette, Genovian history, and European citrus production?

Although this doesn't explain why I know everything about *Star Wars*.

The journaling isn't working yet, and neither is the magnesium. Probably I should have taken Michael up on his offer. (Just kidding.)

Not that I could have even if I wanted to, since he ended up not being able to come over *again* tonight, this time because of some kind of glitch in the consulate's security system. Anytime anyone enters or exits the building from any of the side doors, it sets off the alarm, the one connected to the New York City Police Department.

Which I guess is a good thing (nice to know the system works), but I can't have any overnight guests until they find the glitch, unless I want to pick up the morning paper and see 'Princess of Slut-o-via!' in twenty-point font on the cover again.

Used an eye mask, earplugs, my mouth guard, Tylenol PM, *and* stole a shot from the two-hundred-year-old bottle of Napoleon brandy the consulate general keeps hidden under his desk for visiting dignitaries (which technically I am), but am still wide-awake at five in the morning.

The reporters seem to be having a nice time out there, though, judging by their laughter.

I partly blame my inability to fall asleep on the fact that I made the mistake of FaceTiming with Tina Hakim Baba before bed (even though she lives only a few dozen blocks away, I hardly ever see her anymore either). The whole time, I couldn't stop lying. What kind of person lies to her best friend? Well, one of her best friends.

Our conversation started out normally enough – Tina swore she couldn't see my eye twitching, even when I said the words guaranteed to bring on the twitch:

'Dad's going to lose the election and my cousin Ivan will be the new prime minister of Genovia. He'll do nothing for the immigration problem, but he *will* destroy the country's fragile ecosystem and infrastructure by dredging the harbor and allowing cruise ships larger than the *Costa Concordia* to dock at the Port of Princess Clarisse.'

'Really, Mia, I can't see it,' Tina assured me. 'I'm not saying it's all in your head, but I don't think you need to worry.'

I could feel my eyelid pulsating like Sigourney Weaver's stomach in the movie *Alien,* so I knew she was fibbing to make me feel better.

Maybe that's why later on in the conversation, I returned the favor.

Still, since Tina's in med school at NYU, it was refreshing to hear her take on twitching eyes, which she knew all about since she just did a section on ophthalmology. She confirmed everything Dr. Delgado said. It's nice to know I'm not seeing a quack.

I didn't ask her about the thing Michael told me, though. I didn't want to remind her of her ex, Boris, with whom she's been going through an extremely painful breakup.

'I think it's good for you to get back into journaling,' Tina said. 'I tried it, too, in the hopes it would help me not to think so much about . . . well, you know.'

Well, so much for not talking about her ex. That's when our conversation started going downhill, and I started lying my head off.

I felt forced to ask: 'Did journaling help?'

'No,' she said, with a sigh. 'I really think I might be addicted to Boris. Did you know a medical study showed that participants who had recently experienced a breakup had the exact same brain activity as people going through drug withdrawal?'

Ack.

'Well,' I said, trying to keep my tone upbeat. 'You're a strong, independent woman, and I know you're going to break that bad habit!'

'Thanks.' She sighed again. 'It's so hard, though. I thought Boris and I would stay together forever, the way you and Michael have.'

Ugh. Ugh, ugh, ugh.

Look, I know it's weird that I'm nearly twenty-six and still dating my high school boyfriend. Believe me, I'm *more* than aware of what a cliché it is.

But it gets even worse: almost all my friends are people I went to high school with, too.

But in my own defense, when you find out at the tender age of fourteen that you're the heir to a throne and a billion-dollar fortune (because my mom and dad never got married, and Dad always thought he could have more kids. Due to chemo for cancer that fortunately has remained in remission, he cannot), who are you going to trust, the people who knew and liked you *before* you got on *Forbes* List of Richest Young Royals, or the people you met *after*?

The answer is obvious. I can't even count the number of guys I dated after I found out I was a princess who turned out to only be interested in me for my tiara.

(Well, yes, I can, actually: two. Josh Richter and J. P. Reynolds-Abernathy IV. Not that I'm still bitter about it, or hold a grudge against them, or asked to have my Facebook password taken away and changed so I don't spend hours obsessively looking up every detail of their lives to make sure they're miserable without me, because only a weirdo would do that.)

- *Note to self:* Ask Dominique what the new password is because it would be quite nice to see the photos Lana is posting of her new baby. I'm sure that at nearly twenty-six, I am mature (and self-actualized) enough not to go hunting down my exes. Besides, I am so happy in my own relationship that I don't care what my exes are doing anymore. Very much.

One of the reasons I love Tina so much is that she understands and sympathizes with so many of my issues – being the daughter of an extremely wealthy Arab sheikh who also forces her to be followed around by bodyguards at all times – but she's also the opposite of me in many ways. She's good at math and science, and intends, as soon as she gets her medical license, to join Doctors Without Borders and help sick children. This is so admirable and amazing! I wish I could be more like her.

Except the part where she still hasn't managed to sever all ties to her ex, Boris Pelkowski.

'Tina,' I said. 'Michael and I are an anomaly. Hardly anyone stays together forever with their first significant other, except maybe in YA novels. And usually when they do, it's because he's a vampire or a werewolf or owns a beautiful estate called Pemberley or something.'

'But—'

'Seriously, did you think Lilly Moscovitz and Kenny Showalter were going to stay together forever when they both went off to Columbia after graduation?'

'Well,' Tina said. 'I guess not after Kenny built that yurt in the middle of campus, then refused to go to class anymore.'

'Exactly,' I said. 'It's *normal* for people to change and grow, and for couples to sometimes grow apart.'

'You and Michael never grew apart. And what about Perin and Ling Su?'

I sighed. Just like I have a disproportionately large number of friends from my high school class, a disproportionately large number of the couples from that class have stayed together since graduation.

I blame the faculty. The absurd amount of homework with which they loaded us down every night gave many of us permanent post-traumatic stress. College – even though I attended Sarah Lawrence, one of the top schools in the country – was a breeze compared to AEHS (Albert Einstein High School).

'Okay, well, Perin and Ling Su are an anomaly, too,' I said to Tina. 'But they've had their problems. Remember how they had to pretend for so long that they were only roommates?'

'Only because Ling Su's grandparents were so old-fashioned,' Tina protested. 'They totally support same-sex marriage now.'

'Yeah, because Perin worked so hard to win them over. She even learned *Mandarin*. What's Boris done for *you* lately, Tina, except swap his classical violin for an electric guitar, write a bunch of cheesy pop songs, and then become an international pop sensation who is fawned over by millions of girls who call themselves the Borettes, one of whom he slept with?'

'Allegedly,' she reminded me. 'He still says he didn't do it. He says he misses me and wants to meet with me so he can explain—'

'Oh, *Tina*!'

'I know. But he still insists those pictures of him were Photoshopped, and that he would never, ever cheat on me.'

I could feel myself beginning to clench my jaw, and tried to relax it. Who could have imagined that Boris Pelkowski, the mouth-breathing violin virtuoso from my Gifted and Talented class way back in ninth grade, would become 'Boris P.,' the purple-haired pop singer-songwriter who now plays sold-out concerts all over the world and has girls throwing themselves at him every time he steps from his limo (even though he still hasn't quite learned to breathe through his nostrils, a fact the Borettes have

25

declared 'totes adorbs' on the Internet).

Although there was nothing 'totes adorbs' about the nude photos one of those girls posted online of herself with him in a hotel room.

'What about the texts she posted that he sent her?' I asked Tina. 'Did he have an explanation for those?'

'He said she did interview him for her blog, so the texts are real, but that everyone's taken everything he said out of context, and that all the rest she made up to get more hits on her site. I mean, I guess that's possible, right?'

'Um,' I said. 'Sure. I guess so.'

Lie number one.

Boris had told Michael the exact same thing (the two of them are still friends – they get together to play World of Warcraft a few times a month. The fact that Boris enjoys playing online fantasy role-playing games only endears him more to the Borettes).

Michael refuses to stop speaking to Boris just because he 'allegedly' cheated on my friend. He says there are two sides to every story, and as a fellow celebrity, I should understand how these kinds of things get twisted by the press, and that I should give Boris the benefit of the doubt.

But I've seen the photos. Some violin players develop Fiddler's Neck, a sort of callus along the underside of their chin from holding their instrument there for extended periods of time.

The guy in the photos has the same Fiddler's Neck pattern as Boris (as I know only too well, having seen him shirtless playing water volleyball at the palace pool back in Genovia when he used to be allowed to visit there with Tina).

So despite Boris's protests – and Michael's – those pictures *aren't* Photoshopped. The story *has* to be true.

Although I guess Michael hasn't really driven me sex mad, so maybe it *isn't* true. Ugh.

I always thought when I became an adult everything would become less confusing, but unfortunately, everything's only become *more* confusing.

'Boris says that girl could have hacked into his phone, then wrote all those mean things about me because she's obsessed with him,' Tina went on. 'You know, stalker style. He says she's jealous of me. But none of that seems very likely . . .'

'Tina!' I gasped. 'You say that like there's nothing for her to be jealous of. You know perfectly well how hot you are. You're the hottest, most beautiful woman I know.' This, at least, was not a lie.

'That's sweet of you to say, Mia, but I'm not as hot as her,' she said with an unhappy sigh. 'Have you seen her? She's totally rocking that Brooklyn hipster music blogger thing.'

'And I will be more than happy to yank that ring right out of her septum if you'd like me to. I can always claim I tripped and grabbed it by accident.' To my relief, Tina started to laugh. 'No, really. People will believe me, because I have a reputation for being a klutz, but I'm also a princess, and princesses never lie.'

HA HA HA HA.

'Aw, thanks, Mia,' she said. 'That's what I love about you. You're the loyalist friend ever. Anyway, I don't know what to do. Boris told me that new song of his, "A Million Stars," is about me.'

Ugh! I don't want to be *that* girl – the girl who tells someone not to give her ex another chance, especially right after that person's just called her the 'loyalist friend ever.'

Because, of course, there's always a chance Michael is right, and the thing with Boris really is only a misunderstanding. And this is America. We love forgiving people, then letting them have a second chance.

But that doesn't mean 'A Million Stars' isn't the worst, cheesiest, most horrible song *ever*.

Which, of course, is only *my* opinion. The Borettes love it so much they've made it the number one bestselling song of all time *ever*. You can't go anywhere – any elevator, any store, any airport, any hotel lobby, any restaurant, not even New York's *Times Square* – without hearing it being blared over a set of speakers.

Worse, in the video for it (which is also played everywhere constantly), Boris is singing to a girl who is *dying in a hospital bed*, and Boris is telling her (lyrically) that he'll give her a million stars (plus his love) if she'll just find the strength within herself to not die, and love him forever.

Of course the girl is so moved by this hot rocker dude's amazing song that she doesn't die. Because it is a medical fact that people with fatal diseases only need a hot rocker dude to sit on the edge of their hospital bed and sing them a rock ballad in order to give them the strength to go on living.

People actually believe this stuff! At least the Borettes do.

Both the song and the video have made me hate Boris Pelkowski so much more than I already did (for breaking Tina's heart) that now whenever I hear or see either of them, I begin grinding my teeth. I've even started doing it in my sleep, and have to wear a night guard, which is so not sexy when Michael stays over.

Although he says he'd rather have me wear a big rubber mouth guard in bed with him than for me to have tiny little nubs for teeth someday.

- *Note to self:* Which, if you ask me, is actually way more romantic than some rocker dude singing to a girl on her deathbed. But no one asked me.

'So what did you say when Boris told you he wants to get back together?' I asked Tina cautiously.

'I said I'd have to think about it. Just because he has over five million Borettes following him on Twitter doesn't mean *I'm* ready to follow him.'

Thank God, I thought.

But aloud I only said, 'That was very wise.'

'And maybe it's better we break up now anyway to spare ourselves future heartbreak. What's going to happen when I graduate and have to move away from New York to do my residency? Or when I'm with Doctors

29

Without Borders? I'm not going to be able to follow him around on tour like some little Borette. I have my own career to think about.'

'Totally,' I said, thrilled.

'So I told him that right now I really need to concentrate on acing my exams, but that maybe we could talk later.'

'Well, I think you did the right thing.' This was lie number two. I do think Tina should concentrate on her exams, but I'm not so sure she should talk to Boris later.

'Thanks, Mia,' she said. 'It's just so hard, you know, because every time I go online or turn on the TV, there he is, being interviewed about this forty-city tour, looking all buff from working with that new trainer of his.'

'I know.' Lie number three. Boris doesn't look *that* good, but then, he's never exactly been my type. 'Honestly, Tina, I have no idea what I'd do if I were in your shoes.'

Lie number four. I think about what I'd do if I were in Tina's shoes *all the time,* which is ridiculous, since Michael's the best boyfriend ever (or the best boyfriend he can be, considering what he has to put up with, dating a royal).

But Tina thought Boris was the best boyfriend ever until number one Boris Fan, Brooklyn Borette Blogger, came along.

What if that shadow I keep seeing in Michael's eyes isn't a kidney stone he's too manly to mention, but guilt because he's seeing some little 'Michael-ette' behind my back? I don't know if I'd be able to handle it with as much class as Tina has with Boris, keeping her mouth shut about it (except to me, of course). I think I might go full-on Mrs. ex–Tiger Woods Elin Nordegren on him (even though violence is never the answer and Michael doesn't play golf or even own an SUV like Tiger Woods).

The problem, of course, is that I come from a long line of warrior princesses. Sometimes when I can't sleep – like now – I mentally rehearse how I'd get back at Michael if I found out he'd cheated on me, even though I'm self-actualized enough to know he'd never do such a thing, and that if he did, losing me would be his loss, not mine.

Still, occasionally these thoughts creep in unbidden (I probably should have mentioned this to Dr. Delgado. I bet he'd have given me some medication if he knew) and then I recall how my royal ancestresses handled their business when betrayed by a man:

Princess Rosagunde

The first princess of Genovia, Rosagunde, strangled her husband – the chief of an invading tribe of marauders – to death in his sleep with her braid, an act of heroism for which she was then unanimously named ruler of her village.

I'd never do something like that to Michael, of course, since violence is never the answer (my hair's not long enough anyway), and I do not want to spend the rest of my life in jail like the ladies in *Orange Is the New Black*.

But since I'm descended from Rosagunde, the

capacity for this kind of brutality runs through my veins – even though sadly I can never seem to summon it when I need to, like when teenagers behind me in the movie theater won't stop texting, especially during the dramatic moments. Then I merely get Lars, my bodyguard, to get up and glare at them threateningly.

Princess Mathilde

Upon discovering reports of her intended's multiple affairs, my ancestress Princess Mathilde donned full body armor, rode to his home, then proceeded to smash every piece of furniture in it with a battle-ax.

Then she rode away, taking with her his favorite hunting dogs, servants, and horses, claiming them as compensation for her broken heart.

He was much too frightened of her to protest.

Michael doesn't have any servants, much less any horses, and his beloved dog Pavlov died not too long ago of old age (dogs don't live as long as cats). Michael does, however, have a lot of furniture, plus tons of *Star Wars* memorabilia that he values greatly. He has every single Princess Leia action figure, some still in the box!

Still, I'd feel weird about smashing up his house with an ax, then stealing his stuff. Maybe I'd just light all the boxer briefs he's left over here on fire (in the sink, for safety).

Dowager Princess Clarisse Renaldo

It's a not-very-well-kept secret that my grandmother had a string of suitors before my grandfather, the wealthy Prince of Genovia, fell for her. One of them was a Texas oil baron she met in Monte Carlo while she was vacationing with friends. This gentleman was so smitten that he proposed on the spot (according to Grandmère's version of events).

Unfortunately, it was soon discovered that the oil baron had, in romance-novel parlance, 'a wife yet living' – but not before Grandmère had already spent a hefty amount of money on her trousseau.

So she did what any shrewd Genovian girl would do, and sued him for the cost of her new wardrobe (to the tune of a hundred thousand Genovian francs).

'Those gowns were handmade by Monsieur Dior! They cost two thousand dollars each,' she still says whenever the subject comes up. 'What else was I to do?'

The guy paid up. It was apparently cheaper than getting a divorce.

Oh, ugh. All the insomnia websites say that to ensure a good night's rest, you're supposed to engage in soothing rituals right before you fall asleep, like taking a hot bath or sniffing lavender or drinking warm milk.

Few advise making lists of ways your royal ancestors got revenge on their boyfriends for cheating on them, and *none* mentions discussing your father's recent run-in with the law – or the fact that he did it because he was trying to get back together with your mother.

But that's exactly what Tina brought up later on during our conversation, and probably why I'm wider awake now than ever.

'Things have actually gotten a bit better since this news about your dad broke,' Tina said, just before we were about to quit FaceTiming. 'Now there's a lot less stuff on all the gossip sites about Boris, and more about how people think your dad wants a second chance with your mom.'

'Wait . . .' I was shocked. *'What?'*

'It's true,' Tina insisted. 'People think your dad took up race-car driving to get your mom's attention now that your stepdad has died and she's available again.'

I've seen a lot of wrongheaded and offensive things written about myself and my family, but that one really takes the cake. I'm not going to say it doesn't hurt when people say bad stuff about me, particularly when it's untrue, but I'm young and strong: I can take it.

But to say it about my *mom,* who isn't really a public figure, and can't defend herself, and my *dad,* who's getting on in age, and is clearly becoming a tragic figure like Mickey Rourke, only without the boxing or tiny dogs?

'Well, if that's what Dad's up to, it's a really bad strategy,' I spluttered. 'My mom's so not the type to care about trophies, unless it's a Pulitzer, or maybe a Nobel.'

'I know, right? Your mom would never drop everything and come rushing to be at your dad's bedside after half his face was burned off in a tragic race-car accident, because she'd be like, "He deserved it for being involved in such a dangerous sport in the first place."'

'It's true,' I said, then added, 'Although that would have made an excellent scene in a movie that I would have paid full price to see in theaters, not even waited to watch at home on pay-per-view or HBO.'

'Oh my God, me, too.'

No wonder I can't sleep.

Except that if this turns out to be true, Dad pretty much brought it on himself. Well, at least the part where he's allegedly still in love with my mother, after more than twenty-six years (that's how long ago he impregnated her while they were both college students back in the eighties, when drinking too much and being 'in the moment' was an acceptable excuse for not using birth control, although not really, if you ask me. Well, twenty-five years and nine months ago. My birthday is tomorrow).

'Of course I don't blame your dad for thinking such a crazy stunt might work,' Tina went on. 'Your mother rushed to be at your stepfather's side after he had that heart attack while taking the M14 crosstown bus to band practice last year.'

'Right,' I said. 'But Mr. G. and my mom were *married*. And also, not knowing you have heart disease because you keep putting off going to the doctor is completely different from purposely pursuing high-risk sports.'

At least Mr. G. had plenty of life insurance and a surprisingly healthy 401(k), so he left my mom and my half brother, Rocky, financially secure (and Mom's paintings are still selling really well, considering the market for contemporary realism).

Of course, now that I think about it, Tina – and apparently the media – aren't the only ones with this crazy theory about my dad. Michael's parents kind of brought it up when I was last at their house (for Passover dinner).

This was before the arrest, of course. But somehow the conversation turned toward Dad and how weird he's been acting lately and one of the Drs. Moscovitz – I can't remember which – said my dad'll never be happy because he desperately wants to be with my mother, but she's never been the kind of woman who – like Grandmère – is attracted to men in positions of power.

'So are you saying my dad wants to marry his mother?' I'd asked in horror.

'Well,' Dr. Moscovitz had replied, 'according to Freud, deep down, all men want to marry their mothers, and all women, their fathers.'

I knew there was a reason I don't like Freud. Michael is *nothing* like my dad, and I really can't see how I resemble his mother. She looks like a brunette Dr. Ruth Westheimer, only slightly shorter and with more moles on her face.

Oh, well.

Tina and I hung up after promising each other we weren't going to think about the men in our lives who were bothering us – in her case, her ex, and in mine, my current boyfriend and my father – anymore.

But that's pretty much all I've done since.

I must have gotten a little sleep, though, because I did have a dream earlier that I was asked by Kate, Duchess of

Cambridge, to have lunch, so she could give me tips on how to handle the stress of being a modern-day princess (something I am obviously still not handling well, even after a decade of practice).

But when Kate greeted me at the door, she told me she had no time to talk to me about princess stuff, because she had a date with Bruce Willis. So she left me alone in Buckingham Palace with Prince George!

So I baked a cake for him, then helped him eat it.

Three things for which I feel grateful:

1. Tina Hakim Baba.

2. My noble ancestresses.

3. Cake.

I can't believe this.

I looked out the window this morning because the paps seemed a bit louder than usual. I expected to see them playing some kind of drinking game (per usual) but instead I saw *protesters*!

Not many, but enough. They're holding signs protesting my dad (and me, too).

I called Dominique right away and she said (in her adorable French accent), 'I know, I know, your 'ighness. Don't worry, we are on it.'

(Dominique has a hard time pronouncing the letter *H,* which is silent in French, so asking her things like the name of 'that boy wizard' is one of my favorite pastimes whenever I happen to be stuck in traffic with her. 'You mean 'airy Pottair, Princess?' she always asks, excitedly. ''airy Pottair, 'oo went to 'ogwarts?' Juvenile, but always entertaining.)

'On it?' I asked. 'How are you "on it"?'

'Oh, we 'ave a few ideas . . .'

'Like what? Should we hold a press conference? Do you want me to issue a public statement? What?'

'No, no, nothing like that. It's better that we just ignore them for now.'

'That's what you said about the paparazzi, but they haven't gone away in two weeks.'

'I know, but don't worry. It's only a ploy by your father's opponent to get media attention.'

Oh, right. Of course.

What do Genovians have to complain about, anyway? Genovia has the lowest unemployment, violence, and poverty rate in the world (zero percent), and also the loveliest median year-round temperature (seventy-five degrees), being situated as it is so idyllically on the Riviera. Genovians pay no personal income tax, and business taxes are among the lowest in the European Union.

Even Genovia's royal family is self-supported (unlike the UK's, which is financed by public money). According to Rate the Royals, I have a personal net worth of a hundred million dollars.

HA! Where do these websites get this stuff?

- *Note to self*: Well, of course, I probably do have a personal net worth of that much, but only if you count things like medieval-era jewel-encrusted scepters, which you can't exactly sell on eBay.

So if Cousin Ivan is going to have a chance of beating my dad for prime minister in this next election, he has to do *something* to make people believe things in Genovia aren't all that great.

So why not pay a bunch of lame Genovian expats to stand outside its consulate in New York holding signs making a big deal out of super tiny issues, like allowing cruise ships in, keeping GMOs out, and complaining about that op-ed piece I wrote the other week for the *Wall Street Journal*?

Apparently *some* people feel the heir to the throne of one principality has no right to express her opinion of how the ruler of another principality governs his country, even one who's stripped half his population of what little rights they previously had (the female half, of course), and is threatening to behead his own son for marrying a commoner (fortunately Prince Rashid and his bride have been given asylum in the United States).

All I did was comment on how much I disapprove of the sheikh. I didn't put out a big sign that says HEY, OPPRESSED PEOPLE OF QALIF, COME TO GENOVIA! Like these protesters apparently think I did.

Still, when someone who is being mistreated in their home travels very far and under horrible conditions to get to yours, shouldn't you at least offer them shelter and something to eat and drink until they sort things out? It seems like common courtesy to me.

So what is everyone's problem?

Oh, God, now a television news van has shown up downstairs to film the protesters. *Why?* Why can't a celebrity couple choose today to announce that they're divorcing so the media has something else to cover?

I wonder how much magnesium it's safe to take in one day.

- *Note to self:* Check iTriage.

12:00 p.m., Thursday, April 30
Third-Floor Apartment
Consulate General of Genovia
New York City

Lilly just texted me:

> Lilly Moscovitz 'Virago'*: What are you doing?

*I have to give all my contacts code names in case of hacking. Kate, Duchess of Cambridge, has been hacked 155 times. *Virago* means 'female warrior' but also 'bad-tempered woman.' Not that Lilly's bad-tempered, but lately, since she's been studying for the bar, she's been more difficult than usual.

I guess I'd be difficult, too, though, if I had to study for a test that took two whole days to complete. It's a little disappointing that my best friend, who showed such promise in the past as a television producer, is going into the law, but like Lilly says, her true passion is arguing, so at least in the legal profession she'll be paid to do it.

> **HRH Mia Thermopolis 'FtLouie': What do you think I'm doing? I'm 'working from home.' But really I'm trapped in my apartment, watching NY1 interview Genovian protesters about how much they hate me and my dad.**

There was a pause, and then Lilly wrote:

< Lilly Moscovitz 'Virago'   HRH Mia Thermopolis 'FtLouie' >

Oh my God, there you are! Well, not you, but the consulate, right on live TV. Wow, slow news day. Why don't you come over here and we can live tweet it while drinking tequila?

Thanks, but that is not how the palace is choosing to handle the situation and would also be a violation of diplomatic protocol. Besides, the Royal Genovian Guard has me on lockdown in case any of the protesters turns out to be my stalker.

They haven't caught that guy yet?

No. They think RoyalRabbleRouser must use a VPN (Virtual Private Network software) to hide his IP address since they haven't been able to track his location.

Wow, that is not scary at all. But anyway, that crowd doesn't look too violent.

Don't underestimate them, one of them already threw a Genovian orange at Lars.

Why a Genovian orange?

In addition to their many other complaints, the protesters are anti-GMO and don't think Genovian farmers should be allowed to plant drought-resistant Genovian orange trees (even though genetically modified food could help to end world hunger and the Genovian orange yield increased by 25% last year. And that study with the tumor-ridden rats was proven to be completely faked).

Sorry I asked. I thought Genovia was known for its olives. Or is it pears?

It doesn't matter. The demand for orange juice in Europe is huge, so now all we're growing is oranges.

Of course. What did Lars do when they threw the genetically modified orange at him? PLEASE say he shot them with tear-gas canisters, PLEASE.

He did not. He picked the orange up off the ground and took a huge bite out of it. Including the peel.

❤

Stop.

I swear to God someday I am going to tie that Scandinavian to my bed and do unspeakable things to him.

I know it's been a while since you've had a date, but please keep in mind that Lars has been my bodyguard since I was 14 years old, so I think of him as an older brother.

I'm pretty sure you do unspeakable things to MY older brother on a pretty regular basis.

How many energy drinks have you had today?

Not enough. So all this fuss is over some genetically modified oranges?

Of course not. They also want us to allow bigger cruise ships (3,000 people a day is not enough) and immigration reform.

What immigration? I thought no one gets citizenship in Genovia unless they're born there (or has a parent who was born there, like you) or marries a Genovian.

Yes, and that's the way they want to keep it. But we're offering emergency humanitarian visas to all the Qalifi refugees who've been showing up by the boatload since my op-ed piece.

Is that what those signs they're carrying mean, 'Let Them Live with Mia'?

Yes.

Make your own sign and hang it in the window telling them to suck your [REDACTED].

Thank you so kindly for that piece of advice. However, that is neither princessy nor physically possible.

Actually we are working on finding a more diplomatic solution that includes providing the refugees with emergency shelter in local hotels, but all the hotels are full due to the 125th Genovian Yacht Classic.

Oh, of course. How foolish of me not to know that the 125th Genovian Yacht Classic is taking place right now. I'm sure Muffy and Carrington must be very upset about all the riff-raff dirtying up the beaches.

It doesn't matter since even if there were hotel rooms, no one would take the refugees in, as Cousin Ivan has spread a rumor that they all have tuberculosis and cholera, so border officials are holding them at the Port of Princess Clarisse.

Again, sorry I asked. Can I come over with a sign telling those protesters to suck MY [REDACTED]?

I'm so happy someone like you is pursuing a career in contract law since it's clear you're so calm and levelheaded.

Speaking of calm and levelheaded (no), where's your dad?

Probably the Oak Bar at the Plaza Hotel, where he's been drowning most of his sorrows while waiting to hear from the judge about when he's going to be allowed to leave the U.S.

Typical. What are you doing for your birthday tomorrow?

What do you think?

Wait, let me guess: your grandmother is taking you to Cirque du Soleil. AGAIN.

The magic of the circus is what she lives for.

HA HA HA! How many times is this?

She says we have to put 'a brave public face on' in light of the protesters and Dad's arrest, and act like 'everything is normal' for the good of Genovia.

Is that why there's now a van pulling up in front of your building that says '*Parrucchiere di Paolo*' on the side?

No. Paolo is coming over to give me a blowout so I'll look good as I bravely face the protesters while greeting our guests tonight. Grandmère's decided to throw a dinner party here at the consulate.

What if one sneaks in and throws an orange at you?

That is a risk that, as a royal, I'm obligated to take.

Aw, you're just like that princess from the movie *Brave*. Only you have zero hand-eye coordination. Why is there no e-vite in my in-box?

Because only Genovian expats who pass a background test (and haven't thrown any Genovian oranges at Lars) are invited, so they will see how 'real' and 'caring' we are and hopefully post to social media about it.

If I get invited, I will post to social media about it, and I won't throw an orange at you OR Lars. I'll throw myself at him but not an orange.

Seriously, stop. I can only take so much.

Is my brother invited?

Do you think I'd put his beautiful head at risk over something this stupid?

Well, if he's your future prince consort, he'd better get used to this kind of thing, don't you think?

There are some things I think even a future prince consort should be spared.

Put like a true royal.

3:10 p.m., Thursday, April 30
Third-Floor Apartment
Consulate General of Genovia
New York City

Not a lot of time to write because Paolo is giving me a blow-dry and it's rude to write in one's journal while someone is performing personal grooming services on you (also difficult, especially when that person has applied press-on nails over your bitten-down nails, and the glue/paint on those nails is still drying).

Anyway, Paolo started out the appointment upset because I wouldn't let him cut off all my hair (quote from Paolo: 'It looks better short, it shows offa your long neck'), but I know the truth:

Paolo just wants to do something different that will get my photo onto all the fashion sites, and the best way to do that these days is with a 'daring' pixie cut like so many of the twentysomething starlets are doing.

But I'm not an actress in a movie about someone dying of cancer/tuberculosis, so:

I said, 'No, thank you, Paolo, I like my hair better long, but if your arms are tired, you can leave the blow-drying to one of your assistants.'

This offended him very much. He sniffed, 'No, Principessa! Paolo never get tired,' which is fine with me since now we don't have to talk anymore (Paolo doesn't like to shout over the whine of hair driers. Also a relief: that he can't tell what I'm writing since he's not so good at reading English. Or any other language that I can tell, except the language of beauty).

But unfortunately he did notice my twitch earlier and said, 'Principessa, you look like the pirate, only not the hot one played by Johnny Depp, what is wrong?'

Generally I don't believe in pouring out one's hardships to one's hairdresser, because, as Grandmère is always reminding me, 'Your personal baggage should only be shared with family, Amelia . . . and the bellboy, of course.' This is pretty good advice, except that usually family members are the ones *causing* the baggage problems, so I find that therapists and good friends can be more helpful with it.

But Paolo has been around so long, he's *like* family. So before I knew it, it all came tumbling out.

This turned out to be one of the few times I should have listened to Grandmère.

Paolo wasn't at all sympathetic, especially when I mentioned the fact that right after I logged off from my conversation with Lilly, I went to Google News to see what the media was saying about the protest today, and the first headline I saw was from the *Post*. It screamed:

'Why Won't He Marry Mia?'

Really? *That* is what the editors feel is the most important news to report on today, the reasons Michael Moscovitz hasn't proposed to me yet?

Of course it isn't, it's just what they think will get the most clicks.

And of course it worked, because even *I* clicked on it, knowing I shouldn't have, because Michael and I are mature adults and of course we've discussed marriage at length, and the decision we've come to (and our reason for it) is our business and ours alone.

(Except of course that my grandmother thinks it should be her business and so she's always asking me with elaborate casualness, 'So when do you think you and Michael will be getting married?' the way other people ask, 'So when do you think you and Michael will be coming over for drinks?')

But apparently the *Post* thinks it is everyone's business, since they've printed the reasons they believe Michael doesn't want to marry me, which include (but are not limited to):

1. The fact that after we're married, Michael will have to give up his American citizenship and be called Prince Michael, Royal Consort. (True.)

2. He'll have to be escorted at all times by bodyguards. (True.)

3. He'll have to attend charity benefits practically every night of the week, which, while being extremely worthy and fulfilling, can also be quite exhausting. (True. I can't tell you how much I feel like staying home some nights in my rattiest pajamas, eating pizza straight out of the box while watching Special Agent Leroy Jethro Gibbs and

his team take roguish miscreants to task on *NCIS*, rather than having to dress up and shake the hands of wealthy strangers who only want to talk about their last safari, then listen to a speech about Latvia's rich cultural heritage.)

4. Someone will *always* be sending their hobby drone over to spy on us, usually at the exact moment I've had too many daiquiris and decided it will be perfectly all right to go topless. (Which happened *once*, and I think it might have been the *Post* that bought those photos. Still, once is too many.)

5. Someday he'll have to move himself and his entire business to Genovia full-time. (Sadly, this is also true.)

6. The fact that I only wear platform wedges because I still haven't mastered the art of walking gracefully in high-heeled shoes and that sometimes when I do I'm actually as tall or taller than Michael. (True, but why would this be a reason a man wouldn't marry a woman, unless of course he had very low self-esteem, which Michael does not?)

7. Michael's alleged dislike of my getting involved with the politics of constitutional monarchies. (Blatantly false.)

8. Our having 'drifted apart' in recent days due to our

busy careers. (FALSE. At least I hope it's false. It *better* be false. Oh, God, please let it be false!)

9. My family. (True. So true.)

'I don't suppose it's ever occurred to the editors of the *Post* that if Michael and I have drifted apart – which we haven't – it's because of *them*,' I complained to Paolo after having read this list aloud in a comical voice. Dr. Knutz, my unfortunately named therapist, recommends I do this whenever I see mean-spirited comments or stories about myself. Reading them aloud in a comical voice is supposed to help make them hurt less.

But it doesn't. Nothing does. Except refusing to look at them in the first place.

'The press has a field day with my name every time I get caught in the morning sneaking out of Michael's place downtown, or he gets caught sneaking out of mine. Do you know what *Page Six* called me the last time a photographer spied me coming out of Michael's building?' I asked Paolo. 'The Princess of Gen-HO-via!'

Paolo put his hand over his mouth to pretend like he was horrified, but I could tell he was secretly laughing behind his fingers. Only there's nothing funny about the other names the media has called me, including:

- Shame of Thrones.

- Bad Idea Mia.

- He'll Never Buy the Cow If He Can Get the Milk for Free-a, Mia.

And of course now, *Why Won't He Marry Mia.* (Get it? Why Won't He Marry Me-Ah? Ha ha.)

You would think that in the enlightened era in which we live, a single girl could have a boyfriend and a career and also a healthy sex life (and help her father to rule a country) without getting called names.

But apparently this is too much to ask of some people.

'You know, there are very good reasons to marry – tax advantages, and the fact that married people live longer and report a higher degree of happiness overall than single people, and things like that,' I said to Paolo. 'But Michael and I have just as valid reasons for *not* marrying, like that marriage is an antiquated institution that ends in divorce almost half the time, and that we're perfectly happy with our relationship status the way it is . . . except for the part where we never get to see one another, even though we live in the same city.'

And the part where my boyfriend has started to look every once in a while as if he were harboring some dark, terrible secret. That might be a good reason not to get married, or at least have a very serious talk sometime soon, though I'm really not looking forward to it.

'And what about how we don't think it's fair for us to marry when our many same-sex-oriented couple friends cannot?' I demanded, since there was no way I was going to mention that other thing out loud. 'At least, not everywhere in the world.'

Paolo brightened. 'Yes, but thanks to you, Principessa, same-sex marriage has been legal in Genovia since 2013.'

'Right,' I said. '*You* can marry the man you love in Genovia, but *I* can't. Not without having news helicopters and quadcopter drones flying over my head, vying for as unflattering a shot of my butt as they can manage.'

Paolo looked horrified. 'Why would Paolo want to get married? Paolo has so much greatness to share with many, many men. He would not want to limit this greatness to only one man forever.'

'Yes, I know, Paolo,' I said. 'I'm just saying. Did you hear the part about the drones?'

That is when Paolo laid down the scissors (I'd conceded to a quarter-inch trim only) and said very firmly, 'Principessa, everyone must make the sacrifice for love! That's what makes it worth it. Even the principessas. And I think this is where you have the problem, because you think, "No, I am a principessa, I can do whatever I want. I do not have to sacrifice anything." But you do.'

'Paolo,' I said. 'Have you ever even met me? I've sacrificed *everything*. I can't even walk out my front door right now without people throwing oranges at me.'

'I think you need right now to find the balance,' he went on, ignoring me. 'For life, you never know where the road will take you. Yours took you to a place where you got the diamond shoes, but now all you can says is, "Ow! These diamond shoes! They fit so tight and hurt so much!" No one wants to hear about how tight your diamond shoes fit. You got the diamond shoes! Many people, they have no shoes at all.'

'Uh,' I interrupted. 'I think you mean glass slippers. Cinderella had glass slippers –'

'So you got to decide, Principessa, what are you going to do, put on your diamond shoes and go to the dance? Or take them off and stay home? I know what I would do if someone give me diamond shoes. I would go to the dance, and I would never stop dancing until my feet fell off.'

It wasn't until Paolo put it in quite that Paolo way of his that I realized he was right.

Of course, I don't *literally* own shoes made out of diamonds. (Well, I do own a pair of Jimmy Choos that have diamond toe clips.)

But if you think about it, I have no real problems. Aside from my obviously annoying housing situation, my mentally disturbed family, and the fact that a stalker says he wants to kill me.

I have never even really sacrificed anything for love, or had anyone I loved die, except for a beloved stepfather, and although this was extremely tragic, the doctors assured us Mr. Gianini didn't suffer, and probably wasn't even aware of what was happening once he initially lost consciousness (though it's quite sad that the last thing he saw was an advertisement for Dr. Zizmor, Skin Care Specialist, Don't Accept Substitutes).

But comparatively, I have nothing – absolutely *nothing* – to complain about.

I felt ashamed of myself, and wanted to grab my checkbook and make a large donation to a cause of Paolo's choice right that minute (except of course I've

57

already made several this year alone – not to mention having donated huge chunks of my time, including only last night when I attended that benefit for Chernobyl).

'I'm sorry, Paolo,' I said. 'You're so right. I *do* need to find balance in my life. Only I don't know how. Do you have any suggestions, other than keeping a gratitude journal, which I'm already doing?'

'*Sì!* I think my new boyfriend, Stefano, can help you, Principessa.'

'He can? That's wonderful! How?'

'Stefano has the healing hands!' Paolo cried proudly. 'He can cure you with one touch!'

'He's a masseur? Oh, how—'

'No, no, not the massage! The ancient art of Reiki, laying on of hands. Only the hands, they never touch you.'

I was confused. 'If they never touch you, then how do they heal anything?'

'The flow of energy from the universe! And for you, Principessa, Stefano do it for free. But of course after first half hour, it's two hundred dollars for every thirty minutes.'

'Um,' I said.

Of *course* sweet Paolo has fallen in love with some guy who's convinced he can cure people's problems by waving his hands over them and channeling the flow of energy from the universe.

But if anyone could actually do that, wouldn't all of life's ills have been solved already?

I said, plastering on my fake smile, 'Thank you,

Paolo, that's so kind of you, but I don't think I have time right now. Maybe another day, all right?'

Paolo looked disappointed. I know he's probably been fantasizing about having his current boyfriend magically restore balance to my universe, and then me raving about it to the press. Then the two of them could open some new spa – *Paolo and Stefano's Universal Beauty and Wellness. If we can cure royalty, we can cure you!*

But I think it's going to take more than one pair of healing hands to find the balance in my universe.

Ugh. So glad that's over. At least I looked good. Paolo is a true artist of hair.

I couldn't tell Lilly the truth about why I didn't want her or Michael around tonight. It wasn't that I was afraid of them getting oranges thrown at them (no oranges were thrown; everyone behaved with perfect decorum when Grandmère and I went out to greet our guests. Except for the booing).

It isn't even that the security system is still glitchy and that I'm afraid Michael will get caught entering the building in the wee hours and we'll get more bad press.

It's that Genovians are snobs.

That's why they don't want the Qalifi refugees to be given Genovian citizenship, even temporary Genovian citizenship. They barely think *I'm* good enough to have Genovian citizenship.

My eye was twitching like crazy the entire time (when my jaw wasn't aching from fake smiling), but I don't think anyone except Grandmère noticed.

Of course, even though I overheard half of them making catty remarks about the fact that I'm a 'commoner' and, even worse, an *American* (but of course the other half of me is royal, so to them that makes up for it), they were falling over themselves in an effort to get selfies taken with me (and the portrait of my dad in the Grand Hallway, since he didn't show up – probably a good thing, given his current state of near-constant inebriation).

Now they'll be busy posting their pics to their social media accounts, saying what a fantastic time they had.

Since Michael wasn't there, several of them asked me with fake concern if 'everything is all right' between the two of us. I could tell they were hoping things were *not* all right and that we'd broken up, so then I could date one of their half-wit chinless sons (who would then become prince consort and father to the future heir to the throne).

'No,' I said, with my big fake smile. 'Michael's fine. Just working late tonight.'

'Oh,' they said, giving me smiles that were every bit as phony as mine. 'He works? How wonderful.' (You could tell they didn't think this was wonderful.)

But has Cousin Ivan (who insists on everyone calling him Count Renaldo, even though he isn't a Renaldo and that isn't even a correct title, which I can't believe I know, but that is what over a decade of etiquette lessons from your grandmother, the dowager princess, will do to you) ever invented a robotic surgical arm that helped save the life of a suffering child?

No. No, he has not.

All Cousin Ivan does is manage the properties his father purchased ages ago, and by 'manage' I mean raise the rents so ridiculously high that decent, hardworking Genovians can no longer afford them, which is why there is no longer a single bookstore in all of Genovia.

But when I pointed this out (politely) tonight to one of the count's supporters, he said, 'Books? No one reads books anymore! Look at all the tourism that guy's bringing in with his T-shirt shops and bars. Have you ever been to Crazy Ivan's? That place is the bomb. It has a bar that's topless only! Everyone who comes in – male or female – has to take their top off. It's mandatory!'

I said I have never been to Crazy Ivan's, but I certainly do not want to go there now.

That's when Grandmère took me aside and told me I was being rude.

'*I'm* being rude?' I demanded. 'I'm an adult, for God's sake – nearly twenty-six years old, the age at which neuroscientists have determined most people's cognitive development is fully matured. I can say I do not want to go to a bar where shirtlessness is mandatory if I don't want to, and I can especially say it while I'm standing here on American soil.'

(It's a common misconception that consulates and embassies sit upon 'the soil' of the country they represent. So in all those episodes of *Law & Order* where Detectives Briscoe et al arrest foreign diplomats who then claim immunity because they're on 'Flockistan soil'? They can't.)

So then Grandmère dragged me into the drawing room – she has a pretty strong grip for such an old lady, although of course no one knows how old she is since she won't tell anyone and she had all copies of her birth certificate destroyed, which you can do if you're the dowager princess – and said, 'You *will* be civil when speaking about your cousin Ivan and his businesses.'

I said, 'I don't see why, all the plans he has for Genovia are only going to ruin the place if he wins. Why are we even having these people to dinner? They're obviously his friends. Or, I should say, *spies*.'

Then Grandmère leaned in and hissed, 'They're Genovian citizens, and this is the Genovian consulate, and it will always be open to them. Besides, keep your friends close, but your enemies closer.'

I was appalled. 'Are you actually quoting from *The Godfather*?'

'What if I am?' She exhaled a plume of vapor from her e-cigarette – which, thank God, she's switched to, none of us could take the Gitanes anymore. 'Really, Amelia, you're slipping. And after everything I taught you, too. I suppose you're letting this nonsense about your father's arrest get to you. What is wrong with your eye?'

I flung a hand over it. 'Nothing.'

'Straighten up. You look like the Hunchback of Notre-Dame. And there was no happy ending for him, you know, like there was in the insipid Disney version, which I suppose you adore. Quasimodo lies down in the tomb with Esmeralda – who also dies – and perishes of a broken heart. That's *real* literature, none of this maudlin pap you love so much. That's the problem with your generation, Amelia. You all want happy endings.'

I was so stunned I think my eye stopped twitching momentarily.

'We don't, actually,' I said. 'We want endings that

leave us with a sense of hope, possibly because the world we're living in seems to be falling apart right now. People can't find work to support their families in their own countries, but then when they try to immigrate to countries where they can, they're either enslaved – like in Qalif – or stopped at the border and told they aren't welcome, like in Genovia. And you're inviting the people who are telling them that to dinner! What kind of message is that sending to the populace?'

Her drawn-on eyebrows shot up so high I thought they might cause her tiara to go flying off. Grandmère is old school and still believes in dressing in her evening best for dinner. It's probably what makes her so popular (with the yacht-club and racehorse set).

'It's not the message I care about,' she said dramatically, 'it's the populace itself. Ivan Renaldo is very likely going to be this country's new prime minister, Amelia, thanks to your father's most recent exploits, so we'd do well to position ourselves as his allies now. Although I do blame myself for all this . . . do you have any idea why he dislikes us – especially your poor father – so?'

'No, but I have a feeling you're going to tell me.'

'His grandfather – Count Igor – was very much in love with me, and took it very hard indeed when I chose to marry your grandfather instead.'

I rolled my eyes. 'Of course. Why didn't I figure it out sooner?'

According to Grandmère, there are approximately three thousand men who were once very much in love with her, and took it very hard indeed when she chose to marry the Prince of Genovia, instead. They've all taken their revenge against her in various ways, including but not limited to:

1. Writing books about her.

You might be surprised to know that most major works in modern literature are thinly disguised tributes to my grandmother, including everything written by Mailer, Vidal, and of course J. D. Salinger, even works written before she was old enough to have possibly known the authors. Of course Fitzgerald modeled Daisy in *The Great Gatsby* after Clarisse Renaldo.

2. Competing against Genovia in every sport in every Olympics ever.

You probably haven't heard this, but every single athlete who has ever beat Genovia in any Olympic category (especially sailing and dressage, pretty much the only sports in which any Genovian athletes ever qualify) did so out of romantic spite against my grandmother.

3. Sculpting or painting works of art featuring women.

According to Grandmère, she inspired Picasso's Cubist period by saying to him, 'Darling, I think you're quite talented, but you really ought to develop your own style,' which actually isn't possible because it would mean she is over 127 years old. But when I informed her of this, she told me 'not to be so obtuse.'

'Really, Grandmère?' I said. 'You think the reason Ivan Renaldo is campaigning against Dad is because he's upset that you didn't marry his grandfather?'

'I *know* so,' Grandmère said. 'Though of course you must never mention this to your father.'

'Don't worry, I won't.'

'Poor Igor spent night after night at Maxim's, drinking Chambord out of one of my dancing slippers.'

'Eww.' I made a face, not just because the guy was drinking out of one of my grandmother's shoes, but because Chambord is a raspberry liqueur, and only tastes good when poured over vanilla ice cream. 'Was he before or after the married Texas oil baron?'

She ignored me. 'Finally his parents had to come take him away. They tried to sober him up in time for his own wedding, but it was too late. Delirium tremens nearly took the poor boy off. But I'm sorry to be burdening you with all this, Amelia. This should be a very special time for you, so close to your birthday. You should be flitting from social engagement to social engagement and shopping for folderols, enjoying the companionship of your friends while you still can, before you have to settle down to the very hard work of providing the country with an heir. Let *me* worry about the governance of the monarchy. You worry about being young and having fun.'

It was amazing how she was able to say all this, considering how much *she'd* had to drink – really, it's a miracle of science she's lived this long. Every other week, it seems, they announce the results of some new study warning that women who consume more than one alcoholic beverage a day increase their risk of cancer by quite a few percentage points.

But Grandmère, who has at least six to eight drinks a day, plus smokes the equivalent of multiple packs of cigarettes (though it's hard to tell with these new vapor ones), keeps going strong.

My mother says it's because she's pickled.

Still, Grandmère had a point about trying to get along with Cousin Ivan's supporters instead of antagonizing them. It's annoying how often my grandmother is right.

'Okay, Grandmère,' I said. 'I'll play along with your little game. But Cousin Ivan isn't going to win. We can still beat him. I *know* we can.'

'I'd be quite interested to hear your strategy,' Grandmère said, blowing a long stream of orange-scented smoke (despite the claims of the vapor companies, I'm quite sure there is still nicotine in the 'juice' Grandmère smokes). 'Unless of course you're planning to get yourself photographed with him in a compromising position. But I'm afraid that will only make him more popular, and forever cement your reputation as the Princess of Gen-HO-via.'

This was a low blow, and disheartening to think that even my own grandmother thinks that the only way women can get ahead in this day and age is with their sexuality.

I was so disgusted that I had no choice but to leave

the dining room and go back to my own apartment and lie down with a cool cloth on my forehead and watch television (which is quite hard to do when your eye is twitching nonstop).

12:01 a.m., Friday, May 1
Third-Floor Apartment
Consulate General of Genovia
New York City

Michael just texted.

> Michael Moscovitz 'FPC'*: Wanted to be the first
> one to wish you a happy birthday. Wish I was there.

*Future Prince Consort

> **HRH Mia Thermopolis 'FtLouie': No you don't. I
> can still hear them down there. They're drinking
> shots and comparing Genovian Yacht Classic
> horror stories.**

<Michael Moscovitz 'FPC'   HRH Mia Thermopolis 'FtLouie'>

> What could turn the Genovian Yacht Classic
> into a horror story? Protesters?

> **Worse. Computer programmers.**

> The Chosen People? What have we done now?

You came sweeping in with your advanced technology and won all the trophies and made them feel inferior.

It's not only our advanced technology that makes them feel inferior.

Is sex really all men ever think about?

Not always, sometimes we think about food. Why, is that not what women think about all the time?

No, we think about it – and food – all the time, too, but more in a narrative context where the girl ends up being trapped in a secret room full of cake with a bed in the middle of it and then you come in dressed in full armor and go, 'Put down that cake and prithee get naked.'

Noted, though I'm not sure how the sex works with the armor. What was with going outside with your grandma in front of those protesters tonight?

Oh, nothing.

They weren't throwing fruit over nothing.

What are you wearing?

Mia, I'm serious about this.

I'm serious, too. The armor has a codpiece. I've researched it.

We're going to discuss this tomorrow.

Couldn't we discuss it now? I think I need a professional trained in extinguishing fires. Because there's one going on in my pants.

I meant we're going to discuss the protesters.

Before or after the show of shows, story of stories, sights of all sights?

If by that you mean Cirque du Soleil, how would you feel if we skipped that particular tradition this year?

Uh, Michael, you know Grandmère always pays extra for front-row VIP seats.

What if I've come up with something better for us to do?

What could be better than a dramatic mix of circus arts and street entertainment performed live under a large tent near New York City's main jail complex? Except of course the aforementioned secret room filled with cake.

You'll find out tomorrow.

Michael, you know I hate surprises, right?

I think you'll like this one.

I can already guarantee I won't unless it involves cake and armor.

You really need to do something about that negativity. May I recommend a nice yoga/meditation retreat?

> That isn't funny. Just reading the word *meditate* made my eyelid start twitching more.

> Good night! Sweet dreams . . .

He added an emoji he'd made himself of a gorilla with hearts for eyes. Yes, in his spare time from work, my boyfriend designs emojis.

I think I'm going to have to watch about three more episodes of *NCIS* before I'll be able to calm down.

I wish I were a special agent for the Naval Criminal Investigative Service Major Case Response Team and not the princess of a tiny principality on the Mediterranean. Then I could just save the country from terrorist threats over and over, and never have to hear about oranges (or Reiki, or meditation retreats) again.

Three things for which I am grateful:

- That I've got a TV with streaming Netflix.

- Michael.

- Tylenol PM. Seriously, I'm so sleepy right now, I think I'm . . .

Woke up to 1,479 happy birthday posts, texts, e-mails, and voicemails, several of which are from people I actually know.

This is what happens when you become a public figure. Total strangers wish you happiness on your birthday, which is very, very nice.

But birthday wishes from people who know you (and still care about you, despite being aware of your character flaws) are even nicer.

No sign yet of Michael's 'birthday surprise'.

I'm going to try to be a less suspicious and cynical person now that I'm a year older and wiser, but I can't say I'm a fan of surprises. 'Guess what, Mia? You're the Princess of Genovia.' That's just one example of a surprise I've received that turned out not to be so great.

Michael's a pretty good present giver, though, so I trust his is going to be better.

And it's a new year, so I'm going to spend it taking Paolo's advice: figuring out how to make these diamond shoes work for me.

The people I've heard from so far (that I actually know, though not necessarily intimately) include:

1. My mom and half brother, Rocky (singing 'Happy Birthday' together).

This is the first year I've heard them without Mr. Gianini accompanying on his drum set. That made me a little sad. But when I called them back (I only spoke to Mom, because she'd already dropped Rocky off at school), she sounded upbeat. It's good that she's doing so well, because I sometimes wonder if she's just masking her grief by throwing herself into her work like the bereaved single moms I always see on made-for-TV movies, where the ghost of the deceased husband is watching over her and the kids until they cute-meet a new guy.

This time Mom mentioned she'd seen a piece on Dad's arrest on *Access Hollywood* and wanted to know if I think he's on drugs, and if so, did I think we should get together to do an intervention?

I said no to both.

This actually makes me think Mom's getting back to her normal sassy self (and that Mr. Gianini has moved on to heaven or his next life or whatever, because if he were a ghost he would definitely *never* steer her in Dad's direction).

2. The president (of the United States. I'm pretty sure it was prerecorded, though).

3. Ex–college suite mates, Shawna and Pamela, who now share an apartment over their shop in Williamsburg, Brooklyn, that sells artisanal mayonnaise.

4. The Windsors (despite what some people say about them, they're all actually very sweet).

5. Tina Hakim Baba. (She was trying so hard to sound chipper. I know Michael said I should listen to Boris's side of the story, but would it be so wrong if instead, the next time I happen to be in the same room as Boris, I tell Lars that I thought I saw a weapon on him? A body cavity search by the Royal Genovian Guard could teach him a valuable lesson.)

6. My father, hoping I have a very happy twenty-fifth birthday. Which is great, except that I turned twenty-six today. But since it's my birthday, I'm choosing to be magnanimous. (He's never gotten my age right. Once he gave me a birthday card with my name spelled wrong. But at least that meant he'd addressed it himself.)

7. Ling Su and Perin. I totally made it a point not to mention my b-day to *anyone* at work, so I have no idea how they remembered. This is an example, though, of Perin's extremely high-level organizational skills, and why I'm glad I hired her.

8. Ex-high-school-nemesis Lana ~~Weinberger~~ (I mean Rockefeller. So hard to remember that she goes by her married name now).

This was surprising since I haven't talked to Lana in ages, even though she lives just up the block from here, on Park and Seventieth (in *Penthouse L,* as she always makes a point to remind us. She even had it emblazoned in block letters on her monogrammed wedding *and* baby announcements).

Lana left a long, rambling message about how we need to spend more time together because *Best Friends Are Forever!* and it's been way too long and she knows I'm super involved with this 'after-school thing' I've started for 'all the juvenile delinquents' (even though I explained to her last time I saw her that it's a community center open to *all* students in the five boroughs, not just ones with criminal records), but couldn't I 'take *one day off* from being a politically correct do-gooder to get a mani-pedi and bikini wax, for old times' sake?'

'Also,' she went on, 'there's something really super important I need to talk to you about, just a teeny tiny favor that only you could help me with, Mia, so can you please call back as soon as possible? Okay, bye-yeeee bitch!'

The good thing about being in one's midtwenties is that you know nothing bad is going to happen if you don't return people's texts and voicemails . . . especially the texts and voicemails of people who probably only want to use you for your fortune or political connections.

9. Shameeka Taylor. Shameeka wanted to say how sorry she is about the protesters (who are gone today, thank God. I guess Grandmère was right – either that or Cousin Ivan only paid them to protest for one day) and that everything is going well with the new boyfriend (even though he was

only supposed to be a one-night stand, but he makes such amazing breakfasts that she's decided to let him turn into a thirty-night stand) and she appreciates my wearing the red Vera suit (she does marketing for Vera Wang) to the benefit for victims of Hurricane Julio.

- *Note to self:* Did she send me the suit, or did I buy it? I seriously don't even remember. Check into this.

Am I doing so many public events these days that they've all begun to blur? Am I slipping into early-onset dementia? How early does early-onset dementia begin, and what are the symptoms besides forgetting where my clothing comes from? Is one of the symptoms a twitching eyelid?

Or is it the Tylenol PM? I know I've only just started taking it, but seriously, I can't even remember falling asleep, let alone any of my dreams.

And finally:

10. My ex-boyfriend J. P. Reynolds-Abernathy IV. I can't believe he had the nerve to contact me.

Oh, wait, I forgot: he's J.P.

Anyway, he posted the following on my Instagram (where, of course, EVERYONE can see it).

And even though at the restorative yoga class I took with Grandmère to prove to her that yoga isn't so bad and she should do it to improve her joint health, the yogi said that hatred bars the path to spiritual enlightenment, I really do hate J.P. Or at least dislike him a lot:

Mia, I've been following you on social media. May I just say I'm so proud of the woman you've become? You look more beautiful every day. I don't understand why Michael hasn't proposed yet. I'm sorry the press is now calling you 'Why Won't He Marry Mia.'

Really? He had to bring *that* up? Also, he had to mention that I *look* great, nothing about everything I've accomplished, like founding the Community Center or the op-ed piece I just had published in the *Wall Street Journal*?

Then he made things worse by listing his own accomplishments.

I've been keeping quite busy! As you know, I've always had a creative side. Screen- and playwriting have always been my thing in the past, but to my surprise, this winter I was inspired to write a novel! Even more surprising, it's a YA novel set in the dystopian future featuring a love triangle centered around a racially diverse, strong-minded heroine who is also suffering from radiation poisoning.

Of course it is. Because J.P. knows so much about all of those things, being a white male who has never suffered from radiation poisoning and doesn't know anyone who is racially diverse (except Shameeka and Ling Su and Tina, and they stopped being friends with him long ago, after what he did to me).

The words just seemed to pour out of me. I
think it might even end up being a trilogy!

Of course.

Since you're a published author, Mia, I
was hoping if I sent Love in the Time of
Shadows to you, you'd read it and give me
your thoughts, and also perhaps send it on
to your editor. (Do take your time, I know
how busy you must be, especially dealing
with your father's arrest. And I was so
sorry to hear about Frank, by the way.
Please give my regards to your mother.)

Of course he had to bring up my stepfather's death and my father's arrest. BECAUSE IN HIS MIND THESE TWO THINGS ARE EQUALLY BAD.
OMG, I seriously hope J.P. gets radiation poisoning, then has to go live in the dystopian future.
Oh, wait. Maybe he already does:

Unfortunately things haven't been going

so well for me recently either. My latest
film, which I wrote and also produced and
directed, Nymphomania 3-D, was not well
received by critics (or audiences). I am
really in the hole to my investors, and
have been forced to take a job working here
in the city at my uncle's company. But I
won't bore you with the details!

Too late.

Thank you, Mia. Despite what you might
think, I will always love you and wish
things could have turned out differently
between us.
XOXO J.P.

Ugh. UGH UGH UGH UGH.

Someone with full cognitive development who is also
self-actualized would *never* take pleasure in the pain of
someone else – even their ex-boyfriend who completely
betrayed them and who has now fallen on hard times and
made a movie called *Nymphomania 3-D* (which, by the
way, I looked up and it's about 'a young girl's sensual
journey from frigidity to sexual awakening in the arms
of a skilled older lover' who also happens to be a writer
named John Paul) – but I'm going to be honest:

It's possible this is the best birthday present I've ever
received. Because it gives me free rein not to feel the
least bit bad about COMPLETELY HATING J.P.

But because I'm a princess, instead of reveling in J.P.'s pain, I'll simply write back to him and tell him 'Thanks for the birthday wishes' and to send his book along, but that since I'm quite busy, I don't know how long it will be before I can read it, if ever.

(Wrong: I will read it immediately and laugh and laugh at how stupid it is. Plus I'm going to make sure to get a copy of *Nymphomania 3-D* and play it in the palace theater and laugh at that, too.)

(Well, probably not, because it sounds completely disgusting.)

It's not all good news, though.

RateTheRoyals.com chimed in to let me know my royal popularity rating has now sunk to an all-time low, 'thanks to recent highly publicized events.' This has now made me less popular than a royal baby.

Thanks, Rate the Royals. Happy birthday to me.

9:05 a.m., Friday, May 1
Third-Floor Apartment
Consulate General of Genovia
Rate the Royals Rating: 5

Marie Rose just arrived with breakfast (Belgian waffles still hot from the kitchen downstairs *and* a soft-boiled egg with buttered toast *and* a pot of steaming hot Genovian black tea with milk *and* fresh squeezed juice).

I told her she didn't have to keep doing this – she's supposed to be the chef for the consulate general, not me – but she only rolled her eyes and said, *'C'est pas grave.'*

She is a lovely woman and a true patriot of the sovereign city-state, though she got her green card in 1997, and both her daughters are American citizens.

Of course Marie Rose checked Rate the Royals, too. She says the site is an outrage and ought to be shut down. She says I'm 'definitely a four,' right after Kate, William, and Prince Harry. Royal babies, she said, shouldn't count.

'On good days, after having had your hair blown out, Princesse,' she says, 'you're probably a two, after Kate, or maybe even a one if Paolo's used that airbrush makeup that makes your skin look so smooth on high-definition television.'

I tried to explain to her that Rate the Royals is not an attractiveness rating scale, but a popularity ranking,* but she's staying firm.

---

*Not that rating women on a numerical scale of attractiveness is ever okay, even when we do it to ourselves. It is always sexist and wrong. Popularity rankings are not much better, though, because

83

they're basically about how well a celebrity – in this case, a person born into a royal family – is marketing themselves, which is an exhausting job in and of itself.

I wish I could take Marie Rose with me everywhere I go. But of course it's rude to poach other people's staff.

I'm sure my current unpopularity has nothing whatsoever to do with yesterday's events (sarcasm).

According to Brian Fitzpatrick (founder and developer of Rate the Royals), the lowest-ranked royals in the world right now (besides me) are:

1. His Highness General Sheikh Mohammed bin Zayed Faisal, crown prince and deputy supreme commander of Qalif, who only last night imposed martial law after his own wife was found trying to flee across the border into Saudi Arabia.

2. My father, the Crown Prince Regent of Genovia, Artur Christoff Phillipe Gérard Grimaldi Renaldo (no surprise).

3. My grandmother, the Dowager Princess Clarisse Renaldo (who, I'm sure, would take great pride in her unpopularity, if she knew about it. Grandmère loves being number one, even if it's Number One Most Despised Royal).

This is no doubt due to a paparazzo managing to snap a photo of her taking a long drag from her electronic cigarette outside the Manhattan House of Detention when she went to post bail for Dad.

She probably would have gotten away with this and even had her Royal Rating boosted up a few points (in an isn't-it-funny-when-you-see-old-ladies-smoking kind of way) if Grandmère hadn't noticed the photog and then smacked him in the head as hard as she could with her $20,000 Birkin bag.

Not that I blame her. I feel like smacking paparazzos in the head all the time, though I, of course, would never do so with a $20,000 bag, because I

a) would never buy a $20,000 bag, and
b) restrain myself.

But of course the photog got a picture of my grandmother hitting him, which he's using in a suit against the principality of Genovia for $200 million in damages, something else the protesters brought up, like it's coming out of their personal pockets (no).

- *Note to self:* Would a paparazzo ever earn that much snapping photos of unsuspecting celebrities in his/her lifetime? Probably not unless he/she wins the lottery, and that tiny scratch is hardly going to prevent this guy from buying Powerball tickets.

Anyway, I still feel a bit guilty, because it wouldn't have happened if I'd gone down to White Street to post Dad's bail. He did ask *me* first, but I was so angry that he could have done something so stupid, I said, 'Dad, when someone gets arrested, they're supposed to call their lawyer or their *parents* for help, not their children.'

Then I hung up on him.

Ugh, that sounds awful.

But honestly, he's supposed to be setting a good example, not getting arrested in foreign countries for speeding race cars down public streets, especially right before an election. It's one thing to be going through a midlife crisis because your cousin is beating you in the election for prime minister and the woman you've allegedly been in love with for some time is now finally available but doesn't seem to know – or care – that you are alive.

It's quite another to try to get that woman's attention by driving your newly acquired vintage Formula One race car at a hundred and eighty miles per hour down one of the most highly trafficked highways in the world. He could have been killed . . . or worse, killed someone else.

I hope I impressed upon him the gravity of the situation.

And really, what worse punishment is there than to have to face the Dowager Princess of Genovia after having spent the night in a jail nicknamed 'The Tombs'? I can't think of any.

Frankly, Dad's lucky that paparazzo came along when he did, otherwise *he's* the one who would have been hit by that Birkin.

Still, a part of me can't help feeling like this is all my own fault (not what happened to Dad, of course, or what Grandmère did. They're responsible for their own actions, but how rotten I feel right now). *Why did I click on Rate the Royals????*

Dominique is always saying to me in her thick French accent: 'Your 'ighness, why do you do this to yourself? Stop going online! Nothing good evair comes from going online. You will only see something terrible that will make you feel bad, like that princesses can't be feminist role models, or another comment from your crazy stalker about 'ow 'e would like to kill you!'

Dominique is right. It's ridiculous how one critical remark can ruin your whole day. After all these years, why do I still let it? I should know better. I'm a college-educated, vital, attractive, newly-turned-twenty-six-year-old woman, with meaningful employment, a loving (if sometimes challenging) family, an amazing boyfriend, loads of great friends, and tons to offer the world.

So what do I care what some nutcase on Rate the Royals says? Screw Rate the Royals. Everyone knows that if ninety-five percent of the people don't hate you, you're not doing your job right.

So I'm going to ignore the haters, get out of this bed, and get to work doing what human beings were put on this planet to do: leave it a better place than they found it.

(Which is something Rate the Royals will never be able to say it's done.)

P.S.

Oh, Lord, I see I once again forgot to add tea bags to my grocery-store delivery list, so as soon as I'm done with this pot Marie Rose brought me, I'm out.

But for some reason I have tons of cookies, ice cream, cheese popcorn, and cat food. At least Fat Louie will be all right. He has a plethora of varieties to choose from in his finicky old age.

I'm sure if Rate the Royals saw how incredibly giving and kind I am to the animals, it would be worth another point. Prince Harry doesn't even *own* a cat.

P.P.S.

No! I must stop this! *I don't care!* I'm not going to stoop to the level of Brian Fitzpatrick. You thought you would bring me down, didn't you, Brian? But all you've done is make me more determined than ever to conquer the universe with my wit, charm, and kindness.

P.P.P.S.

Would having the Royal Genovian Guard look up the ISP address of Rate the Royals and then send Brian Fitzpatrick a cease and desist be an abuse of my powers? Check on this. Because this is what I'd *really* like to do for my birthday.

Aside from getting out of seeing Cirque du Soleil tonight. And, of course, sending Brian Fitzpatrick a box filled with deadly scorpions.

Was getting out of the shower when I got the following text(s):

> Michael Moscovitz 'FPC': Picking you up in exactly one hour for a birthday surprise. Take the bag Marie Rose has packed for you and meet me in the consulate lobby. Don't bring your laptop. There's no Internet where we're going.

Before I could text back that I couldn't possibly do as he asked, I got this:

> Don't argue. Just do it.

Then this:

> P.S. Make sure she's packed that bikini you wore to the beach last New Year's. The white one.

He added an emoji of a penguin experiencing what appeared to be a fatal myocardial infarction, since its heart was exploding from its body.

89

I think this was meant to show love or possibly lust, not a marine animal suffering a brutal death, though I'm not entirely sure. Guys are so odd, especially guys who work with computers (and robots) all day, like Michael does, and also like to design their own emojis as a hobby.

I know Michael meant his new emoji to be funny, but considering how Mr. G. died, it's a little insensitive.

Wait . . .

Could *this* be what's behind that strange shadow in his eyes? Simply that he's been plotting something behind my back?

No.

What kind of place doesn't have Internet access, though? Does that mean it also doesn't have cable television? What if it really *is* a yoga/meditation retreat?

God, I hope not. Michael knows I freak out if I go too long without television. It's embarrassing to admit, but television is my drug of choice. And how will I be able to keep abreast with what's happening ~~on all the NCISs~~ in Qalif?

Just dialed Michael's cell, but he wouldn't pick up.

So then I phoned his office number, but his latest assistant (Michael goes through assistants the way I go through tea bags, only because he keeps promoting them, not because he's dunked them in boiling water) said he was in a town car headed up to see *me*.

'Do you want me to put you through to his cell phone, Your Highness?'

I told the assistant that he doesn't have to call me 'Your Highness' because he's not a Genovian citizen and we're on U.S. soil. Then I said no, that I'd tried Michael's cell already, thanked him, and hung up.

- *Note to self:* Is it my imagination, or did Michael's new assistant sound disappointed about the Your Highness thing? I hope he doesn't turn out to be another one of those weirdos who fetishizes royals. I'll have to get his full name from Michael and then have Lars look into him.

Oh, another text:

> Are you just sitting there writing in your diary or are you actually making progress?

Oh my God. How does he DO that?

<Michael Moscovitz 'FPC'   HRH Mia Thermopolis 'FtLouie'>

> Michael, this is very sweet of you, but you KNOW whatever it is you've got planned, I can't go. It's absurd. Why won't you pick up your phone?

Because I don't want to get into it with you. What part of 'don't argue' did you not understand?

> I'm not arguing, I'm telling you facts. Seriously, this is a terrible time for me to leave. The country of Genovia needs me. The center needs me. My family needs me.

I need you. *We* need to have a relaxing weekend away from orange-throwing Genovians and your insane family.

> There's been a DEATH in my insane family, Michael, and another ALMOST death (if you count my dad). And what about my grandmother? I can't leave.

Yes, you CAN leave, and you will. Perin and Ling Su can handle the center – that's why you hired them. And Frank died a year ago. And don't worry about your dad, he can take care of himself. And your grandmother's been taken care of, too.

What? What is that supposed to mean? No one 'takes care' of my grandmother. Grandmère's like that old dowager countess on *Downton Abbey* (only not as nice). She takes care of herself, although occasionally she allows servants to prepare her food and drink and drive her around (thank God, since they took away her license years ago, which they should probably do to my dad).

It's sweet of you, Michael, whatever you have planned, but you know this is crazy. It's because of the orange-throwing Genovians that I can't leave. And in addition to everything else, I have that charity gala I promised to attend on Saturday night. And I can't leave behind my laptop. Neither can you! Do I have to remind you that you own a computer-based business?

I don't want to think of myself as predictable (who does?) but it almost seems as if he anticipated my response, he wrote back so quickly:

We both need to disconnect from work and the Internet. Don't even try to tell me that you didn't see RTR this morning. I know you check it every five minutes to make sure you're in the top three.

This is a scurrilous falsehood! I check Rate the Royals no more than once a day.

But before I could protest, I received this:

I already asked Dominique to give your regrets about the gala and she said she'd be glad to. I know how anxious you are to rebuild what you consider your family's 'tarnished reputation,' but I think throwing your support behind every charity that asks for your help (such as a society hoping to reverse the 'alarming decline of butterflies and moths in urban areas') might not be the most effective way to do it.

He'd spoken to my publicist behind my back? How dare he?

But again, before I could text a word in reply, I received this:

And both your mom AND dad say they'll be fine without you. They agree with me that you need a break after all the stress you've been through this past year. It's making you physically ill.

Lilly would rightfully have accused her brother of being both patriarchal and controlling here, talking to my parents behind my back like I'm a child . . .

. . . though I sort of love it when he tells me what to do, especially in bed, like when we play Fireman, the game we invented where he's the fireman and I'm the naughty resident who ignored the smoke detector and didn't evacuate the building in a timely manner.

Then he finds me sprawled half conscious on my bed in my sexy lingerie, and has to give me mouth-to-mouth to revive me. Only when I get revived, we realize burning timbers have fallen across our only form of egress, so he has no choice but to spend his time waiting for rescue giving me a sexy lesson in fire safety.

Plus I ran the whole trip through the RGG and they cleared it. The youth of New York City, the women and children of Qalif, and the genetically modified oranges of Genovia will be all right without you for one weekend.

Now grab the bag and get downstairs. Are you even dressed? The clock is ticking, Thermopolis. The jet leaves from Teterboro at eleven.

Jet? He's hired a private *jet*?

Who does he think he is all of a sudden, Christian Grey?

I am not okay with this. I'm not some shy virginal college student who only owns one shirt. I am a twenty-six-year-old woman fully in charge of making up my own mind about whether or not I want to go on vacation.

I do love it when Michael calls me Thermopolis, though. Even when it's only in writing, it does something to me, something that normally only happens when he walks into the room after I haven't seen him in a while and hugs me, and I get a whiff of his amazing, clean, Michael smell, or when he comes out of the shower wearing only a towel and his hair is all wet and plastered down darkly to the back of his strong, newly shaved neck, and he announces he smells smoke –

Maybe he's right. Maybe I *do* need a relaxing vacation. Especially away from my crazy family, and the consulate, and the Internet, and . . .

Oh, crap. Might as well admit it: after all these years, I'm still disgustingly, revoltingly in love with him, exploding penguins and all. I'd even go on some kind of weird, wireless retreat with him.

Now, *that's* love.

Sitting downstairs, waiting for Michael to pick me up for the wireless meditation/yoga retreat, or whatever it is.

Everyone who comes in (quite a lot of people for a Friday morning in May, but they were probably put off coming yesterday by the crowd of orange-throwing protesters) is giving me the side-eye.

I suppose they weren't expecting to see Princess Mia Thermopolis writing in her diary in the lobby of the consulate of Genovia when they popped by to get a visa or certificate of nationality. Most of them look quite pleased . . .

I wish I could say the same for the consulate staff. From the moment I set foot down here, I was immediately:

- chastised by Madame Alain, the ambassador's secretary, for entering the consulate staff kitchen (to steal tea bags, but she doesn't know that), and

- told to remove the four gold iPhones and dozens of other birthday cards and packages that arrived for me via the consulate's address.

This was only slightly embarrassing since the Royal Genovian Guard opens all my packages/mail thanks to RoyalRabbleRouser, who pledged to 'destroy my world.'

97

One of the packages sent to me today turned out to be a world destroyer, all right, but it was from my boyfriend's sister (and soon-to-be ex–best friend), not my stalker. It consisted of a waterproof vibrator shaped like a dolphin with a note that said:

I'm FLIPPING out over your birthday!

XOXO Lilly

When Lars handed it to me just now (back in its wrapping paper, though not very nicely; apparently they're out of Scotch tape in the security office, so he used blue medical tape from the first-aid kit), he didn't even bother to wipe the smirk off his face.

'From Miss Moscovitz, Your Highness,' he said gravely, 'with her best birthday wishes.'

The thing is, she knows that Lars opens everything sent to me. So this was her way of birthday-pranking me and also titillating my bodyguard.

Happy birthday to me again.

He must have seen my expression since he asked, 'What?' over his shoulder as he walked back to the security office (he has to pack, too, since he's coming with me wherever Michael is taking me). 'I think it's a highly thoughtful, creative gift. Much more original than a gold iPhone, which you can't even keep.'*

---

*I'm not allowed to have Apple products — aside from my laptop — let alone post anything to the 'Cloud' due to how easily they're hacked/traced, which is why all the iPhones I've received today will have to be returned for store credit. But it's all right, since the products we buy instead will be donated to Mr. Gianini's after-school vocational program.

But see, this kind of thing could have happened no matter where I was living (the part where the Royal Genovian Guard has to go through all my mail). Even if I moved back in with Mom and Rocky (which I'll never do because what if the death threats turn out to be serious after all? I wouldn't want to put their lives at risk. Also, I love my mom and my half brother, but I don't want to move back in with them. Rocky sailed through his toddler years to turn into what's charitably called 'a challenge,' and not because his dad passed away either. He was 'challenging' before that happened).

Mom doesn't even have a doorman (neither does Michael. His loft is in a condo building). RoyalRabbleRouser could get himself buzzed right into Mom's building, walk up to the door of her loft, knock, and then shove a pie in her face . . . or worse. Sandra Bullock found her gun-owning stalker *inside* her bathroom after she stepped out of her shower, and Queen Elizabeth once woke to find hers sitting on the edge of her bed in Buckingham Palace, wanting to chat (he got in through an open window – twice – after shimmying up a drainpipe).

- *Note to self:* Dominique says it's best not to dwell on these things, or let them decide for you how to live your life, but that's easier said than done, especially when you're the one getting the threats about how much better off the world would be 'without you in it.'

Oh, God. Madame Alain just walked over and said, 'Your Highness, do you think you could write in your diary somewhere else? You are distracting the staff.'

'I'm so very sorry, Madame Alain,' I said. 'And don't worry, I'm going to be picked up any minute, and then I'll be out of your hair all weekend.'

Is it my imagination, or does she look relieved?

'Oh, I see. All right, then.'

I know it's wrong since she's a civil servant and has devoted her whole life (practically) to promoting economic development and tourism in Genovia, but I *would* like to have a serious talk with the ambassador about transferring Madame Alain to a different office where I wouldn't have to see her as much. I think she'd be sublime as the headmistress of the Genovian Royal Academy.

- *Note to self:* See if this can be arranged.

I tried to get Marie Rose to tell me where Michael is taking me, but she only giggled and said, 'I can't, Princesse. I promised. But I'll make sure to feed Fat Louie while you're away.'

Fat Louie! I almost forgot about him. I hope he'll be all right. He's getting on in years, which is why it's easier to forget about him than it used to be, as all he does now is sleep and eat. He hasn't eaten a sock in ages, he has no interest in them at all anymore as food, he only eats actual food.

Oh, what am I saying? He's so old he probably won't even notice I'm gone.

Don't even ask me when Marie Rose had time to pack for me without my noticing.

Oh, here's a birthday text from Tina Hakim Baba:

<Tina HBB 'TruRomantic'   HRH Mia Thermopolis 'FtLouie'>

> Happy birthday, Mia! I hope you have a great time. I wish I were going. But that would be weird, ha ha! Plus, I have exams.

> P.S. Don't worry about what it says on RTR. You're #1 to me!

Aw. She's so sweet.
So Tina's in on Michael's surprise, too? How did –
HE'S HERE!

3:00 p.m., Saturday, May 2
Sleepy Palm Cay, The Exumas, Bahamas
Rate the Royals Rating: *Who cares?*

I will admit when Michael suggested a vacation, especially in a place with no television, Wi-Fi, or cell service, I was like 'No way, how am I going to know what's going on with ~~NCIS~~ work and world affairs? I'm the heir to the throne of a small principality and founder of a new nonprofit, my dad just got out of jail, I have to be in close touch with my people and family at all times. I can't *leave*.'

But then when we flew into the Exumas (which are a string of little islands off the Bahamas), and I saw the clear turquoise water stretching so far around us, and the blue sky overhead like a giant overturned robin's-egg-blue bowl, I began having second thoughts. *Maybe I can deal with this. It's only for a couple of days, after all.*

When the limo from the airport pulled up to a *marina*, not the driveway to a hotel, and there was a speedboat waiting, I knew something very unusual was going on.

Michael still wouldn't tell me where we were going, though. 'It's a surprise,' he kept saying, waggling those thick black eyebrows, which I love so much, especially when they get messy and I have to smooth them down with my fingertips.

Then the speedboat took us across the sometimes blue, sometimes green, sometimes aquamarine water to *our own island,* complete with a private dock leading to a thatched-roof cabana, inside of which is a king-sized bed so massive, you need a footstool to climb onto it (at least I do, anyway. Michael is tall enough not to need one).

There are two full his-and-hers baths (with teak shutters that open from the clawed-foot tubs to a spectacular view of the sea, so while you're soaking in there, reading a book, you can also watch the waves, like in a commercial for erectile dysfunction). There's a dining and sitting room, decorated to look like one of those old-timey beach houses from the movies where people wore safari suits and drank gin and tonics to prevent malaria and said things like 'I'm terribly worried about the volcano, Christopher.'

And of course there's an outdoor shower and hot tub, but you don't need to worry about anyone spying on you using them naked, because the whole place is surrounded by a completely private beach, and there are *no other living beings for miles around,* except exotic seabirds and the occasional flash of silver fish leaping from the water against the pink sunset and a pod of dolphins that live nearby and come nosing around, curious about what we're doing.

Dolphins. DOLPHINS.

And then there's Mo Mo, the personal room-service butler assigned to us by the resort, who brings us succulently prepared meals three times a day by boat, and then also restocks the minibar and cleans our snorkel masks, before leaving us completely to ourselves. He rings the bell on his boat very loudly whenever he's approaching to let us know he's coming so we can put on our clothes.

Not that I don't *always* have on clothes when I'm

outside of the cabana, because I'm not about to pull another *Me-Ah-My-Ah!* and get spotted topless by a passing Google satellite or camera-equipped drone copter (though I know Lars and the rest of the security squad are stationed on the closest island with long-range sniper rifles, looking to take any of those out. This has become Lars's favorite new hobby).

At first when I got here, I was like 'Michael, this is insane. This is *way over the top*. How much is this costing you? You are spending *way too much money*. It's not that I don't appreciate the thought, but at least let me split the—'

Michael stuffed a rum-soaked piece of pineapple into my mouth and asked, 'Can't you relax for five minutes?'

So then I concentrated very hard on relaxing, which it turns out isn't that hard to do when the sand is so white and soft and the waves so small and mild that you can simply walk a few steps out onto the beach, lie down, and let the warm water lap gently around you while the sun and sand sweetly embrace you until you finally fall asleep (fortunately having remembered to put on SPF 100).

When I woke up the tide was coming in, so the waves were a bit stronger and the beach had gotten a little smaller and Michael was leaning over me without his shirt on asking if I liked it (and also if I wanted to reapply my sunscreen), and I said sleepily, 'Okay, Michael, I guess I can do this . . . just for the weekend.'

And he laughed and said, 'I thought so,' and kissed me.

Then he asked if I thought I smelled smoke . . .

7:00 p.m., Saturday, May 2
Sleepy Palm Cay, The Exumas, Bahamas
Rate the Royals Rating: Don't know/don't care

It is *amazing* here. We are doing *nothing*. Nothing except kissing and eating and sleeping in the sun and playing Fireman and snorkeling (which is quite easy to do once you get the hang of it) and looking at birds and dolphins through the binoculars.

Although you don't even need the binoculars, that's how close the dolphins swim up.

I'm so relaxed, my eye has even stopped twitching. It could be because of the massive doses of magnesium I've been taking, or it could be because of leaving all that stress behind . . . or it could be because of love.

I'm voting for love.

But the most amazing thing is the sight I'm looking at right now, and I don't need the binoculars to see it either: Michael wearing nothing but board shorts as he lies in the hammock across from mine, reading a book on microprocessing (I do hope the micros and the processors end up happily ever after at the end).

I know how lucky I am, so I shouldn't brag, and of course beauty is in the eye of the beholder, but was there ever such a stunning piece of masculinity in all of history? I don't think so. I happen to like dark-haired men (we won't talk about that brief unhappy period in my past when I was attracted to a fair-haired boy since thankfully I soon came to my senses), the darker the better.

And while I know some girls who like guys without

105

hair on their limbs and bodies, I frankly find that very odd. Fortunately Michael has quite a lot. If he ever started waxing it (like Boris, who, the less said about *him*, the better), I think we would have to have a serious talk.

But the best thing about him isn't his looks; it's that he is someone around whom I can be totally myself. When I'm with Michael, I don't ever have to worry about saying the wrong thing, because to him, everything I say is funny or interesting.

And no matter what I have on (or don't have on), he thinks I look beautiful. I know because we've been together for so long, he can't be faking it when I worry that I don't have any makeup on and he goes, 'You actually look better without makeup on.' (I don't, without mascara I look like a lashless marsupial left too long in an experimental government lab, but amazingly, even in my lashless marsupial state, he's still quite interested in pursuing carnal relations with me.)

Plus, when we snuggle our bodies fit together perfectly, almost as if they were made for each other.

And he never complains when Fat Louie climbs up onto the bed and snuggles with us, even though Fat Louie has gotten quite smelly in his old age, having completely given up bathing (I have to dip him in the bathtub every once in a while or he'd simply never get clean).

Fat Louie, I mean. Not Michael. Michael takes two to three showers a day, depending on whether or not he's done yoga.

Fortunately we no longer have to deal with Michael's dog, Pavlov, climbing into the bed at Michael's place

106

anymore, since Pavlov passed away in his sleep after a long and happy life. Dogs generally don't live as long as cats, except Grandmère's miniature poodle, Rommel, whom she will never allow to die. Rommel's gotten a little dotty in his old age, but because Grandmère never got him fixed, he still has a very active sex drive.

This means in recent months he's been caught attempting to make somewhat aggressive love to: an ottoman; an umbrella stand; other dogs of all breeds (and sexes); Dominique; my father; Michael; me; Lilly; Grandmère; the mayor of New York City; Clint Eastwood (in town for a movie premiere); an $84,000 Persian carpet; sofas of too large a number to name; numerous women's purses; multiple room-service waiters; and almost all the bellmen at the Plaza Hotel.

I told Grandmère that we should write a book – *What Rommel Humped* – and donate the profits to the ASPCA. I'm positive it would make a fortune.

She didn't find the idea very funny, though. Nor did she like it when I suggested that she should get Rommel fixed. She said, 'I suppose when I get old and am still interested in sex, you'll have *me* fixed. Remind me not to appoint you my health-care proxy, Amelia.'

Oh, dear. Michael just asked what I'm writing about. I couldn't tell him the truth, of course.

So I told him I'm writing about how much I love him. It's *sort* of true . . . it's how I got started on this topic, anyway.

He put down his book and looked at me with those big brown eyes of his (such beautiful long lashes! Totally wasted on a man. If only I had them, I'd never need mascara again) and said, 'I love you, too.'

So serious! He didn't even smile.

Never sure what I'm supposed to do when he looks at me so seriously and says 'I love you' like that. I know he does – his love is like this beautiful sea around us, warm and dependable and tranquil and calm, a place where dolphins can safely frolic and play.

But even here, on *vacation*, I'm seeing shadows in those lovely brown depths . . . and I'm getting the feeling that there's rough weather ahead, with dark, deep waters, where you can't see the bottom.

If I could have any wish, it would be that we could just stay here forever under this crystal-blue sky, in these nice warm shallow waves, and never have to face the harsh realities I suspect lie ahead.

But I suppose everyone who comes here wishes for that. Who wishes for storm clouds and wind-tossed seas? Only idiots.

Oh, here comes Mo Mo on the boat, with dinner.

Must write this quickly because I don't want Michael to wake up and discover me out of bed writing in my diary in the bathroom like a lunatic.

But I found out what the shadows in his eyes are all about, and why he's been looking so serious lately. I knew there was something. And it *isn't* because he's passing another kidney stone, been cheating on me with a music blogger, or that he wants to break up so he can have a normal life.

It's the complete opposite of all those things.

I started getting suspicious this evening when Mo Mo brought a helper with him – he'd never done that before when setting up for any meals. The helper was a professional chef named Gretel.

Mo Mo set up a little table for two in the sand, looking out toward the sunset, with a white tablecloth and two rattan armchairs. Then he sank a couple of tiki torches into the sand and lit them.

Meanwhile, Gretel was setting the table and laying out all the food, which I couldn't help noticing included several things that have lately become my favorites, such as grilled shrimp in pasta with mozzarella, jumbo lump crab cakes, and tuna tataki.

Also, Michael had actually gotten dressed – and I was pretty sure it wasn't just for Gretel's sake, because he'd changed out of his board shorts into real pants –

109

long khakis – and a white button-down shirt.

I also spied a bottle of champagne sitting on ice in a silver cooler.

I didn't *want* to think anything was going on other than a nice Saturday-night dinner, despite what the press (and Tina Hakim Baba) has been saying for AGES. I love romance novels, too, but as I keep telling Tina, in real life things don't always work out that way.

But suddenly it seemed possible Tina could be right for once. She's been asking me some odd questions lately, though I thought they were related to her breakup with Boris, or her love of *The Bachelor*.

'Which do you think is more romantic,' Tina asked me not even a week ago, 'finding an engagement ring in a conch shell or a champagne glass?'

'Neither,' I had replied. 'Both are better than a big public proposal, like on a Jumbotron, which you know is the worst, because what if the person being proposed to wants to say no? She'd feel terrible.'

'I know, but if you had to pick one.'

'A champagne glass, I guess. Sticking a ring in a conch shell would probably kill the conch if there were one alive in the shell.'

'True,' Tina said.

'Which did *The Bachelor* do?' I asked her.

'Oh,' she said. 'Uh, conch shell.'

'Typical,' I said.

So when I suddenly saw Michael had put on a shirt, I thought, *What if it isn't because he simply feels like dressing up for dinner? What if he's going to propose?*

Of course there was that ever-present voice of self-doubt in my head (that probably all those people who see me in magazines would never believe exists, because of the way I project myself publicly) that whispered: *Don't be an idiot. He's not going to propose. He's going to announce the news that he can't take it anymore, and break up with you!*

But as Mr. Spock would say on *Star Trek*, that's not logical. No one brings a woman all the way to the Exumas to break up with her. So I quickly squashed that voice.

My next, more rational thought was *Or what if he has a ring in his pocket?*

I decided Paolo was right: I *do* need to enjoy my diamond shoes. Not only enjoy them, but start dancing in them.

So I ran inside and showered and put on the nice sundress that Marie Rose had, thankfully, packed for me. Then I added some mascara and came rushing back out, my hair nicely combed (since, whether I was getting broken up with or proposed to, I didn't want it to be while I was wearing a swimsuit, my oldest Havaianas, and Michael's own New York Yankees T-shirt with the holes under the sleeve, with my hair in a ratty knot on top of my head).

But even though I'd been *very* quick, by my estimation, Mo Mo and Gretel and the boat were long gone, and there was only Michael standing there . . .

. . . at the end of a path of pink rose petals someone had scattered from the porch of the cabana, where I was, to the little table, where Michael stood, holding a glass of champagne for me.

111

'Thirsty?' he asked. Behind him, the tiki torches were flaming merrily away.

Okay. I was probably not getting broken up with.

'Um,' I said. 'Sure.' I followed the trail of roses through the sand to where he was standing and took the champagne glass from him. 'Thanks.'

He smiled and clinked my glass with his and said, 'Cheers,' and all of my insides (and some of my outsides) seemed to melt because I saw that the playfulness in his smile reached his eyes, and though the darkness there might have been as deep as the ocean beyond the reef – which was quite serious, because Mo Mo had warned us there were sharks there – he was finally welcoming me to dive in. In fact, he was grinning from ear to ear.

'Okay,' I said, lowering my glass. 'What is going on?'

'What do you mean?' He lowered his glass, too. 'Nothing's going on.'

'Something is definitely going on. There are rose petals scattered on the beach and you're smiling in a weird way.'

'I'm merely enjoying a romantic meal with the woman I love. Is that so wrong?' He pulled a chair out for me, the one that had the best view of the sea and the sunset, which had turned the sky a dramatic pink and periwinkle blue.

'It's weird,' I said, taking the seat. 'I love you, but you're acting very weird. You have a weird look in your eye. You've had it for a few weeks now. Don't try to deny it. I thought you were having another kidney stone.'

Michael handed me a napkin. 'It's a tragedy when a man can't enjoy dinner with the woman he loves without being castigated by her as weird.'

'I didn't say *you*'re weird, I said you're *acting* weird.'

'You also said you thought I was having a kidney stone.'

'Well,' I said, 'you know how you get.'

'Apparently I do not, since I thought I was behaving in a perfectly normal manner.'

'No, you are clearly hiding something from me.'

'I can assure it's not a kidney stone.'

'Well, then, what – ?'

That's when something hard struck my lip – something that had been inside the champagne glass. At first I thought it was a strawberry – everyone loves cutting up strawberries and sticking them on the side of champagne glasses, which is simply annoying, as it takes up a lot of room where delicious champagne could be.

But then, when I looked inside my glass, I saw that what was in it was not a strawberry, but something that glittered like metal. And stone. A large, glittering white stone on a platinum band.

My heart stopped, and not from a myocardial infarction.

There was no sound (since my heart was not beating) except the sound of the waves gently lapping up against the white shore and the occasional call of a far-off bird. We were the only human beings for miles around (I'm not including Lars and whoever else from the RGG security detail was stationed on the next island over, scanning the area for incoming boats and spy drones).

It was only Michael, me, and the birds (and dolphins

113

and millions of fish a few feet away).

I looked from the ring up at Michael.

'What is this?' I asked him, raising the glass.

'I think it should be pretty obvious,' he said. 'It's an engagement ring. I thought you'd like it because the diamond's laboratory-grown. I know we said we weren't going to get married, but I'm tired of never seeing you anymore, and this seems like the most practical solution to the problem.'

Then, before I knew what was happening, he'd dropped to one knee beside me in the sand, put his hands over mine, and looked up into my face.

'I can take the ring back and get a natural diamond if you want,' he said, 'but I thought you'd like this one since it's conflict-free.'

I wanted to laugh and cry at the same time. Had there ever been a more down-to-earth, more Michael Moscovitzy proposal in history?

'No,' I said. 'It's perfect.'

'You've barely looked at it. Here, try it on, at least.' He took the glass from me, tossed the remains of my champagne into the sand, then fished the ring from the bottom. 'I hope I got the right size. You never wear rings. Tina helped me guess—'

'Tina?' The ring slid neatly onto the third finger of my left hand, where the large colorless diamond caught the rays of the setting sun and flamed like the fire at the end of one of the nearby tiki torches. 'Tina knew?'

'Of course she knew. Well, some of it.'

This explained everything. I can't believe poor Tina

kept herself from breathing a word of it to me.

'Do you like it?' Michael asked again. He actually looked a little anxious, but also excited, like a kid at Christmas. Or Hanukkah, to be exact.

'I *love* it.'

I lowered my head to kiss him, because obviously when a man has gotten down on one knee in the sand to propose to you with a lab-engineered diamond, the natural thing to do is wrap your arms around his neck and kiss him, quite deeply, and for a long time, as the ocean waves lap gently around you.

'But, Michael,' I said a little while later, after catching my breath, 'I thought we were going to wait to get married until—'

He'd had his arms around my waist, and his head was resting quite comfortably against my chest, in a sort of dreamy way. But when I said the thing about how I thought we were going to wait, his head jerked up.

'I'm sorry, Mia, but I'm tired of waiting,' he said, in a decidedly unromantic manner. 'We can't even live together, thanks to those vultures in the press. Think about it, because I have, a lot. What if something were to happen to you? I wouldn't be the first person they'd notify. I doubt anyone would remember to notify me at all. I wouldn't even be allowed into your hospital room—'

'Oh, Michael, how can you say that? It isn't true.' I ran my fingers through his thick dark hair, still slightly damp from his shower and giving off that irresistibly fresh, clean scent of his. 'First of all, nothing's going to happen to me—'

115

His gaze was filled once again with dark hurricane clouds, and I realized *this* was what had been troubling him all along. 'How can you say that after what happened to your stepfather?'

'Michael, we all loved Frank, but you know he was terrible about following up on his medical care. Nothing like that could ever happen to me, because I'm very proactive about my health.'

'Fine, but what about those protesters? Or your stalker? Next time it might not be only an orange that gets thrown in your direction.'

'Yes,' I said patiently. 'But that's why I have the Royal Genovian Guard. There's nothing Lars would love more than to take a bullet for me—'

'*I* want to take a bullet for you,' Michael said, his hands curling into fists in my lap.

'Michael, that's the *last* thing I want.'

'I don't understand why you're arguing with me about this. Do you not *want* to marry me?'

'Of course not! I mean, yes. Yes, of course I do, but—'

'But what?'

'But I don't want you to ask me because you feel like you have to, or because you want to take a bullet for me, or because you feel pressured to do it—'

'Mia, I'm a grown man. No one can pressure me into doing anything I don't want to do.' He looked quite fierce as he said this, his dark eyes flashing. There wasn't a hint of shadow in them anymore. They were very clear. 'I want to marry you because I love you, and I want to spend as much time as I have left on this earth with you. And the most practical way for me to do that is by marrying you. Now, do you want to marry me, or not?'

I slipped both my hands into his. 'Yes, Michael Moscovitz, of course I want to marry you, more than anything. But—'

'Good.' He lifted both my hands and kissed them, then laid them back down in my lap and rose from the sand. 'Now eat your crab cakes before they get cold.'

Really, has there ever been a more sensible – yet loving and romantic – husband-to-be in the entire world? Probably, but you never see or hear about them because they aren't the kind that get written about in books or shown on movies and TV. They just go about their business, getting things done. Like Albert, the prince consort of Queen Victoria. No one ever hears anything about him (except for prank calls about having 'Albert in the can,' and of course references to a certain genital piercing, which in historical fact the real Prince Albert did not have, and of course, as we all know from having watched *Sex Sent Me to the ER,* can actually be quite medically dangerous to both the pierced and their sex partners).

But early into Queen Victoria's marriage to Albert, while they were both riding in an open carriage, the prince consort saw a would-be assassin draw a gun. Instead of freaking out, Albert did the most practical thing on the planet: he pulled Queen Victoria down against the carriage seat (and himself) so the bullet brushed him and not her (at least according to what I remember of

117

the biopic. Obviously I can't fact-check it right now, as I have no Internet access, and also I'm in the bathroom).

How completely sensible – yet utterly romantic – is that?

And how like something Michael would do, if ever given the opportunity . . . which I'm going to do everything in my power to make sure he will never have to. Because protecting your subjects, which includes your loved ones, is what being a royal is all about.

Of course, if they make a third movie of my life, it would be lovely if they show Michael taking a bullet for me, just to liven things up a bit. But only a small one that does minor damage, and not to his face (or anything downstairs).

It wasn't until I saw Michael eating his own crab cakes (with surprising savagery) that I realized *that's* what's been going on in his eyes lately: Mr. Gianini's dying, a possible madman wanting to kill me, and protesters throwing genetically modified oranges at my bodyguard have brought home to him how fleeting life is, and how, when you really love someone, all you want to do is spend all the time you can with that person.

Why delay happiness – even for a matter of principle – if you can have it right away? Of course, we're going to have a talk eventually about all those things that were mentioned in the *Post* article – like that when we get married, he's going to have to give up his name (and U.S. citizenship, etc.). Women give up those things when they marry as a matter of course – well, not their citizenship, generally – so it shouldn't be such a big deal (plus, I think he already knows), but we live in a society where, for most men, I'm afraid this would be nonnegotiable.

But Michael's not like most men.

I did tell him that we are absolutely one hundred percent going to have to elope because there is *no way* I'm going through what William and Kate did on their wedding day. *That* was completely ludicrous. Sweet to watch on television if you weren't there yourself, but the behind-the-scenes drama was insane.

He agreed.

Except a little while later, after we'd finished dinner – I have to admit, I was so excited and happy I could barely finish my shrimp pasta, though I did manage to polish off all my crab cakes and lemon sorbet in limoncello – and we were both in the hammock, looking for shooting stars (I do not think that last one was a satellite no matter what he says), he said, 'My parents are going to be really disappointed if we don't have a wedding.'

'But, Michael, your parents are so progressive! They subscribe to *Mother Jones*.'

'Yes, but they're getting older, and lately they've been dropping hints that there are only two occasions during which families get together anymore, and only one of them is happy.'

It took me a little while to figure out what Michael meant. I lifted my head with a jerk from his chest. 'Yikes!'

'Yes,' he said grimly. 'Think about the number of funerals there've been in our families lately.'

'Of course,' I murmured, lowering my head again. 'Mr. Gianini.'

'My great-aunt Rose.'

'Pavlov . . .'

He laughed and kissed me. We didn't actually have a funeral for his dog. He now lives as tiny cremated ashes in an elegant tin shaped like Rosie the Robot from *The Jetsons* on Michael's bedroom shelf.

'What if we have a very small wedding?' I asked. 'Just family and friends.'

'Do you really think you could get away with that?'

'Why not? Brad and Angelina did.'

He looked skeptical. 'They're movie stars. You're going to rule a country.'

'That makes it even easier, in a way,' I said. 'I have national security to help me keep it a secret.'

'True, but how would we keep the press from finding out?'

'The way Brad and Angelina did. They didn't invite their most talkative family members . . .'

He raised his delectably dark, thick eyebrows. 'Are you saying you wouldn't invite your grandmother to your own wedding?'

'Or we could invite her and not tell her what it actually is until the last minute,' I said with a shrug. 'Think about what will happen if we don't. At her own wedding to my grandfather, I heard there was a two-day public holiday, a military parade, a gown that today would be worth over a couple of hundred thousand dollars, it was dripping with so many diamonds and pearls, a religious *and* civil ceremony, television cameras, enough cake to feed the entire populace, twenty thousand bottles of champagne, fireworks and carriage rides through the town square, a commemorative postage stamp with her head on it—'

'Wait a minute,' Michael said, tensing up. 'Is that something they're going to do to me? Make a stamp of my head?'

'Oh,' I said soothingly. 'No, of course not.'

It was totally something they were going to do to him. There's only one commemorative stamp of me, but there are three of my dad, and *sixteen* of Grandmère (they reissue them every time the postage rate changes, and she's been around for a while).

Personally I'd love to lick a stamp of Michael's head and stick it on an envelope, but I'll wait until after we're married to break the news to him that he has to sit for a state portrait. To misquote Beyoncé, I'm not sure he's ready for this jelly.

'I don't know,' he said. 'I'm beginning to think maybe we *should* risk disappointing my parents, and just elope.'

Damn! He must have detected the hint of stamp-lust in my voice.

'Michael, we can't. I don't want our future together to start off with us disappointing everyone. I'm willing to risk it with my grandmother – she's always disappointed in me anyway – but not your parents. I couldn't bear that.'

He lifted one of my hands and kissed it. 'Well, when you put it like that, how can I say no?' He held my hand up so the diamond on my finger caught the moonlight. 'But I don't want you getting stressed out again.'

I hugged him. 'I'll never get stressed out again with

121

you by my side. Our wedding's going to be *amazing*, just like our future together.'

I don't think I've ever been this happy in my entire life.

Three things I'm grateful for:

1. Shooting stars.

2. Lab-engineered diamonds.

3. That I'm engaged to be married to Michael Moscovitz.

3:05 p.m., Monday, May 4
HELV* from Teterboro back to the consulate
Rate the Royals Rating: ?

* Hybrid Electric Livery Vehicle

So happy. Can't even think of anything to write I'm so happy.

Except that I'm sorry to have left our little island . . . I wish we could live there, swimming and snorkeling and sleeping in the sun all day, then lying in our hammock and watching shooting stars (and satellites) at night. We even invented a new game . . . it's called Space Alien. We pretended one of the satellites we saw was actually a spaceship visiting from a distant galaxy and it happened to land on *our tiny island,* and when the door opened, out came Michael, who was an alien (with many humanoid qualities) who'd been sent to explore the far reaches of space because all the females in his sector had died out from a terrible plague, so he kidnapped me and took me back to his planet to help repopulate it (though I went willingly because he was quite handsome and more gentlemanly and intelligent than any of the men on my own planet).

Obviously, in real life it would not be fun to travel to a planet where you were the sole female and have humanoid males fight over you all day, but that's what's fun about fantasies: they're *not real.* Another fun fantasy would be for us to live in the Exumas, where Michael could fish and I could sell the fish from a little hut on the beach, and we could play Space Alien every night and

123

forget all our other responsibilities.

But that's not real either.

Which is why I just had to switch my phone back on. I need to see how things are going at the center and with my dad and –

. . . and now it's buzzing off the hook. What is going *on*? There had better be an international incident or –

I have 1,372 new e-mails, texts, and voicemails.

I was kidding about there better having been an international incident. *Please* don't let anything bad have happened to my family or friends or kids from the center or the refugees from Qalif or the people of Genovia . . .

3:15 p.m., Monday, May 4
Still in the HELV
Rate the Royals Rating: 1

There hasn't been an international incident. Well, there *has* been, but it turns out to be me. Once again, *I'm* the international incident.

At Long Last:

They're Engaged!

You heard it here first! She's officially 'When Will He Marry Mia' no more!

Longtime beau – multimillionaire biotech entrepreneur Michael Moscovitz, 29 – has finally popped the question to new *Number One*–ranked royal, Princess Mia Thermopolis of Genovia!

RateTheRoyals.com has all the *vital* statistics:

- ❤ The couple became engaged on the princess's 26th birthday this weekend during an exotic getaway in the Bahamas.

- ❤ Before they left, Michael asked Mia's father – Prince Phillipe Renaldo of Genovia – for her hand.

- ❤ The ring is a 10-carat sapphire surrounded by diamonds on a platinum band.

- ❤ The royal wedding will be held this summer at the Genovian Palace in a Catholic ceremony that will be telecast *live* worldwide to an approximate audience of a billion!

- Michael will move his billion-dollar medical business to Genovia, where he and Mia will live in the royal palace once they're married!

- Mia's grandma: 'I've always been very fond of Michael.'

- Mia is 'beyond thrilled,' according to a palace spokesperson.

- Divorce lawyers are already drafting prenups.

- Bookies are placing odds on July 20 as the early favorite for the wedding date.

The official statement released by the Genovian Palace reads:

The Dowager Princess Clarisse Renaldo of Genovia is delighted to announce the engagement of her granddaughter Princess Amelia Mignonette Grimaldi Thermopolis Renaldo to Mister Michael Moscovitz, Esq., of New York City.

The wedding will take place in Genovia in the summer of 2015. Further details about the ceremony will be announced shortly.

Princess Mia and Mr. Moscovitz became engaged on her 26th birthday during a holiday this past weekend in the Bahamas.

Mr. Moscovitz sought the permission of the princess's father prior to proposing.

Following the marriage, the couple will live in Genovia, where the princess and her consort will devote their lives to serving the needs of the people of Genovia.

3:15 p.m., Monday, May 4
Still in the HELV
Rate the Royals Rating: 1

I am going to kill my grandmother.

Michael and I *promised* we'd tell our parents first (which we were going to do tonight after he gets back from a speech he has to give on neural prosthetics at a medical conference in Elizabeth).

Only now they're going to hear it first on the news.

Of course I can't get through to Michael. He took his own town car from Teterboro to the medical conference, and for whatever reason my calls are going straight to voicemail.

Probably he's already been kidnapped by RoyalRabbleRouser and is being held for ransom in an underground bunker for my exact net worth according to Rate the Royals. Only how am I going to pay it, in scepters?

Seriously, though, I know my grandmother is behind this. But how did she find out?

It had to have been Mo Mo. He was so nice, but she got to him. She gets to everyone eventually.

3:25 p.m., Monday, May 4
Still in the HELV thanks to the horrible
traffic on the Upper West Side
Rate the Royals Rating: 1

Still no Michael.
 Am checking all my messages.

<Tina HBB 'TruRomantic'   HRH Mia Thermopolis 'FtLouie'>

Mia, r u back? How was it?

Yes, I'm back. I guess you heard the news?

You mean you didn't announce it?

Of course I didn't announce it.

Oh, Mia, I'm so sorry! I did kind of wonder,
because the details about the ring were wrong.
I was like, 'Did Michael get a different ring
at the last minute'? And it's more your style
to let your closest friends know about things
before announcing them to the press.

129

You think?

Wait, are you being sarcastic?

Yes, sorry. I'm just upset right now.

I'm sorry! But congratulations, anyway! Were you surprised?

Of course I was surprised! It was amazing. Best trip – best birthday – best time of my life! Until now. Thanks for helping Michael to plan it, anyway.

And you like the ring?

I LOVE the ring. I love love love it. I'm just so sorry you had to hear the news from the press. FYI, I've decided not to go on the Internet anymore, especially after all this. You know this morning I saw a majestic stingray leap from the water for the sheer joy of it and now I realize I am wasting too much of the short time I've been given here on this planet worrying about my online social media image.

Oh. That's cool about the stingray, but what's wrong with your social media image? I think you do a fine job with it.

You mean Dominique does, but thanks for saying so. The whole point, though, is why do we even have to have a social media image? Stingrays don't, and they live totally fulfilled lives.

Stingrays don't have higher-functioning cerebral cortexes, so they don't have the ability to worry about things like their online presence.

Oh. Good point.

Also they leap out of the water in order to catch food or avoid predators or to get rid of parasites that are bothering them. I don't think they experience intense emotions like joy.

I'm not going to say it's pointless to argue with Tina about more esoteric things these days (especially given what happened with Boris), but she has developed a tendency since starting medical school to insist there's a scientific explanation for almost everything.

> **OK, Tina.**

That's when I got another message. It was from a member of the Moscovitz family, but not the one I was hoping to hear from.

<Lilly Moscovitz 'Virago'   HRH Mia Thermopolis 'FtLouie'>

> I suppose I should say 'mazel tov' but really? Then again, the best friend is always the last to know.

> **I'm sorry! We were going to tell you in person, Lilly, but 'someone' blabbed to the press. One guess as to who the someone was.**

> Really? You told Clarisse before you told your BFF?

> **Of course not. I think she must have weaseled it out of the help.**

Why doesn't the CIA hire your grandmother to interrogate terror suspects? She does a much better job than they do of getting classified information.

Sadly, Lilly's right.

Actually, now that I think about it, it probably wasn't Mo Mo, but the chef, Gretel, who Grandmère managed to con out of all the intel about Michael's proposal to me. I *knew* there was something sweetly gullible about her. Her hair was flat-ironed. Who bothers to flat-iron their hair in the tropics?

Someone who's anxious to leave there, that's who, and so willing to accept bribes from my grandmother.

I should have known. Paradise, my butt.

And to think, I fantasized about moving there forever.

3:45 p.m., Monday, May 4
Still in the HELV, still on the WSH
Rate the Royals Rating: 1

Finally got through to Michael. He wasn't picking up because he was on the phone with his parents. They heard it on 1010 WINS, New York's twenty-four-hour news radio station.

I told him I was so, so sorry.

'It's all right,' he said. 'They actually didn't believe it until I told them it was true. They thought it was only a rumor, like the time the *Post* announced you were carrying Prince Harry's royal twins.'

Great.

'Are they mad?'

He hesitated. '. . . No, of course not.'

'Michael, I can tell you're lying. You have the same tone of voice that you get when I ask you if I look terrible in khaki shorts.'

'No one looks good in khaki shorts. And they're not mad that we're getting married, just upset that you aren't converting to Judaism. They're very concerned about how I'm going to be able to keep kosher in the palace.'

'Michael! Stop it. It's not funny.'

'Also, that when I become Prince Michael of Genovia, my children are going to be Renaldos and not Moscovitzes.'

I stopped laughing. 'Wait . . . they really did say that last thing, didn't they?'

'Well, I'm their only son, so you can understand their

concern. I think they're torn between the idea of losing a son and the idea of gaining a prince. I told them not to worry, that in the unlikely event Lilly ever gets married, she won't take her husband's name, so her kids will be Moscovitzes. Weirdly, this didn't seem to placate them.'

'Of course it didn't,' I said. 'Lilly swore off men her junior year in college.' I knew better than to mention the thing about Lars, especially with Lars sitting right there in the car. I thought it would be good for him to hear the thing about her having sworn off men, though. Lars's ego is inflated enough. 'She says she's never getting married. How could you forget?'

'I didn't forget,' Michael said. 'What she actually said was that you fall in love with the *person,* their gender doesn't matter. Although to be honest, if you were a guy I don't know if I'd be as into you.'

'Maybe we should call this whole thing off.'

He sounded shocked. '*Why?* Because I said I wouldn't be as into you if you were a guy? I mean I guess I could get used to it, but it might take time.'

'No, because your parents are right. Michael, you know you're not only going to have to take my name, you're going to have to renounce your American citizenship when we get married.'

'I'll be Genovian on paper,' Michael said, 'but I'll always be American in my heart. These colors don't run.'

'Uh . . . maybe we're rushing into this.'

'Mia, I'm kidding. We've been going out for *eight years* – more if you count high school. How can we be rushing into anything? And I couldn't care less what last name I or our kids have, or even if we *have* kids, or what country I'm a citizen of. I just want to be with *you*, and I'll renounce whatever I have to in order to make that happen.'

My heart swelled with love for him. 'Aw. Michael, that's so sweet,' I whispered (I had to whisper because of Lars, and also François, the driver. It would be nice to have some privacy, but privacy goes out the window when you get a chauffeur/personal security). 'I just want to be with you, too.'

'Then how come at the first sign of trouble you're ready to bail? I thought you were made of stronger stuff, Thermopolis.'

I had to ignore the little thrill I always get when he calls me Thermopolis. 'I'm only thinking of you. Things are just going to get worse from here on out, you know. She's trying to *Game of Thrones* us.'

'Who is? What are you talking about?'

'My grandmother! The story about our engagement is going to be everywhere in exactly one hour. Reuters. BBC. TMZ. They're all going to be covering it. Our royal wedding will be the lead on the national news tonight. And after that, there is no way we're going to get our small, private, family-and-friends-only wedding. We're going to have to do what my grandmother says, which means there probably *will* be a national day of celebration declared, and a commemorative stamp issued of your head.'

'I don't care,' Michael said, sounding bravely determined. 'If that's what I have to go through in order to marry you, I will.'

'Oh, Michael, thanks.'

'That's the worst of it, though, right? There's no weird secret royal Genovian marriage ritual I have to undergo, do I? Sacrificial scarring? Ritual cutting?'

'Well, you're already circumcised, so no.'

There was silence from his end of the phone.

'Oh my God, I'm kidding,' I cried. 'The first rule of being a royal is that you have to learn to take a joke.'

'The first rule of jokes is that they have to be funny,' he countered.

'Fine. Can we get down to the real question, which is how my grandmother even found out? I know Tina didn't tell her.'

'It wasn't me,' Lars supplied, from the front seat. 'I didn't tell.'

'Of course it wasn't Lars,' Michael said, having overheard him. 'Tell Lars no one is blaming him.'

Seriously, if my life were one of those romance novels with a love triangle, Lars and Michael would be the sexy paranormal alpha males, but the two of them would be in love with each other and just ignore me.

'We know it wasn't you, Lars,' I said. 'And before we left this morning, I put the ring on my snowflake necklace around my neck so no one on the plane saw it. It had to have been Gretel.'

'Gretel?' Michael echoed.

'The chef. Who else could it have been? I swear, I'm going to write the meanest review about her on TripAdvisor. Unless—' I gasped. 'Unless there were *cameras* in the cabana. You don't think—'

'Mia,' Michael said. 'Calm down. I know who leaked the story.'

'You do? Who?'

'It was me.'

'*You?*' I was stunned. 'Michael, what are you talking about?'

'That part of the press release about me asking your father's permission to marry you was true – well, partly true, anyway. I didn't ask permission – I knew you wouldn't like that, it's sexist. You're not your father's property. But I did see him before we left, to tell him I was going to propose to you this weekend, and ask for his blessing.'

I was stunned. 'Wait . . . is this what you meant when you said before we left that you'd talked to my parents?'

'Yes. I spoke to your mother, too, because she played an even bigger role in raising you. I thought it was the right thing to do. How do you think you got out of doing all those events – and birthday Cirque du Soleil with your grandmother – so easily?'

'Oh, Michael,' I said into the phone. I was feeling a maelstrom of emotions. 'That's so . . . that's so . . .'

'Yeah,' he said. 'I know. Messed up, right? Especially considering the way everything's turned out.'

'No,' I said. 'That isn't what I was going to say at all. It was very romantic of you. In an *ordinary* family it would have been a sweet thing to do.'

'I can see that now,' he said. 'I think your dad must have mentioned it to someone—'

'You don't have to be coy, Michael,' I said. 'You're

family now. You can come right out and say it. My dad must have mentioned it to my grandmother, who turned it into an opportunity to drum up some positive press for my dad after his brush with the law.'

Michael sighed. 'I guess I should have known better after all these years.'

'Oh, shut up,' I said affectionately. 'I wouldn't change a thing about this past weekend for the world, not even this. But why didn't you tell me you'd asked them?'

'I don't know,' he said. 'It never came up. We were sort of busy doing . . . other things.'

I blushed, even though Michael was speaking to me from another state and no one in the car could hear his end of the conversation. 'Er, yes,' I said. 'I guess we were.'

'Anyway, sorry about that. I guess I'll see you in a little bit.'

'In a little bit? What happened to your medical conference in New Jersey?'

His tone was light. 'Oh, it's still happening, but the press found out about my speech and swamped the hotel, and they don't have enough security to handle the situation, so they've politely asked me to reschedule.'

'Oh, Michael,' I cried. 'I'm so sorry!'

'It's all right,' he said. 'There's no way those doctors were going to listen to a talk about the new strides Pavlov Surgical is making in neural prostheses research when they find out the guy who's giving it just got engaged to the Princess of Genovia anyway.'

He said it lightly, trying to make a joke of the whole

thing, but there's nothing amusing about this to me. It actually made me angrier than ever at Grandmère. She isn't only selfishly Game of Throning our wedding: she's hurting Michael's business, and causing vital medical research information to fail to be disseminated.

'Michael, I'm so sorry. I'm going to get to the bottom of this if it's the last thing I do.'

'Mia, it's fine. None of this is your fault. I guess it's all part of being a—'

But I didn't get to find out what it is he thought it was all part of being because his phone died.

Or the Russians had gotten to him, but when I mentioned this out loud, Lars said I've been watching too much *NCIS* and from now on I need to stick to the Lifetime Movie Channel for women.

I've just told him to stop being so sexist since men watch that channel, too, and also, tons of people get kidnapped on Lifetime, particularly pregnant women whose babies are later sold on the baby black market, which is a completely real thing. I once attended a charity event to raise money to help fight it. Mariska Hargitay was there, and we both complimented each other's outfit in the ladies' room.

3:40 p.m., Monday, May 4
Still in the HELV
Rate the Royals Rating: 1

Managed to reach Mom to tell her about the wedding before she heard it on the news (she only listens to National Public Radio while she paints, so there wasn't much of a chance of that, as NPR is not known for keeping its listeners aware of all the latest royal gossip).

Mom asked for the details about Michael's proposal, which I gave her, but briefly. There are some things I've found it better not to share with my mom. When discussing my life with her, I try to keep it to the highlights, like the sports reel in a half hour news cycle.

Unfortunately, Mom has never felt the same about me. I was forced to listen as she told me *every single facet* of Michael's visit to the loft last week to ask her if our union was something she felt she could support.

'He was very gentlemanly about it,' she said. 'He was even wearing a tie. I appreciated that he was respecting my role as your primary caregiver. So of course I told him that I supported your union wholly—'

'Aw.' This warmed my heart. 'Thanks, Mom.'

She wasn't finished.

'— but that to be honest, I didn't think you'd had enough dating experience, so I thought you two should wait.'

'Mom!' I yelled. 'You *said* that to him?'

'Well, of course I did. You're twenty-six and you've only ever slept with one person. Don't you think you

141

ought to broaden your horizons?'

'No, Mom, I do not. And I don't really want to discuss this with you right now.' I eyed Lars and François, who were having an animated discussion in the front seat about how to avoid chafing while wearing a shoulder holster on a hot day. Dropping my voice, I added, 'But just to remind you, I *have* dated other people, even if I didn't actually have sex with them. So I'm a hundred percent sure I'm with the right person.'

'I thought you kids today were all about the casual hookups,' Mom said. 'Friends with benefits, and all of that.'

'Yeah, well, maybe you need to stop watching romcoms that bill themselves as edgy but still end with the guy running through an airport.' Not that there's anything wrong with that, since I still totally watch them, usually with Tina, who can't get enough of them, especially if they involve a heroine who works as a sassy surgeon, as most gorgeous size-two ladies who are unlucky in love are wont to do.

'I just don't understand it,' Mom said, with a sigh. 'Kids today are so different from when I was your age.'

'Yeah,' I said. 'We are. When you were my age, you already had a toddler – me – with someone you weren't even interested in being with long term. I, however, am marrying someone I want to be with forever, and I have never not used birth control in my life.'

'Yes, Mia, I know,' my mother said, in a soothing voice. 'You've always been my little worrywart. That's why I love you. But I loved your father, too, you know. I still do. I wouldn't want you to think that I didn't.'

'Well, that's just great, Mom,' I said. 'So then why don't you let me do the worrying about my own wedding? God knows it's getting off to a rocky enough start. Wait . . . *what did you say?*'

'Oh, I think your wedding's off to a fine start,' my mother said. 'Michael asked you anyway, didn't he? I didn't manage to scare him off.'

'Not that part,' I said. 'The part about you loving Dad.'

'Well, of course I love your father. I always have, and I always will. I just could never live with him. Could you imagine *me,* living in a palace?' She laughed, but there wasn't much humor in the sound. 'I'd make a terrible royal.'

'Uh,' I said. 'I don't know about that, Mom. I don't think anyone could be worse than me.' I couldn't help thinking about Paolo and his diamond shoe analogy. Would mine ever stop pinching?

'Don't be silly, Mia. You've done an amazing job, what with bringing democracy to Genovia and building that community center for the kids and now choosing Michael as your prince consort. You're the best thing that ever happened to that place, and I'm not just saying that because I'm your mother.'

'Aw.' It was silly, but this caused tears to well up in my eyes. 'Thanks, Mom. You have no idea how much it means to me to hear you say that. But seriously, if *I* can adjust to being a royal, don't you think you could? If you really love Dad that much – and I *know* he adores you – don't you think—?'

143

'Oh, Mia,' she interrupted, in the old exasperated tone she used to use when she'd walk into my room to find me taking my temperature before school because I had a test that day and I was hoping I'd spontaneously developed malaria in the night. 'Love is wonderful but it can't solve every problem, you know. It certainly isn't compensation enough for the fact that your father is a grown man who still lives with his mother.'

I winced. Mom had a point. 'No,' I said. 'I guess not.'

'I suppose I'm going to have to buy one of those awful mother-of-the-bride dresses for the ceremony,' she went on with a sigh. 'Nothing kicky from my own wardrobe is going to work.'

'Um,' I said, remembering the last time Mom wore something 'kicky' to a public function. She'd shown up at the opening of Mr. Gianini's Community Center in a blue dress with a red petticoat, covered in purple roses. It had been Mr. G.'s favorite. 'Absolutely. You can wear whatever you want, Mom.'

'Mia,' she said, laughing. 'Of course I can't. Your wedding is going to be broadcast all over the world. I may be a crazy painter, but I don't want to *look* like one on your special day. I think I can stand wearing one of those stuffy mother-of-the-bride dresses for an afternoon,' she added, bravely. 'It was the idea of wearing one of them – with *panty hose* – every day for the rest of my life that I was never able to stand.'

Which pretty much confirms both Tina's and the Drs. Moscovitz's theory.

'That's very sweet of you, Mom,' I said. 'But the

whole idea was that Michael and I didn't *want* you to have to wear one of those dresses, with or without panty hose. We wanted to have a small, informal wedding, no more than fifty people, no commemorative stamps of Michael—'

My mom laughed some more.

'Oh, okay,' she said. 'Well, best of luck with that. Actually, I quite like the idea of a stamp of Michael.'

'I know, right? That's what *I* said!'

I love Mom, but I worry about her. One of the things my stalker likes to harp on in his anonymous letters and e-mails to me (and rants on Rate the Royals message boards) is how women like my mom, who raise children on their own, are evil. His posts go on and on about how women like her (and me) are destroying the fabric of society by being too independent (because we have our own bank accounts, jobs, etc.), and how I should try to make Genovia more like the despotic nation of Qalif, instead of advocating for equal social, political, and economic rights for women.

If only I could find out who he is so I could have him imprisoned and/or publically humiliated, or at least tell his own mother on him.

- *Note to self:* Remind press office to stop letting me read those letters. I would prefer only to read the nice letters I get from little girls who draw me pictures of themselves with their cats.

It's too bad that Mom and Dad were never able to work things out.

But Mom really isn't the panty-hose-wearing type, and unfortunately those are required for most official royal duties, especially when descending private-plane staircases in high winds while wearing dresses. Trust me, I've had this happen enough times in front of photographers to know.

UGH.

Of course neither my grandmother nor my father is answering their phones.

So now I am resorting to texting, which is bad because, considering all the messages I'm getting, my battery is completely dying.

<Dowager Princess Clarisse of Genovia 'El Diablo'

HRH Mia Thermopolis 'FtLouie'>

Grandmère, why are all the gossip sites reporting that Michael proposed to me this past weekend? How would they even know about that? And why is Rate the Royals saying we're getting married this summer? Call me back ASAP because I'd really like to clear up this matter.

Who is this? Why are there words on my phone?

It's called a text message, Grandmère, stop pretending like you don't know what it is, I showed you how to text last year when TMZ hacked your phone and found out about you and James Franco. So I KNOW you know how to do it. And it's the only way I appear to be able to communicate with you right now since you won't pick up your phone.

I don't know what you're talking about. Clearly my mobile is broken. Please make an appointment with my assistant, Rolanda, if you wish to speak with me.

I will not make an appointment with Rolanda. I am on my way to see you (even though we're stuck in traffic right now). So you had better have an explanation ready. Why would you do something so horrible as announce my engagement to the press before we had a chance to tell Michael's parents in person?

Oh, it's you. Amelia, something terrible has happened. Please come see me at once.

> **Something terrible is ABOUT to happen. To you.**

> *Amelia, I am speaking of something of national urgency. I dare not write it here. We could be being spied upon, you know.*

> **Let me get this straight. You sent out a press release that I'm getting married to distract everyone from some OTHER story that you're afraid is about to break? Who are you now, President Snow from 'The Hunger Games'?**

> *Amelia, don't be flippant.*

Sometimes I think Rommel may not be the only one in the family with dementia.

Well, that was . . . I don't even have words to describe what that was.

But I have to write it all down because it's the only way I'm ever going to make sense of it, let alone figure out what I'm going to *do* about it.

It started normally enough – normally enough for my family, anyway – when I walked in and Grandmère didn't want to talk about it (of course).

All she wanted to do was order us 'tea' from room service. She said she couldn't bear the thought of telling me the 'heinous news' on an empty stomach, and of course she'd sent away her assistant, Rolanda, because what we needed to discuss was 'so private'.

Except not so private that certain other people don't know all about it. Only of course I didn't find *that* out until later.

'So let's be honest, Grandmère,' I said, sitting down on one of her overstuffed pink satin-covered Louis Quatorze armchairs (her new decorator has told her that 'everything old is new again,' which is another way of saying, 'I need a hundred-thousand-dollar commission, so let's redecorate').

'There is no heinous news, am I right? You're simply upset that I caught you using my marriage proposal as a propaganda tool to boost Dad's image since he got arrested. Or is it that I'm marrying Michael, and not the

149

heir to some wealthy European family? Well, I'm sorry, but you're just going to have to get used to the idea of the next prince consort of Genovia being a Jewish computer genius who looks incredibly good in board shorts.'

'Don't be a fool, Amelia,' Grandmère said. She was trying to keep Rommel from humping an incredibly ugly antique milking bench for which I happened to know she'd paid sixteen thousand euros. 'Why would I want you to marry anyone other than Michael? He saved our lives that summer he fixed the hi-fi at the palace and I was able to cast my vote for my darling Rudolpho on *Genovia Can Dance*.'

I rolled my eyes. 'You mean when he fixed the Wi-Fi.'

'Whatever it's called. Now get up and help me with this dog.'

I thought she meant Rommel, so I got up to help her place him back in his basket (eighteenth-century French egg-gathering, one thousand euros). But she said, 'Not *that* dog! *He's* fine. The other one. Get the other one!'

Yes, Grandmère now owns *another* dog (although this isn't the national emergency. I *wish*).

And while it is very adorable – for now, anyway, the dog still has all its hair – really, people who can't take proper care of their current pet shouldn't go out and buy a second one.

'Why?' I demanded, lifting the tiny white powder puff I found digging for a stray cocktail onion under the $40,000 white satin-covered couch. '*Why* did you get another dog?'

'She's top of the line,' Grandmère said. 'The breeder

assured me that any puppies she has with Rommel will be of the highest quality, intelligence, and beauty. And you're the one who said I needed to solve Rommel's little . . . problem.'

I was horrified. 'By getting him fixed, not by buying him a wife! And look, he's not even interested in her.' Rommel was humping his thousand-euro French egg-gathering basket.

'Oh, that's because she isn't in heat yet,' Grandmère said matter-of-factly.

'But he'll hump *my* leg, regardless of whether or not *I'm* in the mood. Grandmère, this is worse than *The Bride of Frankenstein,* because instead of building Rommel a girlfriend out of corpses, which he'd have been fine with since he can't tell inanimate objects from animated ones, you actually went out and bought him a *living* girlfriend.'

'Stop worrying about the dog, she's perfectly happy. Show me the ring.'

I put Grandmère's sweet, innocent new dog down in the kitchen with a bowl of food and another of water, then closed the door to keep her safe from Rommel's advances (should he choose ever to make any) and went back to show my grandmother the ring Michael had given me.

'As you can see,' I said, 'your spies got it wrong. It's not a sapphire.'

'Good Lord!' she cried. Of course, while I'd been out of the room she'd put on her jeweler's loupe to examine the stone. 'This must be seven carats at least. I didn't know robot builders made so much money. I have renewed respect for the boy.'

151

I snatched my hand away from her. 'Michael isn't a boy, he's a man. And I've told you repeatedly he doesn't build robots, he designs robotic surgical arms and now prostheses. And it's a lab-grown diamond.'

She immediately dropped my hand. 'It's fake? I take back everything I said about respecting him.'

'Lab-grown diamonds aren't fake like cubic zirconia, Grandmère. They're actual diamonds, they're just grown in a laboratory instead of in a mine, so there's no human-rights or environmental impact in harvesting them.'

Grandmère sighed like I'd just told her that Michael and I were moving to one of those adult gated communities where no one wears any clothes at the public tennis courts because they want to 'express their true selves.'

'I don't suppose this day could get any worse,' she said.

'For *me*,' I said. 'I was hoping to spend this day personally sharing news of my engagement with all my loved ones, and now I'm having to explain to them why they've heard about it via text message or gossip news sites. So why don't we talk about this matter of "national urgency" that you keep saying made it necessary for you to put out a press release that I'm getting married this July, which, by the way, I'm not. And if this national matter is so urgent, why isn't Dad here?'

She regarded me unblinkingly through her tattooed-on eyeliner. 'Because the news I have to impart to you, Amelia, is *about* your father.'

For the second time in seventy-two hours, my heart stopped. The one person I hadn't spoken to (or heard from) all day was Dad.

'Grandmère!' I grabbed her veiny, many-ringed hand. 'What happened? Was it his heart? Was it a protester? Where have they taken him? Can I see him?'

'Pull yourself together!' I think Grandmère would have slapped me if I hadn't already been holding her hand (and there hadn't been a cocktail in her other one). 'Your father is fine. This is no time for hysterics. Have a drink, like a normal person.'

In Grandmère's day, people didn't take antidepressants or go see therapists when they were distressed about something. They had some sense slapped into them, or they had a drink 'like a normal person.'

I have to admit, this does save a lot of time, unless of course you happen to be an alcoholic, or what's bothering you is that family members are always slapping you, which nowadays is called 'abuse.'

Fortunately by that time 'tea' had arrived, so finger sandwiches and 'tea' had been spread out over the antique marble coffee table (7,500 euros). Grandmère was already armed with her traditional Sidecar, so I made myself a vodka tonic because frankly I didn't think I could take whatever was coming sober.

'If Dad's not dead, what is it, then?' I asked, after taking a few fortifying gulps. 'He didn't get arrested again, did he?'

'No, but that's how I discovered all of this in the first place.' Grandmère sat down and bit into an egg-salad sandwich on white bread with the crusts cut off. 'While I was searching through your father's desk, looking for his checking-account number to post his bail after he was incarcerated.'

'Wait. You paid Dad's bail with money from his *own account*?'

'Of course. It was his foolishness that landed him in jail. Why would I use my own money to bail him out?'

This was cold, even for Grandmère. 'Wow,' I said. 'Remind me not to call you to pay the ransom if I ever get kidnapped.'

'Oh, please,' Grandmère said. 'That's why we pay ransom insurance.'

'Well,' I said. The egg-salad sandwich looked good, so I took one, too, even though my stomach was churning with anxiety. 'Whatever you found can't be that bad. He got arrested weeks ago, and you're only calling it a matter of "national urgency" now?'

'I assigned a member of the RGG to look into it and he just got back to me with a full report on the gravity of the matter this morning.'

'Oh, well, the RGG! And what could the Royal Genovian Guard possibly have found in Dad's personal effects that was so shocking it justifies forcing me to have a wedding I haven't agreed to?'

Grandmère cleared her throat very dramatically and said the last thing I ever expected:

'Amelia, you have a sister.'

Fortunately I'd swallowed before she made this pronouncement, or I'd have choked. 'I'm sorry, *what*?'

'You heard me. You are not your father's only *enfant naturel*' – which means 'love child' in French. 'He has another.'

Stupidly all I could think about at that moment was the scene in *Star Wars Episode V: The Empire Strikes Back* when Obi-Wan sighs that Luke is their last hope and Yoda says, 'No. There is another.'

Of course you have to wait for a whole other movie to find out that 'the other' is Princess Leia, who happens to be Luke's secret twin.

'Wait a minute.' I wasn't aware that I had allowed my sandwich to dangle from my fingers until I felt Rommel's sharp teeth nip them as he stole it. 'Ow!' I cried. Then I said, 'That's not possible, Grandmère. If I had a sister, Dad would have told me. Besides, you know perfectly well Dad can't have any more children because the chemo he had for his testicular cancer rendered him infertile. That's why I'm the heir to the throne—'

'Of course,' Grandmère interrupted, rolling her eyes. 'And when he told you that pretty little story twelve years ago, he *had* just received that devastating news from his doctors. But as we all know, doctors aren't always correct. You will recall the time I was told to avoid smoking and alcohol because it was believed I had a stomach tumor. But it turned out only to be acid reflux. I took a few Tums and I was fine.'

'Grandmère,' I said, still stunned. 'That is *not* the same thing.'

'Well,' she said. 'Be that as it may, you have a sister. She was probably conceived right around the time your father delivered that quaint little speech to you. But as it happened, he still had a few active swimmers left in the old pipeline.'

'Eww!' I did some swift math in my head, which wasn't easy, not only because math has never been my strong suit but also because Grandmère's verbal imagery had completely grossed me out. 'Wait . . . so you're saying I have a twelve-year-old little sister?'

'Yes, that is precisely what I'm saying.'

'How do you know this?' I asked suspiciously. 'What exactly did you find in Dad's desk to prove this? It wasn't another one of *those e-mails*, was it?'

My grandmother is one of the many people who feels compelled to help out whatever down-on-his-luck Nigerian prince (because one royal should help out another royal) comes her way, and she actually believed the one about a close relative needing cash wired to them immediately because they'd been robbed and were stranded in Mexico. Worse, she believed *I* was the person who'd been robbed. Someone managed to find my private e-mail address and use it to scam my grandmother out of $30,000 (which thankfully she could afford) before anyone on the palace staff could find out what she was doing and stop her (not that anyone would have been able to. Once Grandmère gets an idea in her head, there's no talking her out of it).

Grandmère was livid when she found out I was safely in class at Sarah Lawrence and nowhere near Mexico, and that there was a complete stranger running around Mexico $30,000 richer.

The worst decision we ever made was allowing my grandmother to have access to the Internet (although she adores commenting anonymously. She is the worst troll ever. No one on Jezebel.com or Reddit knows that the

Dowager Princess of Genovia is the person making all the mean comments about how the fat children just need to use more self-control and they'll lose weight).

'You know what you saw was probably just another kind of scam, right?' I asked her. 'People contact me *all the time* saying they're my long-lost relative – which, especially with all these genealogy websites, could even be true. Six degrees of separation, and all that. We're all cousins, basically. But I would never send those people any money, or give any credence at all to their crazy claims. Dad wouldn't either.'

'Unfortunately, Amelia, this isn't a scam,' Grandmère said haughtily. 'I can assure you that this person does, in fact, exist, and is, in fact, your sister. Otherwise, I highly doubt your father would have been making child-support payments to her – monthly – for the past *twelve years*. I saw them in his private bank-account book.'

My mind reeled. 'Grandmère, that – that can't be true. The payments must have been for something else.'

'Not according to what José says in his report.'

'*José?*' I was pouring myself another drink, this time with shaky fingers. 'José as in José de la Rive, the director of the Royal Genovian Guard, Lars's *boss*?'

'Well, naturally, Amelia. Despite what you might think of me, I wasn't simply going to *assume* that what I saw in your father's bankbook was true, not after Mexico . . . and not without sending someone to check on it. And José is, of course, the very best, and quite experienced in this kind of thing. He used to work for Interpol. The terrorism unit.' She got a faraway look in her eyes that I recognized. It was the same one she'd worn around the time of the James Franco affair. 'José is surprisingly gentlemanly for a man skilled in the use of torture.'

This was getting worse and worse.

'Oh, Grandmère,' I said. 'Please tell me you didn't send José to waterboard this little girl's family!'

'Of course not, Amelia,' she said in disgust. 'What do you take me for? I sent José to Cranbrook, New Jersey, to collect DNA from the child for a paternity test.'

'New Jersey? Why New Jersey?'

'Because that's where your father's been sending the monthly support payments for nearly twelve years now, Amelia. Are you dense? I thought it would be nice to know he's not been doing so unnecessarily—'

'*New Jersey?*' I shouted. 'Are you telling me that I've had a half sister living across the river since I was fourteen years old, and no one ever told me?'

'*Us*, Amelia,' Grandmère said, looking annoyed. 'Your father never told *us*. And must you shout so? It's hardly regal. And that is precisely what I asked José to find out, which he did. He said he's shocked that no one – such as your insufferable cousin Ivan, or that blackguard Brian Fitzpatrick – had discovered it sooner. Your father has been making the payments *in his own name* from an account here at Chase Manhattan Bank. The fool!'

I couldn't believe it. Not the part about Dad having had a secret love – he's a prince, after all, who'd never married after my mom refused his proposal in college, choosing instead to 'wander the globe in search of a woman who might be able to provide the balm to soothe his wounded heart,' as Tina liked to put it (although really he'd simply had dozens of short-lived relationships with supermodels, actresses, television news journalists, and the occasional high school English teacher).

It was the part about my having a little sister that I couldn't believe . . . and the fact that my father had never told me about it. Not telling Grandmère I could understand. Though underneath her flamboyant exterior, she has a warm (well, warmish) heart. How else has she tolerated her horrible dog all these years?

But there is no doubt that she disapproves of nearly everything her only child (my father) does.

This is most likely why he'd fallen for the one woman in the world he couldn't have – my mother, his own mother's exact opposite (in complete defiance of Dr. Moscovitz's theory about him).

But I'd always thought my father and I were close.

Now I realized I knew nothing about him at all.

This stings a little. Actually, a lot.

I leaped to my feet. 'Well, what are we waiting for?' I said to my grandmother. 'Have your driver bring the car around, and let's go meet her.'

'Certainly not, Amelia,' my grandmother said. 'According to Lazarres-Reynolds, that's the *worst* possible thing we could do. We can't risk exposing this story to the media, especially after all the trouble we went to today in order to provide the perfect distraction for them, in the form of your wedding.'

'What are you talking about? Who on earth is Lazarres-Reynolds?'

'The crisis management firm I hired to handle this affair, of course. Why do you think I announced your engagement this morning?'

I sank back down onto the couch, stunned. 'I thought you did that to distract the press from Dad's arrest.'

'Well, of course I did, Amelia. Have you seen his most recent numbers in the polls for prime minister? He's five points behind your cousin Ivan – who just today announced that, if elected, he'll make genetically modified fruit illegal *and* deny all humanitarian entry visas into Genovia. But if news of this latest debacle of your father's gets out – well, he'll be crushed in the election. *Crushed.*'

I shook my head. 'Grandmère,' I said. 'This little girl's existence isn't a political scandal you can hire a publicity firm to cover up. She's a human being. She's *family.*'

'I'm aware of that, Amelia. But Lazarres-Reynolds really is very good. Do you remember that incident last year with the son of the Sultan of Brunei and the monkey?'

'No.'

'Exactly. Do you know why you don't remember it? Two words: Lazarres-Reynolds.'

'But, Grandmère,' I said desperately, 'do you really think if people found out Dad had another kid, they'd think badly enough of him to vote against him?'

'For keeping it a secret so long? Yes. No one likes a liar. Think about it, Amelia. How do *you* feel about your father right now?'

'I . . . I . . . I guess I feel a little confused.'

She snorted. 'Nonsense. What you feel right now, Amelia, is *hurt*. Personally, I'd like to hack off his testicles – the one he has left, anyway – but that would only give Lazarres-Reynolds another crisis to manage. And they may have one anyway, because according to José, this uncle who's helping to raise her has accepted a lucrative contracting job overseas and is planning on moving the whole family—'

'*What?*' I didn't care about Grandmère possibly cutting off my father's remaining testicle. I was more concerned about the welfare of my newly discovered sibling. 'Why is the *uncle* helping to raise her? Where is her mother?'

'Her mother, Elizabeth Harrison, passed away ten years ago in a tragic Jet Ski accident—'

'*What?*' I yelled. Every time my grandmother opened her mouth, it seemed, the news got more terrible.

'If you would allow me to finish, Amelia, instead of constantly interrupting, you'd understand. The girl's mother was a private charter jet pilot – that's how your father met her. You know how he is about hopping on a private plane every time the fancy strikes him, and he can't always be bothered to wait for the royal jet. Anyway, apparently they were quite hot and heavy for a time, but then it fizzled out and the woman died while on vacation. I never did agree with personal watercraft, so dangerous, I'm glad we had them banned from Genovian waters.'

I sat there, completely shocked. My father had been in love – in love enough to have a child with someone other than my mother? I was going to have to go back and reread every page of my diaries from that time period to see how I'd missed it. There must have been a clue, some indication of Elizabeth Harrison's existence. Otherwise, my father was the greatest actor who had ever lived.

Or I was a completely insensitive daughter.

'Like your mother,' Grandmère was going on, 'Elizabeth preferred that her child be raised in ignorance of her birthright. She left her in the care of her sister, Catherine, who, by José's account, is perfectly acceptable, but has questionable taste in men, since she's married what I believe is commonly referred to today as a "bohunk" who owns a construction business that—'

I'd taken all I could take. 'Grandmère, what is Dad *thinking*? I can understand wanting to keep this girl a secret from the media, but how could he keep her a secret from *us*?'

Grandmère sniffed and poured herself another drink. 'And have your mother find out and think ill of him? Not likely!'

'But why would *Mom* care? She fell in love and had a kid with someone else, too.'

'That is the point, Amelia. Your father fancies your mother *would* care . . . as much as he did when she married that algebra teacher of yours. Not that she noticed, cruel woman that she is.'

'My mother isn't—'

'Here.' Grandmère handed me a dossier. She looked as self-satisfied as Fat Louie after he's managed to stick his head in my cereal bowl and lap up all the milk. 'This is José's report, you can read all about it. There's quite a bit about the bohunk. It's extremely unsettling. He's a ginger.'

I frowned at her. One of the signs of dementia in older people is a loss of social inhibitions, and that's certainly true of my grandmother, who barely even bothers to hide her prejudices anymore, especially the one she has against red-haired men. Despite all evidence to the contrary, Grandmère believes that Ron Weasley, not Voldemort, is the villain of the Harry Potter series.

I would totally have ratted her out to Dr. Delgado for this, except that Prince Harry of England and A-list actresses with auburn tresses are completely exempt from her wrath. So she isn't prejudiced against *all* redheads, only those she considers socially inferior to herself.

I'm completely demanding an autopsy on my grandmother's brain when she's dead so I can see what I'm in for as I age.

'I'm sorry, Grandmère,' I said crisply as I flipped through the neatly typed pages, each stamped with the official seal of the Genovian Guard. 'I can understand why it might be dangerous for the girl if the truth gets out – no one should have to grow up with bodyguards and press hounding her the way I did. But these are enlightened times. I really believe, if we handle it properly – even without the help of a crisis management team – neither the voters *nor* the press is going to make a big deal out of . . .'

My voice trailed off because I'd turned to the

page with my sister's photo on it.

'Oh,' I said. *'Oh.'*

Grandmère nodded knowingly. 'Yes,' she said. *'Now* do you see the gravity of the problem, Amelia?'

'It isn't a *problem,*' I said. 'Except maybe to some people, who might be surprised to see that she's . . . she's . . .'

'Black,' Grandmère said.

Seriously, sometimes I can't even deal with her.

'African American,' I corrected her.

'She's not *African,*' Grandmère said. 'She was born in New Jersey, and her father is Genovian.'

'Yes, Grandmère, but today people say—'

'That makes her *American Genovian,*' Grandmère went on, blithely ignoring me. 'I suppose you'll argue that the proper term is biracial, but in Europe they'll call her black, just as they'd call her uncle a ginger.'

'No one but you would call her uncle that,' I said. 'And hopefully in Europe they won't call her anything but Olivia Grace, which according to this is her name.'

'Do you really think that's what your cousin Ivan is going to say when he finds out?' Grandmère asked acidly. 'I highly doubt it.'

It would be nice to think she's wrong, and that we live in a world where no one notices things like skin color (or hair color) and that prejudice and bigotry don't exist. Certainly many people claim they 'don't see' these things, and that we live in a 'post-racial society.'

But I don't need a crisis management team to tell me that this is untrue.

'Yeah,' I said. 'Well, in Cousin Ivan's case, it might have been better if she were a redhead—'

'Bite your tongue!' Grandmère cried, horrified.

We didn't get to finish our talk, though, because at that moment we both heard loud male voices from the hallway outside Grandmère's penthouse condo. Curiously, they appeared to be singing a popular Genovian drinking song, which goes, roughly translated:

Oh, forgive me, Mother, for I am drunk again!
Forgive me, Mother, for I am drunk again!
Forgive me, Mother, for I am drunk,
Forgive me, Mother, for I am drunk,
Forgive me, Mother, for I am drunk again!
(Repeat)

It is possibly the most annoying song of all time (besides Boris's 'A Million Stars'), but its annoying qualities multiply times infinity when you realize that it's being sung by your father, who you've just found out has been lying to you (by omission) about having another child, and who only a few weeks earlier got arrested for recklessly speeding his race car in Manhattan.

'What's *he* doing here?' I hissed, hurriedly closing the dossier.

'Oh, he's been downstairs in his own suite this entire time,' Grandmère said, 'with your fiancé.'

'*What?* Michael?' Suddenly I recognized the second male voice. 'When did *Michael* get here?'

'I believe he arrived while you were imprisoning

165

Rommel's bride-to-be in the kitchen,' Grandmère said drily, 'to try, as he put it, to straighten out this wedding nonsense. I sent him to speak to your father. It sounds like the two of them have been celebrating your impending nuptials. You can keep that.' She pointed to the dossier. 'I have my own copy. But I wouldn't allow your father to see it.'

'Wait . . . *Dad doesn't know you know?*'

'Of course he doesn't. You know how sensitive he is. Ever since he was a little boy, he never liked me knowing his business. I remember when he was at school, he used to collect comic books – the one who dressed as a spider, what was his name? Well, whatever his name was, your father loved him, but he never wanted me to know about it. Why do you think your father would be so ashamed of loving a spider man?'

'I don't know, Grandmère,' I said, shoving the dossier into my bag, which was fortunately large enough to hold it since it was my carry-on. I hadn't yet had a chance to unpack from my trip, so I was still carrying around all my clothes and bottles of sunscreen. 'Maybe because he secretly wanted to be Spider-Man. Anyway, we have to talk about this with him. He can't go on keeping his own daughter a secret.'

'Of course he can,' she said with a sniff. 'At least until after the election. He's done it for twelve years, he can do it for three more months.'

'But he can't allow Olivia to be taken overseas!'

'Why not? The press will have a much more difficult time finding her there than in New Jersey. And this is the family she knows and, presumably, loves and feels comfortable with.'

'But it's not right,' I said. 'We're her family, too. And we may never have a chance to see her again. Like in the 1991 docudrama starring Sally Field, *Not Without My Daughter*, based on the true story of the kidnapping of American citizen Betty Mahmoody's daughter by her own husband, who refused to return her from Iran after his two-week visitation.'

Grandmère frowned at me. 'I said overseas, Amelia, not Iran. You do know that I only shared this information with you so you would understand how essential it is that you provide a distraction in your role as royal bride this summer, not so that you could turn it into the plot of some terrible movie only you have ever seen.'

'That movie wasn't terrible,' I said indignantly. 'It was a moving portrayal of a brave woman who fought against a misogynistic regime for the return of her child.'

'May I remind you, Amelia, that this is a time of crisis, not a time for film reviews? Your father needs you. Your *country* needs you.'

'Well, I think my *sister* needs me, and I intend to do something about it.'

'You will *not*. You will do as I tell you. And stop twitching at me. It's extremely unbecoming.'

But by then the door to the penthouse had already burst open, and Dad had come staggering in, supported under one arm by Michael, so the conversation (princesses never argue) had come to an end. My grandmother shoved me – with surprising strength for such an elderly woman – toward them, crying, 'Well, hello, gentlemen! How lovely to see you both. This happy news calls for a celebration, don't you think? What will you have?'

Dad is completely blotto – much too drunk to confront tonight – and I'm supposed to be in here making coffee (which obviously I haven't been, because instead I've been writing this all down. I ordered coffee from room service).

Everyone is in too good a mood to notice, though, even Grandmère. Even Michael. He came in and kissed me.

Michael has not had as much to drink as Dad, though he did say that when he tried to broach the subject of toning down the wedding, Dad slapped him on the shoulder and said, 'Now, why would we do that? Got to keep up with those Brits!' then cracked open a thousand-dollar bottle of 2000 Domaines Barons de Rothschild Chateau Lafite.

Even the new dog seems happy: she's currently curled into a little white ball on my lap.

Everyone seems to be bubbling over with joy.

Everyone but me.

What am I going to do?

8:27 p.m., Monday, May 4
In the HELV on the way to the Consulate
Rate the Royals Rating: 1

Ignored Grandmère's advice about not sharing personal baggage with anyone but family and told Michael everything in the car just now on the way home – which means Lars heard it, too, but whatever. The fact that I have a secret sister is possibly one of the shortest-kept secrets of all time.

But I'm *not* not going to tell Michael something like this. We're engaged.

Michael was surprised, but not as surprised as I would be if he'd told me *his* dad had a secret love child he'd been hiding in New Jersey for the past twelve years.

I suppose it's easier to believe this of the Prince of Genovia than it would be of Dr. Moscovitz, a married psychoanalyst who lives on the Upper West Side and likes to read nonfiction about the fall of the Third Reich in his spare time.

'Well,' Michael said, after he'd gotten over his initial shock. 'What are you going to do about it?'

I did not try to hide my bitterness. 'Grandmère says I'm not supposed to do anything about it, for the good of the country. Not until after the election.'

'Right.' Michael rolled his eyes. 'Again, what are you going to do about it?'

'That's the thing. I don't know.' This is very distressing. I usually always know what to do . . . or at least I'm leaning in one direction or another. But in this case, I have no idea. 'What would *you* do?'

'If I found out I had a little sister some ginger bohunk was threatening to take overseas, I'd go find her,' Lars volunteered from the front seat. 'Then I'd put a bullet through the bohunk's head. Probably a nine-millimeter. But possibly a forty-five, depending on how much I disliked him.'

Thanks for the input, Lars.

'I'm not sure that's the most diplomatic way to handle it,' I said. 'Nor would it be the best thing for a twelve-year-old to see.'

'I wouldn't do it in front of her.' Now Lars is disgusted with me. 'And I know enough to make it look like a suicide.'

- *Note to self:* Do not get on the bad side of the RGG.

Grandmère was right. I should have kept my personal baggage to myself.

9:05 p.m., Monday, May 4
Still in the HELV
Rate the Royals Rating: 1

Really must say 'crap' even though princesses aren't supposed to swear.

Pulled up in front of the consulate just now, and half the block has been taken over by blue wooden barricades which the NYPD (working in tandem with the Royal Genovian Guard) has erected to keep back all news vans and photojournalists crowded outside the consulate doors.

I don't want to be the kind of girlfriend/fiancée/wife who says 'I told you so,' but I did tell Michael this was going to happen. It's official:

Our engagement made the national news.

And I'm no longer *Why Won't He Marry Mia*.

I'm the *Princess Bride*.

(So unoriginal. You can do better, Brian Fitzpatrick.)

9:21 p.m., Monday, May 4
Still in the HELV
Rate the Royals Rating: 1

Double crap. Just pulled up in front of Michael's building, and *it's* surrounded by press, too, waiting for us.

Lars is calling José to ask him what the hell we're supposed to do. NYPD flagged us over, and when the nice officer looked inside and saw who we were, she said, 'Do us a favor, would you?'

I said, 'Of course, Officer.'

She said, 'Don't get out of the car.'

'But I live here!' Michael cried.

'I would seriously consider moving.'

So tired. All I want to do is crawl into bed and cry myself to sleep. But right now it appears I have no bed to crawl into.

I never thought having a happily-ever-after was going to be so complicated.

I miss Fat Louie.

See, this is what is making me think I *shouldn't* go rushing to New Jersey to yank Olivia Grace away from her bohunk uncle. When something is keeping you away from home – even if it's only a temporary home, like the third-floor apartment of the Genovian consulate – home is the only place you want to be.

This is *not* how I expected to be spending my first night back in Manhattan as an engaged woman.

Not that I'm complaining, because I know there are many, many people who would trade places with me in an instant. And I am very, very content seeing as how I, along with my fiancé, am currently checked into a premier 'tower suite' at the Regalton (one of Manhattan's finest luxury hotels) courtesy of the Genovian consulate under the name 'Mr. and Mrs. James T. Kirk.' I am not exactly homeless or sleeping in my car under a bridge. I am very much enjoying my diamond shoes.

Still, it's a bit disturbing not to be able sleep in my own bed (or see my own cat) because of the hordes of press staking out our individual domiciles.

'If it's like this now,' Michael asked earlier in the evening while we were enjoying our steak au poivre (room service), 'what's it going to be like closer to the actual wedding?'

'Don't worry,' Dominique assured us cheerfully over the phone (I'd put her on speaker). 'I'm sure there will be a weather disaster or celebrity scandal soon.'

But what if the celebrity scandal is my newly discovered little sister? I thought (but didn't ask aloud since Dominique has not yet been let in on the secret).

I don't want Olivia having a bunch of reporters pointing telephoto lenses at her every door and window, wondering when she's coming home so they can snap a photo of her, whether she's ready for it or not. (There's nothing worse than getting your photo taken when you're not expecting it. I know because I've had countless photos taken of *me* when I was chewing or sneezing or in my bathing suit, then posted online and in magazines, accompanied by unflattering and unfair captions like *Royal Rebel: drunk again!* or *Pity Pity Princess* or *Cellulite Surprise!*)

What saddens me is when I ask young girls (and boys) at the center what they hope to be when they grow up (so lame, I know, and a sign that I'm getting old, because only adults ask young people this question. Why do we do it? Because we're looking for ideas! I'm twenty-six and I *still* don't know what I want to be when I grow up, except of course that I want to help people and be brilliantly happy and with Michael Moscovitz, of course), all too often they answer, 'When I grow up, I want to be famous, like you, Princess Mia!'

At first this made me very depressed. Famous? Being famous isn't a job!

Then I realized that it is. Being famous is very hard work, but it's also empowering, because you have influence over a large number of people and can do amazing things with that power.

And it doesn't even matter anymore how you happen to come by that fame, singing or dancing or posting a sex tape on the Internet or finding out that you're a princess. It's what you *do* with your fame that matters.

· So I began explaining to the children that they could

become famous by doing something helpful in their community, such as being a doctor, teacher, police officer, engineer, or architect. That can be totally empowering, even if it doesn't make them 'famous' internationally.

Of course none of them has fallen for it . . . *yet*. I think I have to work on my delivery. It definitely isn't going to help if my eyelid is twitching as I say it.

And I must say I appreciate the complimentary bottle of champagne and box of chocolate-covered strawberries that the concierge has just sent up, along with her congratulations and a note saying that if we like our room, we should be sure to post about it on our Instagram accounts.

'Well,' Michael just said as he came out of the shower in his fluffy white Regalton bathrobe, smelling of Kiehl's beauty products, his dark hair sticking damply to the back of his neck (how I love when this happens). 'I could get used to this. Did you see that there's a television in the mirror in there? *Inside* the mirror. According to *Inside Edition*, the reason we're getting married in such a rush is because you're carrying my unborn twins. Congratulations. At least they're not Prince Harry's this time.'

'I liked Sleepy Palm Cay better, where there were no TVs,' I said, 'especially not in the bathroom mirrors.'

'I never in a million years thought I'd hear you say such a thing.' Michael lay down on the bed beside me and lifted one of the chocolate-covered strawberries and dangled it over my mouth. 'Open. We must keep you well nourished as you're now eating for three.'

I thought about refusing, but who can refuse a delicious chocolate-covered strawberry? Besides, I hadn't yet brushed my teeth. I'd been busy reading José's dossier on Olivia (the news isn't as bad as I thought. But it isn't great either. Olivia doesn't appear to be happy in her school, though she does make very good grades).

'Don't eat any more of those,' I warned Michael, after I'd swallowed. 'They're blackmail berries. They only gave them to us in exchange for us posting photos of ourselves eating them on our social media network, with a hashtag mentioning the Regalton. But if we do that, it will look like I'm promoting a for-profit business, and you know it's Renaldo royal family policy never to do that. We only promote nonprofits.'

'So?' Michael lifted another strawberry. 'You know in the old days people simply used to accept gifts and enjoy them and not feel guilty about failing to photograph themselves doing it.'

Then he opened his robe to reveal that beneath it, he was wearing absolutely nothing. Then he put the chocolate-covered strawberry on a place I'm not going to write here, but it was quite naughty, even for a visitor to this planet from another galaxy, unaccustomed to our ways and his humanoid body.

All I have to say is, this princess bride thing definitely has its upside.

10:02 a.m., Tuesday, May 5
In HELV on way to the Community Center
Rate the Royals Rating: 1

Michael let me sleep in and was up and gone before I ever even opened my eyes. He left me a text (whatever happened to romantic, handwritten notes left on pillows, along with a chocolate-covered strawberry? Oh, well, we ate them all, and texting is more expedient).

Good morning! There's an E. coli outbreak in California due to bags of allegedly prewashed salad mix. 213 hospitalized. Also, the wife of the Crown Prince of Qalif is alive. She tweeted that she's very angry about this new law her husband has issued that women in his country are not allowed to swim in public.

So we are no longer the lead story! I'm at work, call me when you get up (I thought you'd want to sleep in, as you seemed exhausted. I don't know what could have tired you out ;-). Love you.

He included an emoji of a cartoon alien being blasted through its heart by a laser gun.

I really do need to talk to him about his emojis; he doesn't seem to understand the purpose of them at all.

Anyway, I know exactly what it is I have to do.

177

I read in a magazine once that sleep helps reset the brain, so if you have an important decision to make you should put off making it until morning. As human beings, we make so many important decisions throughout the day (such as what to eat for lunch, whether or not to cross against the light, or whether to friend this person or that person) that by evening our decision-making brain cells are literally depleted.

But by morning they're recharged and ready to go.

This must be why everything seems so clear to me this morning (well, except for the headache).

Obviously, I can't allow myself to be pushed around like this. I plan to go to New Jersey to meet my sister.

I know this goes explicitly against her own mother's (and grandmother's) wishes, but like Lars said, no one is going to keep me from meeting my own sister – especially now that I know we have the same middle name (Mignonette – clearly Elizabeth Harrison did that on purpose. She must have meant us to meet one day).

Of course, Mignonette is also my grandmother's middle name (and a sauce with which raw oysters are served). But this means nothing.

Olivia loves animals (like me) and also drawing and math (okay . . . unlike me. But everyone has their individual talents and we are all unique. Not like snowflakes, though, because they've actually discovered that there ARE snowflakes that are alike. So we all need to stop saying that thing about snowflakes being unique).

She also lives with her aunt and the 'bohunk' uncle and his two older children from a previous marriage.

So I don't want to make her life harder than it already is. Maybe she wants to move overseas.

- *Note to self:* Find out where overseas they are moving. Maybe it's someplace nice, such as the South of France. Maybe they'll be near Genovia!

But where she lives should be up to her. She should know she has a choice.

Although first I have to work on having a choice to give her.

10:15 a.m., Tuesday, May 5
In HELV on the way to the Community Center
Rate the Royals Rating: 1

Just got off the phone with Michael. We had a very serious conversation about what we were going to do about our living situation, and also about my sister, Olivia. (After some initial silliness about whether I was or was not wearing underwear.)

Grandmère's announcement of our wedding plans is forcing us to make decisions about things we hadn't yet discussed in a lot of detail, such as where we're going to live. Obviously Michael can't move into the consulate, because the apartment there is too small and also hideous (the décor is circa 1987), and no one who doesn't absolutely have to should be forced to live under Madame Alain's sanctimonious gaze.

Of course Michael's loft is wonderful but it's in a nondoorman condo building, which means:

- There is no one to keep stalkers from being buzzed in.

- There is no desk for packages, etc., to be signed in/scanned by the Royal Genovian Guard.

- It doesn't have proper walls between rooms (except for the bathrooms), which is fine for us but inappropriate if we're going to be playing Fireman (or Space Alien) while also entertaining overnight house guests, such as a little sister (whom I hope to entertain one day). What if she were to hear us? It could permanently warp her developing little mind.

'Wait,' Michael said, when I mentioned this. 'Are you thinking we're going to adopt her, or something?'

'Of course not!' I said. 'We're going to be newlyweds. We can't have a tween girl lounging around the house, doing tween-girl things like painting her nails and FaceTiming with her friends about her new teen heartthrob.'

'Is that really what you think tween girls do? Have you been watching *13 Going on 30* again?'

'No. I know what tween girls do. I was a tween once.'

'If I recall correctly, when you were a tween, you would walk around with a cat stuffed down your pants while my sister filmed you for her public-access TV show.'

'That is not correct.'

'From my observations, it is. I was there, remember? I don't think you really have a solid grasp on normal tween behavior.'

'Please let's move on. It's not like Olivia can live with my dad. He'd be the worst person to raise a tween. He stays in a hotel room here in New York half the year, and the rest of the time he hangs around Genovia, pretending to govern it.'

'Yeah,' Michael said. 'That's true, but I thought the whole point was that her mom didn't want her to know she's Genovian royalty.'

'Right. But if my grandmother's right, she's going to find out eventually. So it's better for me to be the one to tell her. I can do it gently and compassionately. And so it will be nice if we had a room for her to stay in,' I said. 'So she feels welcome. If she wants to.'

'Okay,' Michael said, sounding skeptical. 'You've decided you're going to tell your long-lost sister that she's Genovian royalty. That will probably go well. When are you going to do this?'

'I don't know,' I said. 'I haven't decided. But soon. Stop making it sound weird. It's no weirder than the fact that we had to stay in a hotel last night because our places were swarming with paparazzi.'

'It's a little weirder than that,' Michael said. 'But that cop did advise me to get a new apartment. I suppose I can just buy one with a spare bedroom for your sister—'

'See?' I said. 'That's the spirit.'

How amazing is he? *I can just buy a new place with a spare bedroom for your sister.* I'm seriously the luckiest girl in the world.

- *Note to self:* Remember this for gratitude-journal entry.

(Wow, it's sad that I have to make notes in my regular journal to remember to put things in my gratitude journal.)

'Why don't I buy it with you?' I suggested. 'Our first place together! Should it be uptown or downtown?

Or what about a place looking out over Central Park? Too bad everyone is having embolisms about the safety of those carriage horses, I bet my sister has never had one of those—'

'Why don't I have my real-estate broker look into where the market is strongest right now,' Michael interrupted, 'and we can buy where we get the most square footage for our money?'

For someone who came up with such a romantic wedding proposal, Michael is certainly practical when it comes to money matters – and without necessarily needing to be. (Fortunately he laughed and said he'd find a way to get over the disappointment when I admitted to him that I did not, in fact, inherit $100 million in cash on my twenty-fifth birthday, as was reported by Rate the Royals.)

'Fine,' I said. 'Maybe I should just put on our wedding invitations that in lieu of gifts people should send money to an escrow account for us to buy our first home.'

'Now, that's a great idea.'

'Michael, I was kidding. We could tell people to donate money to the Community Center or Doctors Without Borders, though.'

'Okay. But look, don't you think you should discuss this whole thing about your sister with your dad first?'

'No, I do not. All my dad's done lately is screw things up. I'm not going to let him screw this up, too.'

All the magazines – and *Star Trek* movies starring Chris Pine as Kirk – say that in stressful situations where you don't know what to do, you just have to follow your gut.

What they don't say is how you're supposed to know what your gut is telling you. Sometimes your gut gives conflicting advice. Often you don't know which path is the right one because *all* the paths seem right, and in cases like that, your gut is no help at all.

Except that in this case, when Michael suggested I talk to my dad, I had a sudden and very strong signal from my gut. It said, *No*.

'Well,' Michael said, sounding dubious. 'Okay, Mia, but I really think you should reconsider. Your dad's going through a tough time right now.'

'I'm aware of that, Michael, and look how he's reacting to it. He's a mess. I left him a message yesterday, and he never called me back. Instead he got drunk.'

'Yeah, but—'

'If he wants to talk to me, he knows how to reach me. In the meantime, I'm going to figure out what to do about Olivia, and my own life. My dad has to take care of his own life, even though I have to say so far he's messed it up pretty badly. One might even say *royally*.'

'Okay,' Michael said. 'But maybe treat the Olivia thing carefully.'

'Thank you, Michael, but I do have a little experience in breaking news to people that they're princesses, you know.'

There were almost as many paps hanging around outside the center – the more intelligent ones who actually know me and figured I wouldn't skip work for nearly a week – as there were outside Michael's apartment building last night.

I felt it would be better to stop and chat with them for a few minutes this time – as well as give them a few photos (it's always good to have photos taken outside the center because it reminds people about it and all the services it provides) – than to ignore them. Despite Dominique's insistence, ignoring them hasn't worked, and I didn't want them pestering the kids, their parents, or my staff.

So I put on my sunglasses to cover my twitch – which sadly started going strong the moment I saw the paps – and stepped out onto the curb.

Unfortunately I didn't notice that one of them was Brian Fitzpatrick until it was too late.

By then he was already holding a digital recorder up to my face and asking, 'Princess, can you tell the readers of Rate the Royals dot-com how you feel about your engagement?'

What I wanted to say was, *Go away, Brian.*

But since that wouldn't have sounded very royal, instead I said, 'I'm over the moon about my engagement, Brian, and that's why I want to enjoy it for as long as possible. No date for the wedding has actually been set.'

185

(Ha! Sometimes being a world-class liar comes in handy.)

Then I showed Brian the ring and made a huge point of telling him that it was a lab-grown diamond and how proud I am that Michael is supporting the effort to create conflict-free diamonds.

Of course Brian had to be a joy-killer and ask, 'But if everyone follows your example, Princess, and buys lab-grown diamonds, how will the poor diamond miners be able to support their families?'

'Well, hopefully governments that earn revenues from the diamond-mining industry will get the message that consumers want diamonds that have been mined in accordance with fair-trade principles and human-rights conditions, and those governments will work to invest productively in their natural resources.'

- *Note to self:* Bazinga!

Brian looked impressed as he checked to make sure his handheld device had recorded this, then asked if he could get a selfie with me for the site. I guess Pippa gave him one last time she was in town.

I know Lazarres-Reynolds would have wanted me to, since we're in 'crisis management' mode and sucking up to the media is an important part of that, but I just couldn't bring myself to move my head close enough to Brian's to pose for a selfie.

I said, 'Oh, sorry, Brian, I haven't got time, I must get into work, I'm running late. Maybe next time, bye-yeee!'

Then I left him standing on the curb.

I don't even feel bad about it. Maybe this will teach him not to rate people (even royal people) like they're appliances on a home-improvement retail website.

Three things I'm grateful for:

1. The aviator sunglasses Tina and I bought so we could look just like Connie Britton, aka Coach Taylor's wife on *Friday Night Lights,* and which also hide my twitch.

2. Press-on nails, so Brian Fitzpatrick couldn't see how badly I've bitten at my real nails.

3. Platform wedges, which caused me to tower over him.

Am attempting to rocket through all my work here (not that I dislike my job, molding young minds and setting them on a path toward success is enormously satisfying, and also important) so I can get busy on my plan for Olivia, but I'm being hampered at every turn by this wedding business (which, of course, is also very important, but not as important as molding young minds or what I'm going to do about my newfound sister).

The kids are so sweet, though! They made me an enormous birthday card and signed their names on it and Ling Su hung it in my office. It takes up most of one wall.

Then yesterday, when they found out about the engagement, they made *another* card, and hung it on my other wall. Some of the kids seem to have seen the report on *Inside Edition* and have wished me luck 'with the babies.' A few of the girls have drawn startlingly tender portraits of 'the babies.' I am somewhat disturbed by this.

- *Note to self:* Must make sure we make screenings of *16 and Pregnant* and *Teen Mom* a regular part of our programming because I understand these shows have helped to lower teen birth rates by depicting how difficult it is to raise a child when you are not yet emotionally or financially ready.

Michael texted that the doctors to whom he was supposed to give his speech last night are willing to let him reschedule it for tonight and would I mind if he's 'home' late.

So sweet of him to ask! And almost like being married already. I texted back no, that I wouldn't mind, but that I'd miss him, and included an emoji of a pair of kissing lips.

In return he sent a picture of an exploding volcano and said that's what I should expect when he got home.

- ~~Note to self: Make sure security-system glitch has been repaired.~~ Forgot . . . I don't have to! We're engaged! No more sneaking around necessary.

E-mail from Grandmère and her assistant, Rolanda, saying they want to put together an itinerary for me for my week and also begin the wedding planning and so need some input. It appears I'm to have some say in my wedding after all! They asked me to fill out and return the following:

=====

The Wedding of Princess Amelia Renaldo of Genovia

to

Mr. Michael Moscovitz

GUEST LIST:

Michael and I would like to keep it small, family and friends only. I know this is asking a lot, but can we keep it under fifty, please? A hundred, tops.

WEDDING PARTY:

I don't know who Michael is going to want, but as my bridesmaids I'd definitely like Lilly Moscovitz, Tina Hakim Baba, Shameeka Taylor, Perin Thomas, Ling Su Wong, and possibly Lana Rockefeller and Trisha Bush (née Hayes), but I'll have to get back to you on that last one. I definitely want Rocky as a ring bearer/groomsman, though.

190

DATE:
   We can't possibly have it on July 18. That's way too
   soon. Maybe in July of next year. Thanks.

VENUE:
   Michael and I don't mind having it at the palace
   but not the chapel, because we don't want a
   religious ceremony and not the throne room (lack of
   intimacy). Outdoors would be nice. I'd love to have a
   beach wedding! But I realize crowd control could be
   an issue. Plus there is always the danger of drones.

GOWN:
   My friend Shameeka works at Vera Wang, so we
   already have an 'in' there. Her gowns are classic and
   beautiful, and it would be nice to have a designer
   who is a woman for a change.

   But I know how important it is to use local vendors,
   so probably we should use a Genovian?

   Since I want a beach or at least an outdoor wedding
   (fingers crossed), I'd like something simple, that I
   can dance in!

ENTERTAINMENT:
   Obviously a DJ.

   Michael wants our first song to be 'Girl U Want' by
   Devo because he says it's our song (since it perfectly
   describes how he used to think of me back in high

school ☺), but I know that will never work since it's much too fast!

So we'll settle for Al Green's 'Take Me to the River' or 'Tupelo Honey' by Van Morrison. See attached playlist for the songs we'd like during the reception.*

FOOD:

While I know how the palace chef feels about buffets, a lot of people nowadays do have food restrictions, so it's nice to be sensitive to that. So I think offering a variety of options, including a gluten-free and also a vegan entrée, would be nice.

Mini grilled cheese sandwiches, fried chicken, mashed potatoes, mac and cheese, and build-your-own taco/nacho bar would also be fun.

HONEYMOON:

It would be great to go to Mykonos. As you know, I've never been there, and I've always wanted to take the royal yacht and visit it as well as the surrounding islands. It's supposed to be the 'Ibiza of Greece'! ☺

*MICHAEL AND MIA'S SUPER AWESOME WEDDING PLAYLIST

'TAKE ME TO THE RIVER'	AL GREEN
'YOU SEXY THING (I BELIEVE IN MIRACLES)'	HOT CHOCOLATE
'DON'T GO BREAKING MY HEART'	ELTON JOHN AND KIKI DEE
'HOT FUN IN THE SUMMERTIME'	SLY AND THE FAMILY STONE
'AFRICA'	TOTO
'LIKE A PRAYER'	MADONNA
'ROCK THE BOAT'	THE HUES CORPORATION
'TUBTHUMPING'	CHUMBAWAMBA
'TARZAN BOY'	BALTIMORA

Just got a text from Tina Hakim Baba:

<Tina HBB 'TruRomantic'

> Hi, hope things are going well with the
> wedding planning, missing you! Anyway, Boris
> texted me this morning to ask if I thought
> you'd want him to perform at your reception.
> He said he's booked that day in Cleveland, but
> he doesn't mind disappointing the Borettes for
> you. I said I'd ask. So do you want him to?

I couldn't believe it. I called instead of texting her back, because I was so upset.

'Tina, why are you even still taking Boris's calls?'

She whispered, 'I don't know.'

'Why are you whispering?'

'I have finals this week. I can't study at home, there are too many distractions, such as my refrigerator and Netflix, so I'm in my study carrel at the library. They don't like it when we talk on our cells.'

'Oh, sorry. I forgot. Do you want to call me back?'

'No. I want you to tell me what it was like.'

'What what was like?'

'Michael's proposal! Was it romantic? Did he put the ring in a champagne glass? I told him that's what you wanted. I know it's kind of cliché, and I explained to him about your fear of choking, but he said he'd make sure you didn't—'

'It was totally romantic,' I said, smiling. I realized what she needed to hear was something to cheer her up. 'And not at all cliché, and super sweet, and he did make sure I didn't choke. He even got down on one knee—'

She *squee-ed,* something people often describe themselves doing on the Internet, but that you rarely hear in real life. However, what came out of Tina's mouth was an actual *squee* sound.

'He did? Oh, Mia, how I wish one of those spy drones had gotten a picture!'

'Well, I'm glad one didn't, because it was just between us.'

'I guess that's good,' Tina said with a sigh. 'So have you picked out a dress? Can I go with you to help choose it, like on that show *Say Yes to the Dress,* when the bride invites all her friends to sit and drink champagne while she tries on different dresses, and then they all hold up signs with thumbs-up or thumbs-down on them?'

I laughed. 'It doesn't work that way when you're a princess. I'll be having a one-of-a-kind gown professionally designed.'

'Oh, *please?*' she begged. 'I have nothing to look forward to since my boyfriend cheated on me. Nothing except taking my stupid finals. Then I'll get to spend the summer with my nosy family, who are just going to hound me about "putting myself back out there." I don't want to put myself back out there, I just want to sit around and eat Doritos and watch bad movies on Netflix.'

'Tina,' I said, in a warning voice. 'Come on. You have so much to offer the right guy!'

'I *found* the right guy, remember? Then he tossed me aside like I was a nothing more than a serving wench to use for his pleasure. Now, come on, you totally owe me for helping Michael give you the perfect proposal.'

I'm starting to realize why weddings are so important, and why people like them so much, even me: when our own lives aren't going so great, weddings give us something to feel happy about. A bride is taking a journey, a magical journey toward a future of happiness and joy, and even though we aren't taking that journey with her, we want to vicariously enjoy the ride.

'Okay,' I said to Tina. 'I'll see what I can do. But you have to promise, no more texting with Boris.'

She sighed. 'Fine, I promise,' and then said, 'What?' to someone who'd apparently opened the door to her study carrel. 'Oh, sorry,' she said to the person. To me, she whispered, 'Sorry, that was Halim. He says the student in the carrel next door complained I'm being too loud.'

Halim is Tina's new bodyguard, by whom she's followed around due to her multimillionaire sheikh father's conviction that she's going to be kidnapped. Her old bodyguard, Waheem, started his own security business (now the third largest in the world) after he got married. He tried to lure Lars away, but Lars said he isn't 'the management type.'

'Well,' I said. 'We should probably talk later, then.'

'Yeah,' Tina said, sounding glum, and hung up.

That's when I saw someone had left a message while we'd been speaking. I hoped it was my dad – in spite of everything, I still wouldn't mind speaking to him – but it was only Grandmère. Not surprisingly, she objected to my replies to her 'wedding list.'

'Amelia, we have a tremendous amount to do in the next few weeks, so I hope you're going to take this seriously. No granddaughter of mine is going to serve *tacos* at her wedding reception, much less something called a mini grilled cheese sandwich.'

Said the woman who'd never had a mini grilled cheese sandwich in her life.

'Now, Lazarres-Reynolds wants to know when you can meet with them,' Grandmère went on. 'They've assigned us a really top-notch man – I quite like him, he's the nephew of one of the founders of the firm. He's free for lunch tomorrow, so I've had Dominique make reservations in one of the private rooms at the Four Seasons. You will be there at one.'

Oh, I will, will I? I was starting to catch on to my role in this whole thing. I'm 'the bride' – the unpaid star of the show, who shows up when she's told, and also does what she's told, but otherwise keeps her mouth shut.

Oh, well. I guess that's what brides – kind of like princesses – are for. We might think we're in charge, but when all is said and done, our main purpose is to give

197

people something to admire, and also to make them feel better about the world.

'I don't understand why you're so fixated on this Vera Wang person. Obviously we have to use a local. Dominique's managed to book us an emergency appointment with your cousin Sebastiano. He's become one of the premier wedding-gown designers in Europe, and is also Genovian, so you know what people will say if we don't use him – that you've snubbed one of your own relatives, and worse, a fellow countryman. He just happens to be in town this week and says he has time to meet you, so make sure to keep all your afternoons clear.'

Of course. And I totally get it. Far be it from me not to hire a Genovian to design my wedding gown.

'And we're going to have to start making a guest list. Find out from Michael's parents who they want to invite so we can start screening them, but please emphasize from me that they can't have more than twenty-five people because we really do only have room for five hundred and my personal list is already at two hundred and of course we have to include our own family and I assume you'll want a few friends.'

How nice of her.

'As for the entertainment, of course we aren't going to hire a disc jockey, nor will we have any of those ridiculous songs you asked for. Madonna? Don't be absurd! You know she and I are still not speaking. And why would we have Dorothy's dog Toto from the *Wizard of Oz* perform at your wedding? We'll have a *live, human entertainer*. I'm having Dominique get in touch with someone I'm told is top-notch – I can't think of his name offhand but I understand he's extremely popular, and more importantly, very keen to perform for us, and *for no fee*. I think he'll do nicely, and I'm positive he can sing that song Michael likes about the river, whatever it is, although I must say I'm surprised, as it sounds like a Christian spiritual, and I thought your intended was Jewish – not that I mind, I'm very open to all faiths, except yoga, as you know. Well, never mind, Dominique is going to send over a copy of your itinerary, so call me when you receive it if you have any questions. You know I don't know why you even have a mobile when you never pick it up. Good-bye.'

I can't.

I can't even.

ROYAL GENOVIAN PRESS OFFICE

HRH PRINCESS MIA RENALDO
Itinerary for Week of May 4

CONTACT: Dominique du Bois
Director of Royal Genovian Press Relations and Marketing
CELL: 917-555-6840
OFFICE: 212-555-3767

WEDNESDAY, MAY 6

9:00 A.M.	Limo to escort HRH Mia to design offices of Sebastiano (119 Mercer).
9:30 A.M.	Meet with Sebastiano to go over Wedding/Bridesmaid Gown Designs
12:00 P.M.	Limo to escort HRH Mia to Four Seasons
12:15– 2:00 P.M.	Lazarres-Reynolds Luncheon.

Private room. Attendees: HRH Mia, HRH Dowager Princess Clarisse Renaldo, representatives of Lazarres-Reynolds.

2:15–2:45 P.M.	Limo will be waiting outside Four Seasons to escort HRH Mia to Plaza Hotel.
2:45–5:00 P.M.	Meeting with HRH Dowager Princess, Dominique, and Rolanda to go over cake, guest list, entertainment choices.
5:00 P.M.	Limo will be waiting to escort HRH Mia home to change.
7:00 P.M.	Limo to escort HRH Mia to the W Hotel.
7:30–10:30 P.M	National Heart Association Benefit Ball to Raise Awareness for Sudden Cardiac Death.

Talking points:

1. Heart disease is leading cause of death in the world for both men and women.
2. 5–10 minutes of running or brisk walking per day can cut risk of stroke/heart attack in half.
3. Don't smoke.

10:30 P.M.	Limo to escort HRH Mia home.

4:30 A.M.	Limo to escort HRH Mia and Michael Moscovitz to Wake Up America studios, Rockefeller Plaza.
5:00 A.M.	Arrive *Wake Up America* green room. Paolo will meet HRH Mia to do hair/makeup.
7:24 A.M.	Interview on *Wake Up America*. Topic: Royal Wedding/Genovia.

Talking points:

1. Sudden Cardiac Death: So terrible!
2. Wedding in July: So happy!
3. Genovia – popular summer tourist destination, especially in July. Rentals/hotel rooms still available!
4. Election – Prince Phillipe's platform: Equality for all!

8:15 A.M.	Limo will greet HRH Mia at stage door and escort HRH Mia to breakfast at Plaza Hotel with HRH Dowager Princess Clarice Renaldo and Rolanda.
9:00 A.M.– 12:00 P.M.	Meeting to solidify wedding invitation, cake, guest list, gown, entertainment choices.
12:15 P.M.	Limo to escort HRH Mia to the NoMad Hotel.
1:00–3:00 P.M.	Renaldo/21st Century Fox Luncheon.

The Parlour. Attendees: HRH Mia, HRH Dowager Princess Clarisse Renaldo, Dominique, representatives from Lazarres-Reynolds and 21st Century Fox.

Talking points:

1. Discussion of granting 21st Century Fox exclusive worldwide rights to film Royal Wedding.

3:00 P.M.	Limo to escort HRH Mia home.
6:00 P.M.	Limo to escort HRH Mia to Gramercy Tavern.

| 6:30–8:30 P.M. | Renaldo–Moscovitz Dinner. |

Front room: HRH Mia and Michael Moscovitz, window table.
Press will be contacted for 'impromptu' photo op of
happy couple dining together.

| 9:00 P.M. | Limo to escort HRH Mia to grocery store. Purchase: cat food. 'Royals: They're Just Like Us' photo shoot for *Majesty Magazine*. |
| 10:00 P.M | Limo to escort HRH Mia home. |

FRIDAY, MAY 8

9:30 A.M.	Limo will be waiting to escort HRH Mia to airport.
11:00 A.M.	Depart Teterboro on board private jet.
10:00 P.M. (GST)	Arrive Genovia.

Perin must have heard me hyperventilating over the itinerary since she just popped her head into my office and asked, looking all concerned, 'Mia? Are you all right?'

I said, 'Fine. I'm fine. Don't worry, it's not work-related. Just . . . something my grandmother sent over. But I'm good. Or I will be, after I make a few phone calls.'

Perin shook her head and said, 'You know, Mia, you don't *have* to stay at work today. I know how busy you must be with, um, everything you have to do with the wedding, and the stuff your dad has, uh, going on. You could leave, if you want to. You don't even have to work from home. Ling Su and I have everything under control.'

I told her not to worry, I plan on coming in every day, as normal . . . well, as much as my schedule will allow.

I never saw myself as one of those women who only worked until she got a ring on her finger, then spent the rest of her life being a professional bride/wife (especially since I'm already a princess, which is basically a profession unto itself). I'm not exactly Lana Weinberger (Rockefeller).

But based on the itinerary Dominique has sent over, I can see how that happens for some people, especially when they have pushy families or spouses-to-be or their

203

wedding is going to be internationally televised. There's just so much to do!

I feel a renewed respect for every royal bride who ever existed.

Honestly, though, I have the best friends (and staff) in the world.

My family, I'm not so sure about.

1:55 p.m., Tuesday, May 5
HELV on the way to the Consulate
Rate the Royals Rating: 1

Ugh. Also, damn. And also, eww.

Now I realize Perin wasn't being sweet when she told me I didn't have to stay at work. She was being practical. And also trying to protect the center . . . and me.

I was trying to get Dominique on the phone to tell her that while I appreciate the itinerary she sent over, we needed to tweak it a little – such as scheduling a meeting with my future in-laws and the fact that my brother Rocky's birthday is May 10, so I can't exactly leave for Genovia before that, especially in light of the fact that I fully intend to be forcing my ne'er-do-well father to be coparenting my long-lost little sister by then – when Ling Su came running into my office to say that *Brian Fitzpatrick* had just been found in the center's women's restroom, standing on one of the toilets, trying to hide a lipstick camera and microphone in the vent.

Of course Brian had another story. He claimed he *found* them in there, having spied them while sitting on the toilet, and that he'd been trying to save us from suffering humiliation by them.

But it's obvious he was the one planting them so he could record my private conversations. Why else would he have been in the *women's* restroom (let alone the building) in the first place?

Seriously. This is my life.

Ling Su insisted we call the police (she is very feisty for

such a tiny person), but cooler-headed Perin suggested this would only bring more unwanted press to both the center and to me.

So we 'escorted' Brian out (meaning Lars and Perin basically carried him, although they didn't get to rough Brian up as much as we all would have liked, since Brian is exactly the type to file a multimillion dollar lawsuit, like the pap that Grandmère hit with her Birkin).

Afterward Perin told me Brian wasn't even the first to have pulled such a stunt today. Apparently since I've been at my desk, several paps who look young enough to pass as teens have managed to sneak in – mainly by wearing hoodies, high-tops, and cross-body messenger bags – only to get caught when they specifically asked for help with their algebra homework from 'Princess Mia' (our regulars know I'm incompetent when it comes to algebra. I can only help with French, English, and papers on European citrus production).

'It might be better,' Perin said, 'if you worked from home again for the next few days . . . just until the excitement over your engagement to Michael dies down.'

I didn't want to make her feel bad by telling her that I *have no home* and that this *is* the excitement dying down, thanks to the Crown Prince of Qalif outlawing swimming for women and of course the E. coli outbreak.

Instead I said, 'Thank you, Perin. That's a good idea,' and gathered my bodyguard and left.

I was feeling a bit depressed, but rallied after Lars and I grabbed sandwiches at Murray's Shop (also Fritos, Butterfingers, and sodas from a bodega, where I saw that on the cover of the *Post* it says: 'Michael Makes His Move!' and there was a photo of Michael kissing me in the backseat of the HELV. The accompanying article explained the tax breaks to which both Michael and his corporation, Pavlov Surgical, Inc., will be entitled once we've been married five years, since Genovian citizens – and companies – pay no taxes, and a 'close friend' of Michael's is speculating that Pavlov Surgical will soon be reincorporating on Genovian soil to avoid paying American taxes).

(Yes, I bought the paper and read the article.)

It must be a slow news day if this is the most scandalous reason they could come up with for why Michael's finally proposed. The tax break? I like *Inside Edition*'s theory – that I'm carrying his twins – better.

Got a message that the crowd outside the consulate had dissipated enough for me to be smuggled in through the back service entrance, so I'm home (well, my temporary home). So happy to see Fat Louie.

He did not even appear to notice I'd been gone, having apparently slept the entire time, judging by the fur matted on the left-hand corner of my bedspread.

But he purred quite happily when I petted him, and even let me pick him up and carry him around like a big fat baby (for about one minute. Then he got cranky and growled and I had to put him down and give him a chunk of ham from my sandwich. But it was a lovely minute, until he bit me).

Weirdly, Madame Alain greeted me even more warmly than Fat Louie. At first I didn't understand why, since I've never been her favorite person, or even seen her smile.

Then I saw that she was packing all the things in her office into boxes. She's being transferred back to Genovia.

I completely forgot that I suggested she might be happier elsewhere. Apparently someone agreed with me.

Fortunately she couldn't be more pleased. She's always hated her job here (and me) and now she'll never have to see the consulate (or me) again.

I wonder where she'll be working. But actually I don't care so long as it's well away from me.

Since we didn't bring our laptops to the Exumas, I haven't checked my e-mail in ages.

Well, I just did, and guess what?

J.P. sent me his dystopian YA novel, *Love in the Time of Shadows*.

I have sent it straight to Tina.

I read the synopsis, and I've decided I'm not in a place right now where I want to know more about J.P.'s vision of the future, especially since in it:

1. One percent of the population owns all the wealth and property while being catered to by the impoverished 99 percent who have no chance of attaining any of that wealth and property (except through armed rebellion or a randomized lottery system).

2. The police are militarized.

3. Everyone has skin cancer/radiation poisoning because the ozone layer is being destroyed by humankind's disrespect of the environment.

4. The media is highly biased and censored.

5. All anyone does is watch reality television to escape their problems.

6. Everyone is overweight (except of course the lithe heroine and her two love interests) because healthy food options are so expensive/unavailable.

J.P.'s vision of the future seems eerily similar to the world we live in NOW!

Why would I want to read this book in what little free time I actually have, considering the fact that it doesn't seem to offer any realistic solutions to the problems it presents its characters, is very depressing, and is also written by my ex-boyfriend?

That's why I've sent it to Tina. Maybe *she* will find something to like about it. Or at least find it a nice distraction from *her* ex-boyfriend.

Just spent a half hour on the phone arguing with Dominique over my itinerary. She says it's 'too late' to change anything on it, and 'after all, Princesse, you do want to get married this summer, *non*? Well, then, we must get started, and that's going to require traveling to Genovia. I'm sure your little brother won't mind your missing 'is birthday.'

Uh, she is evidently not very well acquainted with many nine-soon-to-be-ten-year-old boys. I love Rocky very much, but he is challenging. Most of our conversations revolve around farts (his favorite subject) and dinosaurs (his second favorite subject).

'How much did the dinosaurs fart when the giant asteroid that destroyed their habitat struck the earth?' is one of Rocky's favorite questions.

He guesses quite a lot, but I usually say probably not so much because they were so frightened.

Mom worries Rocky might be held back because of his obsession with flatulence, but Michael says it's quite normal for nine-year-old boys.

For his birthday, Rocky wants a dinosaur-themed cake, preferably one with 'a giant asteroid splatting in the middle.' When my mother questioned Rocky as to whether or not this request was serious, he farted in response, and was sent to his room to 'think about what he'd done.'

I think it might be quite nice to have a female sibling to talk to. Not that girls don't enjoy discussing flatulence and dinosaurs as well, but Olivia Grace looks adorable.

I could take her to the American Girl store and have tea. That is, if she likes dolls. The problem is, she's twelve. Twelve is too old for dolls, isn't it?

I didn't want to admit it in front of Michael, but I have no idea what twelve-year-old girls like to do these days. The ones I meet at the center are all pretty focused on their homework, their families, fingernail polish (obviously, I'm out), video games involving helping puppies find homes and reality stars pick out what to wear, and several boy bands and skimpily clad female singers I've never heard of who are popular, but they don't seem to me to be as talented as either Adele, Taylor, or of course my sweet, sad Britney.

- *Note to self:* Ask Tina what her younger siblings enjoy, and why.

I have no memory of what I liked at age twelve. I'm spending this afternoon combing through my old journals, looking for a hint as to the existence of Elizabeth Harrison, but so far I haven't found a trace, and unfortunately I only started keeping my diaries at the age of fourteen.

Of course, the thing about diaries is that they're always about *you*, not other people. It's even worse if they're the diary of an adolescent. It's dreadful rereading them, because they seem so . . . egomaniacal. How

212

could one person drone on so much about herself? Was I blind? The only thing I ever wrote about was:

1. My grades.

2. My boobs (or lack thereof).

3. Grandmère.

4. Lilly being incredibly annoying.

5. Josh Richter (ACKKKKK).

6. My then arch nemesis, Lana Weinberger.

7. Michael.

My dad possibly conducting a secret love affair across the river is never mentioned anywhere.

Ugh! I am so depressed now.

And even though Marie Rose stocked my kitchen while I was gone, so my refrigerator is full of delicious things to eat – such as a tarragon chicken salad; wild-caught Alaskan salmon poached in a court bouillon with a cumin dill sauce; crisp prosciutto, rocket, and mozzarella paninis; black truffle macaroni and cheese; lobster-claw kebabs; meringue; and Genovian orange crème brûlée – all I feel like eating is the second Butterfinger I bought at the bodega. I am not following Dr. Delgado's advice at all!

But I have to admit, the Butterfinger is helping, as is the fact that there's an *I Found the Gown* marathon on TLC.

It would be so much simpler if I could just drive to a discount store like the girls on that show do and find the perfect gown (for $400)!

But I have a sneaking suspicion that after all the Butterfingers I've just eaten, there's no gown in existence (especially for only $400) cleverly enough designed to hide the food baby I've developed and the press seems to feel compelled to comment on.

Okay, I think I just did something really stupid.

It probably doesn't help that I've taken a couple of nips from the bottle of hundred-year-old Williams pear schnaps* that Michael and I were sent as an engagement gift from the chancellor of Austria (it was already open anyway, since the Royal Genovian Guard had to make sure it wasn't poisoned – not by the chancellor, obviously – which they did by tasting it themselves).

*Austrian schnaps is completely different from what Americans call schnapps. For one thing, if it's prepared correctly, it actually tastes like something other than toothpaste.

I was just feeling so bummed out about everything after reading parts of *Love in the Time of Shadows* (radiation poisoning is *so* depressing! Why would anyone write about this? Unless it was a book about Hiroshima, of course) and all my own diaries that I was like, 'Oh, whatever. It's five o'clock somewhere! *Skol!*' and helped myself to a sip. Or maybe two. I don't remember anyway.

And not just because my rank on Rate the Royals has sunk from number one (not that I care, since that website is a stupid blight on humanity and is best ignored) down to *seven*.

I am now even less popular than General Sheikh Mohammed bin Zayed Faisal, the Crown Prince of Qalif! And, apparently, the Sultan of Brunei (the one who did something with a monkey, though we'll never know what, thanks to Lazarres-Reynolds).

There is absolutely *no reason* for this to have happened other than my having kicked the founder of the website out of my community center for planting listening devices in the women's restroom (which I now regret not having him arrested for. Ling Su was right).

But *even worse than this,* there was a post from Royal-RabbleRouser, who was stalking me all last year. He disappeared for a while, most likely due to having joined a cult or a radical terror group, or possibly the cast of a reality show. Reality-show casting agents recruit the same kind of people as cults and terror groups do, ones who feel like there is something missing from their lives, very often romantic love.

And since the only way woman-haters like my stalker are going to get a date is if they kidnap one or one is assigned to them by a cult leader or central casting, often such people's decision to join up proves to be a good one . . . until they get blown up or kicked off the show.

It must have been the latter since RoyalRabbleRouser has shown up again – probably due to the news that I'm getting married, at least based on his message about being glad that 'the princess slut' is finally letting 'Mike' make 'an honest woman of her.'

'It's about time, too,' writes RoyalRabbleRouser. 'Maybe now she'll let him work while she stays home and squeezes out a few puppies, like a decent woman should. Hopefully she'll learn to cook, too. But probably she'll just keep on making her asinine speeches about how women should work, while letting her servants do the cooking.'

Um . . . yes. Yes, I will. Because that's the job for which I employ them, and if I didn't employ them, they would have no paycheck, and without a paycheck they would have no way to feed their families, and then they would starve. It's called *economics*, RoyalRabbleRouser. Look it up.

At the center we're trying hard to provide teens with the mentoring, education, and job training they need so that when they leave school they'll be invulnerable to the kind of thinking RoyalRabbleRouser supports, but sometimes I worry it's not enough. Obviously the Frank Gianini Community Center needs to expand globally.

I really have to start following Dominique's advice and stop reading this stuff.

But I can't stop reading texts from Lana Weinberger (whose birthday wishes I'd forgotten to return). She sent another, even more alarming than the last:

<Lana Weinberger 'TheRock'

> *Bitch, how could you get engaged and not even tell me? I had to hear it from Trish who heard it from her mom who saw it on TMZ! You are a twat and a half!*
>
> *But don't worry, you can make it up to me by making me and Trish bridesmaids! And we're not just going to be lame bridesmaids who do nothing but look good and carry your train. We're actually going to do stuff. See the attached – we have your bachelorette party all planned out! It's going to be at a place in Genovia called Crazy Ivan's. You'll LOVE it!!!!*

CRAZY IVAN'S BACHELORETTE PARTY FROM HELL!

She's your best bud and soon she's gonna be stuck in the kitchen whippin' up chicken fingers for a passel of brats while hubby's out bromancing his best buds!

So show 'er the last good night of her life! Give her one to remember with our no-holds-barred bachelorette abuse 3-alarm party package, including:

Special X-rated bridal cake!

BJ shots for the bride! No hands allowed!

Penis party beads galore!

Sashes and tiaras like Miss America contestants wish they had!

Dicklickers!

And more!

Sorry, we cannot hold seats for late arrivals.
Be there or be BUMMED!

CRAZY IVAN'S, LOCATIONS IN ALL MAJOR CITIES WORLDWIDE.
Tokyo – London – New York – Paris – Genovia – Rio – Berlin – Sydney

Now I have to figure out how to explain to Lana that I do not care for BJ shots, nor do I particularly want to know what a dicklicker is.

It's not just because I don't care to support businesses owned by Ivan. It's because it's almost one hundred percent guaranteed that someone is going to photograph me wearing penis party beads and then put the photograph on the Internet. I'll be raked over the coals . . . though of course it's horrible that public figures can't go out (or even stay in) and have a good time and be photographed doing it and not be judged for it.

It's one thing to say, 'Oh, have a sense of humor about it,' but there's such a double standard. The populace does *not* have a sense of humor about it, especially if they feel you are somehow representing their country. Was Kate Middleton ever photographed wearing 'penis party beads'? I think not.

Of course I get Lana's plea that 'we all need to spend more time together because Best Friends Are Forever and high school was the best time in our lives' (okay, well, I don't get that part. High school may have been the best years of Lana's life, but it was definitely not mine. Except that AEHS is where I met Michael). Yes, it would be fun to take *one day off* from being politically correct, but that's much easier said than done, especially when there are cameras around, and I'm guessing there are cameras everywhere at Crazy Ivan's, considering you're required to take your top off as soon as you enter.

This is so sweet of you, Lana! Of course I'd love for you and Trisha to be bridesmaids.

But I think Crazy Ivan's may not work for a number of reasons. Maybe we can settle for a private bachelorette party at the palace. We could do it at the pool. You know Lars loves nothing better than an excuse to sit on the roof with his long-range sniper rifle, looking for camera-equipped drone copters to take out.

Fine!!!! You can make it up to me by writing Iris a letter of recommendation. You know, with a letter from the Princess of Genovia she'll be a shoo-in.

Sure, I'll be happy to do this. What school are you trying to get her into?

Oh, the application isn't for school! Iris has been referred as a possible candidate to the National American Baby Awards in the four-to-six-month Miss Junior Princess Division of their pageant!!!!

Lana. No. Not a baby beauty pageant.

Why? This one has more than $1,500,000 in cash, prizes, and scholarships. It says if I don't register her, I will be denying her the opportunity to learn valuable new skills that will help empower her and enable her to accomplish her future goals.

Lana, you are being scammed.

No, I am not! Purple Iris is the most beautiful baby in her playgroup. Everyone says it. I'm sure someone spotted her there and entered her name. Or maybe from my Instagram or Facebook page about her.

Then how did they get your home address?

It's public record. And anyway, the pageant is real, I looked it up. This is the tenth year of the program. They are dedicated to helping girls build character and appreciate their self-worth.

Your kid isn't even one year old yet. How is this going to build her character?

It's going to teach her how to show poise and confidence in front of an audience, the way you do, Mia, when you're giving one of your boring speeches. Only Iris doesn't have to give a speech because there's no talent required for this pageant. The contestants are judged on confidence and charisma.

Lana, did you read the fine print?

The entrance fees are to offset the costs of producing the pageant.

How much are they?

It is an investment in her future!

Lana, what's wrong with you? You used to be able to see through obvious cons like this. Did your brain slip out through your vagina along with the baby when you gave birth?

No, since I had a cesarean. I wasn't going to let my joy hole get all out of shape from squeezing that thing out of it. You've probably noticed she inherited Jason's ginormous head.

Both your husband's and your baby's heads have always looked average-sized to me.

Well, they aren't. Everyone on his dad's side of the family has a huge head. After I saw the ultrasound, I told the doctor if she thought I was squeezing that thing out from my joy hole, she could just think again. Jason's mother never recovered from having three boys. She still walks funny.

I really do not know what to say in reply to that.

Are you going to help me or not??? There's an essay part of the application, and you know writing's not my strong suit, so I need your help, Mia. You're the best writer I know.

I will help you, but I strongly disapprove.

> *You'll feel differently when you have a baby. Then you'll see what it's like!*

> **Fine. E-mail the application to me, and I'll help you. But just this one time!**
> **And only if you promise no surprise bachelorette party at Crazy Ivan's!**

> *I promise! Oh, thank you! You won't regret this.*

> **I already do.**

By the time I was done having this conversation, my eye was twitching like crazy. I had no choice but to stretch out on the couch and watch Judge Judy yell at a man named Bud for moving in with his new girlfriend, Tiffany, and then, after promising he'd pay half the rent, spending all his rent money on tattoos, a new Corvette, and a trip to Atlantic City with his ex-girlfriend.

The judge decided in favor of the plaintiff – Tiffany – in the amount of $5,000, but only because Bud had paid his half of the rent for one month, and had written on the canceled check the word *rent,* which showed statement of intent. Case dismissed.

It was very soothing.

Three things I'm grateful for:

1. Fair judges.

2. My mother, for never entering me in a baby beauty pageant.

3. Austrian schnaps.

I didn't think things could get much worse, but everyone knows the minute you think this, they do. It's like saying, 'I think I'll go to the pool today.' The second you say this, the sun disappears behind a cloud.

I was filling out baby Iris's beauty pageant essay when my phone rang.

It was my father's office, wanting to know when was the most convenient time for me to meet with 'the Prince of Genovia and his lawyers.'

'His lawyers? Why does Dad need me to meet with his lawyers?' I asked.

'I believe it's to discuss your prenuptial agreement, Your Highness,' his assistant said. 'What day is best for you?'

'*Prenup?* My father wants me to get my fiancé to sign a *prenup?*'

'Why, yes. Yes, Your Highness, he does.'

I cannot believe this.

I suppose I shouldn't be shocked, given what I know about my family.

But this is low, even for them. And frankly, the kind of thing I'd expect from Grandmère, not Dad.

But Marielle, Dad's assistant, assured me that the prince is very concerned about protecting my (and the family's) 'financial interests.' A prenup is 'standard' in

226

all Genovian royal marriages (oh, really? Because there have been so many?) and are really meant to protect the assets of both parties.

But I know what all this actually means:

It means that somewhere deep down inside, Dad must believe the stupid rumor started by the *Post*. As if *that* is why Michael has been dating me on and off since the ninth grade: because he has been plotting to take advantage of me – like Bud took advantage of Tiffany on *Judge Judy*.

Only instead of refusing to pay half the rent and taking off to Atlantic City with an ex-girlfriend in a new Corvette, Michael is only marrying me to reincorporate Pavlov Surgical in Genovia in order to reduce its tax burden.

Except that I don't need Judge Judy to rule on how stupid this idea is. I told Marielle that a good time for me to meet with the prince and his lawyers about my prenup would be 'never.'

'I beg your pardon?' she said, sounding surprised.

'You heard me. Never. Also, please tell my father to call me, as I have something important I'd like to discuss with *him*.'

When Marielle asked politely if she could know 'the nature of the matter' I'd like to discuss with my father, I said: 'Yes, please tell him it has to do with Olivia Grace Clarisse Mignonette Harrison.'

Then I hung up the phone.

What is wrong with me? I don't know.

I can't even blame the schnaps because I only had a few sips.

I was eating cheese popcorn while checking on my phone to see if there is a Wiki-How for 'How to Discuss Your Dad's Secret Love Child with Him' (there is not. This seems like a missed opportunity), when the RGG buzzed up and announced, 'Your Highness, your father is here.'

'Uh . . . send him up,' I said into the intercom (after I'd got done choking). What else was I supposed to do?

Then I ran around really fast, getting rid of all evidence that I'd been drinking, even though of course I am an adult, and should be able to drink if I want to.

When I opened the door, I was shocked. Dad looks awful. I mean, he hasn't been looking too good anyway since his arrest, all pasty-faced and sort of green around the gills (although that could have been partly due to the excessive celebration in which he engaged last night over my engagement. Or possibly he's been eating prewashed lettuce from California).

But then I realized that for some reason he'd taken it into his head to *shave off his mustache,* which he's had for quite some time now, and which has become as distinctive a part of his look as his bald head (the hair on his scalp never did grow back after the chemo, but he's been rockin' a 'stache since growing one for a Save the Children charity drive one 'Mo'-vember, and we all said how sporty he looked in it).

228

It's frightening how horrible he looks without it!

'Dad, what *happened*?' I couldn't help blurting when I saw him.

'What happened? What do you mean, what happened?' he demanded. 'You know about your sister, that's what happened.'

He barged in past me, and then went to lie down on my couch like he was in his analyst's office, or something.

'No,' I said, shutting the door. 'I mean what happened to your face? Where's your mustache?'

'Oh, that.' He touched his upper lip, which for the first time I realized he doesn't have – an upper lip, I mean. It's been hidden under a patch of sandy-colored hair for so long, I stopped noticing he only has a lower, no upper, lip. 'I shaved it off. Apparently only men who work in the pornography industry have mustaches anymore.'

'Dad, who told you that? It isn't true. You should grow yours back. You look—' I wanted to say *naked without it,* but thought that might hurt his feelings, so instead I said, 'Less dignified without it.'

'Your cousin Ivan mocked my mustache in his last ad. He said it made me look old. Like "an old, balding Ron Burgundy" were his exact words. Mia . . .' He looked up at me helplessly. 'Who is Ron Burgundy?'

'Never mind, Dad,' I said, feeling sad that my father was so unfamiliar with the comic stylings of Will Ferrell. 'There's nothing wrong with looking like Ron Burgundy, and that's even more reason not to shave it off. You need to grow it back right away, to show Cousin Ivan that he can't get to you.'

He folded his arms over his face and sighed. 'But he *has* gotten to me, Mia. I'm afraid that was the last straw. Do you have anything to drink?'

I told him about the schnaps and he said, 'I meant anything *good*,' so then I had to explain that it was schnaps, not schnapps, so he agreed to have some.

He took the glass and then got mad because Fat Louie jumped onto his chest (which is actually a compliment; Fat Louie has grown much less athletic in his old age, so when he jumps onto anything, it's only because he's put a lot of effort and thought into it).

So I moved Fat Louie back into his little bed and then Dad began to talk . . .

. . . and talk, and talk.

He talked all about how he'd been wanting to tell me about Olivia forever, but he hadn't known how, because he was terrified of what I was going to think.

I guess I shouldn't be surprised that a man who has, upon occasion, spelled my name wrong on my birthday cards wouldn't know I'd be delighted to have a little sister, especially one I could take with me to every single Disney musical on Broadway so people would no longer give me the side-eye for going by myself as an adult.

'It wasn't as if it was just a one-night stand,' he went on. 'I was in love with Elizabeth, but she didn't want to settle down any more than your mother ever did, let alone raise Olivia in the stifling environment of a palace. And then she died, and it was so terrible. Why do I keep falling for women who are so afraid of commitment, Mia? Why?'

'Well,' I said, thinking about what the Drs. Moscovitz

had said. Is there ever a good time to tell your father that his future son-in-law's parents think he has an Oedipus complex? No. Some things are better kept to yourself.

'Naturally, I can understand why an independent, free-spirited woman like your mother – or Elizabeth – wouldn't want to settle down with a man like me, who has as many responsibilities as I do—'

'I know you can't help that you were born a prince,' I interrupted, 'but no one is *forcing* you to stay on the throne, or run for prime minister year after year.'

He looked a bit startled at this. 'But I have to. For the good of the country. And what reasonable woman would want to live with my mother, even in a palace on the Mediterranean, in the most beautiful country in the world?'

'None,' I said, thinking about what my mother had said to me on the phone about Dad when we'd discussed Michael's proposal. 'But Grandmère does have her own place, you know. You could always ask her to actually stay there.'

He looked even more alarmed. 'Stay in the summer palace? *Year-round?*'

'The summer palace isn't exactly an outhouse, Dad. It has seventeen bedrooms.'

'I don't think your grandmother would hear of it,' he said.

'Dad!' This just goes to show that you can have all the money in the world – even a castle and a crown – and it still can't buy you happiness. Or common sense. 'Listen to yourself. You sound like someone complaining that your diamond shoes are too tight.'

He looked taken aback. 'My what?'

'Your diamond shoes. I know you don't literally own a pair of diamond shoes, but someone quite wise told me that we need to be more appreciative of the things we have. You have to make sacrifices for love, you know.'

'By wearing overpriced, uncomfortable shoes?'

'No, Dad.' I took a deep breath and tried to find another way to make him understand. 'It's like what Robert Frost said in that poem about the road less traveled. It may not get you to where you were headed, but it will get you *somewhere,* and that place may be even better than where you thought you were going.'

Dad glared at me. 'You know, I prefer following maps, Mia. GPS is even better.'

'I know. But I don't think maps or GPS are working for you anymore, Dad. Prenups and living with Grandmère and keeping all these secrets and promises you made to people who aren't around anymore? Olivia's mom has been dead *for ten years now.* I think the statute of limitations on your promise to her is up.'

He nervously chewed his lower lip, which was upsetting, because then it looked like he had *no lips at all,* like a bird. I wanted to tell him to stop, but it's not really the kind of thing you can say to your parent.

'I . . . I don't know, Mia. I've never been a father before. Not like this. With you, I always had your mother. I knew she'd never do the wrong thing.'

'Dad, being a single parent was never easy for Mom,

even if to you she might have made it look that way. Do you think she's having an easy time with Rocky? She's not. The school sent him home with a note the other day asking that Mom take him to a psychopharmacologist because of his obsession with farting.'

Dad got the faraway look in his eyes he always has when the subject turns to my mother. 'That's not your mother's fault. The boy has just suffered the loss of his father. And besides, that school obviously isn't a very good one if it can't handle a young boy's perfectly normal interest in flatulence.'

'Well, be that as it may, parenting isn't easy for anyone. It's the hardest job in the world, but I think you'd be good at it. You've always done pretty well with me.'

'Your mother did all the heavy lifting with you. I think I could make things much, much worse for that little girl.'

'Worse than not being there at all?' I raised my eyebrows. 'I don't see how.'

I shouldn't have said it. I should have said something else – pulled out one of my many platitudes, or lies – or simply shut my mouth and said nothing at all.

But I didn't, and the result was that tears filled my father's eyes.

It's pretty horrible to watch your dad cry. I'm not going to say it's the worst thing in the world, because there are definitely worse things, like that time I went to Africa to oversee the installation of some water wells. Seeing a man driving a hollowed-out Sealy box spring on wheels pulled by a donkey down the highway, his family sitting inside it (because that was the only form of transportation they could afford), was definitely worse than watching my dad cry.

But awkwardly patting my dad's shoulder and telling him things were going to be okay when, to be honest, I wasn't sure they were going to be (just like with Africa, even after installing the wells) was up there on my list of worst things ever.

Finally, I got up and grabbed my phone to check out the menus the RGG had provided me from all the restaurants in the area that had been approved to deliver to us.

'I'm going to order some dinner now,' I said. 'Is there anything you particularly feel like eating?'

I think this surprised Dad so much that he forgot about crying, which was partly my intention. 'I . . . I don't know,' he said, looking shocked. *Food? Who can think about food at a time like this?* Uh, Mia Thermopolis can.

'Well, you have to eat something. Hunger and dehydration can lead to impaired decision making, and also mood swings.' At least according to iTriage, and also Ling Su, who always makes sure the kids at the center have plenty of healthy snacks to eat while doing their homework. It's led to a lot less crying-while-doing-algebra. 'Marie Rose left a lot of stuff in the fridge, but I really don't think I could handle black truffle mac and cheese right now. What about you?'

'Well . . .' He blinked a few times. 'Maybe I could eat a little something. It's been a while since I've had anything other than nuts at the bar at the hotel, and there's something I've always wanted to try . . . but no, I couldn't. It's silly.'

'What, Dad? Just tell me.'

'Well, I keep seeing advertisements on the television for something they call cheesy bread. I've always wondered what it tastes like.'

He sounded wistful, like King Arthur in the musical *Camelot* when he and Guinevere wonder what the simple folk do. People always laugh at that part of the show, because it's so ridiculous that royal people don't know what 'simple folk' do.

But in my dad's case, it's true. Growing up all his life in a palace, he really doesn't know. I think it's another reason he probably found my mom – and Olivia's mom – so appealing.

'Fine,' I said, feeling a little sorry for him. 'Cheesy bread it is.'

I figured cheesy bread might actually do him some good (it turns out he hadn't eaten solid food in days, maybe since before his arrest, he'd been freaking out so much over everything that's been going on – and of course is freaking out even more now that I'd told him he actually needed to do something about Olivia), so this explained a lot about his current behavior, especially the mustache.

So I ordered some . . . which meant I also had to order some for the RGG and the paparazzi stationed outside.

But whatever. The more cheesy bread, the merrier.

Oh, God, I certainly hope this doesn't become the legacy for which I, Princess Mia of Genovia, am remembered.

Dad ate like one of those starving children you always hear about on the news who somehow get separated from the rest of their families and have to spend a few nights wandering around the woods alone, subsisting on nothing but acorns and snow, and then someone finds them running down the highway days later in nothing but a diaper and it always turns out they're from Indiana and you go, 'Uh-huh, I knew it.'

Then he dozed off on the couch while watching a home renovation show on HGTV. I wanted to avoid anything too stressful, such as the news or any *Law & Order* reruns that might remind him of his arrest, and of course the election and how horrible he looks without his mustache.

He chose a show where a couple is given a choice of either 'loving' their newly renovated home, or 'listing' it for sale and buying another. He couldn't stay awake long enough to find out what decision they made (they listed it).

When I was sure he was really asleep, I put a blanket over him (given to me as a birthday present by the Queen of Denmark), which only acted as a magnet for Fat Louie to jump back on top of him and curl up on his chest . . . but even that extra twenty pounds didn't wake him up. Maybe his crying jag (or the cheesy bread) had been cathartic.

236

I just texted a photo of the two of them (Dad and cat) to Michael, along with this message:

> **Hi, hope you're having fun telling the doctors about your robot legs. You might want to make other plans for later tonight since I don't know how interested you're going to be in coming over for volcano time with THIS on my couch. XOXO**

Michael texted back:

> Why have you left me for a middle-aged band teacher? ;-)
>
> I understand. I'll see you tomorrow. I love you.

He signed off with an emoji of a melting snowman. Poor Michael. Since getting engaged to me, he's:

1. Had the fact that he was getting married announced to his parents over the radio.

2. Had the small, family-and-friends-only beach wedding we planned turned into a monster affair that will be internationally televised and at which there apparently won't be mini grilled cheese

sandwiches or a mashed potato or a build-your-own taco bar.

3. Lost his apartment to news vans and paparazzi and been forced to live out of a hotel.

4. Discovered his future father-in-law has a secret younger daughter.

As much as I adore Michael and think he's the type who can weather any storm, I don't know how much more he can take.

I don't know how much more *I* can take either.

After I texted Michael, I texted his sister:

<Lilly Moscovitz 'Virago'   HRH Mia Thermopolis 'FtLouie'>

What are you doing?

What am I always doing lately? Memorizing the black letter rules. Thanks for having your wedding a week before New York State holds its bar exam in July, by the way. That is not at all inconvenient for me, nor is it freaking me out in any way.

Sorry, it wasn't my decision. So, has anyone told you the one about the princess who turns out to have a long-lost sister living in New Jersey?

I am coming over RIGHT NOW.

You can't.

I sent her the photo I'd texted Michael.

Why is there a dentist from Scottsdale, Arizona, sleeping on your couch?

He shaved. He's upset that I found out about that thing I mentioned, and is basically having a midlife crisis.

Give me the 411 about that thing you mentioned and I'll LexisNexis her.

English, please.

God, you are such a princess. It's the database we use to access legal and business documents online. I just need her name and city of birth.

A 'dossier' on her was already prepared by the RGG.

And I'm sure Grandma's dossier was very thorough. Now it's time to let Big Lilly take charge.

Lilly, the RGG is a military organization that has been in existence since the 1200s.

Oh, yeah, and they've done a great job catching your stalker.

Fine. Olivia Grace Clarisse Mignonette Harrison, Cranbrook, NJ.
   Delete this message.

Done. One moment please while I research. Here is some soothing music for while you wait. 'A Million Stars' by Boris P.

Not funny.

Quiet please, processing.

You know Tina is still in love with him.

HA! She would be.

She doesn't have a heart made of stone like you do.

THERMOPOLIS!! YOU WERE SERIOUS!!! YOU HAVE A $!$T5R!

Yes, I know, I just told you that.

Well, what are you going to do about it?

I don't know.

GO GET HER, Liam Neeson in *Taken* style.

She's only 12 and not in any known danger of being sold into sex slavery.

You need to get to know her and instruct her in the ways of the princess force.

That's not a thing.

It is, actually, I've seen it in action. Also, she needs to be your flower girl at your wedding to my brother.

How do you even know what one of those is? I thought you hated weddings!

Only other people's, not yours to my brother. Actually, she's too old to be a flower girl.

Wait, how do you know how old flower girls are supposed to be?

Nothing. I don't.

Lilly! Have you secretly been watching all those bride shows on the Learning Channel on Friday nights like the rest of us?

No. Take me with you when you go to get her, though. I have a particular set of skills . . .

Are you drunk studying again?

. . . skills I have acquired over a very long career.

OK I'm going to bed now, I don't have time for this.

Skills that make me a nightmare for people like you.

Lilly, this is serious.

> I know. We're seriously doing this tomorrow. I'll clear my schedule.

> **Good night, Lilly.**

> ;-)
> Good night, POG.*

*Princess of Genovia. It's been years and she still won't stop calling me this. I've given up.

Even so, it's nice to know that beneath that hard outer shell, she's still got that sweet gooey middle. All the law school in the world can't change that.

Three more things I'm grateful for:

1. My friends, who really are wonderful (even if they're lunatics).

2. My dad (even though he can be a lunatic, too, at times).

3. Cheesy bread.

Dad's gone. He's left Queen Margrethe's blanket neatly
folded on the end of the couch, along with a note. The
note says:

Mia, thank you for the hospitality. Sorry about my
behavior last night. I don't know what came over me. I
feel much better today. Perhaps it was the cheesy bread.

In the light of day I feel that it is much better if we
don't pursue the subject we discussed last night. It is, after
all, an election year, and that particular subject could
hurt me in the polls. And as mentioned, I don't know
that I have the necessary qualifications for that particular
position.

Then there's always your wedding to think of. I
don't want such a happy occasion to be marred by
foolishness from my past. So I think it's best that, as
soon as my legal entanglements are cleared up, I return
to Genovia.

As for the other topic we discussed, on that I cannot
budge. It's the height of fiscal foolishness for you not to
obtain a prenuptial agreement. You are the heiress to one
of the largest fortunes in Europe, and it makes no sense
for you to enter a marriage without some legal protection.
Please reconsider.

Truthfully, Mia, I don't think I'm the type to travel without following a map.

Sincerely,

Your father
Artur Christoff Phillipe Gérard Grimaldi Renaldo
Prince of Genovia

I can tell he means it, too, because he's used all his names in the right order.

He's also taken all the leftover cheesy bread with him.

Foolishness from my past? That's how he's chosen to refer to his own progeny?

Nice.

Well, if he thinks he's going to intimidate me into backing down about Olivia – and the prenup – he's wrong. I'm *not* giving up. I'm going to have a relationship with my little sister, and like Michael said about marrying me, it's going to happen sooner rather than later.

Apparently not at this precise moment, however, because the deputy prime minister wants a conference call, and then after that – according to my itinerary, anyway – I have my first wedding-gown fitting.

Seriously. This is my life, as if things weren't bad enough. Last night I dreamed that Bruce Willis took me to the ballet, and when, during intermission, he turned to ask me what I thought of the performance, I wasn't wearing any clothes. *I dreamed I went to the ballet naked with Bruce Willis.*

In a way I almost wish RoyalRabbleRouser *would* try something – just a very minor assassination attempt (to get it over with so he could be arrested already; one that only slightly wounded me and of course didn't hurt anyone else) – so I'd have to be hospitalized for a little while and not allowed any visitors. Then I could drink Sprite and watch the Food Network for a day or two and have total peace and quiet.

But I realize this is hardly a healthy fantasy.

Although certain reality stars seem to check themselves into the hospital quite a bit for 'exhaustion.' An assassination attempt would be a legitimate excuse, at least.

10:15 a.m., Wednesday, May 6
In the HELV on the way to Sebastiano's
Rate the Royals Rating: 7

Just had the most disturbing conversation with Suzanne Dupris, the Genovian deputy prime minister (who said she's been trying to reach Dad, but he won't return her calls. Honestly! Is Dad so scared of women he can't even return their *business* calls?).

Apparently they've run out of camp beds (and 'sanitation stations,' which is the polite word for portable toilets) at the Port of Princess Clarisse for all the Qalifi refugees who've fled there.

Worse, several of the refugees' TB tests have come back positive.

They're being treated in the hospital, and are in good condition, but Cousin Ivan has lost no time using this as ammunition in his campaign. He is now declaring that *Diversity = Disease.*

Really! This is his new campaign slogan!

And some of our citizens seem to believe it, not understanding the basic facts that what *actually* causes disease is bacteria, or, put more plainly, overcrowding, poverty, lack of clean drinking water, and idiots like Cousin Ivan.

So Madame Dupris wants to discuss other 'options' for dealing with the refugee crisis.

Meanwhile, Cousin Ivan has threatened to ask Parliament to raise Genovia's 'security threat level' to *high,* saying that the only reason the refugees want to come to Genovia at all is that they wish to attack us 'with their germs.' He wants to ask Parliament to allow the Genovian Navy to use 'aggressive military maneuvers to blow the incoming refugee boats out of the water.'

'Perhaps we should use the Genovian Navy's aggressive military maneuvers to blow my cousin Ivan out of the water,' I said to Madame Dupris.

'I would love that,' she said with a sigh. 'Perhaps they could also use it on the mega-cruise ships he wants to let in, too.'

If only.

I promised her I would find my dad, but that even if I couldn't, I would get back to her with an answer by the end of the day (Genovian time). But that first – embarrassingly – I had to go try on wedding gowns.

'Ah,' she said. *'Comme c'est romantique!'*

Of course she's never tried on wedding gowns with my grandmother in the room. There is nothing *'romantique'* about that.

Well, Tina got her wish. I did not get mine – of having
Vera Wang as my wedding-gown designer – but I suppose
I got the next best thing: my cousin Sebastiano. (No.
This is not the next best thing. It is not even close. But
Sebastiano is Genovian, and also family, and also free, so
he is what I get.)

Tina's here – along with Shameeka, Ling Su, Lana,
Trisha, and my mom – to watch as I try on wedding gowns,
and also to have their measurements taken for bridesmaid
gowns, which Sebastiano will also be designing.

Apparently, this decision was unilaterally made by
Grandmère. She had her assistant, Rolanda, send out
invitations to all the women I mentioned on my list
of potential bridesmaids, along with my mother. Only
Perin did not accept, saying she could not attend, as
she had to work – this was very smart of her. Lilly said
she was going to be late (I shudder to think what that
means).

When I walked in, I was shocked to see them all
sitting on the slinky black leather couches Sebastiano has
all over his studio, sipping mimosas.

'Surprise, bitch!' Lana said as my jaw dropped.

I was already having a bad day, but I wasn't expecting
things to go quite as badly as *this*.

'Wow,' I said, giving my mom a hug. 'I'm so happy
to see you guys . . . I guess. Are you drinking already?'

'Duh,' Lana said. 'Didn't you know you can't try on wedding gowns sober?'

'I did not know that,' I said.

'It isn't true,' Shameeka assured me.

'Don't make her drink if she doesn't want to, Lana,' my mom said in an icy tone. My mom has never been able to forget Lana's mean-girl past.

'Yeah, I think I'll pass,' I said, remembering that later I was going to have to make important decisions with Madame Dupris regarding the Qalifi refugees.

'Don't be a twunt,' said Trisha, and handed me a champagne flute.

'I beg your pardon?'

'A twunt,' Trisha said cheerfully. 'That's a cross between a—'

'A lot of people don't know the secret to a really good mimosa,' Lana interrupted. 'It's not just orange juice and champagne. You gotta put triple sec in there, too, to really bring out the flavor of the juice. I added vodka, too, for kick.'

She said this right after I'd taken a sip.

'Princessa!' Sebastiano hurried over to raise one of my hands and air-kiss it. 'You are here at last! You don't know how long I've been waiting for this day, all so that you can walk down the aisle in one of my gowns, like the princess bride you were born to be. I have so many designs for you to try. Almost ready, all of them, they just need for you to say *sì* and then I will put on the fin touch. So we try now, yes? What do you like best, the mer? Or the ball?'

Sebastiano's grasp of English has always been tenuous, even though he's had studios in both New York and Europe for some time. He prefers to say only the first syllable of multisyllabic words, so that *mermaid* (as in, mermaid skirts) becomes *mer* or *ball gown* becomes *ball*.

'I don't know, Seb,' I said to him. 'To be honest, I don't really care.'

'Don't *care*?' Grandmère looked like she'd been hitting the mimosa (or screwdriver) bar pretty hard herself, especially since she'd brought Rommel along and he was running around loose, humping the legs of all the couches and anyone who'd stand still long enough to let him.

'Mia,' Tina said, sounding anxious. 'You have to choose. It really matters.'

'Yeah.' Trisha looked appalled. 'Don't wear a sheath, like I did, that's too tight. Then you can't sit down, even in double Spanx. And trust me, it blows not to be able to sit down on your wedding day. Getting married is really tiring. There are so many people you have to snub by not smiling at them.'

Grandmère tipped her glass in Trisha's direction in a silent little toast of approval.

'Mia will look great in whatever she wears,' Shameeka said generously. 'It doesn't matter.'

'But since she's a princess, wouldn't a princess ball gown be most appropriate?' Tina asked.

'But that's what everyone's *expecting*,' Ling Su said worriedly.

'Sebastiano, what do you think looks best?' Shameeka asked. 'I'm thinking modified A-line.'

I had no idea what anyone was talking about, and I had, upon occasion, watched those bridal shows on TLC on Friday night, on the rare occasions I hadn't had a function to attend and Michael hadn't been over to demand that we change the channel.

'Of course, of course,' Sebastiano said, steering me toward the dressing room. 'I have it all. *You* sit here, princessa.' He stuck me on this little couch in a room far away from everyone. 'I bring you dresses. My assistant CoCo will help you change.'

Then he ran out, and ever since CoCo has been coming back here at regular intervals with gigantic garment bags containing half-finished one-of-a-kind Sebastiano creations which she's been helping me try on, and in which I then parade out into the studio to model for Sebastiano, my mother, Grandmère, Rolanda, Dominique, Tina, and the rest of the girls to comment on.

Truthfully, they're lovely dresses. And everyone seems to like all of them. I have the most supportive friends and family (and bodyguard) in the whole world (except for Grandmère, who said the mermaid gown made me look 'like that woman who likes to show her backside, what is her name? Oh, yes, the Kardashian').

But none of them have made me catch my breath and cry, like women do on that one show when they know they've 'found the gown.'

Maybe that only happens on TV? A lot of stuff, I've

noticed, gets manipulated by writers when it's shown on television – even so-called reality television – and makes us think we're supposed to think and act and look certain ways, when the true reality is totally the opposite. Often there's no 'right way' to look or think or act, but because we've been so conditioned by the media to think so, we actually mistrust our own better judgment.

Like Sebastiano, who just took me aside and asked worriedly if 'Every all right?' He left out the word *thing*.

'Yes, I think everything's all right,' I said to him. 'I'm sorry, Sebastiano, all your gowns are beautiful. I just can't pick one.'

'You need focus!' Sebastiano urged me. 'Wedding day is most imp day of your whole life!'

Oh, God! The minute he said that, I wanted to throw up. It wasn't the screwdriver or that I don't want to marry Michael, or that I'm having second thoughts. Not at all.

It's the wedding itself that's causing me anxiety. How can I plan a wedding right now with all the other crazy things going on in my life, like my dad thinking he's got to 'follow the map,' or the fact that I have a little sister I haven't met yet, or hundreds if not thousands of refugees possibly about to be hit by streams of water from Genovian naval ships?

Maybe this wedding thing is happening a little too fast.

Or maybe there is no 'one' perfect gown. Maybe I'm not the only liar: maybe we've all been lied to our entire lives, not by the government as J.P. insists in his stupid book, but by the *$51 billion wedding industry*! Why doesn't someone write a book about *that*? . . .

'Princessa? Are you all right?'

Sebastiano has begun to sweat profusely, since he's run through all of the one-of-a-kind bridal gowns in his collection, including the ones he made with me in mind. 'Princessa, I can't start from scratch. I have noth I'll be able to fin in time! I'm go to be ruin!'

I've told him it's okay. 'It's just a dress.'

This was the wrong thing to say, apparently, since it made him catch his breath and go back into the studio, looking as if he were about to cry.

Dammit. What is wrong with me? Why couldn't I lie when I needed to?

And it's *not* just a dress. A bridal gown is never just a dress! It's a symbol of hope, a source of inspiration, a thing of beauty in a world where there's so much sadness and despair! What is wrong with me?

And where is Lilly? I know her studying for the bar is way more important than my choosing a stupid wedding dress, but I sort of wish she was here right now, even if it was only to tell me to—

11:57 a.m., Wednesday, May 6
Limo in line at the Holland Tunnel
Rate the Royals Rating: 7

Lilly came barging into the dressing room just as I was giving up all hope of finding the 'one,' or of maintaining my sanity.

'Look,' she said, shoving a stack of papers into my face.

'Where have you been?' I practically shrieked. 'I can't decide which is The One! It's really upsetting Sebastiano.'

'What is the one?' she asked. 'Do you mean Keanu Reeves from *The Matrix*? And who cares about Sebastiano? He only wants you to pick a dress so he can get his name on all the fashion websites. You're the bride, not him. Tell him to suck your [REDACTED].'

'No, not Keanu Reeves. The One is what Tina keeps calling my wedding gown. And do you have to swear so much? I'm choosing a dress to marry your brother in, show a little class.'

'What's wrong with the one you have on? You look pretty [REDACTED] hot.'

I looked down at myself. 'I don't know. It's a ball gown. Ling Su says everyone will be expecting me to wear a ball gown, because I'm royal, and everything.'

I'd been staring at myself in dismay in the mirror for ten minutes, afraid to go out of the dressing room since I knew Lana and Trisha were going tell me I was being boring (and also that there was a chance Grandmère might have heard about Cousin Ivan's threat to raise the security level, since that will adversely affect tourism, and I'd have to hear about it).

Lana and Trisha wanted me to go with something backless or at least so sheer it basically looked like Princess Leia's gold bikini from *Return of the Jedi*, only in white, which I knew Michael would like, but I definitely did not have the confidence to wear on international television.

Boring as it might be, I like having a bodice no one can see through (the one I had on happened to be embroidered with diamonds – or as Sebastiano called them, 'real dimes'), and a tulle skirt so wide, it would take up the entire aisle of the throne room. Talk about raising the threat level.

'Of course it's a ball gown,' Lilly said. 'As you just reminded me, you're a princess, stupid. Why wouldn't you wear a princess ball gown? Here.'

She scooped up a layer of the tulle and created what Sebastiano (who'd come back to stand beside me, his tears temporarily stifled), clapping his hands, declared a 'pickup.'

'Okay,' Lilly said. 'If that's what you want to call them. Do one on either side. Like Cinderella's ball gown in the cartoon. Do a couple of those thingies, out of the crystals you have on the bodice. That might make it less grotesque, and I won't want to throw up as much.'

Suddenly the gown took on a whole new look. Not that I've ever been a huge fan of Cinderella – although of all the Disney princesses, she's one of the most relatable.

She had to do domestic work for a living, after all, and didn't simply lie around in a coma waiting for someone to kiss her awake.

I could completely see this dress being The One. I got shivery, I could see it so much. I even wanted to cry a little.

'Wow,' I said. 'I want to throw up less, too.'

'This wonderful,' Sebastiano said, clapping his hands in delight. 'I'm so glad I make you not want to throw up! And I know exact the thing to make it most perfect of all. Stay here, Princessa, I come back quick.'

'You do that,' Lilly said, eyeing him as he rushed out like a madman (which he is, but really, all creative people are, sobbing over how great their own accomplishments are, like that's perfectly acceptable behavior). 'Here.'

I took the stack of papers Lilly shoved at me. They were mostly long rows of numbers.

'Uh,' I said to Lilly. 'Mr. Gianini was a great algebra teacher and all, but you know the minute I graduated high school I never looked at a single math problem again, right? I send everything with numbers on it to my accountant, or I make Michael deal with it.'

'Great. Spoken like a true feminist,' Lilly said. 'I'm sure your mother must be so proud. Well, those pages hold bad news about that bohunk your sister's aunt married. He's been using large amounts of the child support your dad's been sending her to finance the business he owns with her aunt, O'Toole Construction and Home Design.'

I sank down on the little bench in the dressing room,

my tulle skirt ballooning around me like a huge fluffy white cloud. 'I can't take any more bad news today, Lilly. I really can't.'

'Well, I'm sorry, but it gets worse.'

'What could possibly be worse than this?'

'Uncle Richard's planning on moving the whole family to the Middle East.'

'The Middle East? Where in the Middle East?' There are many lovely places in the Middle East. I've had state visits to Bahrain and Jordan and Abu Dhabi. I've been to Egypt and Israel and Saudi Arabia. All of them are lovely countries (not without their challenges, but then, every country has its challenges).

I certainly did not expect Lilly to reply: 'Qalif.'

'*Qalif?*' I felt as if my heart had sunk to the bottom of my tightly corseted bodice. '*Why?*'

'O'Toole Construction's been contracted to build a new mall there. It's going to have the world's largest indoor wave machine in it. Or maybe it's the world's largest indoor ski slope. Oh, well, it doesn't matter since only men can use it because the crown prince there just banned women from swimming and skiing in public.'

My eye began to twitch like mad. 'You found all this out through a *public records search*?'

Lilly looked slightly guilty. 'It's possible I may have searched a few records that weren't so public. But it isn't my fault. People really shouldn't use the word *password* as their password.'

'Oh, God,' I breathed. 'This isn't happening.'

'I wish it weren't, but it is.'

'So, essentially,' I said, feeling like I was going to throw up the single sip of screwdriver I'd had, 'my dad is paying for an indoor ski park – or pool – to be built in Qalif, a country with some of the worst human-rights violations in the world right now.'

'Don't be stupid, he doesn't pay *that* much child support. She's just one little kid. But he's paid for some of the front loaders that are being shipped there to build it. Sorry to be the bearer of bad news.'

I sat there in a big puddle of diamonds and tulle. 'How come the Royal Genovian Guard didn't figure this out?'

Lilly shrugged. 'They're not as smart as I am.'

I could not deny this. No one is as smart as Lilly, with the possible exception of her brother, but he isn't as ruthless as Lilly, which makes Lilly slightly smarter, but only because she always sees the worst in everyone.

'The kid's physically okay,' she assured me. 'At least so far as I can tell. I mean, they're feeding her and stuff. I Google-searched her home and school, and she lives in a nice place – well, obviously, her aunt's listed as one of the top interior decorators in the area – and goes to a nice school—'

'But how do we know?' I asked. Lilly's deep suspicion of everyone is catching, especially to someone who watches a lot of *NCIS*. 'They could be making her sleep in a closet under the stairs!'

'That seems unlikely. The house is a four bedroom on a cul-de-sac. It's currently on the market, listed for sale at one point four million dollars. I would imagine, with a home like that, if there's a closet under the stairs, it's probably where they keep extra paper towels and soda and stuff they bought at the local big box store.'

'I am not okay with this,' I said. 'And if my dad were in his right mind, he wouldn't be okay with it, either!'

'You don't have to shout,' Lilly grumbled. 'But I wouldn't be okay with it either if it were my kid sister.'

'The problem is, my dad's been in no condition lately to make decisions.'

'Yeah,' Lilly said. 'I saw the mustache. Or should I say, lack thereof. Your dad needs to be kept away from sharp objects and probably everything else right now except YouTube videos about cute puppies.'

That's when I made a decision. I stood up and started taking off my princess ball gown.

'What are you doing?' Lilly asked.

'We're going to Cranbrook, New Jersey,' I said. 'Help me get out of this thing.'

'Um, okay.' Lilly started helping me out of my wedding dress. 'What are we going to do in Cranbrook, New Jersey?'

'We're going to do what you said – go get my sister.'

'Okay,' Lilly said. 'When I said that last night, I might have had a few too many energy drinks, like you'd suggested. Transporting minors over state lines without permission of their legal guardian is a felony.'

'I don't care,' I said. 'I'm a princess.'

'True. But do you maybe want to discuss other, less criminal ways we could deal with the matter first?'

'No.'

'All right. Great. I kind of anticipated you'd have this reaction, to be honest, which is why I took the liberty of—'

'Lilly, just shut up for once in your life, and unlace me.'

'Yes, Your High Holiness.'

So now we're on our way to Cranbrook, New Jersey. (Lilly keeps yelling at François, the driver, that we should have taken the bridge, but that makes no sense, we'd have had to go way out of our way.)

Of course Grandmère was furious when I came out of the dressing room with no gown on and announced we were going to have to reschedule our lunch with Lazarres-Reynolds.

'What could possibly be more important?'

I didn't tell her, or anyone. I simply said that something very important had come up and I was going to have to meet them another time.

(Dominique took me aside and pointed out one of the reasons Grandmère is so angry is that Lazarres-Reynolds is still going to bill us, and that they cost $500 an hour, or as she put it, 'Five 'undred dollars an hour.' So I said she could tell Grandmère to send the bill to me.)

That's when Grandmère caused a scene and said she was taking my hybrid electric livery vehicle – she only did this to hurt me – leaving me her obnoxious black stretch limo with the Genovian flags on it that she takes everywhere because she doesn't believe in traveling inconspicuously like I do (in this way Grandmère has a lot in common with some popular rappers).

But the joke's on her, because the limo has Wi-Fi and also a bar (though unlike Lilly, I am staying away from it).

I gave my mom a lift home in it. She was only going a block away, back to the loft on Thompson Street. Still, it was fun to ride with my mom in a limo – we don't get to do it very often.

I thought about using the opportunity to tell Mom about Olivia, but it didn't seem like the right time. Also, breaking the news that he has a child by another woman is obviously my father's responsibility.

But when Mom asked where Lilly and Tina and I were going (Tina was going back to the NYU library to study, so I offered her a lift too, then secretly texted her what was up, which might have been a mistake because now she's sitting on the jump seat looking very pale, mouthing *I can't believe this is happening* over and over), I couldn't exactly lie, not only because I've been getting worse and worse at it – not even counting my twitching eye, I've still never learned to keep my nostrils from flaring when I tell a fib – but because she's my *mother*. I knew she was going to be able to tell something was up (besides Genovia's security threat level).

So I said we were going to Cranbrook, New Jersey.

'Oh, really?' Mom asked. 'What's in Cranbrook, New Jersey?'

Lilly smiled at me expectantly from over her laptop and the whiskey sour she'd mixed for herself from the mini-bar, clearly enjoying the situation.

I had to think of something my mom totally wouldn't want to come with us to do, because as an artist her schedule is pretty flexible (except for having to pick up Rocky from after-school karate practice, but she could easily get one of her equally artistic, flexibly-scheduled friends to do that).

'Um, we're going to look at bridesmaid dresses to get inspiration for Sebastiano,' I said. 'There's a shop out there someone told us about. I hear they have amazing mother-of-the-bride dresses. Do you want to come?'

Fortunately the lighting in the limo is pretty dim, so Mom didn't notice my nostrils or eyelid. Also I knew she'd be so turned off by the words 'shop' and 'mother-of-the-bride dresses' there was no way on God's green earth she'd ever want to join us.

'Oh, no, sweetheart, but thank you so much for the invitation,' she said, smiling warmly. 'I really can't afford to take any more time away from the new painting I'm doing. I'm calling it *Woman with a Weed Wacker*. I'm hoping it will break new ground in the battle against the Men's Rights Activists.'

'Oh, no problem, Mom,' I said. 'The new painting sounds amazing. Good luck with it.'

'Thanks, Mia. But send me some photos! I'd love to see what kind of dresses you girls find.'

Great. So now when we get to New Jersey, we're going to have to find some store that sells bridesmaid dresses and look at them, in order to take photos to send to my mom.

Although Lilly said there's another way to accomplish this. She started looking up bridesmaid dresses online so we can send those to my mom instead.

'Oh, look, Mia. One shoulder empire waist in electric green. Mia, *please* can you get Sebastiano to go with one shoulder empire waist in electric green as our bridesmaid dresses? I'm *begging* you.'

Naturally, this got Tina upset. 'Stop it, Lilly. Your best friend – who is marrying your brother – has made a *life-altering* discovery. She has a sister she never knew existed, a little girl who's grown up without a father or a mother, and you're sitting there joking about electric green bridesmaid dresses? Really?'

Lilly looked a little ashamed of herself . . . at least until Tina went on to add, 'Besides, you *know* I look terrible in green. That cream color that Sebastiano picked out for us this morning is going to be really flattering on *all* of our skin tones, even if it's derivative of what Kate, Duchess of Cambridge, chose for the bridesmaids in her wedding to Prince William, and I think we need to stick to it. Even Trisha liked it, and you know she hates everything that isn't made out of black lace stretch Lycra—'

I'm seriously going to check myself into a rehab center for stress and anxiety after this, I swear to God.

'Can we please stick to the subject?' I demanded. 'Once we get to Cranbrook, here's what I'd like to do: go to Olivia's uncle's business to talk to him – and the aunt – like normal, rational adults about my meeting my sister. Nothing accusatory, nothing confrontational. Just "Hi, hello, I'm Mia Thermopolis. Would it be okay with you if I meet your niece?" Then we can go from there.'

'Oh,' Lilly said. 'Okay. That seems like a great idea,

especially without any sort of advanced planning or consulting your lawyers or your dad or anything first.'

'It will be fine,' I assured her. 'It's not like I haven't been trained in the art of diplomacy.'

'Right!' Lilly laughed over her whiskey sour. 'By your grandmother, the queen of tact!'

'We're two separate generations,' I said. 'We might do things differently, but we still get things done.'

'And the aunt might not even be aware her husband is using her niece's money to buy bulldozers to send to Qalif,' Tina pointed out. 'She could be perfectly innocent in the whole thing.'

'Exactly, Tina.'

Lilly laughed some more. 'Oh, my God. You two are so naïve. It's like watching Bambi and Thumper go after Tony Soprano.'

Lilly is such a pessimist.

Oh, great, the car is finally moving.

Tina is reading aloud from J.P.'s dystopian YA novel, *Love in the Time of Shadows*, which she downloaded to her phone.

Lilly is laughing so hard she says she's going to wet her pants.

I'm not finding it very amusing, particularly as the heroine, 'Amalia,' has light gray eyes and long sandy blond hair, which gets whipped around a lot in the unforgiving desert wind.

But I suppose hearing J.P.'s book read aloud is better than the alternative, which was listening to Tina play all of the voicemails Boris has left her recently, swearing that he was never unfaithful, and begging her to take him back. Some of them were accompanied by long violin solos.

Lilly said if she had to hear one more, she was going to fling herself from the limo and into oncoming traffic.

I'm starting to think Tina should take Boris back just so we don't have to hear about him anymore.

I've left four messages for my dad, including two on his private cell, but he has not returned them. His assistant Marielle says she has no idea where he is, but as soon as she hears from him, she'll let him know I've called.

Except that wherever he's gone, he has to have taken his bodyguards. So the RGG knows where he is.

But they aren't talking, either.

267

This is not a good sign.

No one told me it takes an hour and a half to get to Cranbrook, New Jersey, during periods of high traffic. This could be a very long trip.

But my resolve is not flagging.

People are honking at the limo as they drive by. It's like they've never seen one before, which is ridiculous. I've watched the show *Jersey Shore*, and they rode in limos all the time.

Well, not ones with Genovian flags flying from them, but still. I suppose I should get François to pull over so we can remove the flags and not draw so much attention to ourselves, but I'd rather save the time and get there, already.

Tina is continuing to read. The two rivals for Amalia's affection, 'Mick' and 'Jared,' come from enemy factions. Jared is blond and warmly creative, whereas Mick has dark hair and is more coldly analytical. Amalia seems to be leaning more toward Jared.

But none of it really matters since they're all dying of radiation poisoning.

Lilly just said she's going to give *Love in the Time of Shadows* 'a million stars as soon as J.P. self-publishes it somewhere.'

This caused Tina to look teary-eyed. '*A Million Stars*,' she echoed, with a sigh.

'Oh, for God's sake,' Lilly said in disgust. 'If you miss Boris that much, why don't you take him back?'

'How can I?' Tina asked. 'He betrayed my trust.'

'Did he?' Lilly asked. 'Or did you destroy it by believing some bimbo blogger's word over your boyfriend's?'

269

I widened my eyes. 'Lilly!'

'Well, it's true,' Lilly said, as Tina appeared stricken. 'Look, as a lawyer, you know I'm obligated to look at the facts, and weigh everyone's testimony impartially, regardless of their sex. But as a feminist, I'm far more likely to show solidarity for my sisters, and believe a woman's word over a man's. Hos before bros, and all that.'

I sucked in my breath, glancing at Lars and Halim, who fortunately weren't paying the slightest bit of attention. '*Lilly*. Sisters before misters.'

'But in this particular case, I just can't,' she went on, ignoring me, as usual. 'I know Boris too well. He's the type of man who, if he did cheat, would immediately confess to it, because he wouldn't be able to bear the guilt for one second. So the fact that he keeps saying he didn't do it makes me think he really, honest to God, didn't do it, and in this one individual case, we have got to believe this particular bro over this particular ho.'

I bit my lip. 'I hate to say this, Tina, but Lilly has a point. For a musical genius, Boris is pretty uncomplicated.'

Tina continued to look upset. 'I know, okay? But photos don't lie. Unless . . . do you think it's possible that girl *drugged* him, or something? Maybe she—'

'Okay, let's not get carried away,' Lilly interrupted. 'He definitely wasn't drugged. He seemed pretty . . . alert.'

Tina glared at her. 'You *looked*? You looked at the photos? I can't believe you looked! *I* haven't even looked at the photos!'

'Hey,' Lilly said with a shrug. 'I'm single. I have to have *some* fun.'

'I can't believe you,' Tina declared, hotly. 'I know you used to go out with him, Lilly, but that's a violation of—'

'Uh, Tina,' I interrupted, guiltily. 'I looked, too. I mean, it was by mistake, and I clicked away as soon as I realized what they were. But Lilly's exaggerating, as usual.' I glared at her. 'They were only from the waist up so you couldn't really see anything. In fact, they were actually kind of innocent—'

'I can't believe you!' Tina cried. 'You guys are disgusting!'

'How did you click on them *by mistake*?' Lilly, grinning, kicked me in the leg.

'Shut up.' I kicked her back. 'Tina, don't be mad. I'm telling you, the photos aren't anything like what people are making them out to be. In fact, they're kind of sweet, and the lighting's surprisingly good. Maybe you *should* look at them, because the more I think about it, the more I wonder if Boris could be telling the truth about them being Photoshopped – at least partly – and if Lilly is right about the bro thing, which I think she is, maybe that girl really is some kind of editing genius who—'

'No!' Tina looked as if she were feeling sick to her stomach. 'I'll never look at them. And I think we should change the subject now. Let's talk about what you're going to say to your little sister when you meet her.'

I agreed, but only out of pity for her.

This turned out to be a huge mistake. In addition to

being knowledgeable about fingernail polish, it appears that if I'm going to get along with a twelve-year-old, I'm also supposed to:

- Have read all the latest semi-erotic boy band fan fiction on something called Wattpad.

- Know how to Snapchat.

- Follow all the haul video stars on YouTube.

- And be up on all the gossip about an actress I've never heard of.

I'm dead.

1:25 p.m., Wednesday, May 6
Still on Interstate 295
Rate the Royals Rating: 7

Michael/Mick just texted.

<Michael Moscovitz 'FPC'   HRH Mia Thermopolis 'FtLouie'>

> Why are you in New Jersey?

Who says I'm in New Jersey?

> Someone just Instagramed a photo of you eating at a place called 'Lou's Lucky Deli.' You're with two women who look suspiciously like my sister and Tina Hakim Baba along with three men who, unless I'm mistaken, are Lars, Halim, and your grandmother's chauffeur.

Oh! Ha. Yes. We stopped for sandwiches because we were starving.

> That's a long way to go for deli. What's wrong with Katz's?

We're looking at bridesmaid dresses.

I thought you were sticking with Genovian designers.

They have those in New Jersey.

I know there's only one reason you'd go to New Jersey these days, Mia, and it isn't for bridesmaid dresses.

I'm sorry! We're pulling into her town now. Tell you about it later?

Fine. But this means when I tell you what Boris has planned, you can't get mad.

Wait . . . what? What does Boris have planned? Michael, seriously, no. Tina is too fragile right now.

Not for Tina. For me.

Why would Boris have something planned for you?

It's called a bachelor party. You've probably heard of them.

No.

No, you've never heard of a bachelor party?

No, you are not having one. Especially given by Boris.

We'll talk about it, and your trip to New Jersey, when you get home.

No, we won't, because when I get home we have that benefit for Sudden Cardiac Death Awareness tonight at the W. And anyway, Boris P. is not throwing you a bachelor party. I can't believe you even WANT one.

Even one where Boris is chartering a private jet to fly me and some of our other closest *World of Warcraft* friends to Buenos Aires to eat gigantic steaks?

Never mind.

What? You don't want to come?

Thank you, no. It sounds like a delightful outing, but I'll pass. Take Lars with you, though. I'm sure he'd enjoy it.

You only want me to take Lars with me so he won't be with YOU at your bachelorette party at Crazy Ivan's.

Dammit! Who told you about that?

Tina told Boris, who told me. He says you girls shouldn't be the only ones who have fun. Something about 'dicklickers'?

I'm going to kill her . . .

He replied with an emoji of what I believe to be a house with flames coming out of the windows and the words, 'When you get home expect to be severely reprimanded by the fire marshal.'

!

J.P. is completely wrong. Michael is the opposite of cold and analytical.

2:45 p.m., Wednesday, May 6
Limo outside Olivia's school
Cranbrook, New Jersey
Rate the Royals Rating: 7

Well, that did not go as well as I'd hoped.

When we pulled up outside Olivia's aunt's house – which was a lovely split-level – I saw that, along with a perfectly respectable Mercedes minivan, there was a yellow Ferrari parked in the driveway that had a vanity plate that said *Hers* on it.

'A Ferrari?' I shook my head. '*I* don't even have a Ferrari.'

'You never got your license,' Tina pointed out.

'I'm helping to stimulate the economy,' I explained, 'by keeping professional drivers employed.'

'There's another Ferrari that matches that one exactly sitting in the manager's parking space in front of O'Toole Construction and Home Design,' Lilly said. 'Did you guys notice? But it says *His* on the vanity plate.'

I had not noticed. We'd gone to the O'Tooles' place of business first, as planned, only to be told by the wide-eyed receptionist (she'd been reading a copy of *OK!*, so might have recognized me, as I frequently appear on the cover of *OK!*) that Mrs. O'Toole was 'working from home today,' and Mr. O'Toole was 'at a site.'

He'd evidently taken a different car to the 'site.'

'*Two* Ferraris?' I cried. 'They have *two*?'

'Of course it's entirely possible that Olivia's uncle's construction business is doing so well financially that he bought those Ferraris with their own money and not the child support money your father meant for your sister,' Tina said.

It's amazing how she can see the best in everyone, including her boyfriend (the fact that he may have cheated on her aside).

'I saw their tax returns from the last five years,' Lilly said. 'The business is doing well, but not *that* well.'

I got out of the limo without even waiting for François to open the car door for me, then stalked up to Olivia's aunt's front door and rang the bell.

After a moment or two, a nice-looking lady in yoga pants and a cowl neck sweater opened the door and said, 'Yes?' expectantly.

It only took a second for her eyes to open very wide as she recognized me and then noticed the limo.

'Oh, my God,' she said, in an entirely different, much less welcoming tone. She'd evidently seen the *OK!* magazines with me on the cover, too.

'Hi,' I said, putting on my best smile and holding out my right hand. 'Are you Catherine? You can call me Mia. I'm here to see your niece, Olivia. Is she at home? Or is she still at school?'

Catherine O'Toole didn't reach out to shake my hand. Instead, she tried to slam the door in my face.

I, however, had learned a thing or two in my years working on Lilly's cable access TV show, *Lilly Tells It Like It Is* (and also volunteering for various political campaigns, both here in the U.S. and back in Genovia), and that is that if you don't want someone to slam a door on you, you should insert your foot between the jamb and the door they are attempting to swing shut. This makes it impossible for them to close it all the way.

What I had forgotten is that you should only do this if you are wearing combat boots with reinforced toes, not faux-suede platform Mary Janes.

'Ow!' I yelled as Catherine O'Toole slammed her door on my foot.

'Sorry,' Catherine O'Toole cried. 'There's no one here by the name Olivia!'

'Help,' I cried, certain many of my metatarsals were being broken or at least sprained. 'Help, help!'

'Oh, my God,' I heard Catherine say again, probably because she'd gotten an eyeful of Lars, who was already hurling himself at us with a considerable amount of speed.

Lars can look intimidatingly large to people who've never seen him before, even when he's a dozen yards away. He is well over six feet tall and weighs two hundred pounds ('most of it muscle,' as he is fond of saying). He can bench press my weight several times over (he claims. I've been spared the sight of him doing this, thank the Lord).

But hurtling toward you at close range, with his face contorted in rage, he's an even more intimidating sight, sort of like a bull charging at an anthill.

The next thing I knew, Lars had crashed through the O'Tooles' front door and pinned Olivia's aunt Catherine to one of her living room walls.

'Princess was attacked, but suspect subdued,' I overheard Lars murmur into his headset. I had no idea who he was talking to. Probably Royal Genovian Guard headquarters back at the consulate. 'Repeat, princess was attacked, but suspect has been subdued.'

'Lars,' I said, as I hopped around, holding my injured foot in one hand. 'I was hardly attacked.'

I couldn't help thinking, though, that if I'd actually been wearing diamond shoes, my foot would be hurting a lot less.

Meanwhile, Lilly was standing there with a large grin on her face, her camera phone up and on, having filmed the whole thing.

'Don't worry,' she said, when she saw my disapproving expression. 'I'm not going to post it anywhere. This is for my *personal* collection.'

Oh, God.

'What's going on?' Tina was crossing the lawn with Halim in tow, both of them looking bewildered. 'Mia, are you all right?'

'I'm fine,' I said, even though my right foot was throbbing with pain. 'There was just a little misunderstanding.'

'There was no misunderstanding,' Lars said firmly.

'No.' Lilly continued to film. 'There was definitely no misunderstanding.'

'Please.' Catherine O'Toole's voice was muffled. This was because Lars was still pressing her against the ornately plastered wall. 'I'm sorry. I didn't mean it. Olivia does live here. Please just tell this . . . *man* to let me go.'

I felt sorry for her, even though I was pretty sure she

had broken or at least sprained my foot.

'Lars, this is ridiculous. Please release her.'

Lars released her, and Catherine O'Toole came away from the wall and adjusted the neckline of her fancy sweater, then one of her fake eyelashes that had come loose when her face had been pressed up against the Venetian plaster. Then she said, 'Excuse me, Your Royal Highness, what I meant to say was, won't you please come in? May I offer you and your friends some refreshment?'

'Yes,' I said. 'That would be lovely.'

So I hobbled over to her white couch (everything in her house is white. The marble floors. The Venetian plaster. The furniture. Everything. It's hard to believe she has three kids – or at least, one niece and two stepkids – and manages to keep everything so clean. They must be very well trained, or she has an amazing cleaning service).

'I'm very sorry to have alarmed you, Mrs. O'Toole,' I said, after she'd brought us iced tea in tall highball glasses that were etched with the letters C and R . . . in white, of course. Lars had accompanied her to the kitchen on the pretense of 'helping' (but really he'd gone to make sure she didn't call the police, press, or her husband), and he'd brought out a little bowl of mixed nuts. The bowl was also white. 'But all I want is to talk to you about your niece, Olivia. I think you're aware that she's my half sister.'

Mrs. O'Toole blinked at me through her crooked eyelash and said, 'Oh. Yes. Yes, of course. Actually, I thought your father would be the one who'd show up. I never expected you.'

I had no idea how to respond to that despite my earlier claim to extraordinary powers of princess diplomacy.

So it was probably a good thing Lilly leaped in and introduced herself.

'Lilly Moscovitz, Mrs. O'Toole,' Lilly said, setting her iced tea down on the pricey – white – coffee table, and sticking out her hand. 'Columbia Law School, Royal Attorney-at-Law to the Princess of Genovia—'

I elbowed Lilly in the gut, causing her to lower her hand with a cough, because Mrs. O'Toole had begun to blink very quickly at the word *attorney*.

'Never mind her, Mrs. O'Toole,' I said, hastily. 'I'm here because, in spite of your sister's wish that her daughter Olivia never know about her royal lineage, I'd very much like to meet her. Having been lucky enough to have had a sister yourself, you can probably understand that.'

Catherine blinked even more, rapidly, and I realized she was only trying to adjust her loose eyelash. 'I suppose I can,' she said. 'Though Elizabeth and I didn't have all that much in common. I've never understood why she didn't marry your dad when he asked. I'd have loved being a princess.'

Tina nearly dropped her iced tea. Her dark eyes had widened to approximately twice their normal size. 'Prince Phillipe asked your sister to marry him?'

'Well, yes,' Catherine said. She'd got her eyelash back on, and was now blinking at Tina like she'd only just gotten a good look at her, and realized how gorgeous she is. Tina has her father's dark coloring and soft roundness, but her mother's British supermodel bone structure and fashion sense, which had caused Sebastiano to moon over her earlier in a manner that made me suspect he wished *she* were the royal bride.

'But Elizabeth always said she wasn't the royal wedding type,' Catherine went on. 'She liked flying those stupid jets. I don't suppose they'd have let her keep doing that if she was a princess.'

'No,' I agreed. 'That would be too dangerous a career for the wife of the Prince of Genovia.'

'I thought so,' Catherine said, knowingly.

Tina swung her bewildered gaze toward me. I could tell she was crushed. She wanted to believe my father had only ever loved my mother for his entire life.

But it's possible for people to have more than one soul mate . . . even though if I ever lose Michael, I'll probably don all black and sit around forever in mourning like Queen Victoria did after she lost her beloved Prince Albert.

'Your sister sounds like a wonderful woman,' I said to Catherine. 'I wish I could have known her. But since I never had the opportunity, I'd like to get to know you, and of course my sister, before you and your family move to Qalif—'

Catherine O'Toole looked relieved. 'Oh. So that's really all you came here for?'

I exchanged glances with Tina and Lilly. 'Uh, yes. Why?'

'No reason.'

Ha. She totally suspected another reason for my visit . . . that we'd found out the truth about her and her bohunk husband stealing all my sister's money!

But of course I had no proof of this . . . yet. And as Tina kept insisting, maybe it wasn't even true.

'Well, maybe one other thing,' I added, wickedly.

Was it my imagination, or did she appear flustered? 'Yes?'

'There's actually a warning out from the State Department right now advising Americans not to travel to Qalif due to the civil unrest—'

Catherine O'Toole made a pooh-poohing gesture with one of her long-nailed hands. 'Oh, that. I talked to a girl at the embassy, she said it's all being overexaggerated. It's perfectly safe so long as you stay in the American compounds.'

'Uh,' I said, watching as Tina's eyes got rounder and rounder with astonishment. 'Okay. Well, if it's all right with you, my father and I were wondering if Olivia could stay with us for a while—' I was lying left and right now, so many lies I could hardly keep track of them. 'Maybe for a few weeks this summer while you and your family get settled in to, uh, your new home in Qalif? How does that sound?'

Catherine O'Toole bit her lower lip. 'Oh, well, I don't know. I'd have to discuss it with Rick . . .'

'Oh, you don't have to worry about the oranges,' Lilly leaped in, breezily. 'The rumors about the rats aren't true.'

I glared at her, then said to Olivia's aunt, 'I really

would so value this opportunity, Mrs. O'Toole.'

'Oh, please call me Catherine.'

'Catherine.'

'Well,' she said, hesitating.

Tina leaned forward and laid a hand soothingly on her knee. 'It would be such a kindness. Olivia's the only memory you have left of your sister, but Princess Mia's never had a sister at all, so think what a chance this would provide her.'

Lilly shot Tina a look that said, *Laying it on a little thick, aren't you?* which Tina ignored.

'Oh, my,' Catherine said. 'It's not that I wouldn't love to help you. It's just that Rick already paid the deposit for Olivia's new school in Qalif. It's year round there, so they have it even in the summer. Extended learning, they call it – and it wasn't cheap. And it was also nonrefundable.'

Tina looked confused. 'Wait. Are you saying – ?'

Lilly leaned forward to pluck Tina's hand from the older woman's knee.

'I think I know *exactly* what Mrs. O'Toole is saying,' Lilly said. 'Don't you, Mia?'

I was already reaching inside my bag for my checkbook. 'Absolutely,' I said. The thing is, you can't hang around the beaches of the Riviera without noticing all the grifters, and then learning to recognize a shakedown when you see one. 'Why don't you let me pay you back for Olivia's summer term, since it looks like she might be staying with us?'

'But—' Tina sputtered. She still didn't understand

what was happening. 'What?'

'Oh, that would be lovely,' Catherine said, smooth as silk. 'You can make the check out to me personally. That's Catherine with a C.' She mentioned an astonishingly large sum of money that, when Tina heard it, caused her to make a squeaking noise.

Lars calmly passed her the bowl from the coffee table. 'Nuts?' he asked.

'No, I'm not hun—'

Lilly jammed a handful of nuts into her palm and signaled for Tina to eat them, which she did, still wide-eyed, but only after Lilly gave her a warning glare.

'That's great,' Lilly said, watching as I made out the check. 'And if you, Catherine, would just look over this contract I took the liberty of drawing up this morning' – she pulled a stapled sheaf of papers from her messenger bag – 'then sign it, I think we can be on our way.'

Catherine took the pages from her and thumbed through them while I gave Lilly a surprised look. A contract?

And Lilly had made such a fuss about us coming here unprepared.

But Lilly Moscovitz was never unprepared for anything. Well, not since tenth grade or so, anyway.

'Standard language, really,' Lilly went on, more to me than to Olivia's aunt, 'about how you don't intend to share any information about this meeting or your niece's parentage with the press, and an addendum on the back giving Mia permission to pick her up from school today so they can have sister-bonding time. Sound good?'

'That sounds fine,' Catherine said, and turned to the back page, where Lilly had placed a little pink sticky arrow. She signed with a pen Lars gallantly offered from the front pocket of his suit jacket.

Olivia's aunt seemed to be in a much better mood when we left. She waved, the check I'd written her fluttering in her hand, from the front porch as we walked back to the limo.

'You guys,' I said under my breath as we crossed the lawn on our way back to the limo. 'She is seriously hiding something. Also, I think she broke my foot.'

'I know, right?' Tina was practically hyperventilating. 'I totally saw this once on a Lifetime movie starring Kirstie Alley. And she ended up in prison!'

'Nobody's going to prison,' Lilly said. 'That contract her aunt signed is binding.'

'You don't even have a law degree!' I reminded her.

'It was witnessed by five people,' Lilly said. 'It will hold up in court, once I get all of you to co-sign it. Now let's go get Mia's sister.'

'Did you check out her room?' I asked.

'What are you talking about?' Lilly looked annoyed with all of us as François popped out of the car to open the door for her, as she was first to reach it.

'When I asked to use their bathroom, I checked out all the bedrooms,' I said. I was trying not to show it, but I needed help walking, and was leaning on Lars for support. My foot was killing me. It had been hard to sneak around the house, but obviously it had needed to be done. 'The two other kids – Rick's from his first marriage – had giant flat screen TVs in their rooms, but not Olivia. Her room was the smallest, and didn't have anything fun in it, not even a computer.'

'I saw that, too,' Tina said. 'But I thought maybe she doesn't like TV. Maybe she doesn't like computers.'

'She's related to Mia,' Lilly said flatly. 'Do you really think that's the case?'

'Maybe,' Tina said, still struggling to find an explanation other than the only glaringly obvious one, that Olivia was the Cinderella of the family, taken advantage of and forced to sleep in the modern equivalent of a garret, 'it was the maid's room.'

'There was a sign right on the door that had the name *Olivia* on it,' I said. 'I think she made it herself. It was in Magic Marker and had little drawings of birds and cats on it. The dossier the RGG made says she likes to draw.'

There was silence as we sat in the cool air-conditioning of the limo, absorbing this.

'Well,' Lilly said finally. 'At least it wasn't a closet under the stairs.'

I narrowed my eyes at her, then said, 'François, the Cranbrook Middle School, please.'

'Yes, Your Highness,' he said.

So now we're sitting outside it, waiting for the bell to ring. When my sister comes out, I'll open the door and tell her who I am and ask her to come for a ride.

Tina says this is the worst plan in the entire universe because kids aren't supposed to accept rides with strangers, even strangers who are world-famous princesses sitting in limos parked outside their school claiming to be their long-lost sister, and that I should do something more subtle, because I'm probably going to scar her for life.

But my foot hurts, and I'm upset about the aunt (and the bedroom), and the fact that my father should be here with me doing this, but that wouldn't be 'following the map.'

Only I can't think of anything more subtle right now.

Tina noticed my limping before we got in the car and made me take my shoe off and is examining my foot and making me press my toes against her hand. She says nothing seems broken but I'm probably going to have a very bad bruise and I should see my own physician.

He'd probably only tell me to journal about it, though, and I'm already doing that.

Oh, God – the bell just rang, and children have begun pouring out of the school.

There she is.

3:50 p.m., Wednesday, May 6
Limo back to New York City
Rate the Royals Rating: 7

Well, I've just ruined my sister's life, forever and completely.

Obviously that was not my goal in coming to Cranbrook, New Jersey. My goal in coming to Cranbrook was to improve my sister's life.

But instead I've inexorably wrecked it.

I don't know why after all this time I continue to listen to anything Lilly says. Obviously I should have consulted with our family lawyers or Dominique or *someone* other than my lunatic best friend before coming out here and causing catastrophic and irreparable damage to the life of a little girl, a life that (probably) wasn't so bad and that now she'll never get back, thanks to me, even though she doesn't seem to be aware of it. She is sitting in the limo beside me, happily doing homework that she thinks she's going to turn in tomorrow.

Ha! By tomorrow news of the fact that she's Prince Phillipe of Genovia's illegitimate love child will be on the front page of every newspaper in the world (I'm surprised it is not already the top trending topic on Twitter).

There is no possible way Olivia will be able to go back to Cranbrook Middle School tomorrow, or ever.

- *Note to self*: I am not qualified to have children. Cancel wedding and secede right to inherit throne? Or just have my tubes tied?

291

On the other hand . . . Olivia *does* appear to be enjoying herself. It turns out I needn't have worried about learning everything I could about a popular starlet since Olivia is much more interested in *me* . . . and riding in a limo and drinking soda with actual sugar in it.

Maybe I haven't *completely* ruined her life. Maybe I've only *changed* her life. For the better!

This is what I set out to do this morning – what I set out to do *every* morning, leave the world a better place than I found it, and that's how I should choose to think of what just happened. Olivia's life is going to be better now, much, much better. How could it not be? She has Coke and me in it now (and soon her father and grandmother, whenever they get around to returning my messages . . .)

OK, who do I think I'm fooling? I've ruined her life. Dominique just called me back because I texted her what happened (*Hey, Dominique, it's me! So, not sure if you heard, but my dad has another kid and I may have inadvertently exposed her existence to the media . . . call me!*) and all I could hear on the other end of the phone was screaming.

Anyway, Tina is the one who spotted Olivia first.

'There she is!' she cried, jabbing her finger against the tinted glass window of the limo.

I saw Olivia standing in the center of a group of uniformed kids by the school's flagpole.

She looked so . . . *little*.

I knew she was going to be because in the dossier, it listed her height and weight, and of course there were photos (the RGG is nothing if not precise).

But photos are very different from real life. In real life, Olivia Grace is all adorable knock-knees and bony elbows and shiny braces and bright blue glasses and curly hair done up in braids.

Was I ever that tiny? I must have been, but it never felt like it. I always felt enormous, too big for my body, and so awkward and ungainly (much too much so for anyone, particularly a member of the opposite sex, to admire).

From the first moment I saw her, I wanted to snatch her up and drive back to New York and throw her in front of my dad and say, 'This! This is what you are so afraid of and have been running from for the past twelve years. *This* tiny little girl in pigtails. You, sir, are a royal jackass.'

But I refrained, obviously. At least at that particular moment.

'Aw,' Tina said. 'She's so sweet.'

This, at least, confirmed that I wasn't the only one who found her to be completely adorable.

'Look, she's wearing high-tops with her school uniform, just like you used to wear combat boots!' Tina went on. 'Oh, wait . . . is she in trouble?'

It was true. As we sat there watching, a little blond girl (who looked not unlike a mini–Lana Weinberger circa thirteen years ago) marched up to my sister, put her hands on her hips, and said something. We couldn't hear what it was, because the bullet-proof windows were rolled up, and there was so much noise all around us, what with the shouting of excited children getting out of school for the day, and the whistle of the very angry volunteer parent who did not want us parked where we were parked (even though the engine was running) and all of the school bus engines and the cars of all the other parents.

But I could tell by the expression of the blond girl – and my sister's face – that it was something rude. I recognized the way Olivia looked, hurt and crestfallen and a little afraid. It was the way I'd always looked (I imagine – I couldn't have seen myself) when confronted by Lana Weinberger, back in the days before she'd mellowed with age.

Suddenly a group of kids gathered around the two girls, blocking them from our view.

'What in the wide world of [REDACTED]?' mused Lilly.

'I believe,' Lars said, 'what we are observing is what is known in America as a *throw down*.'

It was true! Through a gap in the circle the children had formed around my sister and her frenemy, I could see that the blond girl looked like she was about to rip Olivia's hair out.

However much they're paying teachers these days, it is not enough. Middle-schoolers are *animals*. (I don't mean my sister, of course. She is a sweet perfect angel. Well, almost.)

Lars reached instinctively for his ankle holster.

'Lars, no!' I cried. 'They are *children*, not Genovian ex-pats protesting the use of GMOs in their orange juice. I will handle this.'

Because really, when your long-lost little sister is about

to get beat up right in front of you on the playground, you have no choice but to come to her rescue. What else was I supposed to do? I don't see how anyone can blame me.

But of course with my possibly broken foot it was a bit hard to get out of the limo, especially given that my bodyguard is trained not only to keep me from being the victim of assassinations, but to keep me from preventing other people from being assassinated.

'Princess,' Lars said, grabbing my arm as I dove for the closest door handle. 'Really. You must allow me to—'

'Lars, you already smashed the aunt against a wall. Let me take care of the niece.'

'And end up with another broken foot?'

'They're *children*.'

He pointed out that the girls on the popular television show *Pretty Little Liars* are children too, which revealed:

- Lars watches *Pretty Little Liars*.

- Human Rights Watch should probably be keeping an eye on public and private schools all over America because they seem to be breeding enough child murderers that several popular television shows have been based on the subject. There's also one on Lifetime called *Child Killers*, not to mention MTV's *Teen Wolf* and CW's *Vampire Diaries* (although admittedly the latter two feature paranormal entities).

Meanwhile, Tina was wailing, 'There are parents everywhere. Why aren't they doing anything to control their children?'

It was true. All these moms in yoga pants and Tory Burch slides were chatting with one another while sipping lattes grandes, their gazes focused – I hate to admit – on the long black stretch limo with the tiny Genovian flags flying from it (why, oh, why didn't I remove them when I first thought of it?), instead of what was happening beneath their noses.

Now that I think back on it, only Lilly had the common sense to say, 'Uh, Mia, do you really think you should go out there? If you do, someone's going to snap a photo of it and post it to social media, and then the next thing you know, everyone in the whole world is going to know that—'

But like a fool, I left the car without listening to the rest. Because by that time, the little blond girl had hold of my sister's left braid, and there was *no way* I was going to stand for that kind of nonsense.

I threw open my car door and came striding across the schoolyard, calling Olivia's name. It took a minute for any of the children to notice me, because they were too busy chanting the words *Fight, fight, fight.*

But one by one they all did, and when they did, they stopped what they were doing, including the blond girl, who released Olivia's hair and stared at me, dumbfounded.

It's not every day, I suppose, that the Princess of Genovia gets out of a limo in front of your school.

'Olivia?' I said, when I finally reached her.

She stared up at me through the thick lenses of her glasses. It was pretty clear she, along with the little blond girl and most of the kids in the circle around them, knew who I was. I have to say, much as I complain about it, there are certain advantages sometimes to being royal.

'Oh,' Olivia said in a very polite voice, releasing the front of the blond girl's blouse and adjusting her now very messed up braid. 'Hi. Yes, that's me.'

'Er,' I said.

What do you say to your long lost sister upon meeting her for the first time?

Suddenly I became aware of all the gazes – and cell phone camera lenses – that were suddenly upon us. It was only then that I realized Lilly was right: it had been a very bad idea for me to get out of the car. I should have sent Lilly to break up the fight. Or Tina. Tina knew much more about tween girls than any of us, and was also nearly a doctor, or had at least studied child psychology.

'Hi,' I said, feeling a nervous sweat break out beneath my hairline, even though, for such a sunny day in May, it was not particularly warm. 'I'm, uh, Mia Thermopolis.' I had never felt so uncomfortable saying my name in my entire life. 'Your aunt Catherine said it would be all right for me to pick you up from school today.'

The little girl eyed me dubiously through her glasses. I could see why she might find this entire scenario a little on the shady side.

'Oh,' I said, suddenly remembering. 'Here's a note she signed, saying so.'

I was glad Lilly had thought of this at the last minute, and asked Olivia's aunt to sign it, as well. There are advantages to having a best friend who wants to be a lawyer, even one who wants to go into something as boring as contract law, though Lilly says contract law is *not* boring, but the backbone of all legal practice, the way mystery novels are the backbone of all literature. Murder breaks a contract with society, which only justice can set right again.

'Would you like to come with me?' I asked as I handed Olivia the note.

Olivia didn't exactly jump at the chance to climb in the Princess of Genovia's limo, even to get away from someone who was threatening to beat the crap out of her. Perhaps Olivia had not been in as dire circumstances as I'd thought. With dignified calm, she unfolded the note and read it carefully.

There was complete silence from the kids all around us as she did this, although I could hear several of them breathing, including a few who tried to crowd close to read the note over Olivia's shoulder (and mine – well, really my elbows, since the children were so short). I tried gently to shove them away, but they would not budge.

Most children are lovely, but up close some of them are not at all tidy (I don't mean my sister, of course).

'Thank you,' Olivia said, gravely folding the note back up and tucking it into her backpack. 'I'd like to go with you very much.'

Scooooooooore!

'Great!' I said, and snatched up her hand to turn

around and walk back toward the limo before she could change her mind. By that time both Lars and Halim had caught up with me, and had squeezed through the crowd to flank us on either side, busily scanning the school yard for RoyalRabbleRouser or any other enemies of state who might have heard of my sudden arrival in Cranbrook and shown up to rid the world of me. 'Let's go.'

I knew whatever I'd interrupted between her and the little blond girl had been mega-intense, but I wasn't going to ask about it until we were safely inside the car and many miles away, if ever. The last thing I expected was the blond girl – who'd begun trailing after us, along with the rest of the kids – to do so.

'Excuse me,' she said, in a high-pitched voice, 'but is it true that you're Olivia's sister?'

I was so shocked I nearly walked right into Lars, who was barking, 'Make a hole!' at all the curious moms who'd gathered around to stare. How could this little girl possibly have found out such an intimate family secret? And so fast? Had Aunt Catherine been making calls, despite the nondisclosure agreement Lilly had made her sign? Is that what all those yoga-pant-wearing mothers were talking about with one another behind the lids of their lattes grandes? That I was related to one of their kids' classmates?

If so, I was completely canceling that check the minute we got into the car.

'Uh,' I said, yanking on Olivia's hand to quicken her pace. But of course *I* was the one who was slowing us down by all my limping. 'Who are you, exactly?'

'That's Annabelle,' Olivia said with a world-weary sigh.

'My father is her uncle's lawyer,' Annabelle explained in a snotty tone, as if I were a moron for not knowing it. Apparently everyone in Cranbrook, New Jersey, knew that Annabelle's father was Olivia's uncle's lawyer, and I should have, too. 'He's the highest-ranked personal-injury lawyer in Cranbrook. My father says Olivia is related to you. I didn't believe it at first, of course, but now that you're here . . .'

Her voice trailed off suggestively.

Now that I was there, whatever Annabelle had been told had been confirmed.

And despite the confidentiality agreement Lilly had just had Olivia's aunt sign, the news would soon be spread all over the little town of Cranbrook, New Jersey, and a short time after that, the world. Every cell-phone camera in the entire drop-off area of the school was trained on Olivia and me, including ones belonging to the bus drivers. Even the mean lady with the whistle had stopped blowing it and was now pointing her iPhone at us.

That's when I knew. I should have stayed in the car instead of performing a wonderfully selfless act of sisterly charity by saving Olivia myself. I should have done what my dad had been doing all these years, and 'followed the map.'

Why hadn't I been a good little princess bride and gone to lunch with the crisis management team like it had said to on the itinerary? I was only creating a *bigger* crisis for them to clean up, and ruining my sister's life. Nothing was ever going to be the same for her, just as nothing had ever been the same for me after that day my father had taken me to lunch at the Plaza Hotel and told me I was the heir to the throne of Genovia, and a short time later the news had become public and I'd been required to be followed by a security team everywhere I went.

On the other hand, things haven't exactly turned out that terribly for me either.

Three things I'm grateful for:

1. I get to do what I love – make the world a better place by drawing attention to causes that matter to me (well, on a good day. Today would not be an example of that).

2. I have wonderful friends, who are always there to support and help me when I need them.

3. I'm marrying the man I love.

Oh, I've thought of a fourth one! I've already stopped my sister from getting punched in the face (I think. She hasn't *quite* explained exactly what was going on there. I'm hoping we'll get to that soon).

Hopefully, I might be able to continue to make other things better for her, too.

'I'm sorry, Annabelle,' I said to Olivia's little nemesis

in my most princessy tone. 'But this is a private family matter. I'm afraid I don't have time to chat today. Goodbye.'

Then I squeezed my sister's hand and tried to quicken our pace, though it was difficult, given my probably broken (but most likely only sprained) foot.

I have to say, it was quite satisfying to see Annabelle's stunned expression at my reply, but much more so to see Olivia's triumphant one.

But I didn't get to enjoy it long, since Lars was soon tapping the Bluetooth headset he keeps in his ear at all times, and saying, 'Er, Princess,' over the top of Olivia's head so she couldn't hear. 'Police.'

'Someone called the *police*?' My eye began twitching even more than usual. 'But why? We haven't done anything wrong.'

'Well,' Lars said as Halim hurried forward to open the passenger door for us. 'That would be a matter of opinion. Inciting a riot. Making a public nuisance. The uncle might feel differently than his wife about us taking the girl, who has been a significant source of income for some time . . .'

I hadn't thought of that.

Olivia must have overheard – or felt the compulsive tightening of my grip on her hand – since she looked up with concern and asked, 'Is everything all right?'

'Everything is fine!' I practically yelled. 'We just need to go now.' Then I began pulling her with renewed energy toward the limo, which must have been humiliating for her since she is, in fact, twelve and even Rocky objects to having his hand held, and he's nine.

'Back, please,' Lars was barking at everyone who was trying to crowd too close to us, attempting to snap selfies with themselves and either me or Olivia. 'Please give the princess room. No, no photos, sorry – no selfies—'

It was terrifying, and not just because I recently read online that the leading cause of lice transmission is selfies, from kids leaning their heads against other kids' heads, providing a perfect highway of hair on which the lice can transport themselves.

I imagined it was even more terrifying for poor Olivia, who isn't used to it. Even the lady with the whistle lowered it long enough to lift her cell phone to say, in a nasal voice, 'Can I have a photo with the two of you?'

Lars flung out a rock-solid arm.

'No,' he said, nearly knocking the phone from her hands.

'Well!' the woman cried, offended. 'See if *I* ever come to visit Genovia!'

'No one wants you there,' Lars informed her (I thought this a bit harsh).

Once we were all safely inside the limo, though, and Lars had pulled the door closed behind him, Olivia looked more thrilled than upset. She bounced around on the seats, looking out at the children who were plastering themselves against the tinted windows (we could see out, but they could not see in). It was a bit like something out of a boy-band documentary.

François gunned the engine and tried to pull out, but a roar of protest erupted from the children (not unlike the sound I once heard several years ago while visiting Iceland, and a volcano there exploded). Olivia's classmates still had their hands and faces pressed against all the windows, flattening themselves against the limo in an effort to keep us from leaving.

'What are they doing?' I cried, horrified.

Olivia shrugged. 'Nothing. They're just excited. Not many celebrities visit Cranbrook Middle School. Actually, you're the first.'

'Oh. I see.'

If the enormity of what I'd just done had not sunk in before, it did then.

Fortunately, we were able to escape without further incident by François applying a special horn Grandmère had had installed against the wishes and advice of everyone – it plays the first chords of the Genovian anthem at near-deafening decibels. It caused the children to unpeel themselves from the limo and scamper away in alarm.

But Lord only knows what the police found in the school yard when they arrived after we'd gone (we heard the sirens, but in the distance, after we'd already made our escape to the exit ramp to the highway, thank God).

'Olivia,' I said, after we'd had a chance to catch our breath. 'I'm very, very sorry about this. I did not mean for you to find out this way that you're – that we're—'

'It's okay,' Olivia said. She didn't look the least bit upset. Her gaze had been roving around the interior of the car, lighting up as it landed on the minibar, where there were full cans of soda on display as mixers for Grandmère's alcohol, not to mention bags of chips and other assorted favorite snacks of my grandmother's. 'I already knew. Annabelle told me.'

'Yes, I realize that. But that's what I mean. It shouldn't have happened that way. I'm *very* sorry about that.'

'That's okay,' Olivia said. 'This is fun.'

'*Fun?*' I glanced uneasily at my adult companions. What had been fun about any of what just happened? 'Really?'

'Yes,' Olivia said. 'This is my first time in a limo. Do those go on?' She pointed at the fiber-optic lighting in the limousine's ceiling, which Grandmère had had installed because she enjoyed being bathed in the most flattering colors at all times.

'Yes,' I said. 'Those do go on.'

Like magic, we were all suddenly bathed in a rosy hue from both the sides and roof of the car.

'Cool!' Olivia cried, smiling broadly, especially as François, who'd overheard us, had chosen the 'twinkle' effect, so the rose color began to turn to purple, then to blue.

When you ride in limos all the time, it's hard to remember that to some people – especially a twelve-year-old – it's a new, exciting experience. That's the great thing about being twelve.

'So,' I said to Olivia, 'I'm sure you must have a lot of questions—'

'Yes, I do.' She looked at me very intently. 'Is it really true?'

'That we're sisters? Yes, it's really true. I'm so sorry you found out this way, but it's very, very true—'

'No, is it true what that paper you showed me said? That you have my aunt's permission to take me to any destination of my choosing?'

I threw Lilly a startled look. The truth was, I hadn't read the agreement Olivia's aunt had signed.

'Er, yes,' I said, when I saw that Lilly was nodding. 'Yes, it's really true. Why? Is there somewhere you'd like to go?'

'Yes,' she said, her dark eyes sparkling. 'To meet my dad.'

I'm not sure what I'd expected her to say, but not that. I don't know why, since it should have been obvious.

Those four little words, however, momentarily robbed me of breath with their sweet simplicity.

Of course. *Of course* she wanted to meet her dad. How could I have been so stupid? What else was a little girl who'd never known her father – never really had a parent at all – going to want?

'Oh. Right,' I said, my heart rolling over in my chest. Up until that second, I hadn't even thought about where we were going. *Away,* was all I'd said to François. Just take us away . . . away from that awful school and that terrible Annabelle and all those kids throwing themselves against the car and Aunt Catherine and Cranbrook.

But clearly I needed to take her to meet her father, and right that second, before I did another thing.

I wasn't sure Dad was going to agree, but I didn't care.

'Of *course*. François? New York City, please.'

He nodded. 'Yes, Your Highness.'

Olivia looked a little nervous at this development. 'Wait . . . my dad is in New York City?'

'He is,' Lilly said, leaning forward to thrust her right hand toward Olivia. 'Only sixty-four miles away, and you never even knew it, did you? Lilly Moscovitz, by the way, but you can call me Aunt Lilly. I'm your sister's cool friend.'

'Hey!' Tina protested.

'Lilly's teasing you,' I explained to Olivia as she politely shook Lilly's hand. 'All my friends are cool.'

'Not true,' Lilly said as she continued to pump Olivia's hand. 'I'm the one you're going to want to come to with all your questions about boys—'

'No.' I reached out and disengaged their hands, laying Olivia's back in her lap. 'Do *not* go to her.'

'Come to *me*,' Tina said firmly. 'I'm your aunt Tina. I'm in medical school.'

'Okay,' Olivia said faintly. 'But I'm only twelve.'

Hoping to distract her – and myself, since I'd been feeling a little teary-eyed since she'd asked about meeting her father – I asked Olivia, 'Would you like a soda?' It was the only thing I could think of to say. Who wouldn't be thirsty after an ordeal like the one we'd just gone through in the parking lot?

'Yes, please,' Olivia said, looking bewildered by her exchange with my friends . . . and no wonder, since they're psychotic. 'So we're going to New York City *right now*?'

'Yes,' I said as I was pouring her soda. 'That's not a problem, is it?'

She shook her head, her braids flying.

'I guess not. Dad always said we would meet someday, but not until I was much older.'

I nearly spilled the soda. 'He did? When did he say that?'

'In his letters,' she informed me matter-of-factly. 'We've been writing letters to each other for a long time.'

I couldn't believe it. My dad, who'd been so freaked out the night before about being Olivia's sole parent, had been in communication with her this entire time? Well, written communication, but communication just the same. He'd led me to think horrible things about him – that he'd allowed this child to live in total ignorance of his existence – that weren't even true!

'He gives me all kinds of advice,' Olivia prattled on, accepting the soda I passed her. She certainly isn't shy, which is definitely a positive if you're going to be thrust into the international spotlight. 'Like he said it was good to keep a diary. He told me it really helps to write down your feelings when you get overwhelmed.'

'Gee, I wonder where he got that idea,' I murmured.

'What do you mean?' she asked curiously.

I hadn't meant for her to overhear me.

'Oh, nothing. My mom told me to do the same thing – write down my feelings in a diary when I thought I was getting overwhelmed – when I was about your age.'

'Really? Your mom is still alive?'

'Yes. She lives in New York City, too.'

'With our dad?'

My heart, which had been on the verge of melting all

afternoon, turned liquid, especially when I glanced at her face and saw that her expression had suddenly become guarded. I had no idea what Dad had told her in his letters, but obviously nothing about me, and clearly very little about himself.

'No, Olivia,' I said. 'Our dad and my mom split up a long time ago – right after I was born. Dad is single. He doesn't live with anyone.'

'Except his mother,' Lilly added darkly.

Olivia didn't seem to hear her, however. She said, staring out the window at the trees whizzing by along I-95, 'It makes sense that he doesn't live with anyone. Probably the death of my mother, who was very beautiful, still haunts him to this day. That's most likely why he never wanted to see me before, because I look so much like her, and the sight of me would be too painful a reminder of his lost love.'

I was so astonished by this, I didn't know how to reply. I don't think I'd ever seen Lilly clap a hand over her mouth so quickly to keep herself from bursting into laughter.

'Oh!' Tina whispered. 'The sweet thing. The sweet little thing!'

Olivia looked away from the window and back toward us, completely oblivious to the fact that she'd sent one of us into near-hysterical gales of laughter and the other into near-tears. I was torn between both.

Olivia's expression was stormy. 'I understand now why Aunt Catherine said I'm not allowed to go there.'

'Go where?' I asked. 'To meet your father? Your

aunt and I talked about that, Olivia, and we decided that it was okay.' Well, not in so many words, but whatever.

'No, go to New York,' she said. She took a big swallow of soda. It was clear she liked the stuff. We had so much in common already. 'My aunt always said New York is too dirty and dangerous for kids. But I can see now that she probably never wanted me to go there because I might run into my dad, and then I'd find out I'm really a princess, and seeing me would probably cause him emotional damage.'

I thought it best to avoid this last topic – especially since it sent Lilly into peals of laughter that she didn't even bother to hide – and instead asked her what she wanted to be when she grew up (which was both ridiculous and pathetic, because obviously now she's going to be a princess, and I've told myself a million times to stop asking kids what they want to be when they grow up and here I was doing it to my own sister).

But Olivia was all too happy to show me, flipping through her 'diary' – actually a notebook – where she'd sketched many cats, horses, and – for unknown reasons – kangaroos.

'I want to be a wildlife illustrator,' she said, explaining that this was one of the reasons she'd always wanted to go to New York City. 'They're the artists who draw all the animals on the plaques outside the exhibits at the zoos and on websites and in books and stuff. It's a dying industry, thanks to photography, but I'm pretty sure I can make it because I've always gotten really good grades in art. My teacher says I've just got to keep practising.'

'Well,' I said, impressed. I mean, really, how many other twelve-year-old girls want to be wildlife illustrators? My little sister is obviously superior. 'I think it's about time you got to go to New York City, then, because we need more wildlife illustrators in this world.'

'We really do,' Tina burst out excitedly.

'Definitely,' Lilly agreed. 'You can meet your grandmother, too. I know she's going to be very excited to meet *you*, and hear all about wildlife illustration.'

I shot her a warning look, but it was too late. Olivia was already asking what kind of cooking our grandmother enjoys. 'My best friend Nishi's grandmother makes authentic Indian samosas and chicken tikka masala every Sunday night.'

Lilly choked on the cocktail she'd prepared for herself. 'Yeah, Mia,' she said. 'Tell your sister about the home-cooked meals your grandma loves to make on Sunday night. What's her favorite ingredient again? Bourbon?'

'No,' I said, more to Lilly than to Olivia. 'Our grandmother doesn't cook. But she has many other talents. She's very . . .'

How to describe Grandmère? For once, words failed me. And that's saying a lot, because besides filling pages and pages of diaries like this one, I got As on every essay test I took in college, and occasionally they were described by my professors as examples of 'exemplary work.' Well, okay, once.

'Your grandmother is very *knowledgeable*,' Tina said, finally.

Well, that's certainly true.

'That sounds good,' Olivia said, pulling a sheet of paper from her backpack, which seemed to be filled with endless amounts of them. 'Because we've been doing genealogy in my biology class, and I had to leave all these spaces blank on my work sheet because I didn't know the answers. I was going to write to Dad to ask, but I knew by the time I heard back, the work sheet would be overdue. Maybe my grandmother could help me fill them out?'

I looked down at the work sheet. 'Who Am I?' it read across the top in bold lettering.

Lots of people go through life not having the slightest idea what names to put in the blanks on their 'Who Am I?' work sheets, and they aren't bothered in the least by it. What does it even matter, anyway? You can get your blood tested now and find out what you have the genetic tendency for.

But it seemed terrible that my own sister shouldn't know.

'And the truth is,' Olivia was going on, prattling with perfect ease, like she'd known me her entire life, 'I sort of would like to know a few things for my own personal interest, like if diabetes runs in my family, and heart disease. Aunt Catherine never would tell me anything about my dad, just that he was too busy to take care of me because his work was so important. I understand that now, he has to run a whole country. But maybe' – Olivia had dug a pen from her backpack, along with the work sheet – 'you know some of these answers? It's due tomorrow, and it's worth twenty-five percent of my total grade.'

'Oh, God,' I heard Tina whisper. I think about the aunt saying 'Dad was too busy' to take care of Olivia, which caused my heart to break a little as well.

Lilly, however, only shook her head and said, 'Yep. She's your sister all right, Thermopolis,' probably as a result of Olivia's concern about the possible diseases she might have inherited from the Renaldo side of the family, which I frowned at her for, both because Olivia's worries are well founded (who isn't worried about diabetes?) and also because I am *not* that much of a hypochondriac.

- *Note to self:* Remember to look up later on iTriage what could be causing my boobs to hurt so much. They've been killing me for days. Could it be a side effect of all the magnesium?

'Well, fortunately I'm here to help you now,' I said to Olivia. 'Shall we get started?'

'Yes!' Olivia smiled so broadly that I only just noticed the bright turquoise bands she has on her back teeth. 'That would be great!'

So that's the homework we're doing. Filling in all the missing information on her 'Who Am I?' work sheet as François drives us back to New York so that Olivia can meet her father (and grandmother), and maybe even go to the Central Park Zoo to see some of the wildlife illustrations there, if there's time.

- *Note to self:* Are there even illustrations on the plaques there? I've spent a lot of time at the zoo,

but I've never noticed – because I was always
too busy feeling traumatized from finding out
I was a princess (or dealing with various other
crises) – the signage.

I'm letting Olivia eat all the junk food she wants
out of the minibar, and not just because she said, 'Aunt
Catherine doesn't let me have sugar.'

(Tina disapproves, since 'sugar really isn't that good
for children, or anyone,' but as Lilly put it, 'How often
do you find out you're a princess? The kid ought to
celebrate while she can, since I imagine her entire world
is about to fall apart very, very soon.')

This, like the rest of the day – this whole week,
actually – is probably going to be a disaster.

But oh, well.

What else is new?

4:35 p.m., Wednesday, May 6
Limo back to New York City
Rate the Royals Rating: 7

Michael just phoned. It hasn't taken long at all for the [REDACTED] to hit the fan.

Well, I sort of suspected that already, since Dominique stopped screaming long enough when *she* phoned earlier to say:

'I will take care of everything. Do not speak to anyone. Do not stop the car to eat, or even to go to the *toilettes*. Do not answer your telephone unless eet eez someone you know.'

'Uh . . .' I'd said. 'Is there anything I can do to help?'

'No, you have done quite enough,' Dominique said crisply, and hung up.

Publicists are a lot like cats: super lovable until you cross them. Then the claws come out.

Michael's the one who let me know what was going on:

'Are you aware that someone posted a photo of you with a child they're calling "Princess Mia's illegitimate sister" on social media a little while ago, and the post has been picked up by just about every news outlet in the western hemisphere?'

'Ugh,' I said. I couldn't show too much emotion about it with Olivia sitting there beside me. We'd finished her 'Who Am I?' work sheet and had begun her math homework (or rather, Olivia has begun it, with Lilly and

Tina giving her occasional help when she asks. I have no idea how to multiply and divide fractions. Why do they even make children learn this when there are calculators? Although some of them – like Olivia, apparently – want to do it).

'Oh, well,' I went on. 'It was bound to happen sooner or later.'

'Mia, I just had two agents from the RGG show up in my office,' Michael said. 'They say I've been assigned extra security due to anonymous threats from people who don't approve of interracial relationships that result in illegitimate princesses.'

'Well, that is just *ridiculous*.'

I glanced over at Lars but saw that, like any highly trained bodyguard, he was already in contact with the office, murmuring swiftly in French about the *danger public*.

'Mia, I know it's ridiculous, that's not why I'm calling. I'm worried about *you*. Where are you?'

'Michael, I'm fine, I'm still in the car. I'm so, so sorry about all this—'

'Don't be sorry. Obviously it isn't your fault. But where are you going?'

'Home.' I tried to keep my tone breezy so as not to alarm anyone else in the car. 'Olivia wants to meet her father.' Olivia looked up at the sound of her name and smiled at me. I smiled back. Breezy. Everything was breezy.

'Her father?' Michael echoed. 'Do you even know where your father is right now?'

'No, as a matter of fact I don't. I've been trying to

reach him all day, but he won't pick up my calls or return my messages—'

'Of course not, cell phones are prohibited in the courthouse. Everyone knows that. Haven't you ever served on jury duty?'

'No,' I said, a little defensively. 'Remember? I wanted to but they waived my summons because they were afraid it would be too much of a media circus if I showed up – wait, he's in *court*?'

'Yes, you didn't know? I just saw a clip of him on New York One, headed up the courthouse steps with his lawyers. His case was finally called today. He wore his ceremonial dress uniform, including his sword. They confiscated it, of course.'

Obviously I didn't know. No one ever tells me anything.

I signaled to Lilly to check her phone. She did so, casually keeping the screen from Olivia's view. Olivia had informed us that her aunt Catherine said she isn't 'allowed to have a phone,' though her stepcousins, Justin and Sara, each have one, as well as a tablet and laptop.

(The list of items Olivia is not allowed, besides sugar, cell phones, and trips to New York City, is long and somewhat curious, and makes me question her aunt's parenting skills somewhat, although I realize, not having children, I have no right to judge. The list includes:

No pierced ears.

No bedtime any later than 9:30 p.m., 'even on weekends.'

No books above a sixth-grade reading level, which is problematic since Olivia 'is reading at an eighth-grade level,' or so she proudly informed us.

No pets of any kind, as 'Uncle Rick is allergic.'

No shoes inside the house.

No friends over, as 'they might bother Uncle Rick.'

No going online, except for homework.

No video games – too violent.

No gluten – although neither Olivia nor anyone else in the O'Toole household has been diagnosed with celiac disease or a gluten intolerance.

No television shows that haven't been rated okay for kids eleven or under.

No Boris P. 'Too sexy.')

Tina was so profoundly upset by this list (especially the part about no adult books and Boris being considered 'too sexy') that she handed Olivia her phone, which was encrusted with pink crystals, and of course loaded with Boris P. videos.

'Here,' Tina said. 'You can have this until you get your own.'

Olivia was delightedly shocked, and cried, 'Thank you, Aunt Tina!'

I was shocked, too, but probably not for the same reason as my sister.

'Tina,' I hissed. 'You don't have to give her your phone. We'll get her one. Besides, what are you going to use?'

Tina pulled another phone from her enormous Tiffany-blue tote. 'Don't worry about it. That's my game and music phone. This is my *real* phone.' This one was Bedazzled in zebra-stripe crystals.

Lilly turned her own phone toward me. She's trying hard not to swear in my little sister's presence, so all she said was, 'Zoinks.'

The main page to TMZ (now no longer one of the nation's leading gossip sites, but its leading breaking-news site) had split its screen so that one half showed a photo of my dad outside the Manhattan courthouse, and the other a photo of me taken outside Cranbrook Middle School, surrounded by Olivia's classmates.

'Prince Meets the Judge,' screamed my dad's half.

'Princess Meets Her Sister?' screamed mine.

My heart dropped.

'Mia? Are you still there?' Michael asked in my ear.

'Of course I'm still here,' I said.

'Have you and your father ever considered coordinating your efforts?' he asked. 'Because if you teamed up, you might possibly be able to take over the world.'

A little harsh, but not totally off base. 'Point taken.

In my own defense, though, I never meant in a million years for any of this to happen—'

'Of course you didn't,' he said, his tone softening. 'You never do. So, what's she like?'

I glanced at Olivia, who was still bent over her fractions, the tip of her tongue sticking out slightly from between her teeth.

'Amazing,' I said warmly.

'Good. Why don't I try to make a few phone calls and see if I can reach your dad? There's a guy who plays World of Warcraft who works in the IT department at the courthouse. I think I can get your message delivered.'

'Oh my God, could you? That would be great—'

My heart got the rosy glow in it that it always did when Michael did or said something particularly wonderful – or even when he simply walked into the room. He really is the most spectacular man on earth.

Then I remembered something.

'Oh, but if you do reach his lawyers and they ask you about signing a prenup,' I added in a whisper, 'just ignore them. I told them we weren't doing that.'

'I will do no such thing,' he said, sounding offended. 'A prenup makes good fiscal sense.'

'Michael!'

'What? It's a good idea for both of us to protect our personal assets.'

'Oh, God.' I dropped my head into one of my hands. 'Your mother was right.'

'My mother? About what?'

'She said we marry our parents. "A good idea for us

to protect our personal assets?" You sound exactly like my dad.'

'Well, your dad's not always wrong, Mia. And you *are* always trying to help people. Who does *that* sound like?'

I flung a glance across the length of the limo at Lilly, who was now bathed in sapphire blue from the fiber-optic lights while she bent over Olivia's homework.

'Not your sister,' I whispered in a horrified voice.

'No, you nut,' he said. 'My parents, who are psychotherapists, one of the ultimate helping professions. You always want to help everyone. It's one of the many reasons I fell in love with you, but also one of the reasons you're always getting yourself into trouble.'

'Well, I can assure you,' I said, 'after today, I'm quitting.'

'I'll believe that when I see it. Look, I'll text you as soon as I hear anything. In the meantime, if you get pulled over by the cops, don't let Lars show off his gun to them.'

'Obviously,' I said.

After we'd hung up and I crept back to my original seat, Tina looked at me worriedly and mouthed, 'Everything okay?'

I gave her a reassuring smile. Of *course* everything's okay. It's me! When *hasn't* everything been okay?

- Found out I'm a princess of a country no one's ever heard of, but everyone wants to move to? Check!

- Getting married in less than three months on live international television and don't yet have a dress, or anything else ready? Check!

- Discovered I have a long-lost sister? Check!

- Exposed her identity to the entire world by showing up at the wrong time, getting my picture posted on every website in the world, and ruining her life? Check, check, *and* check!

5:32 p.m., Wednesday, May 6
Traffic jam on Houston Street
Rate the Royals Rating: 1

When I phoned just now to say that I was on my way to her apartment with her long-lost grandchild, Grandmère's reaction was unsurprising but still not satisfactory.

'But I don't even have my eyebrows on! I can't meet my only other grandchild with no eyebrows.'

I told her that we still have to drop off Tina and Lilly at their respective domiciles, which should give her plenty of time to draw on her eyebrows.

Olivia, who'd been eavesdropping, asked brightly, 'Our grandmother likes to draw, too? That's so great!' and held up her notebook. 'We have something in common already!'

When she finds out all Grandmère likes to draw are eyebrows (and from her Swiss bank account, of course), she's going to be crushed, but I tried to sound encouraging. 'Yeah! It's great!'

'Is that her?' Grandmère demanded. 'I cannot believe you've done this, Amelia. It's going to ruin all my careful plans.'

'Yes, it's her,' I said, then switched to French. Never in a million years did it occur to me I'd be using my ability to speak French – learned over the many summers I spent visiting my grandmother, then perfected with Mademoiselle Klein in high school – to keep my secret sister from knowing what I was saying about her over the phone to our grandmother. 'And that's a nice attitude

323

to take about your grandchild. Why don't you have your eyebrows on? It's cocktail time.'

'I, er, had an afternoon visitor, and somehow they must have become smudged—'

'Oh, sure, *somehow*. Who was it this time? Please don't say Chris Martin. You have got to leave that poor man alone.'

'José de la Rive, if you must know, though I don't see why you—'

'You were *making love* with the director of the Royal Genovian Guard while your son was in court?'

'Amelia, must you be so coarse? José merely stopped by to share with me the very interesting results of his continuing investigation into Olivia's uncle's personal finances, and I suppose one thing led to another, and before I knew it, we'd—'

'*Continuing?* I didn't know he'd *begun* a secret investigation into Olivia's uncle's personal finances.'

'What do you think the director of the Royal Genovian Guard does all day, Amelia, besides check for bombs along my shopping routes? In any case, he discovered something else very important. Are you aware that Ivan's grandfather – my own sweet Count Igor – owned a controlling interest in Monarch of the Seas Cruise Lines, one of the largest cruise-ship companies in the world?'

'Uh, no.'

'And that when Igor passed, he left his controlling interest in the company to his only grandson, Ivan?'

I was aghast. 'But, Grandmère, that would mean—'

'Of course. He never disclosed that conflict of

interest, did he? And while running on a platform of economic reform that included a promise to dredge the harbor to allow for larger – and more – cruise ships. Naughty, naughty boy.'

I was stunned. 'But that's criminal!'

'Of course it is, Amelia,' Grandmère purred. 'That's why José's on his way to the airport right now to catch a flight back to Genovia and meet with Count Ivan. He's going to ask the count whether he prefers to quietly withdraw from the race – for medical reasons, I think – or face public humiliation and arrest.'

'Don't tell me. José's going to cause the reasons for Ivan's medical withdrawal if he doesn't agree to go quietly, isn't he?'

'Don't be so cynical, Amelia, it isn't becoming in a young bride. Now tell me about my granddaughter. What is she like? Will she make a trainable flower girl? I already asked some of your second cousins to fill that role, but as you know they're not particularly telegenic, having inherited your grandfather's troubling jawline. You were so fortunate to have inherited mine, Amelia. What about your sister? Is her jaw shaped normally?'

'Grandmère, stop. What about Dad? Have you heard anything from him?'

'Your father's on his way here. He was only given a fine by the judge. And they returned his sword.'

'Grandmère, that's wonderful!'

'Yes. You would think that – plus the news about Ivan – would make him a very happy man. But I'm afraid he was quite abrupt with me on the telephone. I suppose your antics today have spoiled his celebratory mood a bit.'

'*My* antics? More like his antics twelve years ago.'

'What was that, Amelia?' she demanded. 'I've told you before not to mumble, it's unbecoming.'

'Nothing. He's not seriously upset with me, is he? Because if so, he knows where to reach me.'

'He's far too busy fielding calls from the deputy prime minister about his illegitimate daughter. Why that woman can't deal with the press herself is beyond me.'

'Um, maybe because Olivia is *Dad's* daughter, and they're questions *he* should be answering?'

Grandmère sniffed. 'Well, she shouldn't have chosen to be deputy prime minister of Genovia if she can't take the heat. She couldn't run a book club, let alone a country.'

'That's far from true, Grandmère, she graduated first in her class at the Sorbonne. And what do you know about book clubs, anyway? All you ever read anymore is the entertainment news from BuzzFeed.'

'Which is how I know someone spoke to that horrible Brian Fitzpatrick from Rate the Royals about all this. He's saying terrible things about your father while making *you* out to be some kind of saint.'

'Well, *I* don't have any publically unacknowledged children in New Jersey.' Still, it was surprising that Brian Fitzpatrick had anything nice to say about me considering the way I'd treated him the other day.

'Don't be fresh, Amelia, it isn't attractive. And now

326

Lazarres-Reynolds is saying the best way to handle the situation is for you to bring the child instead of Michael when you go on *Wake Up America* tomorrow morning. They don't want you to talk about the wedding anymore, they only want you to talk about *her*. They say it will be the best way to, uh, how did they put it? Oh, yes . . . come out ahead of the story.'

'Well, you can tell Lazarres-Reynolds from me that *that* will only happen over my dead body,' I said, throwing a quick, protective look at Olivia, who was now on her third bag of mini chocolate cookies and showing Tina how to draw a giraffe.

'I'll do no such thing,' Grandmère hissed in her scariest voice. 'And you're going to this benefit to raise heart-attack awareness tonight, as well. We've got to show the world that nothing is amiss. Dominique can send someone to fetch a gown for you to change into.'

'Uh,' I said. I'd totally forgotten the event at the W. 'No, Grandmère. I realize sudden cardiac death is an important issue, and moreover, it was my choice to bring awareness to it after Mr. Gianini passed away from it, but considering today's events, I feel the best thing to do is cancel and stay home with—'

She cut me off faster than Ian Ziering cuts sharks with chain saws midair.

'No one is interested in your feelings, Amelia. Lazarres-Reynolds is sending a representative over right now – one here, and one to the bohunk uncle's house – to start planning the offensive.'

'What offensive?'

'On the media! What on earth did you expect, Amelia? This revelation about your father was bound to bring him worldwide attention, and not the pleasant kind either!'

She was shouting so loudly I had to hold the phone away from my ear. I could tell everyone else in the car could hear her, because they all looked over at me inquiringly. Fortunately, she was shouting in her native French, so Olivia, at least, couldn't understand. I gave her an embarrassed shrug.

'Grandmothers,' I mouthed, and Olivia smiled, but it was clear from her slightly troubled expression that she knew something, at least, was up.

'Now do you understand why Genovia so desperately needs a large wedding right now, full of pageantry and elegance and cannon fire?' Grandmère continued to shout. 'Between this and the refugee crisis, I don't know how else we're going to get out of it, Amelia. This is our annus horribilis. Being a bride, particularly a princess bride, you can turn it all around by becoming a symbol of hope and beauty and joy.'

'Yes,' I said, wincing a little at the shrillness of her tone. 'I understand. But in the meantime I can't allow my little sister to be paraded around like a prizewinning show dog. I thought the whole point of the wedding was to *distract* the public from her existence—'

'It was, until you thrust her into the spotlight,' Grandmère said.

'I didn't mean to do that, but at least *someone* did the right thing and stepped up and—'

328

'Excuse me.'

I paused as a voice I recognized chimed in. Only it was my sister Olivia's voice, and it was speaking perfect French, and it shouldn't have been. I slowly turned my head to find her looking at me expectantly.

'Pardon me,' she said, again in perfect French. 'I don't mean to interrupt, but may I make a suggestion?'

My normally shaped jaw dropped.

'Who is that?' Grandmère demanded. 'Who is that speaking, Amelia?'

'Your other granddaughter,' I said. 'You better get your eyebrows on. You're going to need them.' I hung up on her, then stared some more at my sister. 'I'm sorry, what did you say?'

'The refugees,' Olivia said, this time in English. 'I'm sorry to have interrupted, but I couldn't help overhearing Grandma talking about them? And the cruise ships? Well, I have an idea that might help.'

I shook my head in astonishment. 'How could you have understood any of that?'

'Oh, I don't know, Mia,' Lilly said. She held up the notebook Olivia had been doodling in. 'Maybe because of the language class Olivia is taking. *French.*' Then she mouthed the words *you moron* over the top of my sister's head.

I felt sick to my stomach. 'Oh, wow. So you understood everything I was saying to Grand, er, ma, Olivia?'

'Not *all* of it,' Olivia admitted. 'You guys talk pretty fast. But I understood a lot of it. Definitely the part about the guy and the cruise ships. And that's when I started thinking, why don't you let the refugees live on the cruise ships until you can find them some better place to stay? That's what they did for refugees of Hurricane Julio. We saw a documentary about it in school.'

I stared at her some more. I've heard the expression *out of the mouths of babes* hundreds of times, but I'd never really understood it until that moment.

'Oh, Olivia,' I cried, joyously throwing my arms around her to hug her. 'Where have you been all my life?'

'Um,' she said, a bit startled, but hugging me back. 'New Jersey?'

I don't think I've laughed quite that hard in a long time. It felt good. Almost good enough to make me forget the throbbing pain in my foot, where her aunt had smashed it with a door.

After I released her, Olivia reached up to push her glasses back into place.

'What was *that* for?' she wanted to know, meaning the hug.

'You just solved a big royal headache,' I told her.

'I did?' she asked. A pleased smile crept across her face. 'That's great. How?'

'Thinking outside the box,' Lilly told her, since I'd gotten back on the phone, this time to text Madame Dupris. 'Finish your homework.'

'I wasn't thinking outside any box,' Olivia said. 'Sometimes I color outside the lines, though.'

'Keep doing it, kid,' Lilly advised. 'You'll go places.'

HRH Mia Thermopolis 'FtLouie' to Deputy Prime Minister Madame Cécile Dupris 'Le Grand Fromage'

Madame, you're going to hear some news from Monsieur le Directeur José de la Rive (about which I cannot go into detail at this time) that will be quite startling, but welcome. When you hear it, the proposal I'm about to write will make perfect sense:

When the time is right (you will know when), ask Ivan Renaldo to donate three cruise ships for the use of the Genovian government so that they may house the Qalifi refugees for a time period of no less than six months.

If he refuses, tell him that everything the Renaldo family knows about him will be made public.

This should, I trust, alleviate the refugee crisis for the present time, until we can come up with a more permanent solution.

XOXO
M

Deputy Prime Minister Madame Cécile Dupris 'Le Grand Fromage,' to HRH Mia Thermopolis 'FtLouie'

!!!
I am, as the Americans say, very gung ho about this and dying to know what it's all about, but for now will proceed as requested.

I was quite startled, Princess, to hear the news about your sister, but am quite gung ho about this as well. Any addition to the family is always pleasant, is it not?

XOXO
C

I'm not entirely sure Madame Dupris knows what *gung ho* means, but it's reassuring that we have one normal, intelligent person on the team, anyway, and might possibly pull this whole thing off, after all.

7:05 p.m., Wednesday, May 6
The Plaza Hotel
Rate the Royals Rating: 1

I don't know how I could have been so stupid. All the signs were there. I suppose I was ignoring them because I didn't want to have to face the truth.

But I can't ignore them anymore, especially after I hobbled into Grandmère's condo a little while ago and there stood *J. P. Reynolds-Abernathy IV*.

Well, he did say that after his latest movie was a flop, he'd had to take a job working for his uncle.

It's my own fault for not asking *what kind of job,* or recognizing that the *Reynolds* in Lazarres-Reynolds is the same Reynolds as in Reynolds-Abernathy IV.

Isn't this another kind of conflict of interest, though, not unlike Cousin Ivan's? J.P. really should have turned down this assignment when it was offered to him. *'Oh, no, she's my ex-girlfriend from high school. I couldn't possibly work for her family.'*

But no. To do that, J.P. would have to have developed some empathy, and why would that have happened? All the signs point to him having only gotten *more* manipulative since high school. He's already cornered me once in Grandmère's kitchen (where I hobbled to get some ice for my foot. I didn't want to bother anyone by asking for some), where he said in this completely sincere (fake) voice:

'Mia, I hope it doesn't bother you that I'm here. I thought about messaging you to let you know, but then I realized how insulting that would be, since we're both mature adults and what we had was so long ago – I mean, it was high school, after all. And you're engaged to Michael now, so it seemed hardly worth mentioning.'

'Ha ha!' I said breezily. 'Of course! Exactly.'

'So no worries, then,' J.P. said. 'Water under the bridge.'

Meanwhile, I'm not even sure his uncle's firm is competent at crisis managing. When François pulled up to the hotel, the entrance was a madhouse. Press was *everywhere,* trying to elbow their way to a prime spot in front of the red carpet (there really is a red carpet leading up the steps to the front doors of the Plaza Hotel, I guess to make guests feel like celebrities, which is all a lot of people want anymore).

'Ready?' Lars asked us, as François opened the door to the side of the limo. 'One, two, *three.*'

For Olivia's first time walking a red carpet, she did pretty well – much better than I would have at her age. She had her own cocky grace despite the flashes – which do blind you a bit – and the deafening noise, smiling and waving.

'Olivia, how does it feel to find out you were abandoned at birth by your rich white father?'

'Olivia, are you going to be in your sister's royal wedding?'

'Olivia, look over here!'

'Olivia, do you think they didn't acknowledge you before now because you're black?'

'Olivia, could you sign my cast?'

'Olivia, what's the first thing you're going to buy with all the money you're going to have?'

'Olivia, over here, honey!'

But I kept her hand in mine so she wouldn't be scared . . .

Although I don't think she actually was. When she reached the top of the stairs, she did the last thing any of us were expecting, which was to turn to take a quick photo (with the cell phone that Tina had given her) of all the press that was photographing her.

'Well,' Olivia explained, when we got inside and I looked at her questioningly, 'I want to remember this.'

I don't think she quite realizes that this isn't all going to vanish tomorrow. It's going to go on and on, forever. Of *course* she wants to remember it . . .

. . . unlike me, who'd give anything to forget it. In fact, I'd be drinking right now to numb the pain (and my memory), except that my foot hurts too much to get up and go to the liquor cabinet, and I'm certainly not going to ask J.P. to get me a drink, even though he's asked three times if he can 'get me anything.'

Yes, you can, J.P. You can get away from me.

I haven't had the nerve to tell Michael that J.P. is here (Michael texted to say he's on his way. His HELV is stuck in all the traffic outside, and the RGG won't allow him to get out and walk due to 'safety' concerns).

J.P. has never been one of Michael's favorite people. Michael even threatened to punch him once, but managed to restrain himself. I don't know if he'll have that kind of self-control now, seeing as how J.P. has grown a mustache (though not as nice as the one my dad used to have) and wears skinny jeans.

Shudder.

Of course there's one part of all this I *do* want to remember, and that's the look on Grandmère's face when she first opened the door to her condo and saw her only other grandchild (besides me).

I could tell she was touched, though she was trying hard not to show it. Her mouth was squeezed into a tiny frown (some of the muscles in her face are permanently frozen from all the Botox she's had shot into them, but she's still able to move most of her mouth to varying degrees).

'So this is she?' Grandmère asked grammatically correctly, if not exactly warmly.

'This is she, Grandmère,' I said, poking Olivia in the back. I'd coached her in the car on what to do and say when she met her grandmother, and she pulled it off perfectly . . . almost.

'It's so nice to meet you, Grandmoth – is that a miniature *poodle*?'

Olivia's curtsy wasn't very graceful to begin with, but she practically fell over herself when she saw the little white powder puff peeking around Grandmère's still shapely ankle (Grandmère is inordinately proud of the fact that her legs haven't gone).

'I love poodles!' Olivia cried. 'They're the most intelligent breed of dog. And they're also very excellent swimmers.'

I hadn't coached her to say *that*.

The tiny frown on Grandmère's face curled ever so slightly into a smile.

'Yes,' she said, trying but failing to sound cold. It's very difficult to speak coldly to a child expounding on the virtues of your favorite breed of dog. 'Poodles *are* very intelligent, aren't they?'

Then the two of them stood there going on about poodles. I'm not even kidding. It was like watching a couple of announcers at the Westminster Kennel Dog show, only one was a nine-hundred-year-old dowager princess from the Riviera, and the other was a twelve-year-old from New Jersey.

'My *other* granddaughter only likes cats,' Grandmère said, finally remembering I was standing there, and giving me the evil eye.

'I don't only like cats,' I protested. 'I've only ever had a cat. Grandmère, could we come in now? I hurt my foot earlier and it's very uncomfortable and I'd really like to sit down—'

Grandmère opened the door to her condo to allow Olivia to enter, which she did, hurrying after the dog, who had evidently taken a liking to her since it turned around and began to romp alongside her, its tongue lolling out excitedly . . . not surprising, since its only other companions were my grandmother, who doesn't do much romping, and of course Rommel, who only humps, not romps.

'Well?' I asked Grandmère as I hobbled past. 'Does she pass muster?' Like I even needed to ask. The two of them were clearly madly in love.

'She has a certain gamine charm,' Grandmère said, pretending not to care. 'Your hair was much worse at her age. It still is. I suppose you inherited it from your father. He's lucky his all fell out. Perhaps yours will, too. Then you could simply start wearing wigs.'

'Thank you so much. Speaking of Dad, is he here?'

'Yes, he's in the—'

She was cut off by a scream. Olivia's scream, to be exact.

But not because the girl had injured herself on any of the admittedly odd collectibles Grandmère keeps around her New York apartment, such as a complete fifteenth-century suit of armor and a mounted narwhal tusk.

It turned out to be because she'd found Dad standing in the library and recognized him instantly (apparently she'd done a little research on Tina's phone, since he'd never sent her any photos during the course of their written correspondence). Not a shy child, she'd shrieked and thrown herself into his arms. By the time Grandmère and I got there to see what was going on, they were hugging as if they never wanted to let each other go.

I don't think it was just a trick of the non-energy-saving lightbulbs Grandmère insists on using that there was a glimmer of tears in all of our eyes.

Now Dad and Olivia and Grandmère are chatting in the library – they appear to have ordered everything on the evening room-service menu, since it's spread in front of them on the coffee table – while J.P.'s uncle and Dad's lawyers are in the study making calls to see what they can do to win full custody.

Oh, Lord, now someone's pounding on the door. Who on earth would they even let up here? It can't be Michael. The hotel staff let him right up, and all the agents on the RGG staff know him . . .

OMG. It's my mother.

And she is not happy.

Grandmère's staff didn't recognize my mom because she never comes here, so that's why they wouldn't let her up at first.

I can't really blame them, since she doesn't look anything like her normal self (even herself in her ID photos). She's still wearing her clothes from the studio – paint-spattered overalls and a man's T-shirt – and she'd piled her hair on top of her head with a bungee cord.

I was the first one to reach the door, despite my limp, and the crazed look in her eye startled even me.

'Do you know this woman?' the Royal Genovian Guards who had her by the arms asked.

'Mia,' Mom said acidly. 'Tell them you know me.'

'Of course I know her,' I said, shocked. 'She's my mother.'

Beside her, Rocky said, 'Hi, Mia. Mom's really mad.'

'Mom,' I said, opening the door wider to allow them both to come in, 'what's wrong?'

I should have known, of course.

'Oh, nothing,' she said. There were tears sparkling at the corners of her large dark eyes. 'I just heard on the *radio* that you have a half sister, that's all. God forbid I should have heard this news from your father himself. Or you. You went to New Jersey to look at bridesmaid dresses today, Mia? Really?'

Uh-oh. I guess National Public News does

341

occasionally report things not necessarily of national or cultural importance.

'Mom,' I said, my eyelid beginning to throb uncontrollably. 'Look. I can explain—'

'Oh, don't worry,' Mom said. 'You're not the one I'm angry with. None of this is your fault. *He's* the one I'm going to kill for leaving that poor child parentless in New Jersey.'

'She wasn't parentless,' I said, even though of course I'd been thinking pretty much the same thing ever since I'd found out. 'She has an aunt—'

'Mia,' Mom said, her mouth shrinking to the size of a dime, a sure sign she was about to blow. 'You know what I mean.'

'Helen,' my dad said, suddenly appearing in the foyer. I guess he'd heard all the knocking and finally come to investigate. 'What are you doing here?'

'What do you *think* I'm doing here?' Mom demanded, her eyes flashing wetly. 'How *could* you, Phillipe? How *could* you?'

She shouted this with such explosive force that the door to the study flew open, and J.P. and his uncle, along with the Royal Genovian legal team, all stepped out into the foyer in alarm.

(Fortunately Grandmère and Olivia were too consumed by whatever they're doing in the library – probably training the poodles to do circus tricks – that they didn't seem to hear.)

My dad took it like a mensch. He held up a hand to stop the RGG agents from throwing my mother out on the spot and said, 'No, no, gentlemen. I'll handle this.'

Then he took her by the arm and steered her out onto the balcony, where I suppose he thinks none of us can hear the massive argument they're currently having.

But of course we can.

(Well, probably not Grandmère, Olivia, and Rocky, who Dominique just shut up in the library as well.) But I can.

I know it's probably wrong of me to record what they're saying on my cell phone, but how else am I going to preserve it to play back for Tina later? She's going to want to know every detail, and they're talking too fast for me to write it all down.

Besides, I keep hearing my name mentioned. How can I *not* listen?

Mom: 'Phillipe, what could you have been thinking? I don't care what her mother said, of course you should have stayed in contact with her. She's your child.'

Dad: 'I did stay in touch with her. We write once a month. Helen, Mia told me about Rocky.'

Mom: 'Rocky? What about Rocky?'

Dad: 'That he's having trouble in school.'

Mom: 'What does that have to do with any of this? Phillipe, we're talking about you, not me. Writing once a month is not the same as being there for a child physically and

emotionally. You're a grown man, how could you not know this?'

Dad: 'I was thinking that since you're coming to Genovia in July anyway for Mia's wedding, perhaps you could take a tour of the school I'm thinking of sending Olivia to—'

Mom: 'Sending Olivia to? I thought she lives with her aunt!'

Dad: 'But I'm working right now to get legal guardianship, because of course her place is with me. And this school has an excellent program for gifted children, just like Olivia and Rocky.'

Mom: 'Gifted? Rocky's not gifted, Phillipe. He's in trouble at school because of his obsession with farting, that's all. Farting and dinosaurs. I just caught him building something in his room today out of cardboard boxes that he claims is a spaceship powered by his own farts.'

Dad: 'Such a brilliant mind, just like his mother. You must be feeling overwhelmed raising such a clever child on your own.'

Mom: 'No, I'm not, Phillipe, because I already raised a child on my own. Your daughter Mia, remember?'

Dad: 'Yes, but you had summers off when she came to live with me.'

Mom: 'She came to live with you and your mother. Who you still live with.'

Dad: 'Yes, but not for long. Things are going to be different now. Did you know there are more than seventeen bedrooms in the summer palace?'

I'm the one who told him that!

Mom: 'So what, Phillipe?'

Dad: 'So I'm saying a person could be perfectly happy living there year-round.'

Mom: 'Phillipe, you're not making any sense.'

Dad: 'The Genovian art scene needs someone like you, Helen, someone vital and real. Vulgar giclée prints of nude women riding dolphins into the sunset sell for tens of thousand of euros there. Won't you at least consider – ?'

Mom: 'But, Phillipe, according to NPR, that little girl's uncle says—'

Dad: 'I swear all of that is going to be worked out, Helen. But first there's something I need to tell you, and it isn't only about Olivia. It's something I came to realize today while I was standing in court in front of that judge. The truth is, Helen, I—'

'Princess?'

It's Dominique. She's blocking my view of my parents. I can dimly make them out through the gauzy white curtains over the panes in the French doors to the balcony.

'*Yes?*' I'm trying to see around her.

'Mr. Moscovitz is 'ere, but I'm sorry to say 'e's in the 'allway, beating Mr. Reynolds-Abernathy—'

2:05 a.m., Thursday, May 7
Third-Floor Apartment
Consulate General of Genovia
Rate the Royals Rating: 1

Any day that begins with trying on wedding dresses and ends with your fiancé beating up your ex-boyfriend is a good one, right?

Especially if, in between, you manage to introduce your long-lost little sister to her father, and no one ends up in jail.

Okay, well, maybe not. Maybe that's why I can't sleep.

Probably also because my foot is throbbing like crazy, no matter how many bags of frozen Chinese dumplings I keep on it.

And also Michael is still up, tap-tapping away at his keyboard in my bed (conspicuously shirtless).

He doesn't think he did anything wrong, of course. His side of the story is:

'I walked into your grandmother's condo, completely minding my own business, and the next thing I know, out into the hall comes your ex-boyfriend, and he doesn't see me, but he's on his cell phone, and he's saying, "Oh, yeah, I can score you tickets to the royal wedding. I have a complete in. She's still into me. So how many do you want?" So I jumped him. What else was I supposed to do?'

'Oh, I don't know,' I said. 'Deal with it diplomatically, *like a prince.*'

347

'Ah,' he said, raising one of those thick dark eyebrows. 'But I'm not a prince yet. So it seemed more logical to kick his ass.'

'Oh, yes, Michael, what you did was very logical. Very unemotional, just like Mr. Spock from *Star Trek*. The two of you have so much in common. Now, thanks to you, our own crisis management firm is suing us, and I have no idea how things turned out with my mom and dad. She took Rocky and left right after the RGG broke up your little fight. And I also don't know what's going on with Olivia, since Grandmère kicked us out, too. She says you behaved like a hooligan, and I should give back your ring and marry that nice ex-boyfriend of Taylor Swift's instead.'

'A hooligan!' Michael grinned. 'No one's ever called me a hooligan before. I like it. But you might want to notice something.' He held out his jaw. 'Not a scratch on me. Dude didn't even get close.'

'Wow,' I said sarcastically. 'You're more physically intimidating than a guy who wrote a screenplay and a dystopian YA novel. You must be very proud.'

'Hey,' he protested. 'He tried to bite me!'

'How upsetting for you. Do you have any idea, Michael, how hard I had to work on Grandmère to convince her to like you? And you ruined it all in one night. We might as well cancel the wedding. She's never going to approve.'

Michael closed his laptop and put it on the nightstand, then flipped back the comforter on my side of the bed. 'Well, maybe now we can have the wedding we wanted.

Why do you need her approval, anyway? Come over here and let's discuss it.'

He grinned and patted the clean white sheet beside him.

'Seriously, Michael,' I said. 'Are you suggesting what I think you are? After a day like today?'

'I thought *I'm* supposed to be the alien visitor to this planet. But it looks like you're the one in need of gentle humanizing right now. So get over here.'

Well, I guess it's worth a try.

I'm really feeling quite a bit better now. Even my foot hurts a bit less.

Wait . . . what was it I was worrying about again? I'm so sleepy I forgot . . .

Oh, well.

Three things I'm grateful for:

1. Fat Louie (who is curled up beside me, purring).

2. Little sisters.

3. Michael. Michael. Michael.

8:45 a.m., Thursday, May 7
Inside the HELV on the way
to the Doctor's Office
Rate the Royals Rating: 1

When I got up and tried to walk this morning, I nearly fell down. The foot Olivia's aunt slammed in the door is twice its normal size.

Michael took one look and said, 'That's it. We're taking you to the doctor for an X-ray,' even though I protested that I felt fine, really.

(I was trying to sound brave. I don't feel fine. I'm pretty sure my foot's not broken because I already checked on iTriage and I can put my weight on it – the nearly-falling-down thing aside – and that means it's probably only bruised. It's definitely turned a hideous blue and green in some areas. And it's so swollen my only shoes that fit are my UGGs, which is bad, because princesses can't wear UGGs in public. It isn't DONE. Except on ski slopes.)

So now we're in the HELV on the way to Dr. Delgado's office. I'd have made him come to the consulate, but we only have metal detectors, not X-ray technology.

In spite of my own pain – which isn't really that bad, but then again, I've taken a Tylenol – I can't help wondering how Olivia is doing. Dad texted that she spent last night at Grandmère's. After the news broke about her true parentage, it was deemed too unsafe to take her back to Cranbrook.

That's *all* he texted, though. Nothing about Mom, or whether or not she's forgiven him.

351

And of course all Mom had to say about the situation (in a voicemail she left in response to all my voicemails, probably while I was in the shower) was:

'Mia, please, stop worrying about me. I'm fine. Just a little embarrassed at the scene I made in front of everyone last night. I suppose I just never realized before how . . . complex a man your father is, deep down inside. Anyway, I'll call you later. Have a good day, sweetie.'

I forwarded this message to Tina, to whom I'd also forwarded the recording of my mom and dad's conversation the night before (although most of it turned out fairly muffled – I am not exactly Carrie from *Homeland,* though I like to pretend I'd be as good at her job at the CIA as she is – and I'd ended up having to transcribe a lot of it anyway).

Tina texted back promptly:

> Your dad did it! He finally impressed your mom! And he didn't have to injure himself in a high-risk sport to do it!

Yeah, right. All Dad ended up having to do to win my mom's admiration was alienate his own country's populace by hiding a love child for twelve years in a small town just off the New Jersey Turnpike. Easy!

He's screwed things for us so royally, the consulate even had to cancel our appearance on *Wake Up America* (not that I would have gone anyway) due to the 'unprecedented amount of death threats' they'd received.

The RGG says not to worry, though, the death threats aren't serious (no more than usual, anyway). In addition to the usual antiroyalists, anarchists, misogynists, and general wackos, we've now acquired a few white supremacists and even some anti-Semites (Michael says he's very proud he was finally able to bring something to the family, even if it's only a hate group).

I instructed Dad that under no circumstances is he to leave Olivia alone with his mother for a period of more than two hours. There is no telling what that woman might do. I have a sneaking suspicion a makeover might be in the works. While this did not end up being the worst thing in the world for me, there is no reason to give Olivia one. She's only twelve, and besides which she doesn't suffer from the many style maladies that plagued me at age fourteen (such as the 'bad hair' Grandmère reminded me last night I inherited from Dad).

Meanwhile, the news from the tabloid press couldn't be worse. Of course they're making much of the 'scandal' of a newly discovered illegitimate princess (though I fail to see how this is any big deal, since everyone's been there, done that with me), but some of the more sensationalist sites/networks are trying to suggest that my father took advantage of an innocent watercraft tour guide (since Olivia's mother died in a Jet Ski accident), not a sophisticated woman who actually piloted multimillion-dollar Learjets.

Is there no low to which the media won't sink in its quest for hits/ratings?

Oh, we've reached Dr. Delgado's office –

9:55 a.m., Thursday, May 7
Back inside the HELV
Rate the Royals Rating: 1

I am in total and complete shock. Such total and complete shock that I can barely even write, my hand is shaking so badly.

But I *have* to write this, because – as Olivia reminded me yesterday – sometimes when you're overwhelmed, the only way you can make sense of what's happening is to write it all down.

So here's what happening:

First of all, the wedding isn't canceled. I think the date is going to have to be moved up, actually.

Also, my foot isn't broken.

Well, we don't know if it's broken, because Dr. Delgado wouldn't give me an X-ray. He said he *couldn't* give me an X-ray. He seemed very surprised I didn't know why. He came bustling into the room where the nurse ushered us, having directed Michael onto a chair and me onto the examination table, and took off his glasses and said, 'Oh, there you are. I see you finally got my message.'

I said, 'No, what message? I called *you*.'

And then I showed him my foot, holding it in the air as I lay on the examination table (fully clothed, I might add, even though the nurse had told me to undress and gave me a paper gown, which I'd thought was extremely odd. Why would you put on a paper gown when all that was wrong with you was a possible broken foot? Michael

354

had found it odd, too, so obviously, I had not undressed, except for taking off my sock and UGG).

'The message I left for you on your phone days ago,' Dr. Delgado said. 'I left a message telling you I'd received the results of the blood and urine tests that I took the last time I examined you.'

'Oh.' I glanced helplessly at Michael, who'd put away his phone and was staring at Dr. Delgado as uncomprehendingly as I was. 'Well, I guess I didn't get your message. I get a lot of messages. Like a thousand a day. I have people who are supposed to sort through them, but a lot of stuff has happened since I last saw you. You might have heard about it on the news—'

'News?' Dr. Delgado looked impatient. 'I don't have time to follow the news. It's too depressing.'

'I have to agree with you there,' Michael said.

'Well, not all of it,' I said, annoyed. Those two had never met before, and there they were, instantaneously bonding over how the news is so depressing. 'Some of the news is good, like that I'm getting married. Dr. Delgado, this is my fiancé, Michael Moscovitz. Remember, I told you about him?'

Dr. Delgado smiled and reached to shake Michael's hand, saying, 'Well, that *is* good news. Very nice to meet you.'

'Nice to meet you, too,' Michael said. 'Sorry about missing your message. We went away for the weekend.'

'Well, that's fine,' Dr. Delgado said, still smiling, 'just fine. Always good to get out of the city for a bit.'

He reached for my medical file and opened it. 'Well, I guess it's better this way.'

'What's better this way?' I asked.

'I can tell you in person,' he said, putting his glasses back on so he could read the file.

'Tell me what in person?'

But I knew. Or at least I thought I knew: I had a fatal blood disease.

It made complete sense. Of *course* I would finally get engaged to the love of my life, only to discover I'm dying.

But it was all going to be fine, because my dad had Olivia, so the throne's succession was secure. It wouldn't go to any of my alarmingly odd cousins. I could die knowing I'd given my best for my country.

But it wasn't entirely fair, because there were still so many things I wanted to do, such as dance with Michael under the stars on our wedding night; tour the Greek islands with him on my honeymoon; and possibly have children of my own someday, and teach them to be sane and careful leaders of the country I'd come to love so much.

How could this be happening, especially *now*, when I was finally so close to getting everything I had ever wanted?

'You're pregnant, of course,' Dr. Delgado said, still looking down at my chart. 'And according to your HCG levels, you are very, very pregnant indeed.'

I nearly fell off the exam table. In fact, if Michael hadn't reached up and grasped my wrist – he couldn't grab my hand, because I was clutching the white paper lining the exam table too tightly – I probably would have hit the floor.

'Uh,' I said. 'No, that is not possible. There has to have been some kind of mistake.'

'Oh, no,' Dr. Delgado said. 'There's definitely no mistake. Both urine and blood work confirm it. But we can do an ultrasound right now if you like, just to make sure.'

Dr. Delgado's office is on Eightieth and Park, quite far from any subway, and definitely not on a geological fault.

But I was sure I felt the examination table sway underneath me, anyway, as if there'd been an earthquake, or a train passing beneath me.

'Dr. Delgado, that is impossible, because I am on the pill, and I never miss one. I take them very responsibly.'

'She does,' Michael said somberly. 'At the same time, every night, right before she puts in her mouth guard.'

'That's very interesting,' Dr. Delgado said, closing my file. 'And you're telling me you're experiencing no pregnancy symptoms whatsoever? No morning sickness?'

'Of course not,' I scoffed.

'No fatigue?'

'Well, I mean, I'm tired all the time, sure, but who wouldn't be with my schedule? It's inhuman.'

'No changes in appetite or unusual food cravings?'

'Well, yes, I'm starving all the time, but that's normal, given all the stress I've been under lately. I love salty things like cheese popcorn, and who doesn't love Butterfingers? Those are very, very delicious. And wasabi peas . . . and chocolate cake frosting.'

I noticed both the doctor and Michael looking at me oddly.

'No nipple tenderness?' the doctor asked. 'Bloating?'

'Well, yes, but—' I clamped my mouth shut, beginning to realize why they were looking at me so strangely. 'That's completely normal. It's probably just that time of the month.'

'Of course,' the doctor said gently. 'Speaking of which, when *did* you have your last period?'

'Well, that's easy. It was . . . um.' Panic began to sweep over me. 'Being a busy career woman, I don't have time to mess with things like cramps, so I'm on that extended cycle pill, the one where you get your period only every four months, so it's been a while, and with everything going on, I can't remember off the top of my head, but I know it's been . . .'

'You haven't had it since Christmas,' Michael said firmly. 'You should be having it now. But you're not.'

'Well, that's not true,' I said. 'How would you even know?'

'Believe me,' he said. 'I know.'

'Well, you're mistaken. Let me see, I started my last pill pack on . . .'

And then I realized I had *no idea*.

Which is the worst, most embarrassing thing for a hypochondriac (or any responsible human being who lives in the modern age) to have to admit.

'I would have to go home and check,' I said. 'But I'm sure I've taken them all exactly as prescribed. I haven't missed one.'

'Yes,' Dr. Delgado said, in a bored voice, looking at my chart. 'So you said. You do realize that most studies show that birth control pills are only ninety-one to ninety-nine percent effective against preventing pregnancy, even when used correctly.'

I swallowed. 'Well, I mean, yes, I know that, but—'

'And you are a woman at peak fertility, Ms. Thermopolis,' he went on, 'who travels frequently between time zones.'

'Well,' I said. 'Yes, but I still always try to take my medication at the same—'

'Plus I would imagine you and your fiancé have frequent intercourse.'

I wanted to die when Michael said, 'As frequent as possible.' I don't think the magnitude of what was happening had quite hit him at that point.

'So it is not unreasonable to suppose that there was perhaps a systems failure at some point,' Dr. Delgado said. 'Mazel tov. You're going to be parents. Now, what do you say to an ultrasound?'

That's when I realized I'm one of *those* people: One of those women on that show *I Didn't Know I Was Pregnant*, which Tina and I love to watch together and mock. Especially when the women go camping, and then suddenly they're like 'I was sitting on the toilet in the outhouse, and then *plop!* Out came a baby!'

Tina and I always swore we'd *never* be one of those women, because who is so out of it that they don't know they're pregnant?

Me! That's who. *I am! I* am that out of it! I could be

on that show! *Hi, I'm Princess Mia of Genovia, and I didn't know I was pregnant.*

What kind of monster am I? Think of all the weird things I've been putting into my body lately, such as:

- Austrian schnaps.

- Two-hundred-year-old Napoleon brandy stolen from the consulate general's office.

- Champagne in the Exumas.

- Tylenol PM!

- Chocolate-covered strawberries.

- Bag after bag of cheese popcorn.

- Eleven billion cups of Genovian tea (which is NOT herbal).

- Not to mention approximately a million pounds of magnesium, Butterfinger candy bars, wasabi peas, Screwdrivers (courtesy of Lana Weinberger Rockefeller), and more.

'I highly doubt you ate a million pounds of anything,' Dr. Delgado said in a calm voice after I'd hysterically confessed my shameful Food-and-Drink-a-Log. 'And I have never heard of a developing fetus being harmed by

Genovian tea, nor an occasional shot of Austrian schnaps or a few Tylenol PM. Studies show that moderate drinking early in a pregnancy rarely does any harm. In fact, I believe it's safer for a pregnant woman to have a glass of wine now and then than one of those horrible prewashed salads—'

He is clearly deranged.

'Michael,' I said to my fiancé. 'I'm sorry. But our baby's going to be born with three heads.'

Dr. Delgado coughed. 'I think it's important to remember that people from my generation were born to mothers who drank alcohol and caffeine – and even smoked – while pregnant, and most of us turned out just fine. Not that I in any way advocate that women smoke or consume alcohol while pregnant. I'm only saying that there's no reason to panic just yet. We'll do the ultrasound to be sure your child doesn't have, er, three heads.'

After Dr. Delgado left the room to go get the nurse and the ultrasound machine, Michael patted me on the leg.

'Well,' he said, 'you Renaldos are almost as good as the Lannisters at making weddings interesting.'

I turned my tearful gaze upon him, only to find that he was *smiling*.

'Michael,' I cried, shocked. 'How can you be laughing at a time like this?'

He shrugged, still smiling. 'You have to admit, it's kind of funny.'

'How is any of this funny?'

'Oh, Michael, *nothing like that could ever happen to me, because I'm so proactive about my health,*' he said, in what I guessed was supposed to be an imitation of my voice, since it was in a falsetto. 'That's what you said when I proposed to you.'

I glared at him. 'That's mean. And like *you* really helped the situation.'

'Hey,' he said, leaning back in his chair and spreading his legs wide. 'I'm more than willing to change my last name and give up my citizenship for you. I'll even walk two steps behind you in public after we're married, like a proper prince consort. But the birth control thing is going to have to be up to you, because obviously nothing can contain what these bad boys are packing.'

'Did you seriously just refer to your testicles as "bad boys"?'

'I did. It's not as if you didn't have warning, Mia. As has been previously stated – by that bastion of fine reporting, *In Touch,* no less – I *am* the world's greatest lover.'

'More like the world's greatest idiot.'

He got up from his chair, leaned against the exam table, and kissed me.

'Come on.' He pressed his forehead against mine, grinning. 'You're happy about this. I can tell. It wasn't exactly what we had planned, but it's a surprise, not a disaster. A surprise is a *good* thing. Right?'

The frustrating thing about being in love with Michael Moscovitz is that it's impossible to stay angry with him, especially when he's got his hand wrapped around the

362

back of your neck and he's resting his forehead against yours and that clean Michael smell of his is filling your senses.

Then all you want to do is throw your arms around him and say, 'Oh, all right, I give up, I'll do whatever you want. What does it matter?'

He's very hard to resist.

'If that ultrasound shows that I'm having twins,' I snarled, 'I will kill you.'

'If that ultrasound shows that you're having twins' – he grinned back – 'you have my permission to kill me.'

And then – as if from our lips to God's ears – that's *exactly* what showed up on the ultrasound.

'I would say you're around eight weeks along,' Dr. Delgado said, looking pleased, as I wavered between wanting to laugh, cry, and throw up (but not because of morning sickness. Because the ultrasound showed that I was having twins). 'Everything looks fine . . . times two. Congratulations.'

Congratulations? Congratulations? No, not congratulations!

'Thanks!' Michael said, looking completely delighted. 'When can we start telling people?'

I'd never seen him looking so pleased . . . well, except for a few minutes earlier. He'd been proud of himself for having defied all laws of nature and science by impregnating me with *one* baby while using birth control. The fact that he'd managed to knock me up with *two* had sent him over the edge.

(In fact, he's *still* grinning ear to ear next to me here in the car.)

'Well,' Dr. Delgado said, 'most couples wait twelve weeks before sharing the news.'

Michael's smile disappeared. 'Oh. Even with their parents, who are getting older and have been looking forward to grandchildren for years already?'

'Well, that's up to the individual,' Dr. Delgado said, which brought some of the wattage back into Michael's smile.

'Wait,' I said. 'This can't be right. I can't be having *two* babies. I'm not ready to have *one* baby.' I looked at Michael, who was still grinning ear to ear, and belatedly remembered everything Lana had told me about her childbirth experience. 'I want a second opinion.'

'Well, you can get one, of course,' Dr. Delgado said, mildly. 'But you aren't going to hear anything different. You're very definitely carrying two eight-week fetuses. Of course, since you don't have regular periods, I suppose they could be ten weeks . . .'

'Ten!'

'My receptionist has some literature she can give you on how to begin preparing your home for your new arrival. Or arrivals, I should say.'

'That's all right, Doctor,' Michael said. 'We're going to be moving soon anyway.'

'That's right,' the doctor said. 'To Genovia?'

Michael looked at me questioningly. 'That probably isn't a bad idea. We're going to need a lot of room for the babies. And what you pay in New York is ridiculous compared to what you'd get elsewhere for the same money.'

'It's really true,' Dr. Delgado agreed. 'That's why my wife and I are looking for a place upstate.'

'Oh,' Michael said. 'That's a great idea. The city's way too overpriced.'

I thought my head might be exploding.

'No,' I cried. 'We are not moving to *Genovia*.'

Michael looked thoughtful. 'It's something to think about,' he said. 'It would be safer, both for you and the babies, especially considering everything Dominique said this morning about those new threats.'

Babies? *Babies?* What kind of alternative reality was I now living in, where suddenly my boyfriend is talking about *babies*?

Then Dr. Delgado (who is only an internist, after all, not an ob-gyn) glanced at my foot and said it was bruised, not broken, told me stay off it for the next few days, gave me the name of an ob-gyn (for 'future appointments'), loaded me down with prenatal vitamins and information, told me everything was going to be all right, and sent us both along our way, cheerfully wishing me luck with the 'babies.'

- *Note to self:* Do not sign up with any more physicians who are male. Female physicians only, from now on. Male physicians cannot relate, and *do not understand*.

10:05 a.m., Thursday, May 7
Inside the HELV

What am I going to tell Sebastiano? He's going to kill me. The design I picked out for my wedding gown is never going to work now.

Wait, what am I thinking? Wedding gown? Who cares about a wedding gown. There are human lives growing inside me.

But seriously, that dress is going to look hideous.

I guess I'm still in a state of shock because all I can think about is not my 'babies,' but how hungry I am.

But what are women who are pregnant even allowed to *eat*?

It turns out women who are pregnant can eat whatever they want, unless it's raw, unwashed, or undercooked, seafood, has caffeine or alcohol, is unpasteurized, or contains the word *herbal,* because there's no data on what 'herbs' do to developing fetuses.

(Michael has already downloaded seven pregnancy books to his phone.)

Weirdly, I don't feel like reading any of the pregnancy books (even though he really wants me to) or the literature Dr. Delgado gave me. I'd rather just eat my eggs (thoroughly scrambled, because undercooked eggs can contain bacteria) with whole-wheat toast.

I figure I should eat as much as possible now, before the morning sickness hits (although, according to one of the books Michael has downloaded, not everyone gets this. Maybe I'll be one of the lucky ones. Except my boobs are killing me, so I don't know).

I think Michael's going to make a good dad. Not that I ever thought otherwise, but it's been only an hour since he found out, and he's already canceled all my appointments for the day (informing Dominique vaguely that I'm 'under the weather') and has the names picked out. Adam for a boy and Leah for a girl. It's entertaining to watch.

'Oh, really? What if it's two boys?' I asked. 'Or two girls?'

Now he's looking frantically through the baby-name app he just downloaded. 'Crap. I never thought of that.'

'Also,' I added, 'if we have a girl, we can't call her Leah. Because then she's going to be Princess Leah.'

'Oh my God.' His eyes lit up. 'I didn't think of that. Princess Leia of Genovia? That's fantastic.'

'No, it's not. Of course, we could name the other one Luke if it's a boy—'

He sucked in his breath, his eyes lighting up even more.

'Michael, I was kidding,' I said. 'We can't name our twins Luke and Leia.'

'Well, we *could*—'

'No, we can't. And don't you think it's a little early to be picking out names? We have a lot of bigger problems.'

'I'm already on it,' he said, growing serious. 'I called my real-estate broker and told her we now need a classic six—' Three-bedroom, three-bath apartment, with a separate living and dining room in a prewar building, very difficult to come by in New York. 'She's got four viewings lined up.'

'That's not what I mean, Michael. I meant—'

'Oh, I know what you meant. I think we should move to Genovia, and be settled there before the babies are born. I think it's important we have a place here so our kids can get to know the city the way we did when we were growing up, but the rest of the time they should live in Genovia so they can go outside to play and not have to worry about being stalked by the paparazzi or some psychopath waiting for them outside the door.'

Every time he says the word *babies* I feel a little nauseous. (Could I actually have morning sickness after all? Probably it's only the maple syrup I keep smelling from the table next to ours.)

'Michael, I totally agree with all of that. But we can't just drop everything and move to Genovia. What about my community center? What about Pavlov Surgical?'

He shrugged. 'I told you when we went out of town: Perin and Ling Su can run that center blindfolded. That's why you hired them. They're amazing. And I can run my company from anywhere. Eventually I planned on reincorporating it in Genovia anyway, like everyone was accusing me of wanting to do.'

I gave a mock scowl. 'I knew you were only marrying me so you could take advantage of Genovia's low tax rates.'

He reached for my hand across the diner table, then squeezed it, gazing lovingly into my eyes. 'That was my scheme all along, baby. To knock you up with twins so you'd never be able to get away, then turn to the dark side. I mean, significantly lower my overhead.'

'I should have run the moment I first saw you.'

'You couldn't,' he said. 'Vice Principal Gupta would have given you detention for leaving school property during class.'

Now he's poring back over his books, looking so worried, I've almost forgiven him for getting me into this situation. Although I do realize there were two of us there, and I'm the one who invented the whole fire-marshal thing.

It couldn't have been Space Alien. I only came up with that one last weekend.

It's very strange how things that used to really matter to me already don't matter anymore. Like it doesn't matter to me that Michael says he's going to take over cleaning Fat Louie's litter box from now on because of the risk of my getting toxoplasmosis and transmitting it to the babies. I'm not even going to argue with him that only cats who hunt and kill rodents – or are fed raw meat by their owners – get infected with this disease, and that it's much more likely I'd get it from gardening (ha! Like I've ever gardened) or eating raw meat myself than from Fat Louie. He's never fed raw meat and, as an ancient indoor cat, has never caught a mouse in his life (though he used to sit on the windowsill – back when he could fit on it – and stare wistfully at the pigeons on the fire escape).

I don't even care what my ranking is anymore on Rate the Royals. Not that I ever cared, but I *seriously* do not care now. I can actually see Brian Fitzpatrick standing outside the window of this diner gesturing frantically to me (*how?* How do paparazzi always know where I am?) and it isn't bothering me at all.

It's like a great calm has come over me. I know exactly what I've got to do.

And that is go home with Michael, put up my bruised foot, then binge-watch every single episode of *Buffy the Vampire Slayer* in a row without stopping (except for meals) until I'm done.

Then maybe – just maybe – I'll feel prepared for parenthood.

I can't, though. We have too many other things we have to do. Such as break the news to our parents. And grandparents.

I know Grandmère is going to love the news that days after finding out she's a two-time grandmother, she's now also a great-grandmother (no. No, she is not going to love finding this out).

I don't *want* to do this. Look what happened when Grandmère found out Michael and I were getting married.

But we don't have a choice. Because this, unlike a royal engagement, isn't exactly something you can hide, especially since by the time the wedding rolls around – unless we change the date – I'll be showing. Even Sebastiano is not a skilled enough designer to disguise the belly bump of a woman who is eighteen weeks pregnant with twins.

Oh, God! I can barely take care of myself. How am I going to take care of a baby, let alone *two*?

Oh, I forgot. I'm a princess. I have staff.

And if we move to the palace, we'll have even *more* staff. Dad always complains that when he was a kid, he had a night nanny, a day nanny, and various tutors, and this was in addition to all his riding and fencing and language instructors. He said he saw his parents only twice a day, at breakfast and at teatime, and he thought this was normal and how all children lived until he was sent away to boarding school and the other boys immediately stuck his head in a toilet.

Thank God for Michael. When I pointed all this out to him just now, he said, 'Well, that won't happen to our children because we're never going to send them to boarding school and they're going to have only one nanny, who'll be a lovable robot like the one on *The Jetsons*. I'm working up the plans now.'

'Michael,' I said, laughing, 'be serious.'

'I *am* being serious.'

'If you invent a robot nanny, then I'll have to deal with the ensuing social unrest that inevitably comes when automaton technology puts humans out of work. Thanks a lot.'

He looked contrite. 'Sorry. I didn't think of that. Maybe I'll hold off on the robot-nanny plan.'

Then he ordered three extra-large blueberry muffins, in a to-go bag, from the server.

'Who are these for?' I asked bewilderedly. 'Lars? You know he doesn't eat muffins. He calls them fattins because he thinks they're nothing but fat.'

'No, they're not for Lars,' he said, looking at me like I was crazy. 'They're for you and the babies, in case you get hungry later.'

He's going to be the best dad.

3:00 p.m., Thursday, May 7
Grandmère's Limo

Haven't gotten a chance to break anything to anyone yet.

That's because when Michael and I walked out of the diner, Brian pounced, and for some reason – possibly hormones – I was feeling magnanimous, so I actually stopped to listen to him for once.

'Princess, I know you must be very upset about the vile lies some of my colleagues are spreading about your father,' he said very rapidly. He's obviously been rehearsing. 'Would you like to take a moment and give the readers of Rate the Royals a chance to know the truth?'

And though I knew Dominique would disapprove, since Brian isn't affiliated with a major (or even cable) network – and of course he'd done something completely unethical in the ladies' restroom at the center the other day – I decided that while I didn't have to forgive him, I could still use him to my advantage.

(That's a very important distinction, and one often pointed out in *Game of Thrones, Mad Men,* and various other television shows. You don't have to like *or* forgive someone to work with them.)

'Yes, Brian,' I said, noticing that he'd stepped it up a notch in recent days and had actually hired a cameraperson – well, a woman who was recording our conversation with a camcorder. 'I would like everyone to know that my father, the Prince of Genovia, is the first to admit that he's made many mistakes in his life, but his

374

daughter Olivia is not one of them. In fact, he considers her one of his proudest accomplishments – and I agree. The only reason you've never heard about her before now is that her mother, who sadly passed away a decade ago, very wisely asked that she be raised out of the glare of the media. As someone who's experienced what it's like to be a teen princess in the spotlight, I can definitely understand her concerns. But now that the information is out there – for which I take full responsibility – I only ask that Olivia be given the space and time she needs to adjust to her new situation, and get to know her new family.'

When I was through, Brian appeared dumbfounded with joy.

'Oh, Princess,' he breathed into his recorder. 'That was . . . that was . . .'

'Was that enough?' I asked him as Michael tugged on my hand. Other paparazzi, having heard through their mysterious paparazzi underground that I was giving interviews, were rushing over to shout questions of their own, and the scene outside the diner was getting a little chaotic. Lars was beginning to lose it. He doesn't like uncontrolled venues.

'More than enough,' Brian gushed. 'I'll post it right away. Thank you. *Thank you!*'

'No, thank *you*,' I said, and allowed myself to be rushed into the waiting car.

Brian was as good as his word. He did post the interview about a half hour later. And less than fifteen minutes after that, it was picked up by every major news outlet, where it's received overall positive feedback (though Dominique is upset that I didn't clear it, or my talking points, through her first).

That's the good news. The bad news is, when I finally located my grandmother, my worst fears were confirmed:

She was trying to give my little sister a makeover.

Maybe it's the hormones (I guess I'll be saying that a lot for the next few months), but suddenly I found myself running around Paolo's salon, screaming, *'There's nothing wrong with my sister's hair!'*

Everyone stared at me in complete shock, especially Paolo.

'Principessa,' he said, holding a hair dryer over a smocked Olivia's soaking-wet head. 'Calm down. I only give her the blowout. You want I let her catch the cold going around with the damp hair?'

Okay, maybe I overreacted. Olivia obviously loves her new blue nails and spiral curls (and Grandmère, and I don't think it's only because Grandmère has allowed her to name the new poodle Snowball, of all things).

But sometimes I think the entire world has gone mad.

That's when Michael realized he'd forgotten an important meeting at the office and left.

- *Note to self:* Is it possible Michael left only because he couldn't handle all the estrogen in the room from three – possibly more, if either of the babies is a girl – female Renaldos?

~~Check with his assistant to see if he really had a meeting.~~ No, don't. Do not be this person.

After everyone had calmed down a bit, Grandmère and Olivia and 'Snowball' and Rommel and I went to lunch at the Four Seasons (for 'bonding' time), where I ordered every dessert on the menu because Olivia didn't seem particularly enthusiastic about anything else, and that's what I felt like eating anyway.

(Although Grandmère remarked about how I ought to be 'slimming' before the wedding, not trying to increase my caloric intake as much as possible. HA! Wait until she finds out the truth.)

Now we're going back to the hotel because Grandmère says that's where Dad is and he's going to 'hear about' my appalling behavior.

He's going to 'hear about' a lot more than that.

Things to do:

1. Make appointment with ob-gyn.

2. Break the news to Mom that she's going to be a grandmother. Make sure she knows none of her friends can have the placenta for their weird art projects!

3. Tell Lilly she's going to be an aunt. Ask her to be godmother? But no fairy jokes.

4. Start interviewing nannies. No robots.

5. ~~Ask Lana what labor feels like~~ No, better not ask Lana anything.

6. Ask the vet how to prepare Fat Louie for a new baby. Will he be jealous?

7. What if Michael wants Boris to be godfather? NO.

Everything is a disaster.

When I got to Grandmère's this afternoon and went into the library to speak to my dad, I interrupted a meeting he was having. A meeting with Olivia's aunt and uncle and their lawyer, Bill Jenkins, Annabelle's dad.

Actually, I didn't know it was Olivia's uncle because I'd never seen him before (except in the surveillance photos José had taken), but he had red hair and was wearing a light gray suit with a shirt that was open at the collar to show a lot of gold necklaces. So naturally I assumed he was Grandmère's nemesis, the 'bohunk ginger.'

Annabelle's dad looked exactly like her, only much larger, male, and wearing a suit and tie instead of a schoolgirl uniform.

It turned out neither of my guesses were wrong.

'What it boils down to, Your Highness,' Mr. Jenkins was saying as I walked in, 'is that my client is not willing at this time to give up her—'

'Oh,' I said, startled. 'I beg your pardon.'

'It's all right,' my father said, looking weary. 'You might as well hear this.'

'Hear what?' I asked. I instantly had a very bad feeling about what I was about to hear.

Unfortunately, I wasn't aware that Olivia had followed me into the room (as little sisters, and poodle puppies, apparently have a tendency to do).

When her uncle saw her, he leaped from his chair and said, 'Finally. There she is. Olivia, get your things, you're going home right now.'

I was appalled. I thought we'd had the visitation thing all worked out.

But evidently not.

True, in typical Genovian fashion, we *had* kind of left it up to a recent law school grad who hasn't yet passed the bar, a New York law firm employed by the royal family of Genovia, and a crisis management team belonging to my ex-boyfriend's uncle, who is now suing us. This probably hadn't been the best idea.

So that made it even worse when I heard Olivia say, in the sweetest voice possible, 'Oh, I know I missed school today, Uncle Rick, but it was an excused absence. Grandma totally phoned in—'

'I don't care,' her uncle said, without the slightest hint of sympathy. 'Go and get your things.'

I hadn't even officially met him, but already I strongly disliked him. And I could tell from the dangerous glint in my dad's eye that I wasn't the only one.

'Rick,' Catherine said. She looked as if she'd been crying. 'Must you—?'

That's when I heard Olivia's uncle snap at his wife to shut up, and inform her that everything was all her fault in the first place for having been stupid enough to have allowed Olivia to leave Cranbrook with me in the first place.

When my dad rose so quickly from his desk that his chair fell over and barked, 'Would you like to say that again, Mr. O'Toole, this time to someone your own size?' I whirled around to seize my sister's hand.

'Let's go into the other room,' I whispered to her. I realized the library was not a particularly safe atmosphere for either Olivia or myself to be in at that moment.

As I was dragging her out onto the balcony on which my father and mother had stood the night before and possibly rekindled their love, Michael came up, smiling, having returned from his fictional office meeting. He was completely oblivious to everything that was going on.

'Did you tell—?'

'Not yet,' I said quickly, cutting him off. 'Bad timing.' I tilted my head toward the library. He looked inside the door, saw what was going on, and quickly lost the smile.

'Got it,' he said, and slipped inside the library to help my dad. I hoped this help would come in the form of reminding him to wait for his legal advisers to get here before making any rash moves, and not the kind of 'help' he'd given J.P. last night.

'Soooo,' I said to Olivia in as cheerful a voice as possible (which I also tried to make as loud as possible so it would drown out what was going on in the library). 'You can see a lot of stuff from up here, can't you? There's the park, and the place where my boyfriend, Michael, once took me on a carriage ride before everyone decided it was better to ban carriage horse rides, and if you look really, really hard, you can almost see the zoo, where they have those wildlife illustrations you were talking about—'

'No, you can't,' Olivia said. 'It's too far away. Am I in trouble?'

'You?' I was surprised. 'Oh, Olivia, of course not! Why would you be in trouble?'

'Then why is my uncle Rick so mad?' she asked. 'And why is Mr. Jenkins here? I thought Aunt Catherine told you it was all right for me to come with you to New York.'

'She did,' I said, with a sigh. 'But things have gotten a bit more . . . complicated since then.'

It was only when I saw the anxiety in her eyes that I realized nothing I'd said had been the least bit comforting. What was I doing, telling her things were complicated? She knew that already!

And my telling her not to worry was no use. Children's fears are perfectly legitimate, and deserve to be validated, not dismissed, especially when, like in this case, they were over something that very directly concerned her.

What kind of big sister was I being to her by not answering her questions? What kind of mother was I going to be to my own children if, in an effort to protect them, I tried to shield them from everything that might possibly hurt them? Shielding them from bullets, the way Prince Albert had shielded Queen Victoria, was one thing.

But kids whose parents shield them from the truth – censoring their reading material, lying to them about who their parents really are, cushioning them from every possible blow – are the ones who tend to get hurt the worst once they get out into the real world . . . not because the truth is so awful, but because they haven't been taught the skills they need to handle it.

And suddenly it hit me – with even more force than Dr. Delgado's announcement a few hours earlier – that *this* is what my grandmother's princess lessons, tedious as they'd seemed, had been about all along. Not standing up straight, or using the correct fork, but preparing me for the real world. The wonderful, amazing, but occasionally distasteful and sometimes even horrifying world where most people are incredibly decent and well meaning, but occasionally you do encounter someone who is going to try to use you, or even abuse you, and when that happens, there isn't always going to be a bodyguard – or a parent – around to rescue you.

Grandmère never cushioned a single blow, and this is why: I needed to know the truth, just like Olivia, because a princess needs those skills to survive.

Well, I wasn't going to be quite as brutal with Olivia as our grandmother had been with me, but I wasn't going to sugarcoat it either.

'There's some stuff about your uncle that we recently found out – it's why I came out to Cranbrook in the first place to get you, aside from the fact that I wanted to know you, because you're my sister,' I explained to her, pulling her down beside me on the wrought-iron bench as, below us, taxi horns honked. 'Nothing's been proven yet, since the Royal Genovian Guard is still investigating. But we believe your aunt and uncle have been using money meant for you to fund their business—'

Olivia didn't look particularly surprised to hear any of this. In fact, it almost seemed as if she'd suspected it herself.

'Oh,' she said. 'I get it. They don't want to give me up because they don't want to give up the money Dad sends for me every month.'

'No,' I said quickly. 'We don't know that at all. I'm sure your aunt loves you very much.'

Seeing the skeptical look she shot me, I added, wanly, 'In her own way.'

'Then why,' Olivia demanded, 'did they bring Annabelle's dad with them?'

'Well,' I said, 'your aunt has legal guardianship of you. So if she's changed her mind and doesn't want you to stay with us any longer, there's nothing we can do . . . at least for now.' Seeing the look of growing dismay on her face, I added, wrapping an arm around her shoulders, 'But, Olivia, I promise that Dad will never rest until he gets permanent custody of you, if that's what you want. It just might take a little—'

'Noooooo!'

This is what Olivia cried as she leaped from the bench and ran back inside, Snowball bounding after her. It took me completely off guard, since it was so totally unlike her. She was a quirky kid, but normally pretty calm . . .

Until she wasn't.

I hurried after her to see where she'd gone, and was relieved when I saw that she'd only rushed back into the library . . . to throw her arms around her father.

He, of course, looked as surprised as me, but was running a hand through her new spiral curls, saying, 'Shush, Olivia, it's going to be all right.'

'I won't!' she yelled, quite loudly for such a tiny thing.

384

'I won't go back with them to New Jersey!'

My dad leaned down to whisper something in her ear. I have no idea what it was, but it caused her to loosen her hold on him a little and appear somewhat more composed, though she was still giving her aunt and uncle the stink eye.

I could see then that she'd inherited more than a love of poodles from her paternal grandmother's side of the family. She'd also inherited Grandmère's ability to dress someone down with a single look.

'Well,' her aunt Catherine said nervously. 'We'd better be going if we want to beat the traffic.'

From the look in Dad's eye, I could tell he wanted to beat something, too, but it wasn't the traffic. He was nobly holding himself back, however.

Grandmère appeared in the foyer as Olivia was leaving, Snowball on a sparkling rhinestone leash.

'Do not forget this,' she said with regal calm, and handed her younger granddaughter the end of the lead.

'Grandmère, I can't!' Olivia cried. 'Snowball is *your* dog.'

'Not anymore,' Grandmère said, and refused to hear anymore about it.

This seemed to cheer Olivia up a little, though Uncle Rick didn't look too happy about it. He started to say something about his allergies until Grandmère, too, gave him one of her patented evil stares.

I've never seen anyone shut his mouth faster.

'Listen,' I whispered to my little sister as I hugged her good-bye. 'I'll see you soon, okay? Thanks for the help with the cruise ships. And keep writing in that diary.'

She nodded, as teary-eyed as I was. 'You, too,' she whispered.

After they left, we all felt low and dispirited, even Rommel, who retired to his French egg basket to lick off what little remaining fur he had left. Dad tried to make himself feel better by getting on the phone and shouting at his lawyers for being incompetent.

I sidled up to Grandmère and – in my new capacity as a mother-to-be, in which I felt I now understood not only her, but what's actually important in the universe – whispered, 'I saw what you did there.'

Grandmère had lit a cigarette – not even a vapor one, which is a sign of how upset she was. 'I haven't the slightest idea what you are blathering about, Amelia.'

'Yes, you do. It was very kind of you to give up your new little dog. It meant a lot to Olivia. And thank you, Grandmère, for always telling me the truth, and preparing me for the real world. I should have thanked you before, but . . . well, I never realized before now what an incredible impact you've had on my life.'

I shouldn't have been surprised when she turned and blew a stream of smoke right at my face.

'I never wanted that bitch in the first place. She nipped Rommel every time he came near her.'

I assumed she was referring to Snowball, not her long-lost granddaughter, but it was hard to be sure. I was coughing too hard, trying to make sure no smoke got into my lungs and threatened my unborn fetuses.

'Why are you just standing there?' Grandmère went

on as Michael hurried over to make sure I was all right. 'Make yourself useful, and get me a drink.'

'Is everything okay?' Michael asked, concerned, as he dragged me out of the line of secondhand smoke.

'Yes,' I whispered, gagging. 'I don't know what I was thinking, trying to have a tender moment with her. I hope someday she gets what she deserves.'

'I think she's going to,' he whispered back. 'She's going to be a great-grandmother. To twins.'

I looked up at him and smiled. 'HA! Thanks for rescuing me, Fire Marshal.'

He smiled back. 'Anytime.'

Dad was saying, in an exhausted voice, after having hung up with the lawyers, 'They think we'll have Olivia back by tomorrow afternoon.'

Michael raised a skeptical eyebrow. 'Really?' To my grandmother he said, 'And should you really be smoking that in here? I thought your doctor said—'

'I need a drink as well.' Dad grabbed a whiskey decanter from the bar shaped like a globe where my grandmother hides all her best hooch, and began pouring. 'Well, who wouldn't, after something that unpleasant? Who's with me?'

Dad assumed everyone was with him, since he poured four glasses. Michael and I exchanged glances. I tried to get him to read my mind. *Not now. We are not telling them now. Now is not the time.*

I couldn't tell whether or not I'd succeeded.

'Uh,' I said as Dad passed me a glass. The fumes from inside it made my eyes water. 'None for me, thanks. I'm not really in the mood.'

'Well, you should be,' my father continued. 'Because it's not all bad news.' He raised his glass. 'As of a few hours ago, Cousin Ivan has officially withdrawn from the election for prime minister of Genovia.'

I kept my glass in the air as Michael and Grandmère said 'Cheers' and took a sip. 'Oh, wow, Dad. That's great.'

'It *is* great,' my father said. 'For Deputy Minister Dupris.'

'Wait . . .' I lowered my glass. 'Why is it great for her?'

'Because I've decided to withdraw from the race as well,' Dad said. I noticed he didn't make eye contact with his mother as he said this. 'And when I do, that will make her the only viable candidate.'

I heard the sound of smashing glass. When I turned, I saw that Grandmère had thrown her whiskey into the marble fireplace. She was shaking almost as much as Rommel usually did, only from rage, not from having no fur.

'I *knew* it!' she cried, her face a mask of fury. 'I *knew* it! It's because of *that woman,* isn't it?'

Stunned at this outburst, I swung my astonished gaze back toward my father. Amazingly, he looked calm . . . and almost cheerful. Certainly happier than he should have been, given what had happened moments before with Olivia, and the fact that he'd just announced he was giving up on a campaign on which he'd spent millions of his own money.

388

'Yes, it is, Mother,' he said happily. 'I've decided to take the advice of my daughter, and stop following the map.'

'Map?' Grandmère cried. 'What map? What kind of nonsense is *that*?'

'The kind I should have listened to a long time ago,' Dad said, setting down his whiskey glass and heading toward the foyer. 'I'm taking the road less traveled. It may not get me where I thought I was going, but it could take me somewhere even better. Right, Mia?'

'Sure,' I said as Michael and I followed him. He'd reached for his suit jacket, and as he did, I noticed that there was stubble on his upper lip. He was growing his mustache back. 'You never know. Where are you going?'

'To have dinner with Helen Thermopolis,' he said. To Grandmère he said, 'Mother, do not wait up for me.'

'Helen Thermopolis?' Grandmère looked apoplectic. '*Amelia's* mother?'

'Yes,' Dad said. 'We're going to a new vegetarian restaurant that's opened around the corner from her place. Helen says the baba ghanoush is excellent.'

'Baba ghanoush?' Grandmère looked as if she were about to have a stroke. 'You're going to eat *baba ghanoush*?'

'Yes, Mother.' Dad stopped in front of the floor-length mirror Grandmère had hung next to the front door to her condo so that she can check herself before she goes out in order to make sure her eyebrows aren't drawn on unevenly. He adjusted his tie, then smoothed down the imaginary hairs on his bald head. 'Helen has decided to give me another chance. And I am going to win her back, no matter what I have to do, even if it's eat baba ghanoush.' He glanced at us, then added deliberately, 'Or step down from the throne.'

Grandmère was so shocked, the cigarette dropped from her limp fingers to the marble floor. Michael stepped forward and quickly stamped it out.

'*Abdicate?*' my grandmother cried. 'B-but what would you do instead of rule?'

Dad gave her a look that was as stony-eyed as any she'd ever given me.

'Live, Mother,' he said softly. It was the softness in his tone, in fact, that caused the chill to creep up the backs of my arms. If he'd said it loudly, it wouldn't have sounded half as convincing. 'I'm going to live.'

Then he left the penthouse, closing the door behind him as softly as he'd spoken.

In the ensuing silence, all I could hear was Rommel's panting. When I risked a glance at my grandmother, I saw that her face had gone the same color as my bruised foot . . . a sort of purplish gray.

When she noticed I was looking at her, she snapped, 'Well, I hope you're happy now, Amelia. If he abdicates, you're going to have to take his place on the throne. And it will all be your own fault.'

'How is it *my* fault?' I demanded. 'Just because I told him he didn't have to follow the map?'

'Yes, whatever that nonsense even means. You know perfectly well sacrifices have to be made when one inherits a throne. Well, now that responsibility is going to fall on *you*, young lady. Enjoy planning your wedding while also planning a coronation! Enjoy the honeymoon, because as soon you get back, you'll be princess of a country that's *falling apart*!'

'You forgot to add pregnant,' I said. 'With twins.'

She stared at me. 'What did you say?'

'A baby.' I pulled the copy of the ultrasound from my pocket and stuck it to the suit of armor next to the baby grand. 'I'm having one. Times two.'

Grandmère wandered toward the suit of armor to stare at the ultrasound, Rommel trotting along behind her. 'Baby?' she murmured. For once, I'd managed to render her speechless. Well, almost. 'Two?'

'Yes,' I said. 'And I'm going to do just fine ruling Genovia. The wedding's going to be fine, too. Though we're going to need a bigger dress—'

'Okay.' Michael crossed the foyer to take me by the arm. 'That's it. We're going home now. We'll see you later, Clarisse.'

'Pregnant?' She stood there murmuring, still staring at the ultrasound. '*Twins?*'

I don't know what she did after that because Michael shut the door behind us. He doesn't really approve of the way I broke the news to my parents (well, paternal grandparent).

But I think I did the best I could under the circumstances, which admittedly were not ideal.

Now I'm in bed with my foot up (finally), eating Rocky Road ice cream (I'm totally going to set up an appointment with a nutritionist like Michael wants us to, but until then, I'm just going to finish this ice cream) and watching *Buffy the Vampire Slayer* with Fat Louie and Michael beside me.

I suspect tomorrow is going to be a bad day – like, epically bad – so right now I'm going to take Dr. Delgado's advice and practice gratitude.

Three things I'm grateful for:

1. That I'm safe in bed with the person (and cat) I care about most in the world, watching this awesome TV show.

2. That I have a sister, even though I don't know how she's doing. I hope she's okay. She hasn't responded to any of my text messages.

3. That I sent the RGG to sit outside her house and monitor her movements, including when she's at school tomorrow, because I don't trust that Annabelle Jenkins girl.

   And I don't care what anyone says: it's *not* spying, or intrusive. It's simply making sure my little sister is safe, and being well looked after.

4. That unlike Olivia, I have a mom, even though I can't necessarily call to tell her my news, because it's not really the kind of thing you should tell someone over the phone, especially when they live

in the same city as you do . . . *Hello, Mom? I'm having twins!*

It would be nice just to hear her voice. But I know she's with Dad right now, dealing with whatever it is the two of them are dealing with. I don't even want to know, really. I just hope they're happy.

5. And that it's the episode where Buffy's class gives her the special award of an umbrella, to thank her for protecting them, which she wasn't expecting, because she didn't know they knew that she was the Slayer, and that she was protecting them the whole time. But they did, and they're grateful. It makes me cry every time.

Hmm, that's more than three things. I have *so much* to be grateful for. I feel like I might burst.

<Lilly Moscovitz 'Virago'   HRH Mia Thermopolis 'FtLouie'>

Why do you keep calling me? I'm studying. Unless the consulate is under attack by protesters again and Lars is eating GMO oranges whole, I do not want to know.

Sorry. I just have something important to tell you. But it's not about Lars.

I saw your statement on the news about your sister. It was good.

Thanks. It didn't do any good. Her aunt came and took her back to New Jersey.

What? We had an agreement!

She has legal guardianship, therefore your agreement was not valid. But she may have violated terms of said guardianship. Dad's lawyers are going to be up all night working on it. Anyway, what I wanted to tell you before you hear it somewhere else is 1 M pr3gnt.

Ha ha ha, I know, I read it on the covers of like three tabloids this week. It's twins.

No, for real, I am, and it is.

Is my brother telling the truth about administering a 'mouthful of fist' to J.P. at your grandma's place?

Yes, it's true, Michael did. Although he didn't hit him in the mouth. And I don't know how the press figured out about the twins before I did. Maybe it's because they watch me 24 hrs a day and noticed my very slight weight gain.

You really need to cut back on the meds, Thermopolis. I know you're under a lot of stress, but this is crazy.

I'm not on any meds. I just thought you'd want to know since you're going to be an aunt for real, but if you don't want to believe me, that's fine, too. I'd say ask your brother, but he's asleep next to the now-empty carton of Rocky Road.

Okay, now I KNOW you're hallucinating. It's okay, we did a case about this in class once, over 30 percent of people experience hallucinations right before or after waking and they can feel very convincing . . .

Okay, well, I look forward to your abject apology when I turn out to be right about all this stuff and you're wrong, especially since it happens so rarely.

Okay. Good night, POG. Try not to operate any heavy machinery.

Good night, Auntie Lilly!

9:35 a.m., Friday, May 8
Third-Floor Apartment
Consulate General of Genovia

Apparently Grandmère isn't one of those people who believe that you should treat pregnant women – even women who are pregnant with twins – like they are delicate flowers.

(Michael isn't either, but he's decided to work from home anyway – at least this morning, since he has a meeting this afternoon – because I'm supposed to be resting my foot. He brought me breakfast in bed.)

Although I think he's regretting this decision, because Grandmère's been calling the apartment since nine, demanding that I come back to the Plaza immediately to explain myself.

Obviously I'm not picking up. I decided to text her because I really can't bring myself to speak to her right now, and also I'm enjoying my eggs and toast too much.

<Dowager Princess Clarisse of Genovia 'El Diablo'
HRH Mia Thermopolis 'FtLouie'>

> I thought I explained myself pretty thoroughly last night. I left my explanation on your suit of armor.

397

Amelia, you are being obtuse. Have you spoken to your father yet this morning? Because I have, and do you know what he told me? He said in addition to giving up his position as prime minister, he's officially stepping down as regent. He and your mother are 'in love,' whatever that means. Abdicating, Amelia! He's officially abdicating!

And I have just officially had my first round of morning sickness.

Or maybe it was only vomiting at the thought that in a few months, I'm not only getting married . . . I'm also going to have to rule a country.

(In name only, since it's a constitutional monarchy, and Madame Dupris is going to be the one actually running it. But still.)

Poor Michael! The lovely breakfast he made me! All gone.

And now I'm starving again.

Well, that was awkward. As I was scarfing down the second breakfast Michael made me, there was knock on the door, and who should walk in but my parents. Together!

I don't suppose I should have been too surprised, since Dad is still officially the Prince of Genovia and I live in the Genovian consulate, but still.

They said they wanted to tell me 'the big news' in person.

Of course I had to act like Grandmère hadn't already spoiled it, and also like I hadn't just been vomiting in the half bath, and also like my boyfriend hadn't just spent the night, which obviously they must know he does sometimes, since Michael and I have been going out forever, are engaged, Dad receives full reports on my activities – I'm only guessing – from the RGG, and I was wearing pajama bottoms and a VISIT BEAUTIFUL GENOVIA! T-shirt while sprawled with one foot up in the completely unmade bed.

But it was embarrassing nonetheless.

'Well, Mia,' Dad said, smiling more broadly than I'd seen him smile in years . . . maybe ever. 'Your mother and I have something to tell you.'

'Great,' Michael said, rushing over with coffee for both of them. He loves playing host. 'Mia and I have something tell you two, too.'

'Oh, you go first,' Mom said. She was walking

around, poking nosily into all my stuff. This is what she does. She doesn't mean anything by it.

'No,' Dad said. 'I think we should go first, actually, Helen.'

'Let the kids go first, Phillipe,' Mom said. 'Don't be such a spoilsport.'

Dad seemed a little surprised at being called a spoilsport, but after thinking about it a minute, he said, 'Well, all right,' with perfect equanimity.

I could tell this was how his life was going to go from now on: Mom was going to boss him around, and he was going to love it. He's used to having a woman boss him around – Grandmère – but Mom is much better looking and also not his mother.

Michael walked over to the bed and took my hand.

'Well, go on,' he said, giving my fingers an encouraging squeeze. 'You're going to have to tell them sometime.'

This was embarrassing. It's one thing to tell your grandmother in a fit of pique that you're pregnant with twins . . .

It's quite another to announce it to your mother and father, especially after you've found out that they've gotten back together after twenty-six years, and that your father was giving up his throne to make it happen.

Also, I've noticed that online there's this trend where young couples film their parents unwrapping a box containing baby clothes, or whatever, then announce, as the sweet but puzzled old fogies hold up a set of booties, 'We're having your grandchild!'

This usually makes the grandma-to-be burst into tears.

I wish Michael and I had prepared something this creative. Oh, well, maybe for the Drs. Moscovitz.

Instead I decided to go with the truth.

'Well,' I said, 'I went to the doctor yesterday to get an X-ray of my foot, because Olivia's aunt slammed it in her door, and it turns out I'm pregnant with twins. So we're probably going to need to move up the wedding date. I hope this won't be a big problem.'

I wish we had thought to film their reaction, because it was pretty great. They *both* burst into tears, which was pretty gratifying, and started hugging us and weeping and telling us how happy they were.

Except that as they were hugging us and weeping and telling us how happy they were, Dad got a little *too* emotional. When I told him to throw out the map, I didn't mean for him to throw out all his filters, too. He told me that Mom had made him the happiest man on earth, and now I was making him the happiest man in the galaxy, and all he needed was for the lawyers to come up with an agreement so that he could get at least partial custody of Olivia, and he'd be the happiest man in the universe.

'Your mom and Rocky are moving to Genovia this summer, you see,' he told me, 'just as soon as I can renovate the summer palace. Hopefully by then I'll have things straightened out with Olivia, and you'll be married, and I'll have abdicated, and we can all be one happy family.'

'Hold on,' I said. 'Renovate the summer palace? If you and Mom and Rocky and Olivia are – hopefully – going to live in the summer palace, then where's Grandmère going to live?'

'In the main palace,' Dad said, squeezing me tightly. 'With you and Michael. She can help you with the babies. It will be *wonderful*.'

Wonderful for who? Not wonderful for me. Not wonderful for my new husband, to have to live with his grandmother-in-law. It's nice that Dad's so happy, and great that Mom's happy, too, and yes, I realize I'm complaining about having to live in a palace, which is like complaining about my diamond shoes being too tight, but it's a palace with *Grandmère,* who likes to smoke indoors while perusing the morning paper . . . and then the whole rest of the day until she removes her false eyelashes and turns out the light to go to sleep.

Deputy Prime Minister Dupris just called to congratulate me on becoming the new reigning monarch. I congratulated her back on becoming the new prime minister.

Of course, none of this is going to be formally announced until next week, which is good, since by then hopefully we'll have Olivia's guardianship sorted out. Dad is on the phone with the lawyers now. Apparently, some sort of headway is being made.

Before hanging up with the deputy prime minister, I asked what Cousin Ivan had said about donating three of his company's cruise ships to house the Qalifi refugees.

She said, 'He was perfectly agreeable to the idea!' to which I replied, 'Great.'

She said she thought we were going to make an amazing pair. I said I agreed.

I hope she couldn't tell that the whole time I was talking, I had my head resting on the bathroom floor.

The lawyers have worked out an agreement with Bill Jenkins (and, allegedly, Olivia's aunt and uncle).

The details are confidential – I could find out if I asked, but I haven't asked. I'm assuming it's either a sizable deposit into Rick O'Toole's bank account, or a promise not to have him arrested for child-support fraud.

In any case, I'm on my way back to Cranbrook – this time with Dad – to pick up Olivia.

Hopefully. I'm keeping my fingers crossed that nothing's going to go wrong. Things have been going a little too well today for me to get my hopes up – aside from the part where I found out Michael and I may have to live with my grandmother, and the morning sickness, or whatever it is.

I'm feeling a little better. Ginger ale helps.

Grandmère's always insisting that the secret to aging gracefully is remaining well hydrated, but I sometimes wonder if this isn't actually the secret to life itself.

Dad is obviously following this advice. Either that, or it's simple, old-fashioned *loooove*. All his color is back to normal, and I can see a faint hint of shadow on his upper lip (he didn't shave there this morning. He's already looking better). He's chattering away a mile a minute about Mom, and how great she is, and how great he feels now that she's letting him back into her life, and what a great mother she's going to be to Olivia (although we both felt it would be better if Mom – and Grandmère –

405

stayed home for this trip. Their personalities are a bit strong).

And now that I've gotten over the initial shock of it – kind of like the initial shock of having twins – I think I'm going to be awesome at ruling. Madame Dupris, Olivia, and the twins and I might actually make something of that tiny little principality on the sea. If Lilly passes the bar, I might see what I can do about getting her hired as attorney general. And Tina, if she ever finishes medical school, to be surgeon general.

(Although we really ought to hire locals. But there aren't that many Genovians who are interested in pursuing careers in the legal or medical professions, due to the distractions provided by the crystal beaches and many casinos.)

Truthfully, I'm not even that worried about Grandmère. She has other palaces that she inherited from the Grimaldi side of the family, just a stone's throw from the rue de la Princesse Clarisse in Genovia. Once the twins come, I have a feeling she's going to want to move into one of them, especially if she's going to be entertaining romantic guests, like Monsieur de la Rive.

So I'm letting Dad prattle away, telling me how right I was all along about throwing away the map, and how if he'd only 'gone for it' sooner, he could have saved himself a lot of heartache.

I'm even restraining myself from pointing out that if he'd 'gone for it sooner' with Mom, he'd never have met Elizabeth Harrison, and then Olivia wouldn't have been born. I'm fairly certain he'll work this one out for himself, eventually.

Oooh, Tina's texting:

<Tina 'TruRomantic'   HRH Mia Thermopolis 'FtLouie'>

Hi, how's it going? Sorry to bother you, but I wanted to say I loved the piece you did with Brian F.! Your hair looked really good! Also, you're still going with cream for the bridesmaids, right? Because I saw this dress online that's really pretty, maybe S. could look at it? Or would suggestions make him upset? I know how designers can be. At least on TV and of course in Danielle Steel novels.

Thanks! Go ahead and send me the dress. I'll forward to S. He's going to have a lot of design challenges on this project anyway for other reasons.

Really? Why? Don't tell me your grandmother is making you change everything you wanted to do again ... Mia, it's not fair, it's YOUR wedding! You should be able to have a nacho bar at the reception if you want to! It's a bit unorthodox but it's not like it's never been done.

It's not the nacho bar. 1 m p3gnant.

Tina, I think there's something wrong with your phone, the last 3 texts you sent me didn't have any writing in them.

No, I accidentally hit send before I could write anything, I'm so excited! Oh, Mia!!!!!

But are you sure? Because you know you thought you had dengue fever last month.

No, a blood test and ultrasound confirmed it. But now that you mention it, I think I know now why I thought I had dengue last month.

WHAT DID MICHAEL SAY?????

He's very proud of himself.

Himself? Why? What did HE have to do with it? I mean besides the obvious?

I have to tell you later when we can talk in person. Right now I'm in the car with my dad. We're going to pick up Olivia.

Oh, Mia!!! But what about your GOWN?????

Yes, exactly. Priorities.

You know what I mean. What are you going to do????

Work around it. Have you talked to Lana lately?

No. Why would I have talked to Lana?

Stop it, T.! I know you guys are planning a 'surprise' bachelorette party for me at Crazy Ivan's in Genovia.

Oh, no! How did you find out?

Lana already asked me about it. Then Boris spilled the beans about it to Michael. Which means you've been talking to Lana AND Boris.

Well ... we wanted to do something special for you both!

I don't need anything special. I already have you guys! And there's no point in throwing me a crazy bachelorette party when I can't even drink. And it would be more fun to do something all together. Maybe we should go with the boys to Buenos Aires to eat steaks.

But it won't be a bachelor party if WE go!

None of them are really bachelors, though, are they? At least Michael isn't, he's going to be the father of twins.

TWINS??????

Oops, Tina, I've got to go, we're at the O'Tooles'. Later!

WAIT! TWINS?????

Well, that certainly did not go the way I was expecting it to.

Although the people here in the waiting room at the Cranbrook Memorial Hospital are being very pleasant, which is more than I can say for Olivia's aunt and uncle.

Actually, Catherine did try to be gracious at first, inviting us in and serving coffee, which of course I didn't actually drink, but no other refreshment was offered.

But her husband acted like a sullen schoolboy, saying, 'Really, it's up to Olivia to decide where she wants to live, and I can tell you, she wants to stay here. She knows she's better off moving to Qalif with down-to-earth people she knows than to Genovia with a bunch of royals she never met until a couple days ago.'

Seriously? In what universe? I wanted to ask.

I couldn't tell if he was angling for more money or simply being obtuse (to quote a favorite phrase of Grandmère's). It seemed pretty obvious to me that Olivia wanted to live with her father, especially after the heartrending way she'd cried *Noooo!* when she'd learned her aunt and uncle had arrived in New York to take her back to New Jersey.

But I said, exercising some of my diplomacy skills, 'Well, when Olivia gets home from school, we'll see what she has to say. Until then, let's sit and enjoy this delicious coffee and these lovely gluten-free cookies.' Note: They were not lovely. 'Whatever her decision is, that's what we'll abide by.'

Dad did not like my saying this one bit, I could tell, since he kept shifting on the white couch and looking at his Rolex.

But what were we supposed to do? We'd arrived too early, and Olivia wasn't home yet, and in any case, it *was* her decision, no matter what the courts said. I knew my dad would never want to make her unhappy, and he'd certainly do everything he could to keep any sort of legal battle with her aunt – and Rick O'Toole – out of court as well.

I was making small talk with Catherine O'Toole about her wedding to Rick – they had a very large photo of their outdoor beach ceremony on the wall – when the front door opened and in walked my sister, the front of her white school uniform blouse *covered in blood*.

I don't think I've ever screamed so loud in my life.

Then I jumped from the couch and ran over to Olivia, crying her name, trying to figure out where the blood was coming from.

It's strange how differently people react in times of crisis. Dad did the exact same thing I did, minus the screaming. Lars, who'd been slouched against a chair, sprang up as if he'd been electrified and began calling the units of the RGG I'd asked to be sent to protect my sister, demanding to know what had happened.

But how did Olivia's aunt and uncle react? The two of them didn't even get up off the couch! Not until I spilled my coffee (when I jumped up).

Only *then* did Aunt Catherine leap to her feet. And then it was only to clean her precious white carpet.

'Olivia.' Dad was running his fingers up and down

his younger daughter's arms, looking for broken bones. 'Where are you hurt? Where is the blood coming from? Who did this to you? *Who did this to you?*'

'I'm okay,' Olivia said, through some cotton toweling she was holding to her face. 'It's only my nose.'

'She's fine,' we were assured by a red-haired girl who'd come into the house behind her. 'Annabelle Jenkins just punched her in the face.'

All I could say in response to this was 'Thank God.'

That may sound horrible, but what I meant was, *Thank God it was only Annabelle Jenkins and her fist, and not RoyalRabbleRouser with a gun, or a knife, or acid.* It could have been so, so much worse. I felt so relieved.

But a split second later, I got angry. Not because I'd been wrong, but because my little sister had been punched in the face, and apparently some people – like the school, and her uncle Rick's two kids, who'd come slinking inside along with her, and were standing around, smirking at me – had allowed it to happen.

Obviously you can't protect kids from everything – like I said earlier – but there should be some reasonable protections, especially if you're paying for them, which P.S., I am.

'Where was the Royal Genovian Guard?' I demanded, glaring at Lars, who was still on the phone. 'I sent them to shadow her all day. Why didn't they stop Annabelle?'

'Annabelle's dad said he would sue them,' Olivia said, through the cotton toweling. 'And the entire Cranbrook school district, if they laid one finger on his daughter. They said they called to tell you, but you were in a meeting and couldn't be disturbed. I didn't know the meeting was *here,* about me.'

Uncle Rick laughed from his place on the couch. 'Ha ha. That Jenkins. You gotta admit, the guy's good.'

That's when Dad lost it. I think he actually might have done some punching of his own if I hadn't intervened and said, 'Okay, that's enough. I'm taking Olivia to a doctor right now.'

'Oh, please, you don't have to do that,' Catherine said, looking embarrassed. I couldn't help noticing that throughout the whole thing between my dad and her husband – which had gotten a bit ugly – she hadn't once stopped scrubbing at the coffee stain I'd left on her carpeting. 'I'm sure it's nothing serious, but our pediatrician is perfectly capable—'

'You should notify your pediatrician that our doctor will be requesting Olivia's records.' I took my sister's hand. 'Because I believe this incident has more than adequately proved that this isn't a safe – or stable – environment for her to live in. If you disagree, you may have your lawyer contact ours. Come on, Olivia. Let's go get your things.'

I began tugging my sister toward the stairs so we could start packing up her stuff. I was really mad.

But even though she was in obvious physical discomfort – something I understood; my foot wasn't feeling too great either – she lingered a little, wanting to see what was going to happen next.

What happened next was that our father stopped glaring at her uncle Rick and said, 'Yes. Yes, of course, Mia, you're right. Let's go.'

And he bent down to pick up Snowball – who'd become very fascinated by the coffee stain, as well – and followed us to the stairs.

But of course the aunt couldn't let it go.

'But what about the promise I made to my sister?' she asked, coldly. 'I promised her that I would raise her child to be as normal as possible—'

'You and I both know, Catherine,' Dad said, in as crushing a tone as I'd ever heard him use, even in Parliament, 'that what Elizabeth wanted most of all was for her child to be loved. And from what I've seen so far, that's far from what's happening here.'

I saw Olivia's aunt and uncle exchange a look. I might have been reading more into that look than was actually there, but I thought I saw guilt – guilt and maybe even a little shame – in their eyes.

The next thing I knew, Olivia had been pulled from my grasp, and Catherine was kneeling down before her.

'Olivia,' she said, in a tearful voice. 'You know perfectly well that we love you. I know we didn't exactly spoil you, but that's because my sister wanted you to know what it's like to live among the common people. She didn't want you to grow up to be some snobby, rich princess who only cares about her looks and getting on the covers of magazines.'

She had the nerve to narrow her eyes at me. What? *I* was the snobby rich princess she was talking about?

'That's not what you want, is it, Olivia?' Catherine asked. 'To grow up to be some rich, snobby princess?'

'No,' Olivia cried, looking horrified. 'Of course not!'

Catherine smiled. Her grip on Olivia's arms loosened a little. 'Oh, thank goodness,' she said. 'You had me worried.'

'I don't want to live with you because all you cared about when I walked in was getting the stain out of your stupid carpet.' Olivia pointed at my dad and me. '*They* cared about what happened to me. That's why I want to go live with them. Now, could someone please give me some ice? Because my nose really hurts.'

If the twins turn out half as wonderful as Olivia, I'm going to feel like a complete success as a mother. Not, of course, that I've had anything to do with how Olivia's turned out.

As soon as we get the X-ray results to let us know for sure whether or not her nose is broken (if it is, we're going to have a consult with a plastic surgeon), we can all go home.

Which, in Olivia's case, is going to be Manhattan, and from there – most likely tomorrow, via the royal jet – Genovia.

No offense to my sister's birthplace, but if I never see Cranbrook, New Jersey, again, I will be very, very happy.

Oh, Michael's texting:

<Michael Moscovitz 'FPC'   HRH Mia Thermopolis 'FtLouie'>

Why is TMZ posting photos of you in an ER in New Jersey? Is everything all right???

LOL, everything is fine. Well, with me. O., on the other hand, got punched in the face by the school bully. She's going to be OK though.

Good. That scared me. I thought something was wrong with you. Or the babies.

Everything is fine with me and the babies. Except I am starving and there is nothing to eat here.

Come. Home.

I am coming home. But first we're taking my sister to her favorite restaurant as a special reward for being so brave.

I'm afraid to ask.

You should be. It's Cheesecake Factory.

When you get home I'm going to have a special reward waiting for YOU for being so brave.

Oooh, is that a promise?

Better than a promise. It's a vow.

Palais de Genovia

By the order of

*Prince Artur Christoff Phillipe Gérard
Grimaldi Renaldo of Genovia*

you are cordially invited to the marriage of

*Her Royal Highness Princess Amelia
Mignonette Grimaldi Thermopolis Renaldo*

with

Mr. Michael Moscovitz

*in the Throne Room of the Palais de Genovia
on Saturday, 20th June 2015 at noon
A reply is requested to: Lord High Chamberlain
Palais de Genovia
Dress: Ceremonial   Reception to Follow*

419

Reader, I married him.

Ha! I've always wanted to write that!

It's so perfect, I wish I'd made it up. But I can't take the credit: it's from *Jane Eyre,* which I have to confess I've never read in its entirety (even though it's one of my favorite books) because I've never been able to handle the depressing bits at the beginning where she's stuck in the orphanage.

And I'm certainly not going to read the depressing bits *now*. I'm under doctor's orders to read only lovely, cheerful, nonstressful things, which even my mother – who is one of the people who forced me to come up here to 'rest' between the ceremony and reception, though I told them I'm not tired – says is good advice.

'I read J. R. R. Tolkien's *Lord of the Rings* series when I was pregnant with you,' she admitted. 'I've always wondered if that's the reason you turned out the way you have.'

I assumed she meant a natural-born leader, like Aragorn, and not an anxious troll-creature, like Gollum, who is always going around speaking in a lisp about his 'precious.'

I didn't ask, because frankly, I don't want to know. Too many people from my past have told me too many things I do *not* want to know lately. This is probably only to be expected when you get a large group of people from your past together all at the same time, but it's still a little disheartening. The bachelorette party was bad enough – though it turned out exactly the way I wanted, just us girls at the pool here at the palace. No trips to Crazy Ivan's!

Except, of course, Lana had to show us Baby Iris's beauty-pageant portfolio (literally. Lana engaged a professional photographer and had head shots taken of her baby).

Then Lilly had to cause a scandal in the RGG by being seen on security cameras emerging from their barracks at 0600 (that is six o'clock in the morning) wearing only a secret smile and beach cover-up (and obviously nothing underneath it).

She's dying to tell us what (and who) she was doing in there, but every time she starts to, I put my fingers in my ears and go, 'La, la, la, la, la.'

I do not *want* to know (though of course I already do).

My goal was to have as drama-free a wedding as I could.

But this, I've discovered, is nearly impossible if you're trying to put one together in a little over a month (Grandmère insisted we move up the date, just as I suspected she would, so I wouldn't be 'showing in front of the entire world'), especially one to which two thousand guests are invited, and that the entire world will be watching.

This is partly why I haven't had time to update this journal in so long: it's no joke moving yourself – and your boyfriend – to a foreign country, planning a royal wedding, getting your little sister settled into her new school, and having morning sickness all at the same time.

- *Note to self:* Remember to check if motion-sickness medication is safe for pregnant women. The doctor (and Tina) said it was, but double-check with iTriage. Now that I've finally stopped vomiting, I don't want to start again on my honeymoon, just because we're spending it on a yacht.

Then of course there was 'the incident.'

I'm not sure I want to bring it up on such a joyous day, especially since it was really just a blip on my happiness radar. I wouldn't even know anything about it myself if Michael hadn't canceled his bachelor-party trip to Buenos Aires.

'I don't want to leave you alone,' he said when I asked him why, as casually as if he were saying, *I'm going to go take a swim in the royal pool,* which he does quite frequently. I often watch him from the balcony off our bedroom. It's an amazing sight.

'Michael, that makes no sense. I'm never alone. I live in a palace with my grandmother, a hundred employees – many of whom are trained in Krav Maga, the art of Israeli contact combat – and my mother, father, half brother, and half sister, who are staying here until their own palace is finished being renovated. I never get a *minute* to myself. Go and have fun eating dead animals with Boris and your little online friends.'

So then he tried to say he didn't 'want a bachelor party,' and didn't 'feel like' going to Buenos Aires anyway, which I *knew* was a lie, because I often caught him looking up 'Best Steak Restaurants in Argentina' online (the way other people catch their significant others looking at porn).

So really I had no choice but to sic his sister on him. I had to know what was really going on. Truthfully, I asked Lilly to look into it more for Tina than for me, because I was beginning to suspect there was something even creepier going on with Boris than that he'd cheated on her with that single blogger. Maybe Michael had found out Boris was running an underage teen prostitute ring, or something, with the Borettes, and he wanted to steer as far away from him as possible (understandable).

But Lilly soon had the real story, and this was far from it. It had nothing at all to do with Boris:

Michael had discovered the true identity of RoyalRabbleRouser . . . and it was someone we knew! Someone from my past.

Someone so unlikely, I'd never even considered him as a suspect.

Lilly was still in New York, and I was here, in Genovia, so she had to call me. She didn't even text. Or look at the time difference before dialing.

'It's J.P.,' she said, before even saying hello.

'What? Who's J.P.? What are you talking about? Did you know it's one in the morning here? I was asleep.'

'Sorry. But RoyalRabbleRouser is J.P. I just got off the phone with Michael, who confirmed it.'

'Michael? Michael is downstairs in the billiard room, playing pool with Lars.'

'Yeah, he is now. Before that, he was talking to me. And he said not to tell you, but when he punched J.P. that one time in your grandma's apartment, he also stole his phone, because he wanted to see who else he'd been trying to sell tickets to your wedding to. And that's when he saw all J.P.'s posts as RoyalRabbleRouser, your stalker.'

I'd gasped. 'Oh my God!'

Looking back, it makes perfect sense. I don't know why I didn't see it right away. It's just so unbelievable that someone I know would be so angry with me, and make so many hurtful remarks about me and my family.

But who else would have so much reason to? Or *perceived* reason to, anyway, since ever since I met him, J.P.'s always wanted to use me, for one reason or another, and I was never willing to go along with any of them.

Now all I can think about is how many hours he wasted sitting there in front of those various computers, logged in as someone else, spewing hatred, when he could have spent them doing something positive for himself and the world. He had the talent – his book wasn't my cup of tea, but a lot of people would have loved it. What twisted path was he following?

The wrong one, obviously.

'Why didn't Michael tell me?' I asked Lilly.

'Because the next day you found out you were pregnant with twins, dummy. He didn't want to upset you. Anyway, he says there's nothing to worry about, because it's all taken care of.'

'What does that mean, it's all taken care of?' I'd demanded. 'How is it all taken care of?'

'Well, have you heard from RoyalRabbleRouser lately?'

'No.' It was true, when I thought about it. There hadn't been a single post or threat since that night I'd seen J.P. at Grandmère's. But that wasn't necessarily a good thing. 'Oh my God, Lilly! What did Michael do to J.P.?'

'Michael didn't do anything to him. Don't be stupid. He turned the phone in to the RGG.'

'Oh, no,' I groaned.

'Oh, right,' Lilly scoffed. 'You think J.P. is locked up in a holding cell somewhere under the palace like the president did to Olivia Pope's boyfriend on *Scandal*?'

'No,' I said. 'Grandmère's new boyfriend used to work at Interpol. I bet that's where they've got J.P.'

'Well,' Lilly said, 'good. Then I guess his douchey dystopian novel is never going to get published. And J.P. has learned a valuable lesson: don't mess with the Princess of Genovia.'

Obviously, none of this explained why Michael didn't want to go to Argentina, so I had to confront him about it as soon as he returned to our bedroom.

But he only expressed dismay about his sister's betraying his confidence and said not to worry: Lars had told him that J.P. had 'volunteered' to go work on a Russian icebreaker in order to 'clear his head,' and wouldn't be back to the United States for several months, possibly years.

'Michael,' I said skeptically. 'Volunteered? That doesn't sound like J.P. at all. He hates physical labor. And none of this explains why you don't want to go to Argentina for your bachelor party.'

'I already told you,' he said, climbing into bed. 'I don't *want* a bachelor party. If I go to Buenos Aires to have steak, it's only going to be with you.'

It was hard to argue with that.

Oh, speak – or write – of the devil: Michael's just come in to check on me. He looks so handsome in his morning suit! When I was coming down the aisle and saw him standing there, looking so nervous – partly because of the many camera people buzzing all around us, shining their extremely bright lights directly into our eyes – I could hardly believe my luck.

But of course luck had nothing to do with it. We both have worked very hard – and have been through a *lot* – to get to this day. We should get some sort of hazard pay just for putting up with Grandmère these past few weeks. There were several times I thought I might actually pack up and run off to Bora Bora to live under an assumed identity to escape her.

After tonight, though, it will be all over.

At least for two weeks, while we're on the yacht, and we don't have to listen to her constant yammering about how every single solitary thing we do is wrong . . .

'Why aren't you resting?' Michael wants to know.

'I *am* resting.'

'Writing in your diary is not resting.'

'Really? You're going to criticize me, too?'

Once you become pregnant – especially with twins, apparently – all anyone cares about anymore (including your partner, sometimes) is what is growing inside your uterus, especially if you're a person of royal heritage. Once they realize the tabloids were right all along, and you really are carrying twins, all anyone wants to know is:

- What sex your babies are. (Michael and I don't even know. We've requested to be surprised.)

- What you're naming them (and they will have plenty of suggestions, even though you didn't ask. We have our own ideas for names, even better ones than Luke and Leia, such as Frank and Arthur and Helen and Elizabeth. But of course everyone will hate these, so we're keeping them secret).

- Touching your stomach, either for luck or just because you're the new 'People's Princess' . . . which I guess will make the twins the 'People's Babies,' which is good. But seriously. Boundaries. *Boundaries!*

- Offering advice, from parenting tips to how much you ought to be resting, what you ought to be eating or not eating, drinking, doing, wearing, etc.

But it's good to be liked, I guess.

Michael grinned and sat down beside me on the bed, slightly jostling Fat Louie.

'I'm not criticizing,' he said. 'I'm taking care of you. That's my new job, besides following two steps behind you at all times, protecting you with my life, and calling you "ma'am." '

'You don't actually have to call me "ma'am" until after the coronation,' I said, reaching out to give his hand a squeeze. 'How are they doing down there?'

He nodded toward the open balcony doors, through which I could hear our parents and siblings, all the groomsmen, bridesmaids, visiting dignitaries, and other wedding guests – but most especially Grandmère – raucously laughing and enjoying their champagne and mini grilled cheese sandwiches (I did win on those. But there's no taco or nacho bar. We are, however, having lobster mac and cheese later this evening) in the royal gardens below.

'You can't tell by that racket?' he said. 'They're having a terrible time. Just awful. The ceremony was a disaster.'

'No, it wasn't,' I said. 'I've been watching it.' I held up the remote. 'It's recorded. They showed it on CNN. Do you want to see?'

He groaned. 'No. Why would I want to see my enormous head on CNN?'

'Your head isn't enormous. Lana's husband's head is enormous.'

Michael's eyes widened. 'I know! Have you seen

that guy? What's wrong with him?'

'I don't know, but if our babies have heads that big, I'm getting a C-section for sure. I totally understand now what Lana was talking about when she was telling me why she got one.'

'That is cold,' Michael said. 'What else do girls talk about, besides their husbands' enormous heads? Wow, I just heard that come out of my mouth, and it sounded way dirtier than I meant it to.'

'I don't know,' I said. 'But I do know I'm starting to feel infantilized. When am I going to be allowed to bust out of here and rejoin the party?'

'What did the doctor say?'

'The doctor said two hours. Tina said the doctor was being reactionary.'

'Oh, and Tina has her medical degree, so we should definitely listen to her.'

'Well, I think Tina is feeling a bit better than she has in a while.'

'Yes, I think you could say that,' Michael agreed with a grin, but he was too much of a gentleman to add, *I told you so.*

Tina was not the only one who'd been surprised to discover Boris P. was the 'top-notch live entertainment' Grandmère had lined up for the reception instead of the DJ Michael and I had requested.

I was a little miffed at first. Was I to get *nothing* I wanted at my wedding?

Well, except a groom who's the man of my dreams, of course. And my parents, happily together for the first

429

time in my memory. And a new little sister, and all of my best friends showing up, as well as what's turned out to be a truly gorgeous gown, Sebastiano having de-emphasized my belly by raising the waistline a little, and adding diamond *M*s – for Michael and Mia – instead of bows as the 'pickups' Lilly had suggested. They not only 'pick up' the full tulle skirt, they pick up the light and glitter outrageously!

But even Boris being here has turned out all right, because he's agreed to sing every single song on Michael's playlist, and also – quite dramatically, at last night's rehearsal dinner in the grand reception hall, no less – showed Tina that the photos of him and that blogger were, indeed, Photoshopped, as he had insisted all along.

'Look, they're of you and me,' he insisted (which, if she'd ever bothered to look at them, like Lilly and I had encouraged her to do, she'd have known). 'Remember the ones we took that weekend in Asheville? She cut and pasted copies of her own head over yours. I don't know how she got hold of them. Hacked my phone, I guess. You always told me I needed a better password than the one I use . . . Tina.' He blushed. 'I guess it wasn't that hard for her to figure out.'

This, of course, mortified Tina – she didn't want any of us knowing she and Boris had nude photos of each other.

But I thought it was sweet . . . and it also allowed me to be able to sagely point out, 'Let he – or she – who does not have a set of nude photos cast the first stone.'

(This did not amuse Grandmère, however, especially since I said it in front of the pope. But I think it must have amused him, since it's currently one of the top quotes on social media, I noticed a while ago.)

'Maybe the next wedding we go to,' I said, reaching up to adjust Michael's pale gray tie, 'will be Tina's to Boris.'

He considered this. 'Maybe . . . I think it's more likely to be your dad's to your mom.'

'Another royal wedding?' I tried to raise my arms over my head in a dramatic gesture to show my frustration, but doing so caused the bodice of my wedding gown to slip, exposing more of my cleavage than I intended.

That's when Michael stood up and began removing his jacket.

'Excuse me,' I said. 'What are you doing?'

'Making myself more comfortable,' he replied. 'Aren't I supposed to wear something different tonight, anyway?'

'Yes. A tux. But that's in like four hours.'

'This isn't a tux?'

'No. It's a morning suit.'

He shook his head. 'I'm never going to get used to this royal thing. So many rules. *Too* many . . . that's what your sister says.'

'When did she say that?'

'Earlier, when your grandmother told her to be less liberal in her throwing of the flower petals from her basket.'

I groaned some more. 'She wasn't even supposed to

be a flower girl! She's too old. She was supposed to be a bridesmaid.'

'It doesn't matter. I think she was really happy today,' he said, draping his jacket over the back of a chair. 'She told me just now that she loves her new school. She's taking art lessons.'

'Well, that's good.'

I'm the only one who isn't wild about the Royal Academy, and that's because Madame Alain, from the consulate, is the headmistress, which is totally my own fault. I'm the one who asked for her to be transferred back to Genovia.

How was I supposed to know it was going to be as headmistress of the school my long-lost little sister was going to be attending?

Now I still have to see Madame Alain all the time, like whenever Olivia has a school concert or horse-riding competition.

But whatever. Olivia's happy, and that's what matters.

Michael began stripping off his tie, and then his shirt.

'Michael,' I said curiously, leaning up on my elbows. 'What *are* you doing?'

'Joining you.' Once he was down to his boxer briefs, he bounded onto the bed beside me, greatly disturbing Fat Louie, who gave him an offended stare and retreated to the opposite side of the mattress. 'If you have to rest, so will I.'

'But, Michael – you'll miss the party.'

'No, I won't,' he said, lifting my left hand and kissing the new ring on my wedding finger – this one having once graced the finger of my royal ancestress Princess Mathilda. 'The actual reception doesn't start for four hours. You just told me that. And the only real party is wherever you are, anyway.'

'Aw, Michael,' I said, my eyes filling with tears at his sweetness.

But then of course nearly everything makes me cry these days, even commercials for Jimmy Dean breakfast sandwiches, and of course when all those sweet little Qalifi children held that tea party for me on the deck of their cruise ship, to say thank you for finding their families a home (even if it's only a temporary one, until we can locate housing for them on dry land) and also to wish me luck as both a bride and the new reigning monarch of Genovia.

Even Paolo made me cry earlier, when he did my hair before the wedding, and leaned down to ask, 'So how those diamond shoes fitting today? Still too tight?'

I'd lifted my skirt to show him. 'Swarovski crystals,' I said, smiling. 'But they're feeling pretty good, thanks for asking.'

Michael dropped his lips to my shoulder, which happened to be bare, as the bodice of my dress kept dipping lower and lower every time I gestured, which I happen to do a lot.

'Isn't there some royal rule that the bride and groom have to show proof that they've consummated the marriage?'

'Michael,' I said, my voice slightly muffled, as he'd lowered his lips to my mouth. 'That's not necessary. First

433

of all, it's the twenty-first century. And second of all, I'm already pregnant.'

'Oh.' He looked down at me, his adorable dark eyebrows furrowed with disappointment. 'Well, I think we should do it anyway, just to be on the safe side.'

'Oh, you do?'

'Yes, I do.'

I grinned at him. 'Who do you think you are, anyway, bossing me around like that, a prince, or something?'

'Why, yes, Mrs. Moscovitz,' he said, and kissed me. 'I do.'

About the Author

Meg Cabot was born in Bloomington, Indiana. In addition to her adult contemporary fiction she is the author of the bestselling young-adult fiction series The Princess Diaries. More than twenty-five million copies of her novels for children and adults have sold worldwide. Meg lives in Key West, Florida, with her husband.